Bloodlines
of
Shackleford
Banks

Also by BJ Mountford

Sea-born Women

Bloodlines
of
Shackleford
Banks

A Mystery by

BJ Mountford

John F. Blair, Publisher
Winston-Salem, North Carolina

*The paper in this book meets the guidelines
for permanence and durability of the Committee on
Production Guidelines for Book Longevity
of the Council on Library Resources.*

*Design by Debra Long Hampton
Cover image by the author*

Library of Congress Cataloging-in-Publication Data

Mountford, BJ.
Bloodlines of Shackleford Banks : a mystery / by BJ Mountford.
    p.   cm.
ISBN 0-89587-292-7   (alk. paper)
1. Shackleford Banks (N.C.)—Fiction.   2. Barrier islands—Fiction.
3. North Carolina—Fiction.   4. Wild Ponies—Fiction.   I. Title.
PS3613.086B58   2004
813'.6—dc22
2004000840

To
Cape Lookout National Seashore
and the Foundation for Shackleford Horses

*for their dedication
to the care and welfare of the wild horses
of Shackleford Banks*

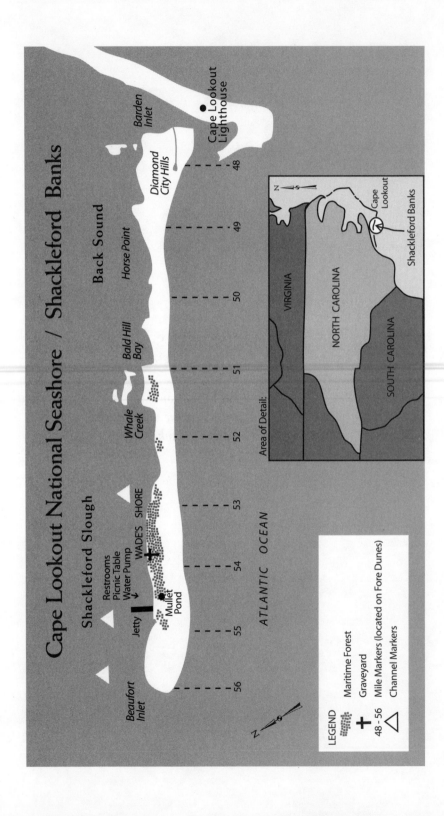

Cape Lookout National Seashore / Shackleford Banks

Shackleford Slough

Back Sound

Barden Inlet

Cape Lookout Lighthouse

Diamond City Hills

Horse Point

Bald Hill Bay

Whale Creek

Restrooms
Picnic Table
Water Pump
WADE'S SHORE

Jetty

Mullet Pond

Beaufort Inlet

ATLANTIC OCEAN

48 49 50 51 52 53 54 55 56

Area of Detail:

N

VIRGINIA

NORTH CAROLINA

SOUTH CAROLINA

Cape Lookout

Shackleford Banks

N

LEGEND

Maritime Forest

Graveyard

48 – 56   Mile Markers (located on Fore Dunes)

Channel Markers

Bloodlines
of
Shackleford
Banks

Prologue

Shackleford Banks, a Tuesday night in January

The chestnut stallion raised his head and stared unblinking into the night. He pawed the ground, tail lashing, as he listened to the restless shuffling of the captured herd.

Swirling sand plowed up by the hooves clouded the air. Blowing to clear his nostrils, Triton paced slowly up and down the barricade. He'd run long and fast for two days before he'd been forced into this enclosure. Even then, he hadn't been able to rest. After rounding up his harem, he had to jockey for the best position, kicking and nipping until even the smallest foal was fed. The young bachelors, excited by the proximity of so many mares, were quick to take advantage of the slightest lapse of vigilance.

Now, Triton's lead mare, Scylla, came to his side, nudging his shoulder. She would stand guard while he dozed. The stallion let his head drop, eyelids closing. His long, white lashes had just touched his cheeks when he jerked up. Danger in the form of man awakened his nose. He rolled his upper lip as Scylla pawed uneasily. In the distance, above the crashing waves, he heard the beat of small hooves. One of the foals was about.

The acrid scent grew stronger. Triton's nostrils flared. This particular scent was familiar—one of his captors. Flicking his ears, he searched for the source of his unease. Yes, an elongated, two-legged form drifted by the gate. Even as he watched, Scylla's foal approached the shadow.

Triton stamped a warning at the foolish youngster, but the colt paid his sire no attention. The little pony was altogether too trusting. Earlier that week, he'd discovered the joy of fingers tickling his head and neck. Eager for more, he butted against the person. A light flashed and was gone. The colt gave a frightened snort.

Immediately, his dam, Scylla, raised her head and pranced toward her wayward foal. The stallion spun around, lifting a foreleg, his eyes fixed on the shadow as Scylla initiated the warning.

Metal rasped.

Ears back, neck arched, nose high, Triton began a forceful, challenging trot toward the intruder.

Something banged against the barricade, sending vibrations along the wire fence. The colt, resisting on stiffly planted legs, was being dragged through the gate.

Thrusting his head forward, mouth open, teeth bared, Triton lashed his tail and charged with a spine-chilling scream. But it was already too late. The gate slammed shut just as the stallion crashed into the bars. The nearby horses snorted, stamping the ground to give the alarm.

Bucking and kicking, the stallion whipped back and forth along the perimeter of the fence, staying as close as he could to the fast-fading scent of the foal and his abductor. Then, raising his head, Triton trumpeted.

From the distance came a shrieking neigh. It cut off abruptly.

A loud crash broke the eerie silence. Triton charged the fence. Time after time, he rammed it, using the force of his shoulders, then his side and his rump, but to no avail. Blood ran down his flanks. The wire fence rattled and rang but held firm. Now, the other stallions began circling and bucking, while the mares stood alert, close to their foals, adding their calls to the general uproar.

But there was no answer. The foal was gone.

Chapter 1

Three days earlier

A shadow pierced the surface of the still water. The black-beaked head of a loon appeared, gliding silently through the shallows.

Motionless, Bert watched, one wader-clad leg slung over the rail of the boat. The loon sensed Bert's presence and vanished again, leaving only a dimple on the slick surface. Farther down the beach, a white egret stalked its prey.

Her mind still on the seabirds, Bert slid off the boat. Immediately, she knew she'd made a mistake. Her foot went down deeper than she expected, leaving her with one leg in the water, the other doubled over the rail, her knee staring her in the face. Cursing herself for her carelessness, she tried to lift her heel over the side, but it was too high. She hopped closer, hoping to pull herself back into the boat. No way.

Help arrived in the shape of a hefty blonde. "That's not how you're supposed to do it," she snickered. "Need some help?" Other passengers turned to stare.

Bert nodded, teeth clenched.

The woman lifted Bert's booted foot higher than necessary, almost forcing her under the boat.

"Thanks," Bert gasped, hanging onto the side and trying to recover her balance.

A park ranger came hurrying over. "You all right?" he asked, concern on his bearded face. Peering down, he broke into a smile. "Bert, girl. Good to see you. What are you up to?"

Damn, it would be Rudy. Pride smarting, Bert greeted the ranger. "Trying to get wet," she said with a grimace. "The water fooled me. It didn't look this deep."

"It's the cold, kills off all the algae," Rudy said, red lips peeping through a flaxen beard like a National Park Service Santa Claus. "Thought we taught you better."

"I never waded in before," she admitted, trying to hide her embarrassment. Bert had worked as a volunteer for Cape Lookout National Seashore last summer. On the southern end of the Outer Banks of North Carolina, the park's three islands were accessible only by boat. She'd spent a lot of her time on the water.

The big ranger turned to the blonde. "You know how to get into the water from a boat?"

"Not that way, that's for sure," she laughed.

Rudy raised his voice to get the attention of the other boaters. "Y'all want to watch this." He had the blonde lie face-down on the wide rail, then pivot and slide feet-first into the water. "This way, if the boat moves, you don't end up hopping along or wet." Even with Rudy helping, the hefty blonde had trouble, to Bert's guilty delight.

Once the woman was safely in the water, the law-enforcement ranger perched on the rail nearest Bert, watching the other passengers slide off. "How's the restaurant coming?"

"Great. You'll be at my grand opening, won't you? Free buffet." This was Bert's big venture. After years of running a restaurant in rented space, she'd bought a place of her own.

"Wouldn't miss it for the world."

"Five to eight, Easter Saturday. See you later, Rudy." Bert joined her fellow passengers wading toward Shackleford, an uninhabited barrier island, home to the wild mustangs of Core Banks.

A ridge of white sand rimmed the water. Above the shore was the maritime forest—what was left of it—a shaggy outline against the pink sky. The sandy, sound-side beach stretched vacant of life, littered with heaps of seaweed and gnarled driftwood, remnants of trees torn from the banks by winter storms.

One of the volunteers splashed through the forty-five-degree water to Bert's side. "Hard to walk, isn't it?" It was the red-faced blonde.

"Yeah," Bert murmured, still annoyed at having made a spectacle of herself in front of this woman. "Especially when you're not awake."

"Does seem like they could bring us over later. A lot of these folks come all the way from Raleigh to Harkers Island and give up their weekend to help with the roundup." Harkers was a tiny island in the sound between the mainland and the Outer Banks.

"Hmm," Bert agreed, her eyes to the east, where the sun tinted the sky. It had been barely light—and cold—when the volunteers crowded onto the boats at the park's headquarters on Harkers Island and roared over the winter waters to Shackleford. Both the park and the nearby mainland towns of Beaufort and Morehead City used the docks on Harkers to access the landings at Cape Lookout.

Staggering through a soft patch of mud, the blonde squinted at the distant beach. "You'd think the park would put in some docks here," she complained.

Bert fought a frown. Why did people bitch about things they didn't know anything about? "There's only one deepwater pier on Shackleford, and it's toward Beaufort Inlet," she told the woman. "Most of the sound side's too shallow for docks, and there's no way they can land on the ocean side—not through the breakers." She pointed at a small, open-hulled boat. "The park uses those flat-bottom skiffs to get around the back of the island, only they don't have enough for a crowd this size."

An hour later, Bert was threading her way through the live oak, cedar, dogwood, yaupon, and wax myrtle that comprised the remnants of a once-dense maritime forest. In the few places where trees formed a canopy, the underbrush was light. But most of the live oaks were gone, ruined by hurricanes and salt spray or cut for ship timbers. The remaining shrubbery was too thick to penetrate except via trails opened by the horses that ran free on the island. The mustangs used these woods for shade, for shelter from storms, and for hiding at times like this. That was why the volunteers were here for the day—to herd the ponies from the thickets to the beach, where they would be driven to pens on the east end of the island for their checkups.

Emerging from the forest, Bert stopped to search for ticks; January temperatures did not guarantee freedom from pests. So far, she hadn't seen a single horse. Ahead was a ridge of old dunes. The group leader, a young man in his twenties, had already started up. Something caught Bert's eye. Damn. The red-faced woman was headed her way.

"How many dunes are there?" The blonde panted as she plowed up the soft sand behind Bert.

Shoving her baseball cap off her forehead, Bert paused before answering. "It's about half a mile to the beach, mostly over hills like this."

The woman must have caught the wariness in Bert's voice. "Don't worry. I'll keep up. I may be overweight, but I don't give up easy. By the way, the name's Julie Piner, in case you didn't catch it."

Liking her better, Bert grinned. "I'm Roberta Lenehan, but everyone calls me Bert. Is this your first roundup?"

"Yes and no. My first time in the field." Julie took sliding steps down the backside of the dune to catch up to Bert, who was trying to stay even with the leader. "I'm the vet tech for the foundation this year. I work at the pens with the blood samples—helped out one day last year. I wanted to see what this part of the roundup was like, not to mention I can use the exercise." She gave Bert a mischievous glance.

Bert's opinion of her companion went up another notch. Partly to keep the conversation open, she said, "I was wondering. What do they test for? All they told us was how not to get kicked in the head by a horse."

"EIA, mostly. We also check out genetics for breeding purposes."

"EIA?"

"Equine infectious anemia. They must have told you about that."

"Oh. Swamp fever." Bert glanced sideways. "It's like malaria, isn't it?"

The blonde waited until she crested the next hill to answer. "When

8

a horse gets infected with EIA, it either dies or becomes a swamper—that's a chronically ill horse with recurring fever." She paused to gulp air. "Sometimes, the horse recovers completely—only it doesn't, really. Like the swamper, it'll be a carrier for the rest of its life." They started down the dune. Julie spread her hands. "EIA can recur anytime, especially if the horse gets run down or reaches old age."

"Sounds nasty. Do people get it?"

The blonde chuckled. "Don't confuse it with the Nile virus or EEE, sleeping sickness. Birds and mosquitoes pass that around to people."

"And EIA is from flies, right?" Bert added, trying to vindicate herself.

Julie nodded. "Horse flies, deer flies, any biting insect. Luckily, the virus is short-lived. The fly has to bite an infected horse, be interrupted, then bite another horse within minutes."

"So that's why they're not worried about the mainland horses catching it." Bert had wondered about that. "Wasn't there an awful fuss about the horses having the fever a couple of years ago?"

"That was quite a few—"

Bert grabbed Julie's arm. Like magic and without warning, a band of wild ponies had appeared in the swale before them. They made no sound and didn't move, but all nine heads were turned toward the women. The sun, just rising over the top of the dunes behind the herd, bathed the sand and cordgrass in gold, silhouetting the ponies with shimmering light. A slanting ray caught the flaxen mane of a small foal, turning it into a silver stream. The pony whinnied, tossing his small head, gold locks flying.

The spell broken, the mares resumed their grazing.

"What I wouldn't give," Julie whispered, "to have hair that color."

But Bert wasn't listening. She was fumbling in her backpack for her digital camera. The low rays had turned the foal's coat a gleaming red. His long, blond mane and tail were iridescent in the light. On his forehead was a white, shell-shaped blaze. Behind the colt, a stallion with similar coloring stood motionless on a rise, his raised head turned toward the women, brown eyes fixed on Bert. Like the foal, the stallion had a whorled, white blaze on his forehead.

9

Must be a dominant trait, Bert decided, cutting her eye contact with the stallion. That had been part of their orientation. "If you want to get close, look away and stop moving until they start grazing again," Purcell, the park's horse administrator, had told them. "If you walk toward a stallion staring him in the eye, you become a threat."

"I do believe that's Triton," Julie said in Bert's ear. "He's one of the smartest, most powerful stallions here, good bloodlines. They say one of his dams was in the War of Northern Aggression." Julie cut a teasing glance at Bert as she emphasized the last two words. "And she was out of a stallion that fought in the War of Independence."

Her eyes on the foal, Bert grinned. Not only could most Southerners name every ancestor that fought against the "Northern Aggression," but apparently they kept track of their horses' military history, too.

Moving slowly, Bert edged over to avoid shooting into the sun. She lifted her camera.

The stallion wasn't having any part of it. Lowering his head, he snorted. Immediately, the colt trotted away, neck curved proudly, flaxen tail high, followed by the other mares and foals, the stallion bringing up the rear.

The horses had already started to move before Bert snapped her shot. "Sorry. I didn't mean to spook them."

"Not to worry. Triton's trouble anytime. Last year, they had only two horses escape the first day of the roundup. Triton was one of them. He's got the Jennetta stamina. It took four men on ATVs to bring him in." Julie gave Bert a curious look. "You've been on a roundup before, haven't you?"

"Uh-uh. This is my first time," Bert admitted reluctantly.

"You don't say? I figured you worked for the park, the way you knew that ranger and all."

"And the way I got into the water?"

Julie laughed.

"But I did work as a volunteer last summer," Bert admitted, cringing as she waited for the blonde's reaction. She'd spent several months on Portsmouth, another of Cape Lookout's islands. Two women had been killed, and Bert had almost become the third. She had not enjoyed the media coverage.

To her relief, Julie didn't appear to make the connection. "I always wanted to volunteer at the lighthouse," she began. Just then, their group leader appeared on a dune to their right. The two women hailed him, hurrying over to report their sighting of the band of horses.

"That way." Bert pointed toward the beach. "Can't have gone far."

The young man sprinted to the top of the next dune, radio in hand. Bert watched with an envious smile. At fifty-five, it took determination to run through soft sand. Julie, who looked to be about thirty, tended to walk around the dunes whenever possible. Now, the leader was yelling commands. "Over there!" He motioned for them to spread out. "Don't let them cut back. That's Triton, all right. He gave us a bad time last year."

Although the two women caught occasional glimpses of the horses, Triton and his family stayed well ahead. The desertlike dunes appeared barren of life. No birds or insects buzzed, and no animal tracks broke the sandy surface, not even hooves. Bert knew there were both rabbits and nutria on the island, but the dry, loose sand, abetted by the wind, filled in any tracks quickly.

Sweating despite the fifty-degree January temperature, Bert's group finally reached the primary dunes. Below it stretched the white-gold of the ocean beach, and beyond that the clear, green waters of the Atlantic—clear thanks to the proximity of the Gulf Stream and the absence of silt-laden rivers.

Triton's band was already up the beach. More horses approached from the south. No, from the west, Bert reminded herself. Compass points on Shackleford were confusing, as it ran east-west instead of the usual north-south of barrier islands.

Bert listened for the ATVs that were chasing the horses up the shore, but the cold wind and crashing surf drowned out the sound of motors. "Who gets to ride herd?" she asked Julie, slipping on her jacket.

"The four-wheelers belong to the park, so the rangers use them. One of the vets is riding with them this year."

A motor roared behind Bert, not on the beach but in the dunes.

Surprised, she swung around. A large, bearded man in an orange jumpsuit appeared on a red Honda ATV. Their group leader was yelling into his radio, waving at the man, and pointing up the beach to Triton.

The bike and rider were hidden from the beach by the dunes. Suddenly, Bert understood. As the other rangers herded the horses up the shoreline, some of the stallions, like Triton, would try to cut back to the safety of the woods. The Honda was there to stop them, as were the volunteers who now lined the primary dunes, poised to turn back any recalcitrant horses.

But it was not to be that simple. When Triton heard the approaching ATV, he swerved inland. The line of waving, shouting volunteers deterred him for a few hundred yards—until he spotted an opening. He shot through, his band rushing to follow.

Immediately, people ran to close the gap. They managed to turn back the mares and even the blond-maned foal, but Triton had escaped. Bert whirled to see the chestnut stallion making a mad dash through the dunes, sand flying under his hooves.

The red ATV spun around and angled over to intercept him. Triton saw the trap. Veering away from the bearded man on the bike, he extended his nose so it pointed into the wind, ears down, flaxen mane and tail streaming, body stretched out, front and rear hooves flying in synchronization. In a race with an ATV, which has a maximum speed of thirty-five miles per hour, Triton could have outrun it, but the Honda had less distance to cross. They came together like two converging lines of a triangle. For a moment, Bert thought the man had won, cutting off the horse's escape. Then she watched the stallion, not even breaking his gait, deliberately shoulder the rider. Like a slow-motion film, ATV and rider tilted to the side, then slowly, still skidding, went down in a shower of sand.

Shouting, Bert and others sprinted toward the downed rider. Being the closest, she reached him first. The man was already on his feet, dusting himself off.

"Are you all right?" she panted.

The man shook himself like a shaggy bear, sand flying from his beard and dark hair. "I'm fine." He reached down. "Did you see that? That horse deliberately pushed me off. Goddamn no-good stallion." With seeming ease, the giant pulled the ATV back upright.

Bert eyed him in amazement. "How'd you do that? When I tipped over, it took both Rudy and Hunter to get the bike up, and Rudy's as big as you."

"Rudy's gone soft." The man stopped to stare at Bert with the clearest, greenest eyes she'd ever seen. "Am I supposed to know you?"

"I'm Bert Lenehan. I volunteered at Portsmouth last year." Now, the others were arriving.

"Is that right?" The giant lost interest. He turned to a ranger who'd just skidded to a stop on another four-wheeler. "Park ought to shoot that stallion. He's gonna kill somebody one of these days."

"Come off it, DeWitt," the ranger snapped back. "You were going too fast. You know we're to take it easy, even if we lose a few today. Don't want anyone hurt, and that includes the horses."

So that's who he was—DeWitt Brigman, the foundation vet. No wonder he'd looked so familiar. The vet was a legend in these parts. Every year, there was a pageant in Beaufort, and DeWitt played the part of Blackbeard. He was supposed to have a temper as fierce as that of the pirate, and he was strong enough to wrestle a balky stallion to his knees. He knew every marsh, water hole, and slew on the island and could ferret out even the most cleverly hidden pony. Fearless, he was hard on himself and harder on his equipment. He'd run park boats aground, ruined motors, overturned trucks, and driven four-wheelers into the ocean.

Now, DeWitt and three members of the Army Veterinary Team, riding double on two ATVs, took off with a roar to fetch Triton. The volunteers continued their march along the ridge of the dunes while the other ATVs, in box formation, herded the horses slowly up the beach.

Ahead, a fence stretched across the island to the water's edge. Volunteers in waders formed a living barricade from the end of the fence to the surf. Here, the horses would be turned inland along a corridor leading to the pens, where food and water waited.

"I think I'll stick around a minute and watch. Want to?" Bert asked Julie.

With a graphic wiggle of her hips, Julie said, "I would, but I got to get me to the porta-potty. See you back at the tents."

Finding a good vantage point on top of a dune with the ocean as a backdrop, Bert settled down to get shots of the ponies. She was hoping for another chance at the blond-maned foal, but she never saw him. Sometimes, the horses clumped up so it was impossible to identify individuals. Other times, one lone animal would shoot through the wide corridor.

A black stallion, coat gleaming with sweat, came galloping down the beach with his band. When he saw the fence, he charged into the ocean, around the volunteers, and into the booming, six-foot surf with total assurance, as if this were inbred behavior. The horses leapt and reared through the foaming breakers, emerging east of the fence line. From there, the band continued up the beach, water and hooves flying.

Finally, the last horse was gone and the rangers were off the beach, leaving behind a quagmire of tire tracks and sand plowed by hundreds of hooves. But the damage was only temporary. Already, the rising tide washed the beach. Pocketing her camera, Bert trudged down the sandy, dung-strewn, aromatic corridor, glad the day was almost over. The boats would take them all back to Harkers. Only two rangers would remain on the island to safeguard the horses.

Suddenly, an ATV bore down from behind. Two men roared past, spraying her with sand. Teeth clenched, blinking grit from her eyes, she swore under her breath. It was DeWitt Brigman, all right. That beard and bulk were unmistakable. As if to confirm her assumption, another Honda approached at a courteous pace, the remaining two camouflage-clad members of the Army Veterinary Team waving as they passed.

Baring her teeth in a nasty smile, Bert turned toward the sound, where her boat waited. At least Triton had eluded capture by the rude veterinarian.

The boat was crowded. Bert found herself standing behind the cabin and away from the rail, nothing to hold onto. As the cruiser reared off, she staggered back—into DeWitt Brigman. "I'm sorry," she muttered, annoyed it had to be him.

To her surprise, he gave her a big smile, his green eyes crinkling. "Here, hang onto this." Somehow, he opened a spot on the rail.

Bert grabbed on. "Thank you." Being practically under the man, she felt obliged to say something else. "Those horses are small, aren't they? But fast," she added, careful to keep a straight face.

"That's the Spanish blood in them," the giant said, catching her dig about Triton's escape.

"One of the rangers said that's just a fairy tale people like to believe. Frankly, I can't imagine enough horses swimming ashore from Spanish galleons to populate an entire island."

He shrugged. "The whalers found wild horses on the banks in the sixteen hundreds, you know. Some were Indian horses stolen from the Spanish. Maybe one or two came from a wreck. When the colonists got here, they began using the banks as free range to pasture their horses and other animals. They didn't have to fence, and there were no predators or Indians to steal them. Then later, the Bankers let their own stock loose, so you got all kinds and breeds mixed in the herd." He paused. "But the ponies got Spanish blood in them, all right. Not so unusual. Most horses did in colonial times, even the English nags and Irish hobby horses." DeWitt smiled down at her. Again, Bert was amazed how the smile transformed his sullen demeanor.

"Really?"

"Ayrabs been breeding horses for thousands of years. Had some of the finest in the world. The horse was like a man's car, you know, only better. The Barbary horses, Barbs, came to Spain with the Moors."

Bert tipped her head in question. She was hazy on early history.

DeWitt squinted toward shore, his bearded chin jutting. "A general by the name of Tariq shipped twelve thousand mounted men over to Gibraltar to invade Spain." He caught her eye, grinning. "Bet you didn't know that's how Gibraltar got its name, Jabal Tariq. Means 'Mountain of Tariq.' "

Chapter 2

Gibraltar, 711 A.D.

Nejmah

"Do not fret, my sweet. Not even the shadow of Jabal Tariq can part us," Wulid whispered in her ear, stroking her taut neck. "I will never leave your side."

Nejmah did not understand the words, but she understood they would be together. She sensed anxiety in his rapid breath and tense hand, but it was muted, not like when they charged into battle. At those moments, his muscles became hard as the decorated saddle on her back.

Leading Nejmah by the braided strap around her neck, Wulid started up the narrow ramp to the boat, but as the mare's hoof struck the plank walk, it resonated hollowly. She shied.

Her master stood firm, holding her steady, his voice a soft croon. "Come, my love, for this day we travel to our destiny; we sail through the Pillars of Hercules."

Reassured by his calm murmurings, she again placed a hoof on the plank. Head low, she trotted rapidly up the narrow gangway to the wooden boat. Behind her, the waiting division of Moors with their Barbary war-horses followed her up the ramp. Then, sail raised and bow turned to the tide, the caravel left Morocco, passing under the towering, dark wall that formed one of the Pillars of Hercules.

The open deck was crowded with mares being calmed by their riders. Braced against the roll of the ship, Nejmah nudged the nose of the horse to her left, nickering to show recognition. Aisha raised her head and harrumphed in acknowledgment.

Aisha's rider, Abu, and Wulid had been together for the past fortnight as they waited for the hired boats to return for another cargo of men and horses. Giving Nejmah an admiring glance, Abu congratulated Wulid. "Without your mare leading the way, it could have taken the better part of the afternoon to load."

"Allah has blessed me with Nejmah." Wulid stroked her nose as she held her head high. "She is more dear to me than my wife." Shading his eyes, he sighted over the bow to a pointed rock that rose like the giant fin of a shark from the mists and the sea. "My mare is strong as the water buffalo and swift as the oryx. Were it not for her, I would fear what lies in wait beneath the long shadow of Jabal Tariq."

The crossing was soon over, and Nejmah was relieved to again be on solid ground. This new country was not so different from the Africa of her origins, with its bright sun, rolling landscape, and dry winds. But as the army of Tariq ibn Ziyad gathered by the banks of the Rio Barbate in Spain, Nejmah sensed the increasing anxiety of her master. He sat heavy as a tent rug on her back, staring across the river at the gathered battalion of horses and armored riders. Those horses were much larger than the small, thin-skinned Barbs, which had been desert-bred for stamina and maneuverability. Hot sunshine glistened off the beaten metal that covered not only the Spanish knights, but also the flanks of their steeds. Then Nejmah noticed something. She tossed her head, swinging her nose and whinnying to her master to tell him not to be concerned, for the enemy rode clumsy, overgrown stallions. She would move like a dervish among the horses, while he brought the riders down with his shining sword.

This soon came to be. As always, Nejmah became one with Wulid on the battlefield, responding to the press of his knee or even the tightening of his calf. When a massive stallion charged at Wulid, Nejmah reared and pretended to meet his charge head on, swerving at the last moment so Wulid could slash off the rider's arm. Quick as a tiger, the Barb parried the attack of another from the side, Wulid decapitating the knight with his scimitar while the doomed man hauled at the reins.

Although the forces of King Roderic were superior in number, they were unable to counter the swift-moving, dark war-horses and their white-clad riders. Spain's Visigoth monarch was slain, his body never found. The Christian battalions melted away before the Moorish onslaught. By the end of the decade, Tariq and his conquering army occupied Toledo and ruled east Spain all the way to the Picos de Europa.

Seven years later, Nejmah pastured in the shade of olive trees while Wulid and his Spanish friend, Don Carlos de Noriega, sat astride the pole fence.

"I tell you." Don Carlos's voice rose in volume, attracting Nejmah's attention. Restlessly, she flicked her tail and moved away to pass water. She was in heat and irritable. Behind her, Noriega continued. "This peace will not last. We have too much to offer here in Cordoba." His hands made a sweeping gesture, indicating not only the orchards of oranges, grapes, and olives, but also the marble balconies, fountains, and hanging gardens of the industrious Moors.

Nejmah's rider frowned. "I pray to Allah, who led us to this place, you are mistaken. This is my home now, and here I stay." He clapped his friend on the shoulder. "Al Andalus—or Land of the Vandals, as they say in the north—has become home to us Arabs with its mountains, the sea, and the warm sun. I should be desolate to depart."

"This is why I seek your patronage. I have a plan."

"A plan?"

"Sí. As you know, I am a breeder of horses."

"Plow horses."

The Spaniard did not take offense. "Exactamente." He pointed to

Nejmah, who ceased grazing to fix her brown eyes on the two men. "You defeated the Visigoth with your superb war-horses, but your little weapons grow old."

"Nejmah may die, but she will never grow old. Her spirit will shine always, like the star on her forehead for which she is named." Upon hearing her name called, Nejmah trotted to Wulid's outstretched hand. He stroked the star blaze on her forehead.

Don Carlos de Noriega smiled. "I have often wondered what her name signified. Now, she will be the star of our new breed."

"Our new breed?"

"Sí, mi amigo. I plan a new breed of horses with you as my partner. Already, I have investors and buyers from Toledo." He looked past Nejmah to the distant mountains. "Your horse was bred for war, my horse for the hacienda and the fields. What Andalusia needs is a horse that is adept for both war and peace, a horse that is intelligent, agile, fast, and surefooted, but also sturdy, strong, able to withstand heat and drought, and," he added with a smile, "because we are a vain race, a horse that is handsome." Vaulting off the fence, Don Carlos whistled.

From behind a red bodega appeared a groom leading a magnificent ruano stallion. He was smaller than the average Spanish horse, standing under sixteen hands, well muscled with a deep chest and long forelegs. He had a wide brow and a Roman nose. A large, white blaze shaped like a bolt of lightning ran from his forehead to his nose.

Anxiously, Don Carlos waited while Wulid inspected the stallion. Finally, the rider nodded.

The smiling groom opened the gate and let the stallion into the pasture. As soon as Nejmah scented him, she knew here was the answer to her undefined yearning—here was fulfillment. She cantered up, nudged the stallion with a shoulder, and then drifted slowly under his muzzle.

As Nejmah's musk rose to his nostrils, the stallion gave a long, low bellow. Tossing his head, he arched his neck and began prancing, feet and tail lifting high as he initiated the courtship dance.

Nejmah stood still, ears signaling her interest. But when the stallion, already in a state of excitement, spun around to give her a friendly nip on the rump, she squealed in pretended fear and dashed off, the stallion in hot pursuit.

The watching men chuckled as their dream became reality.

Three hundred and thirty-eight days later, both Wulid and Don Carlos hung anxiously over Nejmah as she labored. The foal was large for her small frame, and she was old to breed, but finally the newborn lay on the straw in his birth sack. At Nejmah's nicker, he broke free, flopping toward her. His coat was dark, but his mane and tail were white-gold, and on his forehead he bore a white spiral blaze.

"Praise be to Allah," Wulid whispered. "He has combined the blaze of a star with the power of lightning."

"*Sí*. This will be a great stallion, for he bears the mark of Triton, god of the sea."

Chapter 3

The neigh of a stallion with a white, conch-shaped blaze on his forehead greeted Bert as she waded ashore. Triton? She squinted toward the penned herd.

Sunday had dawned gray and damp, forcing the volunteers to huddle behind the boat's cabin for protection against the cold wind and spray. Glad to be on land, Bert headed for the main pen. Inside, the horses clustered around piles of carefully apportioned hay—more piles of hay than ponies, to ensure that even the youngest got something to eat. Bert stopped to watch, inhaling deeply, enjoying the smell of horse manure.

Occasionally, a pony would nip a rump or shove another in vying for feeding position. One mare, kicked out of place, made a big show of dropping to the ground, rolling, and whinnying loudly—all totally ignored by her stallion.

"Reminds me of one of my aunts." A flat face with impish features grinned down at Bert from the top of a long, thin body. It was the young ranger hired to help the Resource division with the wild horses.

Bert chuckled. "Hey, Purcell. I saw you on the ATV yesterday. You looked pretty professional."

"Went good, don't you think?" Purcell flashed his gamin grin, reminding Bert of a mischievous monkey on stilts. "We didn't lose a single horse, didn't even get a sprained knee."

"What happens to Triton and the other ones that got away?"

Purcell pointed an index finger toward the sky. "The spotter plane's been up. DeWitt and I are going out ahead of the crew. There's only a handful still loose."

"You mean the plane will herd them in?"

"No way. That doesn't work. The airplane panics the horses, and they bolt. That's how so many got hurt the first roundup."

"The one that got all the publicity?"

Purcell nodded. "I wasn't here then, praise be. That's when the National Park Service decided it needed a horse administrator."

"I heard the horses were sick and the park put a bunch of them down. The papers accused the park of using the fever as an excuse to get rid of the wild ponies." Bert scanned the horses as she spoke, hoping for a glimpse of the flaxen-maned foal.

"The herd had increased to over two hundred and twenty-five," Purcell said, chin bobbing. "That's twice what an island this size can support. They were starving." He slapped the fence post. "Wild-horse management is always a political nightmare. You can pen them and feed them, like they did on Ocracoke—"

"But then they aren't wild anymore," Bert interrupted, thinking Purcell did take himself seriously at times.

His rather small eyes tightened. "Another alternative is to let nature take its course. That ends up in mass starvation like what happened on Carrot Island years ago. Not a pretty—"

"I know. It's in all the books." Sometimes, she forgot how young he was, younger even than her daughter, Belinda. She hadn't seen Belinda since Thanksgiving, but she was coming down for the grand opening of Bert's new restaurant, thank goodness. Belinda had worked for Bert while she was in college and knew almost as much about the business as—

Purcell cut into Bert's thoughts. "Or we can control the population by culling or using contraceptives."

"Good idea," Bert murmured, moving down the fence.

Purcell followed, still talking. "Would you believe, the media accused me— *me*—of using permanent sterilization? Said I'd come up with a sneaky way to get rid of the horses, that in twenty years they'd all be dead. Willit started that rumor, don't you know." Purcell's lips, already thin, became thinner.

"Willit?"

"Thought you read the paper. Vilma Willit was a freelancer before ninety-six. She jumped onto the wild-pony story like a tick on a dog. It got her a job as a staff reporter for the Carteret newspaper. She even had some of her articles syndicated. Ever read them?"

Bert shook her head. "Never heard of her."

"Just watch what you say to her. She'll twist your words around. She's writing a history of the ponies in her spare time."

"She's here?"

"Vilma's doing a series of articles for the paper. The editor's wife belongs to one of those horse-hugger groups, you know. They hired their own vet this year, DeWitt Brigman, and a photographer."

"I thought DeWitt was the foundation's vet." By law, the Foundation for Shackleford Horses and Cape Lookout National Seashore shared management of the wild horses.

"Not anymore," Purcell said. "I heard DeWitt had words with the foundation. That man doesn't know how to keep his mouth shut."

"The foundation was started after the brouhaha about the park putting down all those horses with swamp fever, right?"

"Right. Anyhow, they hired a new vet this year, nice-looking black gal called Tanisha Hansen. I'll introduce you."

"Oh?" Bert grinned at the young ranger.

He ducked his head and wouldn't meet her eyes.

They reached the end of the pen where the watering tubs were kept. Bert was still trying to locate Triton's gold-maned foal. There were over a hundred horses in the rambling enclosure, and an amazing number sported blond manes and tails. Many also had white blazes on their foreheads. Well, what had she expected? They'd been inbreeding for generations.

Purcell cuffed her shoulder. "Guess I'd better get back to work before Ernie gets on my tail again."

"He's that shy ranger, right?" Bert asked. "The one with the strawberry blond hair. What's he like to work for?" Ernie was chief of Resource. Resource's job was to take care of all the animals, particularly endangered species like turtles and piping plovers. It also kept an eye on the ecosystem with the park's mission statement in mind—preservation for the enjoyment of both present and future generations.

"He's a pain." Purcell scrunched up his small mouth. "Took me off beach patrol two weeks ago just because I forgot to lock the ATV shed—big effing deal." He started toward the tents. "Give my best to Hunter. Is he coming out?"

"Not this time. They're short-handed, as usual." Hunter O'Hagan was park ranger at the cape. He and Bert had met last summer during her tour at Portsmouth. Within the week, they'd been sleeping together. She was staying at his place on Harkers until the roundup was over. Although Harkers Island, connected to the mainland by a bridge, was headquarters for Cape Lookout and had its own residential sector, Hunter's house was off the park grounds.

Volunteers were still disembarking from the boats. Wishing she had a cup of coffee, Bert watched Purcell's jerky stride as he headed toward the staff tent. His face was too flat, his features too small and undefined to be attractive. The slim-cut park trousers emphasized his high waist and long legs, so that he appeared out of proportion, like a stork in green pants. But his personality was so effervescent that Bert was seldom conscious of his physical appearance for long.

No one came out to organize the volunteers. Tired of watching the horses, Bert searched for Julie. She found her, shapelessly bundled in insulated sweats and a ragged jacket, by a chute made of tubular metal. A brown mare, unable to turn in the narrow corridor, rolled a wild, white-rimmed eye at Bert. "What are they doing?" Bert asked, feeling sympathy for the frightened horse.

"Just taking blood from the jugular. Doesn't hurt them." Julie jotted some figures in the log. On a table sitting on the sand in front of her was a rack full of test tubes.

"What can I do?"

"Whatever you like." Julie pointed with her chin to a group of milling volunteers. "You can go over there, or down by the pens. They'll be needing folks to move hay and run water." She leaned over. "Why don't you see if they'll let you inside the chute? Those boys could use another hand. You'll like that."

The main pen, an irregular structure of wire mesh and wood that could be subdivided, ended in a smaller enclosure, which in turn led into a metal chute. From the other end of the chute, a runway took the occupant back to a section of the horse pens. Three men wearing army cammies tucked into leather boots were herding a handful of horses from the main pen into the smaller one. The gate was open. When one man left to close it, the horses doubled around and charged back out through the gap in the line.

Bert slid through the metal bars into the chute, then into the smaller pen. "Need some help?"

An army sergeant eyed her impassively. He was a large African-American, thick in the middle. "Know anything about horses?"

"I grew up on a farm. Had horses there." That wasn't quite true, but she had lived on a farm for a year.

He gave her the once-over, from her steel-toed, leather hiking shoes to her jeans to her old, dark blue Gore-Tex jacket. Bert blessed herself for the sensible clothes. Finally, he nodded. "We could use someone at the gate."

At first, that was all Bert did, open and close the gate for the men as they herded five or six horses at a time into the smaller pen, then into the chute. One young stallion panicked at the last moment, bucking and kicking, forcing his way past the men as he shot around to where Bert stood. Instinctively, Bert yelled and waved her arms. The horse shied away, back to the chute, which allowed the army to finish the job. After that, Bert was allowed to help in the pen, too.

Most of the horses accepted their fate stoically. The scent of hay, manure, and horse perspiration brought back memories to Bert. She enjoyed the activity and was conscious of envious glances from some of the other volunteers. When they broke for lunch, Bert headed to the volunteer tent, pitched between clumps of wax myrtle close to the sound. En route, she glimpsed a familiar head of russet curls.

"Hunter, what are you doing here?" she asked the ranger astride an ATV. Just in time, she stopped herself from dropping a kiss on his head. They'd slept together last night, and it had been so nice to wake up in his bed this morning—something that didn't happen often enough to suit Bert.

"Looking for you, what else?" He slid off the Honda, smiling at her, although she thought he looked tense. "Where you been? I was just about to give up."

"Over there." Bert pointed with pride toward the smaller pen.

Hunter's brows shot up. "Good place to get kicked in the face."

"It was fun. Besides, the sergeant's taking care of me. But why are you here?" She took in the ropes, orange metal flags, and posts tied to his ATV. "Trouble on the beach?"

"Plane spotted another dead stranding, a turtle—a Kemp's Ridley yet."

Bert frowned, concentrating. "You had another Ridley wash up not long ago, didn't you? Isn't that unusual, especially in January?"

Hunter's eyes lightened. "You got that right. Been a real mild winter, so we've had a lot of turtle sightings, more than usual. Loggerheads I can understand, but two Ridley strandings? They're on the endangered species list, you know."

"What killed them?"

Hunter stared out over her head, his slate eyes shuttered against the glare. "Can't really say just yet. The last turtle was too decayed to tell much, except it had some suspicious marks. Ernie said this kill's fresh. Said it had no visible injuries. It could be a drowning, but there's no trawling being done around here."

"They finding them anywhere else?"

His eyes met hers. "You mean like the strandings back in the mil-

26

lennium?" Bert nodded. Twenty-five dead turtles had washed ashore along Cape Lookout one December. Hunter shook his head. "Nothing like that. They reported five other turtles last month—two loggerheads over by Fort Macon, couple of greens, and a Ridley at Hammocks Beach State Park. That was an undetermined cause of death, too."

"You going out to see it now?"

"Yup."

Bert was dying to join him. She'd never even seen a Ridley. But she knew it would smack of favoritism for a ranger to single out a volunteer. "You had lunch yet?" she asked, hoping she could have his company a little longer.

"I'll pick up something when I go off the island." He glanced over to where Ernie Steingart, Purcell's boss, was bent over a map with a group of men on ATVs. Ernie was in charge of the resource rangers, most of whom had degrees in biology. They had little to do with the public, concentrating on the care of the park's fauna and flora.

Like Hunter, Ernie had powerful shoulders tapering down to a long, slim waist and a round butt—which was all Bert could see of him at the moment. As he straightened, she noticed again how much taller than Hunter he was—about six-four, she decided, still admiring the rear view. She was definitely a butt girl.

"Looks like Ernie's sending out another gang to help with the roundup." Hunter leaned toward her. "He'll be awhile yet. We got time to take a run up the beach—if you'd care to see a stinky turtle, that is." His smile crinkled the corners of his eyes.

Bert laughed. He knew her too well. "Won't that get you into trouble?" She glanced at the volunteers.

"Not if we don't flaunt it. Why don't you meet me on the beach in five minutes? I'll go tell Ernie we'll catch him at the 53 when he's ready." The rangers used the island's mile markers to pinpoint locations. With so much flat ground and so few landmarks, it was a necessity.

"Is that where your Ridley is?"

Hunter nodded, starting the motor. "See you in a bit." And he was off.

Bert wasted no time. It was a good half-mile to the ocean, but at least it was flat at this end of the island.

Hunter caught up to her before she reached the beach. Gratefully, she climbed on behind him, clasping him around the waist. He immediately covered her hand with his, sliding back between her legs. "Life don't get any better than this."

Bert cuddled up, dropping her hands to his groin. "How long do you think Ernie will be?"

Hunter jumped. "Not long enough." He pushed her hand away.

"Chicken," she teased. Bert leaned forward so her breasts were pressed to his back, slipping her hands under his jacket and letting them wander slowly up his warm chest. Hunter chuckled.

They'd reached the primary dunes. The track over the ridge was worn, the sand plowed up and soft from all the traffic. Bert hung onto Hunter in earnest as the ATV labored, skidding sideways. Hunter dropped gears, feeding gas steadily. Then the wheels grabbed and the Honda shot forward, cresting the hill. Soon, they were speeding along the damp sand of the beach, the fresh breeze cool on Bert's face. She lifted her head and filled her lungs with the clean sea air.

The sky was still overcast, but here by the ocean even a dull day was bright. Wind whipped the water into whitecaps; waves hissed up the shore. Their wheels crunched over layers of shells. Not all the shells were broken, Bert noticed. Maybe she and Julie could sneak out later and do a little shelling.

A mound close to the dunes caught Bert's eye. Just then, Hunter slowed, turning toward it. With a regretful, final pat, Bert pulled away from Hunter. He grabbed her hand and squeezed it as they dismounted.

"This is the old Ridley, the one that washed up last month," he said. "Purcell found it after a blow."

"What a gorgeous carapace." Bert reached in her pocket for her camera. The heart-shaped shell of the Ridley had been spray-painted with an identifying red slash. The mark had faded and spread as the shell bleached, so the carapace was now a mellow, dusty rose, its plates outlined in darker rose, raised white barnacles marching up the middle. Poking out from under the sand were the turtle's two front flippers, apparently intact. Blowing sand had softened the edges and covered much of the rotting flesh, but the downwind side still reeked of decay.

"You leave them here?" Bert took another picture.

"They did a necropsy, took the head and the back flippers, I believe. Reckon that's all they need." Hunter squinted out to sea. At this time of year, the waters were empty of recreational fisherman, but Bert could see a large boat in the distance. "That's the dredge," Hunter said.

"Think it has something to do with these turtles?" Hit by five hurricanes in as many years, Bogue Banks had taken a beating. The dredge was there to pump sand back to the beach, the lifeblood of the tourist industry.

Hunter shrugged. "They're supposed to have an observer on board to monitor, but the time of death makes them suspect, all right. Nothing else around." He glanced at his watch. "Reckon we'd better be getting on, if you want to see the other one."

As Hunter passed the 52 marker, he slowed, driving close to the sandy cliff of undercut dunes. There was no sign of a turtle. When they reached the 53, he turned around and rode back, both of them searching for mounds. Drifting sand could quickly cover anything on the beach.

Finally, Hunter stopped and got on his radio. "Ernie, I'm down here about the 52.5. Don't see any stranding."

"By the 52.7, thirty feet off the dune, past the tide line," a voice over the radio squawked.

Hunter drove slowly up the beach. "Nothing here." His brows came together. They parked the Honda and walked west, scanning the berm. "Bert, anything catch your eye?"

The sand where Hunter stood did look different. At first, she couldn't figure it out. "I know. This looks like when I sweep away footprints from a turtle nest."

Hunter's eyes narrowed, his lips a straight line. "That's it exactly. You think you can get me a picture?"

While Bert took a couple of shots, Hunter walked down to the water. He took off his shoes, rolled up his pants, and waded into the surf. The cold, surging waves still washed up over the bottom of his trousers. Bert shuddered in sympathy. She figured he was looking for signs of a boat having been pulled up the beach—indentations or a smear of paint in the sand.

When he returned, she asked, "Find anything?"

"Didn't expect to, but had to try. Surf's too high."

"Why would anyone steal a dead turtle? Are shells valuable?"

Hunter sat, using his socks to brush the sand off his feet, which were bright pink from the cold water. "It's illegal to own any kind of sea-turtle carapace or head. Ridleys are listed as endangered. I reckon that would make them valuable to some people." He stared at the breakers. "Man couldn't bring in just any kind of boat here, need a Zodiak or high-prow surf boat." They headed back to the Honda. "Kemp's Ridleys are smaller than loggerheads but still heavy. Full-grown one weighs a hundred and fifty pounds." Hunter's bushy brows were drawn close. Deep lines ran down the sides of his mouth. He got back on the radio. "Two-four-one, Ernie, you leave yet? Good. Wait there. I'm on my way back."

"Is it serious? I mean, more serious than someone snatching a rare turtle?"

"Don't know." Hunter sat on the ATV. "I'd be obliged if you don't mention this to anyone until I find out what happened to it. Got some reporters on the island. This dredging's a hot political issue, and the media's been making a big thing of the turtle strandings."

She nudged against him. "You know I won't." It was pleasant back by the sheltering, ten-foot cliffs, the sand warm underfoot, the sky full of dark clouds, rays from the hidden sun escaping in fingers around the edges. "What are we close to? On the sound side, I mean." Bert was in no hurry to get back.

Brows jutting in concentration, Hunter drew a wavy line in the sand with his foot. "This is where we are now." He pointed at a white post. "The 53 marker is across the island from what they call Wade's Shore. Bald Hill Bay is two miles east of here. That's the bay where you put in the first day."

"I don't remember passing any hills."

"That's on account of the Bald Hill dune washing away a long time ago. But the name stuck. It's a hard place to get to. Real shallow and muddy in there, probably the narrowest part of the island." He looked up, giving her his lopsided smile. "Your eyes are as green as the ocean right now, and I know what that means. How about we get back before you make me forget my duties?"

Bert gave him a hug and put her lips to his neck. He tasted salty and good. She kissed him again. Hunter held her tight for a minute, then with a low grunt pushed himself away. He looked up the beach.

Bert followed his glance. "Someone coming?"

He shook his head, frowning, his eyes dark the way they became when he wanted her. "No." He drew a long breath. "But it's better if we don't take the chance. Too many people on the island."

Bert grinned. "Chicken."

"That's one chicken too many." He took another quick look around and reached for her. "I'll teach you to tease a man when he's on duty."

This was the way to make love, Bert thought—in the sunshine with the ocean crashing in your ears. Then she couldn't think anymore.

They were both quiet on the way back. Bert huddled close to Hunter, still warm and happy.

All too soon, they were at the horse corridor. As Bert slid off the Honda, Hunter's hand clung to her waist. "See you in a couple of hours, all right? Don't get stepped on by any horses." His gray eyes lightened into a smile as he touched her lips with a finger.

Bert watched him drive away, conscious of the hot fluttering deep in her belly. It was amazing how that man could turn her on.

Later that afternoon, Bert followed Julie into the main pen, supposedly to check the watering tubs but really to nose around. Bert had spotted a small, flaxen-maned colt and wanted to see if it was Triton's foal.

"There's Triton." Julie pointed. "DeWitt brought him in this morning." A group of reporters and special guests stood by the fence close to the stallion and a foal. "Isn't that your little pony?"

It was the flaxen-maned foal, having himself a wonderful time. Some of the reporters and guests stretched hands through the wire fence. The colt was standing motionless as eager fingers gently scratched his nose, behind his ears, and down his back and rump.

"Oh, look. Do you think he'll let me touch him?" Bert whispered. They advanced slowly. To her delight, the foal not only let her tickle his head, but also rubbed up against her legs, nudging her.

"He's so cute. Does he have a name?" The question came from one of the women on the other side of the fence.

"Ah believe that's Shony," a slim, gray-haired man who'd just joined the group answered. "Y'all know you're not supposed to pet or feed the horses? Gets them accustomed to folks, and that's not always good." His drawl was heavy, compared to most of the volunteers. Must be from inland, Bert decided. Nice jacket.

"Relax, James. He's just a baby. Probably thinks we're his horsy aunties," said one of the women.

Bert shot the slim man a curious glance. "How do they get named?" she asked, digging in her pocket for her camera.

"Ah believe a professor from Princeton does the naming around here—can't quite recollect his name. Every summer, he travels down the banks with a mess of college students to study the ponies."

Bert smiled as she snapped away at Shony. "Sounds like he's into mythology. Triton the trumpeter, son of Neptune, god of the sea. His blaze really does look like a trident. But what's Shony mean?"

"Ah heard he was some kind of Scottish sea god," the man said.

"That fits." Bert edged around to get a shot of the foal's face.

"Um, ma'am, Ah do believe that youngun's daddy might be getting agitated." The slim man's eyes were focused behind Bert.

She and Julie swung around. Triton was advancing, shoulders down, neck extended, nose flat to the ground, ears back so his head seemed to be just a long extension of his neck, reminiscent of a striking rattler. Julie yelped.

Behind them, the man laughed softly. "They call that snaking. Ah'd say you ladies are being herded off his charges."

"What do we do?" Bert whispered, not thinking it particularly funny from her side of the fence.

"Move away, slowly now. Just keep your eyes forward, and don't turn around."

It took courage not to look back. Bert could feel the horse's breath on her legs. Finally, when she couldn't stand it any longer, she sneaked a peek. Triton was back with his mares, not paying them any attention—but someone else was. Shony was at her heels. "Go away," she hissed, waving her hand. The foal took her flapping fingers as an invitation and trotted up to butt the back of her legs. Bert jumped. "No. Stop it. You'll get me into trouble."

Julie, hand over her mouth, was shaking with laughter. "I do believe he's bonded."

Throwing another nervous glance over her shoulder, Bert hurried to the gate. Even after they were outside the pen, Shony followed them along the fence as long as he could. Bert groaned. "Now, I really feel bad. Do you suppose he'll find his way back?"

Julie patted Bert's arm. "Not to worry. Colts are always getting lost. It's part of their education. The nice thing is, the other horses take care of them until their daddy shows up." As they approached the testing table, Julie paused, dropping her voice. "I wanted to ask you something, but I don't want you to feel obliged or anything, understood?" Bert nodded, curious. "One of the foundation members and me were supposed to stay over Wednesday night. You know, they always leave someone on the island watching the pens. Well, something came up, and she can't make it. I was wondering if you'd care to spend the night. I don't mean to cut in on your time with Hunter or anything." Julie flushed.

So Julie knew about them, too. Well, it wasn't a secret. Bert smiled. "I'd love to. By then, Hunter will need a night off, right?"

Julie's blush deepened. "No way I'm commenting on that, but it will be the last night of the roundup. The test results from DeWitt and the state will be in by Thursday. Then we can let the horses loose."

"What should I bring?"

"A warm sleeping bag and whatever you want to eat. They have cots in the tent and a camp stove. Bring some extra food. Never can tell what'll happen around here."

That was the truth. Bert remembered vividly being stranded at Portsmouth with a hurricane bearing down. She hoped Julie's words were not a portent.

Chapter 4

"That man don't know how to keep his mouth shut." Hunter slammed into the house with a newspaper under his arm, his hair in tight curls around his face.

Bert swung around from the stove, where she had a pan of cratering pancakes. "What's the matter?"

Hunter bent over the paper, cursing. "Couldn't wait, could he? Had to go show up the other vets. I'll get his ass from here till next Tuesday."

Sliding the pan off the burner, Bert leaned over his shoulder to see for herself. The headline read, "Shackleford Ponies Test Clean."

"That's great news!" she said. "Why are you upset? We were hoping for no EIA."

"It isn't that. We expected them to test clean. But DeWitt Brigman didn't have any call to announce this to the papers. Results aren't official till the state tests come in."

Bert put the pancakes back on the burner and flipped them. "The state tests will be back tomorrow, right?"

"You don't understand. Times aren't so good, and these vets all need to make a living." Hunter sprawled at the table. "DeWitt Brigman's using us for free publicity, and it's not right. Dr. Brigman's going to hear from me." Hunter reached for his coffee. After a few more growls, he turned the page and settled down to read.

Relieved, Bert piled the pancakes on a platter. He'd been on the irritable side lately. It was nothing to do with her, she hoped. He was probably just working too hard.

She eyed the clock. Today was Wednesday, the fifth day of the roundup and her night to stay on the island. She still had to get dressed and put together her food. How cold would it be? Hunter's house, like many on Harkers Island, was a converted summer cottage. It had a living-room-and-kitchen combo, two tiny bedrooms, and a big sleeping loft Hunter used for his bedroom. What made it outstanding was the view. The house was built on pilings so the deck extended over the water, the rear wall nothing but glass overlooking Back Sound and its picturesque boat traffic.

Bert squinted through the gloom at the outdoor thermometer—thirty degrees. At five-thirty, the sky was still dark, but ripples ruffled the water's surface. Wind this early was not a good sign. She better wear long johns.

She brought the stack of pancakes over and sat down by Hunter. "I have to be at the dock in forty-five minutes."

"So you're leaving me after just four nights, are you?" He shook his head. "Makes me feel right inadequate, it does."

Bert grinned, patting his thigh. "After last night, you know better. You won't be back until late anyhow."

He slid his hand through her fine, yellow hair, letting it trickle though his fingers back to her shoulders. "I have Friday and Sunday off—if DeWitt Brigman doesn't find some other way to mess things up, that is. You don't have to go back to the restaurant until Monday, right?"

"I'm thinking I should leave Sunday night. I'm hiring servers Monday. You'll need a rest by then anyhow—and not just from me."

"Oh, I wouldn't say that." Hunter gave her a grin. "Besides, I have plans for us on Sunday. But to tell the truth, it's not going to make me sad to see someone else take over this job. Beginning to feel my age."

Frowning, she concentrated on eating. Hunter, forty-seven, was eight years younger than Bert. That had bothered her at first, but she was learning to accept it. He had been acting superintendent of Cape Lookout National Seashore for two months now, ever since the past superintendent had taken a job out west. In her opinion, Hunter should have been promoted to the post permanently. She rose and gathered the plates. This was no time to get into that.

"Leave them. I'll take care of it. I don't pick up Ernie till eight." Hunter and Ernie Steingart, chief resource ranger, were meeting with National Marine Fisheries and Fish and Wildlife at Atlantic Beach to discuss the dredging. Bert assumed it was connected with the dead Ridleys.

Soon, Bert was on the park boat, roaring through the frosty morning to the northeast end of Shackleford. The volunteers were jubilant at the news the horses were free of EIA. They congratulated each other and made plans for the next roundup.

One of the first on board, Bert managed to snag a spot inside the boat's cabin, where she could enjoy the view without having to squint through wind-generated tears. The sun was coloring the sky behind the cape, silhouetting the tall lighthouse with shades of orange and pink. Behind the black and white diamonds of the monolith, wavy lines of dark cormorants flew east to the day's fishing grounds. Suddenly, she was conscious of a pressure against her side—someone trying to edge in. Bert reached for the windshield as if to steady herself, effectively blocking the move.

"I'm so sorry. I didn't mean to jostle you. People are so rude these days." The woman next to Bert twisted around to glare at the man behind. "You're Bert Lenehan, aren't you?" she wheezed, fixing her gaze on Bert. Her eyes were wide apart, a pale, clear blue, and her skin had a myriad of tiny wrinkles. "I've been wanting to meet you for ever so long."

"How'd you know who I was?" Bert flushed. That would teach her to be territorial.

The woman smiled, her lips barely parting. She wore a brimmed hat, her thick, honey-brown hair in a loose braid down her back. She probably wasn't as old as she looked—forties, maybe?—but was in poor health. Besides the wheezing, she was much too thin, and there were red blotches on her neck and hands.

"My dear, everyone in these parts knows all about you. You're the volunteer who cost that nice Hunter O'Hagan his promotion." The woman sucked air noisily.

Bert froze, shocked speechless.

Something flickered in the woman's eyes. "Oh, dear, I didn't mean to upset you." She stopped to draw breath. "I guess I should have kept quiet, but sometimes my curiosity just gets the better of me. I suppose that's why they say I've got a talent for news stories. I trust I didn't hurt your feelings."

Uh-oh, it could only be that reporter Purcell had warned her about. "Are you Vilma, Vilma . . .?" Unconsciously, Bert backed away.

The woman slid forward, capturing Bert's spot behind the windshield. "I guess I should have introduced myself. I'm Vilma Willit. You've heard of me?"

Bert could read no malice or triumph in the woman's face, but she'd learned the hard way that she wasn't good at judging character. Trying to keep any emotion out of her voice, she asked, "What do you mean, I cost Hunter a promotion?"

"Surely, you know. I mean, considering you're living with him and all." The reporter coughed.

"I'd like to hear what's being said."

"Oh, my, I do believe I've started something. Well, it's not like it's a secret or anything." Vilma paused, her concave chest heaving. "Everyone knows Hunter took a demotion last summer for disobeying a direct order when he took that boat out to Portsmouth to help you." The woman's blue eyes opened even wider, pale lashes fanning lined cheeks. "Why, it was a disgrace what the park did. I firmly believe that he should have been given a medal for bravery, not chastised." She sucked air though her nose.

"Then you should know that the demotion was temporary. He's back to GS-13."

Vilma smiled again, this time showing teeth. "That's quite correct, my dear, but then he didn't get a promotion either, did he?" She inhaled. "A man with a record of flouting orders is not likely to be appointed superintendent of a national park. I'm quite sure Hunter's aware of that. Ask him, why don't you?"

Oh, God, was it true? Bert turned away, a sick feeling in her stomach. She edged through the crowded cabin to the boat's rail and leaned over, staring blindly at the water. What a nasty woman. She couldn't be right, could she? Hunter hadn't been appointed superintendent, but he'd given Bert the impression superintendents always came from other parks, not from the ranks. Suddenly, the gray day seemed even darker. How could she ever make it up to him?

Things didn't get better when they docked. Not in the mood for celebration, Bert went up to the pens, where she knew Shony would be waiting for his morning scratch. But no little, blond-maned foal appeared. Bert walked up and down the irregular perimeter. Finally, the sergeant interrupted her pacing. "Want to help us in the chute today?"

His words cut through Bert's thoughts. "I thought we were all done."

"Done with the testing. Time to do some branding."

"The foals?"

The sergeant nodded. Then, mistaking her subdued mood as concern for the ponies, he added, "Freeze branding. Don't hurt them none."

For the next two hours, they picked out the foals that had been painted with numbers during the initial testing. DeWitt Brigman and Tanisha Hansen, the foundation vet, were working inside the testing gate. DeWitt would lean against a foal to hold it steady while Tanisha shaved the horse's hip. Sometimes, an old brand would show up under the heavy winter coat. Julie, standing behind DeWitt outside the gate, handed the branding irons to the bearded vet while making notes in a log. Now and then, DeWitt grunted a command, and Julie scurried back to a log containing pictures and descriptions of each pony. After one such episode, DeWitt climbed out of the pen and strode over to Bert and the sergeant. "We need to be sure whose foal this is. Did you happen to notice whose band he belonged to when you picked him up?"

The sergeant shook his head.

Bert hesitated, then said, "This morning, he was with that dark stallion, the one that has the bony, funny-colored mare."

DeWitt cocked his head. "Blade? Dionysus? Orion?"

"I don't know their names." She'd noticed the foal when she was looking for Shony.

"Think you can find him again?"

"I'll try."

"Julie, you know the stallions, don't you? Go with her."

"Pretty abrupt, isn't he?" Bert commented to Julie as they hunted the stallion.

Julie smiled, tossing her head. "That's just his way, Bert. He's really nice when you get to know him."

"Oh?"

"He let me ride along when they went to get Triton Sunday."

"You kept up with DeWitt?"

Julie laughed. "No way. I stayed on the beach, in case Triton tried to run west." She turned from Bert to point at a dark brown horse. "Is that the stallion?"

After a moment, Bert shook her head. "He has a mare that's sort of a blotchy tan, old. Oh, look, behind the watering tub. That looks like him. Yup, there's the mare."

With the band located, the two women returned to the branding gates. "It was Orion," Julie told DeWitt.

The big vet broke into a smile, white teeth parting his bushy, black beard. Even his eyes softened. He put his arms around both women and gave each a quick hug. His body was warm and, although redolent of horse, not unpleasant to Bert's nose. Maybe Julie was right about the man.

The branding done, Bert was helping the vets pack their gear when Tanisha, the foundation vet, asked DeWitt, "You're handling the adoptions for Croatan Farm, right?"

"They's all spoken for."

"I didn't want one," the black girl said. "The foundation just wants to be sure you keep a record of where each pony is, in case the farm decides to relocate them. We have to do checkups, you know."

Ernie Steingart, the shy ranger with the great build, glanced up and patted the air, as if to quiet her.

DeWitt swung around, hands on hips, his face close to Tanisha's. "What kind of an effing vet you think I am? Damn right I keep records, good ones. You insinuating otherwise?"

Tanisha, almost as tall as DeWitt, held her ground. "You don't have to get nasty. I'm just doing my job."

Purcell, who had been working close to Tanisha all morning, stepped forward. But before he could say anything, DeWitt backed off and spread his hands, palms down. "I apologize. I didn't mean to spout off at you. It's just they all know I keep good records." His eyes narrowed. "Who put you up to this? Clayton Davis? He's always bad-mouthing me." From the way Tanisha's eyes and mouth rounded, Bert guessed DeWitt had hit the mark. The big man slung an arm over the young vet's shoulder. "Why don't you come over to my office tomorrow? I'll show you how I plan to do it, and you can tell me if it meets your approval, okay?"

A gust of wind swirled sand in Bert's face. As she started for one of the tents, she caught sight of Purcell. He slouched as if to minimize his long legs, glaring at DeWitt, who was still talking animatedly with Tanisha. And Purcell wasn't the only one upset with them. Behind him, Julie stared at the pair, her face lacking its usual cheer.

Bert hurried over to her new friend. "So what happens now?"

"Eat lunch, I guess." Julie turned away from DeWitt and began walking slowly toward the tent.

"Is DeWitt married?"

Julie's head snapped around to look at Bert. "How on earth would I know? Anyhow, why would I care?" Then she added quickly, "How was Shony this morning?"

If Julie wanted to change the subject, she picked the right way. All thoughts of a possible romance between her friend and DeWitt went out of Bert's head. "Oh, my God, Shony wasn't with the ponies that got branded. Wouldn't he have needed a brand?"

Lifting the flap of the volunteer tent, Julie said, "Come to think of it, I don't remember seeing him either. Could be they did him while we were searching for Orion, or before we got here."

"But he didn't come up for his morning scratch either. I thought he was keeping warm behind the windbreak."

The tent was packed with volunteers, reporters, and special guests. Julie made a face, pushing her way through to her cooler. "Grab your food, why don't you? We'll take it over to the park tent."

The crowd in the tent faced the rear, where someone was giving a speech. Bert had left her cooler under the cot she planned to use tonight. Pulling out a sandwich and a bottle of water, she glanced toward the disembodied voice. "What's going on?"

"Lida Fulchard, our state legislator, is making political hay. You'd think it was because of something she did that no horse came down with EIA."

"She's the one that's been bucking the park on the Jet Skis?"

"That's her. She's big on beach nourishment, too—at all costs, including the turtles. I heard she picked up a condemned motel on a bankruptcy after the first nourishment proposition was defeated." Julie snickered. "Anytime Lida's involved in something, you can be sure she's got a personal interest."

"Let's go." Bert definitely didn't want to stick around. They left the tents, passing near the horse pens. Bert stopped to zip up her jacket. Although the sun was shining brightly, it was still only about thirty degrees. "I can't figure out where Shony could be."

"Why don't we go take a look? We can eat in the pens." Sandwiches in hand, the two women let themselves into the corral, where most of the horses were standing quietly in groups. Julie pointed at a mare lying with her foal. "Could be he's just napping."

Bert found it hard walking. She had to watch where she stepped and at the same time keep a lookout for moving horses. Luckily, they had no trouble locating Triton. His band had a prime position behind the wind fence. But although Scylla was there, Shony was not. As they approached, Triton snorted a warning, stamping his foot.

"Stay back," Julie said. "I don't want him doing that snake thing again."

Bert frowned, shoving the last of her watercress and onion sandwich into her mouth. "I don't understand," she said. "Where could Shony be?"

They saw several flaxen-maned colts, but most were older and larger. Bert spotted one tiny baby with a long tail just like Shony's, but it was a filly. Then Julie pointed out another foal with a flaxen mane. Bert thought she'd found Shony until she saw the colt's face.

"You certain that's not him?" Julie took a bite of her thick kaiser roll. "Could be Shony wandered away from his band and Triton was just looking after him. That happens a lot."

Bert edged around to get a good look at the foal's forehead. "This one has a star blaze, and look how small it is. Shony's blaze ran all the way down his nose."

Julie shook her head. "Can't say I really noticed."

"I thought you knew the horses."

"Only from last year. Mostly the stallions. I'm a lab tech. I don't get out like this much."

They continued checking. The pens had been enlarged several times and were deliberately irregular in shape to allow the horses some semblance of territory. But the horses, uneasy at being crowded together in less than two acres, were constantly shifting positions. Sometimes, a fight would break out, or one of the mares would charge through, scattering the others.

Julie put an end to their search. "We'd better get out of here before that woman finishes her speech. We're not really supposed to be in the pens."

"Let's find Purcell. He's in charge of them. You can't just lose a horse."

Half an hour later, Bert, Julie, Purcell, Tanisha, DeWitt, and the representative from the Humane Society were in the main pen. The only flaxen-maned male foal they could find was the same one Julie and Bert had noted earlier.

"You're looking at Bunky," DeWitt told them. "That's his band, all right. Satyr's his stallion."

"Bert, this must be the one you saw with Triton," Purcell said in a low voice.

43

Bert shook her head. "Shony had a white, pointed shell, like a horse conch, on his forehead. Just like Triton's."

"You keep calling him Shony. Where did you get that name?" Purcell's flat face turned toward her. He was the only ranger present.

"Oh!" Bert blinked. "I'm not sure. Someone told me. Was it you, Julie?"

The blonde shook her head. "Not me. I'm still learning the names of last year's crop."

Bert's mind was not bringing up a picture. "I didn't make it up, but offhand I can't remember who told me."

"You want to check the horse log?" Julie asked. "They keep a record of all the horses there. Pictures of most of them, too."

But the log showed no foal called Shony. There was a record of a filly born last summer to Charybdis, another of Triton's mares, and a notation that one of Triton's foals had disappeared shortly after delivery. It was presumed dead.

"That's not unusual," Purcell said. "Some births are defective. Sometimes, they're just too weak to make it. Some foals drown trying to keep up with the herd."

A deep voice behind Bert chuckled. "I'm guessing it's that foal's ghost you saw. You do see ghosts, don't you?"

Bert whipped around to confront DeWitt. "And just what are you getting at?" She knew. After the murders last summer at Portsmouth, she'd been stupid enough to tell the media that some of the events remained unexplained. The headlines had screamed about ghosts and brought up the legend of Sea-born Woman.

Instead of backing off at her fury, as most men would have, the bearded vet chuckled again and reached out, cuffing her shoulder. "Just kidding. No need to get hot. You did a great job out there."

"Shony was no ghost. He followed me around, begging to get scratched all the time. Ask . . ." Bert clapped her hands to her mouth. "I remember. It was the man by the fence. I was scratching Shony, and this man said I shouldn't."

"So?" DeWitt's eyes were fixed on Bert's.

Again, Bert noticed their color—Castilian green, they called it. She also noticed his pitted complexion. Was that why he wore a beard? "He's the one who said my foal's name was Shony. He said some professor from Princeton named the new foals."

The big vet tipped his head, listening intently. "That's true. What was the man's name?"

"I don't know. He was nice looking, slim, had on a dark jacket."

Tanisha giggled. "Look around." Most of the men were in orange jumpsuits—like DeWitt and Purcell—or dark jackets.

"But this man looked important," Bert persisted.

"Got more people here who think they're important than we got doers," DeWitt growled.

"Well, hey, we're wasting time. What's the difference if you can't find her horse? We're not missing any, right?" boomed an unfamiliar voice.

He should be on the radio with that bass, Bert thought, swinging around. A tall man with a thick head of silver hair stood a short distance away. The first thing Bert noticed was that his eyes were not in sync. One looked at her, and the other wandered off to the side. Then she saw the thick, raised scar than ran from his brow over the bridge of his nose to his eye. The nose was bumpy and slightly twisted. The only thing that saved him from being downright ugly was the fall of chin-length, silky hair over smooth, sun-browned skin.

"Clayton Davis," Julie whispered at Bert's nudge. "The Humane Society rep—nothing to do with the shelters. He acts as a review and advisory board, and oversees the birth control. Clayton had some great suggest—"

Footsteps sounded close behind them. "They're all here, unless someone let one of the horses out. You girls didn't, did you?"

"Purcell. You know we wouldn't," Julie snapped before Bert could respond.

"The gates were all closed this morning. I didn't see any sign of trouble," Tanisha reported.

An idea floated through Bert's head. "Who picks the horses to be adopted?"

"The foundation," Tanisha said, "with the approval of all the vets and the park ranger in charge. We consider genetics, health, family size, and if the foal's dam is pregnant. We worked on that last night."

"Suppose someone didn't want Shony adopted, so they let him loose. Could it be something like that?"

DeWitt shrugged. On him, it was a big shrug. "Since your Shony's not listed anywhere, I don't see how a body could single him out. Not to mention nothing's been decided yet."

"That foal wouldn't stay away," Purcell added. "If he's as young as you said, Bert, he'd be outside the fence looking for his mother."

The Humane Society rep stepped forward. His good eye was turned to Bert. "She saw the foal with Triton and figured it was his. If it were Triton's foal, then she'd expect it to have a blaze like Triton's. She just got the blazes mixed up. Not her fault. Natural mistake, okay? How about we close shop and get out of here at a decent hour just once this week?"

"What's your rush, Clayton?" DeWitt asked. "Afraid to leave your wife alone too long?"

Clayton stiffened, scar pulsing, bad eye darting to the side. Then he spun about, silver hair flying, and headed for the boats.

Bert clenched her teeth. She had not mixed up the horses. She opened her mouth to protest, but Julie nudged her, shaking her head. Purcell had a finger to his lips.

Swallowing hard, Bert fell in behind them. She'd find Shony if it took her all night. She hadn't mistaken that conch-shaped marking on his forehead either. Hadn't DeWitt said something about it being a genetic trait, handed down through Triton's bloodline for generations?

Julie dropped back to join her, opened her mouth to say something, saw Bert's scowl, and decided against it.

Poor Julie. It wasn't her fault. Bert took a deep breath and said the first thing that came to mind. "You check the ponies for genetics. Can you tell where they originated?"

"You mean, can we tell if they're Spanish?"

Bert nodded.

"Not by genetics, but quite a few Shackleford horses have only five lumbar vertebrae. That's typical of Arabian or Spanish ancestry. Other breeds have six."

"DeWitt said a lot of European horses were of Spanish descent."

"Right. You know those gorgeous white show horses, Lippizaners? They're supposed to have Spanish blood," Julie said. "And I was just reading about a Celtic chieftain that traded seven hundred head of cattle for one Spanish stallion."

Chapter 5

Ireland, 1450

Finn-gall

"*Ce cheval*, this horse, is descended of the stallion Triton," the heavily bearded Frenchman explained loudly with much gesturing. "He is Jennetta. This is fine breed of horse from Andalusia. Very good bloodlines." He peered from under shaggy brows at the Scot, clad in a woolen jacket over a saffron shirt.

The Spanish horse shifted restlessly under the Scot's inspection. For over a year, he'd been traveling, and the stallion was weary of strange lands and owners. Sometimes, he carried a rider, but often he followed behind a mounted escort. Still, his treatment was good. He'd been groomed at the end of each day, and many a night he had shelter while the guide horse and rider shivered in the stable yard. Now, the wool-clad man spoke in a soft, lilting voice. "I had envisioned him to be larger, more imposing."

"Is *son coeur*, his heart, who is large. A Jennetta is not bested. He learn fast, more fast than other horses. In battle, he jump, he go, he turn. Is nothing to stop him. A Jennetta can run over"— he pointed at a rocky field nearby—"that will make fall other horses."

"I understand he's surefooted. The question is, what will Lord Hob think of him?"

"He have but to ride him. He have easy steps, *passé fine*. He walk more fast than big horse trot. Make easy to ride for long time." The Frenchman frowned, searching for words. "He move legs like music. Lift high and throw to side. All stop to see."

"But he is small."

The bearded one threw out his arms, spreading his black cloak in a dramatic gesture. "I am charged by my master, François d'Avignon, to bring to this land *sauvage* the prize of his stables, this horse, Le Spiral."

Walking over to the stallion, the Frenchman lifted a strand of the horse's flaxen mane. "This color horse, like *le soleil*, the sun, come from stable of Carthusian monks. *C'est défendu*, is forbidden, to take golden Jennetta from Andalusia. Much danger before cross sea, ride only at night. In recompense, you are giving me—"

"Yes, yes, I am aware of our bargain," the Scot interrupted.

"*Alors*, you are accepting?"

"Aye." He sighed, patting the purse that hung from his waist. "Come to the tavern, and I shall settle with you. Then you must instruct my groom in the handling of this Spi . . . Spe . . . A pox on his name! I shall call him Finn-gall, fair foreigner." A smidgen of a smile crossed his pale visage as he let his gaze rest on the stallion with the flaxen mane and gold coat.

At dawn the next day, Finn-gall was led from the stable into the frosty morning. The horse, the Scot, and a young groom wound their way down the path to the harbor below. A cold mist condensed on the stallion's shaggy pelt, grown thicker than he'd ever known it in his native warm climes. Finn-gall stretched his neck, raising his muzzle to the breeze. Salt lingered on his lips. He whinnied, making the groom jump. Salt meant discomfort, danger, and death. Early in his journey, a man had led him aboard a wooden craft floating on water, not the sweet water of the rivers but a briny, cold lake. Then ropes had been wound around his body, and he'd been lowered through an opening and left to stand among barrels and crates. Two men had tried to steady him as the boat pitched and rolled but soon discovered it was they, not the quadruped, who needed the steadying. One of the men, slow to move, had been pinned between two crates of sheep as the ship tossed. His screams were terrible.

Soon, Finn-gall's fears proved correct. They came to another salt lake. As they approached the gray water, thick tendrils of fog rose from the edge of visibility. This boat was not large like the others, merely a curragh made of skins over a wood frame. The groom approached with a blindfold. Finn-gall reared, snorting.

"You take reins and speak gentle, he follow you on the *bateau*," called a loud voice from a nearby stable. It was the bearded one watching their departure.

The Scot picked up the bridle. Stroking the horse's nose, he whispered, "Come, Finn-gall. This is the end of your journey, and the beginning of mine. There is no place on earth more suited for horses than the Iron Isle with its spongy turf." As the stallion followed the man aboard, the Scot smiled for the first time, stroking the horse. "You shall be happy, and I shall be rich beyond my wildest dreams."

It was not a long journey. The barge was built to accommodate several dozen head of cattle, so there was ample room for Finn-gall, the groom, the Scot, and the crew. The wind was light and the sun still high as they sailed into the Bay of Weis-ford. The crew lowered the sail and poled into the sheltered but shallow harbor.

Eager to be on shore once again, Finn-gall quickly followed the Scot down the plank ramp to the dark, gravel sand of the beach. Farther up the berm, two horses stood motionless, heads turned toward them. The mare was an Irish black, the other a sorrel gelding. Both horses were considerably larger than Finn-gall.

Although neither mare nor gelding posed a threat to the stallion, it did no harm to establish his status. The Jennetta tossed his head and farted long and loud.

The heavy, bald man astride the Irish black chortled. "He appears to be in fine fettle."

The younger redhead on the gelding dismounted, his freckled face tight with disdain. "I am Henry Carew, firstborn of the earl of Hob."

The Scot bowed. "Ian Mackenzie at your service, my lord." He nodded at the stallion. "I bring you Finn-gall."

The bald man smiled, but young Henry shook his head as he stared at the horse. Finn-gall stared back, feeling his dislike.

The redhead dropped his gaze first, turning to the Scot. "I trust you had a good crossing." He indicated the rider on the Irish black, a heavy man with dark jowls and a gleaming pate. "The lord, my father, Donall Carew, earl of Hob. Ian Mackenzie."

Lord Donall nodded at the Scot in his tartan trews and saffron shirt, then directed his attention to the stallion. "It has been a lengthy voyage. He has not suffered harm?"

"Nay, my lord. The grooms were instructed to care for him as if he were of the House of Lancaster. But it has been a costly undertaking."

While they spoke, young Henry approached Finn-gall. The stallion stood still as carved granite, waiting. Scowling, the youth extended a freckled hand. Finn-gall ignored him for a moment, then passed his lips over the open palm, thus familiarizing himself with this hostile stranger. After a perfunctory scratch of the horse's nose and forehead, Henry began to run his hands over Finn-gall's body.

The stallion permitted the redhead to feel his forelegs and lift each hoof, but when he pushed back Finn-gall's lips to examine his teeth, Finn-gall extended his neck upward, backing away.

"He's a five-year-old, as was on the billet." The Scot stepped forward to steady the horse.

The earl addressed his son. "He is sound?"

"Aye, my lord, from the little I have seen. But considering the cost, might it not be prudent to have another opinion, perhaps the castle groom?" Lifting a strand of Finn-gall's mane, Henry added, "He is handsome enough with his long mane and tail, but he is stunted, and his—"

The Scot broke in. "These Jennettas are as strong as oxen. The foals can walk at birth and feed on grass in a matter of days."

The earl smiled, waving a pudgy hand. "He is here to breed, not to pull carts." He inclined his head to the Scot. "I am satisfied you have kept your bargain. You will find seven hundred head of cattle in the Weis-ford pens awaiting your inspection."

The son winced. A fortune for a horse.

Soon, Finn-gall, on a lead, was cantering behind Lord Donall and his son. When they came to a fork in the road, the earl pulled his mare to a stop. The younger man swung around on his saddle, thin brows raised in question.

Lord Donall guffawed, jowls shaking. "Truly, I am aware the best route to Castle Ur is to the right, but . . ." He turned his Irish black to the left.

Young Henry spurred his mount, cantering back to the earl's side. "It is always a pleasure to ride by the sea, Father," he ventured, "or do we travel this way for some purpose?"

Lord Donall did not answer until they passed a small headland. He reined to a stop, dismounted, and dropped the bridle to trail on the ground. This would leave his mare free to graze, yet she would not stray far. Pointing his whip at a distant stand of woods, the earl said, "Wait here until I pass over the brow of the hill. You may then join me. Bring the *Hineta*." He glanced at the stallion.

Finn-gall began to graze with the other two horses, but he'd barely gotten a mouthful when the young redhead jerked on his lead. With a snort to show his displeasure, the stallion followed Henry up the winding path. As they crested the hill, Finn-gall glimpsed a grassy mound large enough to feed a band of horses. The tomb stood high in the center of a flat meadow. It was longer than it was broad, its ends aligned to the sun.

The freckled youth came to a sudden halt. A wave of fear wafted back. Finn-gall lifted his muzzle to the breeze, but he tasted no danger, only the scent of wood smoke and the presence of a female. However, Henry continued to sweat. He fumbled about Finn-gall's neck, muttering darkly, "What brings my father to this place? The mound is enchanted. Sacred. Haunted by the *Fir Bolg*, the first people. Ordinary mortals such as we do well to keep our distance."

Crossing himself and kissing the crucifix that hung from his neck on a great chain, Henry backed away. A silvery laugh halted him. The mocking sound came from a lass dressed in a simple leine, over which she wore a rough wool cloak. She sat on a three-legged stool outside a small earthen hut between the woods and the mound. Lord Donall sat on a log by her feet. He motioned Henry to approach with Finn-gall.

The lass rose, clapping her hands and running to the stallion's side. With little croons of delight, she buried her face in his neck. She smelled of wood ashes and flowers and green grass. Finn-gall nudged her gently.

"Take care," the bald man warned, "else he will be nipping your shoulder."

"If only I were a horse and could bear your young," the woman whispered in Finn-gall's ear.

"You know why I came this day," the earl said, drawing her back to her stool with a hand.

She nodded, her dark eyes resting on young Henry's dour visage. "Aye, my lord, I do."

Lord Donall, earl of Hob, took his place at her feet, beckoning his son to join them. "Come, Henry. I wish you to bear witness to what is to come. Without this understanding, you will not be able to finish what I begin this day."

The woman laughed again, reaching forward and patting the earl's knee in a most familiar manner. "What, after agreeing to trade seven hundred head of cattle for one magnificent stallion, you fear your son will doubt your wisdom?"

"Even our ruler, the great earl, will say I am befuddled."

The woman addressed the pale youth. "And you, Lord Henry, you now believe you have discovered the reason for your father's madness. That I have bewitched him." She laughed again as red flooded the boy's face. Then she turned back to the earl. "Indeed, he no doubt believes I am one of the old ones in human guise."

"As I, too, have always suspected," the earl answered. "Who else but a fairy could be so comely of face, with eyes and hair that shine like the night sky?"

She smiled. "But now I have a rival. Your stallion's eyes are as black as mine."

"Aye, and as full of devilment," the earl countered.

Happy laughter pealed though the meadow. The sound was so pleasing that Finn-gall reared, joining in with a whinny. All three swung around, staring at the horse behind them.

"The time has come, my son. Take a seat," Lord Donall said, indicating a nearby rock. "No matter what you see or hear, do not move or utter a word."

Henry paled. "It is not necessary to test my loyalty. I shall always do as you, the lord, my father, wishes." He sat heavily, but as the other two turned back to the horse, he groped for his cross, his lips moving in silent prayer.

"The stallion is named Finn-gall," Lord Donall told the woman, "and I have paupered myself for this foreigner. They laugh and call me mad to think of breeding our noble steeds to the Spanish runt."

"Runt! You pay a king's ransom for a Jennetta—or *Hineta*, as they say here—and dare call it a runt?" The woman tossed her black mane. "You with your overgrown Norman horse, bred to carry giants in armor."

"Take care who you chastise with your sharp tongue. Our horses are the best in the world. They were brought over by the Gaels and overcame the first ones, your people, the *Fir Bolg*," the earl growled.

Young Henry's eyes bulged.

The woman sighed. "The rules of war are fickle. Now, I am told men have found a way to send a projectile through armor and kill from a distance."

"Gunpowder," said the earl. "And also how to copy the word of our blessed Lord Jesus with iron pages instead of pen. In truth, the realm is changing, and we must change with it or perish."

She nodded. "This has been foretold. For many generations, the

Fir Bolg have melded with the Gaels, then the Danes, and then the Normans. So, too, must the noble steed of Erin mate with the Spanish horse." She gazed toward the mound, where the mist rolled in from the sea. " 'Tis said the two shall join, and from this joining shall come a new breed, and it shall be known throughout the land." The woman's voice dropped. "This new breed of horse shall bring glory back to the shores of Erin."

She raised a hand, pointing to the mound. Fog rose and swirled, thickening and churning, taking strange shapes. Some seemed almost human; some stood on four legs. The fog thickened, spreading to the trees. Now, Finn-gall saw a darker cloud forming by the woods. It took the shape of a stallion with a rider on his back. "Copenhagen carrying his Iron Duke, Wellington," the woman whispered. "The little Corsican astride Marengo," she sighed as another horse emerged from the fog, cantering toward them.

This was more than Finn-gall could stand. He braced, ready to charge, but young Henry moved first. With a strangled cry, he sprang to his feet, sword in hand. The mist swirled, obscuring the riders. When it lifted, the stallions were gone. All that remained were two white geese waddling over the mound. The redhead moaned, dropping his sword with a clatter. The geese honked. Finn-gall snorted.

"I did not mean to, my lord," Henry said. "The rider, he was armed and strangely dressed."

Lord Donall said nothing, rising slowly to his feet like an old man. The woman, too, no longer appeared fresh and scented with flowers, but dirty and dressed in greasy rags.

"It is done then." The earl dropped a coin in the woman's lap.

Henry turned to follow his sire, coming face to face with Finn-gall. Eyes large, he staggered back and would have fallen save for his father's arm.

The earl appeared to grow in stature. He grasped his son about the shoulders. "Then you did see!" Impatient fingers tapped the young man's arm.

"The horses that came from the fog," Henry gasped. "Their eyes were black as coal, like his, and their manes long and fair." He twisted around to stare at Finn-gall. "They came from the same stable?"

The earl shook his head. "The horses you saw were not this Iberian's brothers, but rather his offspring, many years hence." At Henry's frightened grunt, he added, "Aye, lad, for the blink of an eye, the veil of time parted and showed what is to come. Mark it well, for with this golden stallion lies the fortune of the earldom of Hob. This new breed will be known for its gentle pace and carry great leaders to battle. The Hobbini, the hobby horse of Erin, shall spread the name of our family over the waters to the west and bring greatness to our progeny in a land that has yet to be discovered."

Chapter 6

Small breakers rumbled like cannons on the distant beach as the last park boat finally took off in a flurry of white water. The landing area looked so much flatter and cleaner without all the people and their junk. Maintenance had already removed a lot of the roundup equipment, including the second tent and the testing tables.

Bert picked up a plastic bag rolling like a tumbleweed before the breeze and dumped it into a garbage can on the dock. Three miles of choppy water separated Shackleford from Harkers Island, visible only as a low line of green interspersed with the lighter blots of low buildings. The Cape Lookout Lighthouse stood closer but was blocked from sight by shrubs and small dunes. With the tide at low ebb, the sand bottom was exposed past the end of the long dock. Bert grinned, visualizing what would have happened had there been a boat moored to the dock. She'd seen many a careless boater grounded by the five-foot fluctuating tides of the cape. Oyster clumps, mussels, and other mollusks all lay helpless on the ribbed, sandy seabed.

The volunteers had fed the horses and filled the watering tubs before they left. Bert and Julie had no chores or responsibilities. Their chief reason for being here was in case of fire, injury to a horse, or some other emergency.

Bert strolled over to the ATVs to check the gas. She knew better than to assume the last rider had left them full. Just then, Julie emerged from the tent wearing a huge charcoal windbreaker and heavy gloves.

Soon, the two women were driving down the beach. Every mile or so, they stopped and walked up a dune to check the interior. So far, there was no sign of Shony—or of any horse, for that matter. Bert tightened her hood and the Velcro straps on her sleeves to keep out the cold wind that was running right up her arms.

The sky was a brilliant blue, the sun lacquering the surf to a creamy polish. It was one of those clear days with no water or dust in the air—so clear that it actually magnified objects and made them seem too close, and therefore unfamiliar. This was a weather phenomenon she'd experienced before on the islands. Bert shivered. Clean or not, the air was downright chilly.

When they reached mile marker 51 in the area where Bert had first seen Triton and Shony, she pulled up past the tide line. The high inner dunes blocked their view.

Julie lingered by their Hondas. "I know the ATVs aren't allowed off the beach except during the roundup, but couldn't we ride in just this once?"

Bert shook her head. "They'd see our tracks, and it really does do damage. Why don't you wait here? I'll go."

"No. I'm just being lazy. If the foal did run away, this is where he'd be. From what I heard Blount say, Shackleford horses are territorial." Julie began walking.

Who was Blount? Bert opened her mouth to ask, but Julie had already started across the sand. Bert ran to catch up. It was warmer off the beach, and she found herself unzipping her jacket and removing her cap and hood. It took them twenty minutes to reach the edge of the brush, stopping frequently to sight from the dunes.

"Think we should check out the woods?"

Julie sighed, eyeing the line of thick shrubs. "If he's in there, we'll never see him."

"Let's just make sure he's not on the sound-side beach, okay?"

Julie nodded. "A little one like that, I do believe he'd be looking for other horses, not hiding in the woods."

The sound beach was empty. On the way back, they passed a swale similar to the one where Bert had first seen Shony. She stopped, slapping her head. "How stupid can a person be?"

Julie swung around, mouth open.

Bert dug in her pocket, pulling out her digital camera. "I took pictures. I can prove Shony isn't Bunky. Look." She slid the switch to "Display," and both women squinted over the tiny screen. They could see the band of horses, the swept sand, the turtle pictures, and the snaps Bert had taken inside the corral. But the bright sunlight faded the digital image, and the screen was too small to show details. "A camera this size is convenient, but it does have its disadvantages," Bert said, putting it away. "Wait till I get to a computer. I'll show them I didn't get mixed up."

"Never thought you did." Julie's tone was distant, her usually placid face drawn into a frown.

"What's the matter?"

"You don't want to get some of these people thinking you're a problem. Sometimes, it's best to be quiet."

"About Shony?"

"I don't see how your pictures are going to help him. They'll just make you feel better."

Bert grinned, although Julie's reproach smarted. "You're right. I want to salvage my ego. But if they believe me, maybe we can find him."

Julie shrugged. "He's got to be around here. This is a big island, and he's too small to swim far."

It *was* a big island, as big as Ocracoke, Bert thought as they rode all the way down to the western tip, pausing frequently to search for Shony. Once there, Bert parked her Honda. Across the inlet, she could see Fort Macon and the long, sandy crescent of Bogue Banks curving deep into the ocean. As clear as it was, she could make out the coastline past Emerald Isle and Bear Island to what were probably Browns Inlet and Camp Lejeune. To Bert's right was the state port with its derricks and silos. Morehead City flanked it on one side, Beaufort on the other.

Something moved. Canvas flapped. There was a tent on the beach, sheltered between two dunes. Bert pointed.

"Campers," Julie said.

"At this time of year?" No one was in sight.

"They come over year-round. Surfers, mostly."

Bert squinted against the glare. The wind had whipped up the ocean, and the breakers were close together and choppy. Not her idea of good surfing. Wetsuits didn't protect all that well. Nothing could have made her go into that frigid water on a day like this. Despite her jacket, mohair cap, hood, and gloves, she was cold, the exposed skin of her face numb.

The women climbed on the ATVs and started back, but the east wind blasted sand into their eyes. Julie wore big sunglasses that gave her some protection. Bert stopped to put on her park goggles. Made of cheap plastic, they were badly scratched. She had trouble seeing through them, but she couldn't see without them either.

Keeping a slower pace, they plowed their way back up the island. When they reached mile marker 53, Bert drove up the soft sand close to the dunes.

"See something?" Julie shouted from her bike.

"Not Shony. I was looking for Hunter's Ridley. It was somewhere around here—east of the 53—but it vanished."

"I saw Ernie pulling a turtle up the beach Sunday," Julie yelled.

"Where? Hunter said it was just past the tide line."

Julie stopped next to the slope of a dune. "I thought it was up yonder a piece. I parked below the smelly thing when I was out with

DeWitt hunting Triton. Didn't know it was a Ridley."

"You still don't know that. Hunter doesn't want it broadcast."

They circled, driving down, then slowly coming up close to the dunes. Julie yelled at Bert from the moving Honda. "Wind." She gestured. "Must have covered it."

Bert came to a stop. "I was hoping maybe it exposed it. Oh, well."

Julie glanced toward the western sky. "I don't want to be a spoilsport, but it's going to be dark soon."

It was only a few more miles to camp, and the women were back at their tent well before sunset. Nothing had changed; the horses were quiet. Julie lit the propane heater, and by the time they had their food out and ready to eat, the tent was cozy. Outside, the wind howled.

The warm air soon had Bert yawning. "What should we check? I know it's only eight, but I'm ready for bed."

Bundling up, they took a final walk around the pens, the dock, and the landing. Then, satisfied all was well, Bert went off to brush her teeth and wash her face with some of the water they'd brought with them. She was careful to spit with the wind.

A porta-potty had been set up for the roundup, but it had seen heavy use. After one sniff, Bert decided to dig a hole in the sand instead. By nine, she was wrapped in her sleeping bag. She hadn't undressed, but merely peeled down to her Patagonia long underwear. Julie had pretty much done the same. After making sure that her water and flashlight were within reaching distance, Bert stretched to turn off the propane. Then she pulled the bag's hood over her head. The wind blowing against the canvas was soothing, like waves on the ocean.

A horse snorted nearby. Bert jerked upright, blinking into the cold darkness, clutching the sleeping bag to keep the warmth inside. She knew where she was—sleeping in a tent on Shackleford—but why were the horses making so much noise? Just then, hooves clattered. She flinched, half expecting the herd to come crashing through the canvas.

Then she was standing, yelling for Julie. Socks still on, she forced her feet into her shoes and grabbed her jacket, but she couldn't get out of the tent. The zippers all had fastenings to keep out raccoons and other animals, and the latch was caught on something.

Julie was at her side. "What's going on?"

"The horses are loose, or some of them are. See if you can get this, will you?"

Finally, they got the door flap open. Both women stumbled out, shining their flashlights. Bert saw a shadow shy away, then another. The women ran toward the pen gate. It was wide open. As they reached it, another band of horses ambled out. Bert shooed them back inside, shutting the gate. "Can you lock up?" she said. "I'll go check the other gates."

All the others were securely closed. Bert alternated walking and jogging around the perimeter of the pens, thankful she'd kept in condition. She beamed her light at the horses. It was impossible to tell how many had gotten away. They were stamping and snorting, many on the move.

When she returned to the main gate, she found it closed, the bolts all in place. But there was no sign of Julie. She wasn't in the tent either. "Julie, you here?" Bert shone her light into the tent and around the bushes and paths. Stopping long enough to zip up her partly open jacket, she headed for the porta-potty, expecting to find Julie there.

The horses in the pen were still agitated. Hooves pounded as they cantered about, snorting and whinnying. How on earth had that gate gotten open? Neither she nor Julie had been inside the pen since everyone left, but they'd checked things when they returned from the beach, and again before they went to bed. Bert had heard of horses that were unbelievably clever at escaping from corrals and stables, but never of any that could throw bolts.

A blood-red half-moon hung low in the sky. Bert reached the portable toilet, banged on the door, then opened it. "Julie?"

No one there. Damn, where was she?

Cold crawled up the back of her neck. Someone—or something—was watching her from the dark. She was sure. Holding the flashlight waist high, she turned slowly. Wind howled in her ears. Bushes and stunted trees rustled, and clouds barreled across the sky like sea witches riding oars. Bert could barely hear the surf booming. Wait, something was moving, toward the beach road. Julie? The shadow looked too big.

Suddenly conscious of being a target, Bert turned off her flashlight. Footsteps were coming her way. Whoever it was moved slowly. She strained to see, her eyes adjusting to the dark.

Edging sideways between two bushes, Bert waited. Sand crunched softly. A light glimmered. She must have made some sort of sound, for suddenly the beam was full on her face, blinding her.

Bert screamed, jumping away. Someone yelled back—a female voice.

"Julie?" Bert whispered.

"Bert. Good heavens, girl, you done scared me to death. What are you doing hiding in the myrtle?"

"Looking for you. Where were you?"

Julie sniffed. "I swear, I'm shivering like a leaf."

"You shouldn't have gone off alone like that. Someone let those horses out. He's probably still around."

"You know it, girl. I thought I saw someone running down the road."

Bert's tone reflected her shock. "You went after him by yourself? Why?" Julie was full of surprises. "Who was it?"

Julie sniffed again, wiping her face. "A horse. It was only a horse. Then I was thinking I could catch it, but it got away."

Bert sighed. "What do we do now? Phone the park?"

"What time is it?"

They were walking back to the tent. Bert flashed her light on her watch. "Two o'clock."

"That means we'll wake the ranger on duty. Who is it? You know?"

Bert shook her head, thinking out loud. "The park can't do anything about the escaped horses until morning. But what about who did it? Maybe they could alert the Coast Guard or something."

"You'd better think on that before you call," Julie said. "We don't know for sure there was anyone here. They'll be saying we panicked."

"How about if I get hold of Hunter?"

Julie kicked off her shoes. "You do whatever you think best. Does seem a shame to disturb the man's rest when there's not much he can do, but if it relieves your mind . . ."

Bert hesitated. Hunter had been tired lately. Was she just calling to make herself feel better? Once she woke him, she knew he wouldn't go back to bed. "You're right. There's really not much he can do."

Sleep eluded Bert. Twice, she got up and went to check on the horses, fearful someone would open the gates again. By the time she fell asleep, it was morning.

Julie already had the kettle boiling. Grabbing her ditty bag, Bert went out to the pens and tried to count the horses. Then she washed her face, brushed her teeth, and returned feeling somewhat human. She made herself a mug of instant coffee and checked her watch. It was almost eight. "Did you tell them yet?" she asked Julie.

"Why don't you? You know them better than me."

Bert picked up the cell phone and called the park. The chief ranger, Rudy, answered. "Just fixing to call you girls. The state got a positive. We'll be coming back to do some retesting."

"Rudy, that's what I'm calling about. Some of the horses got out last night."

"Now, that's bad news. How many?"

"I'm not sure, but I think around thirty."

"How did it happen? They break out?"

"I don't know. The horses woke me up around two. The main gate was open. We didn't leave it open. I checked it before going to bed."

"Couldn't happen at a worse time." The phone was silent for a moment. "Leave the phone on. I'm fixing to call you right back."

But the next call was for Julie from Greg Statler, the state veterinarian. Bert watched her grab her logs and flip through the pages. "There's no eighty-seven here." Julie bit her lip, nodding to something he was saying. "It'll take me awhile. I'll have to check each one individually."

"What's wrong?" Bert asked after Julie hung up.

"Just some kind of mix-up." Julie thumbed her notebook. "But it's going to take me awhile to sort it out. Do you think you could water the horses? You know how to turn the pump on?"

"I helped with that yesterday. Can I do anything for you?" Julie was trying to sound casual, but she was upset. Had she messed up the test records? Bert hoped they weren't blaming Julie for the escape.

"No, no. I'm fine. Just have to call Greg back with the information, when I find it."

Bert was still watering the horses when the park staff started arriving. The sound was choppy, the wind and waves bouncing the boats as the passengers tried to slip over the side. To her surprise, one of the first off was Hunter. He came right over to the pen. "Why didn't you call me last night?"

"I was going to, but there wasn't anything you could do, and I hated to wake you up." Damn, she knew she should have called.

"Biggest problem this park has besides money is communication. If you didn't want to wake me, you should have called the duty ranger. Now, you want to let me in on what's happening?"

Bert told Hunter of the horses' escape.

His eyes narrowed. "If you'd called like you're supposed to, we might have caught whoever it was leaving."

"At two in the morning?"

"He was probably camping on the island or had a boat out there."

"There were some campers down by the inlet."

Hunter's brows rose. "How many?"

"I didn't see anyone, just the tent."

"What took you all the way down there?"

"Julie and I went for a ride." At Hunter's look, Bert added, "We were looking for a little pony that vanished." She explained about Shony.

He hesitated. "Understand, I have to ask this. Did those horses by any chance get out while you girls were hunting this mysterious foal?"

He might have a right to be angry with her, but now he'd gone too far. Bert whirled and stomped back to the tent.

Hunter ran after her. "Bert, stop." He grabbed her shoulder. She shrugged him off. "They'll be asking me the same thing, and I gotta be able to say I asked you direct."

"They who?"

"The press. That's why I'm here. Had to use the radio to get the rangers back off the cape, and word got out."

"I'm sorry." Apparently, all she did was make trouble for him. "If I'd called like I wanted to, you would have been able to organize them before they left."

Hunter's voice softened. "What stopped you from calling?"

"No one. It was my fault. I had a feeling I should call in."

He paid no attention to her protest. "Had to be Julie that stopped you. Why? Where is she?"

They went to the tent. To Bert's relief, Julie was gone. They were starting to leave when Bert remembered her camera. She pulled it out of her pack, where she'd stored it the night before.

Hunter frowned. "You fixing to take pictures now?"

"No. It's for Purcell. I have a picture, several, of Shony. They said there was no such horse."

"In there?"

Bert nodded. "Look." She turned the camera to "Display." The screen was blank. She moved the switch to the right, then back all the way to the left. For a moment, she thought her battery was out, but the screen displayed "Busy," then flashed a "No Image" message.

Hunter peeked over her shoulder. "What's the matter?"

"It's not here." Bert opened the case and pulled the card out. It was there, all right. She pushed it back in, making sure it connected, then turned the display back on. Same message. She stared at Hunter. "They're gone. My pictures of Shony aren't there anymore."

Chapter 7

"Your pictures can't be gone," Hunter said. "You think maybe your battery's dead, or so weak it can't read?"

Sitting down, Bert inserted her spare. Then she checked her extra card, in case she'd somehow switched them, but both cards were blank. She shook her head, sighing. "I must have erased them yesterday when I showed them to Julie. Only I don't know how it could happen."

"Easy to do, right?" Hunter grinned down at her, one eyebrow cocked.

"Go ahead, rub it in." During a recent visit to Charleston, Bert had accidentally erased all her beautiful shots of the harbor. "But I didn't do any erasing on the digital yesterday—still had lots of room on the card."

"Worrying won't change things. Let's find your tent mate, why don't we? I need to talk at her."

Outside, the three vets—Tanisha, DeWitt, and Greg—were unloading equipment. Even the testing table had been brought back and was being set up. Bert glimpsed Julie. "Over there." She pointed. As they crossed the path, Bert remembered something. "Your pictures of the brushed sand where the turtle vanished were on that card. Oh, Hunter, I'm sorry." And she'd been so pleased to be of use.

"Damnation! I was fixing to send those to Marine Fisheries. Got ourselves a problem there."

Bert's head snapped up. So there *was* something else bothering him. But before she could say more, Vilma Willit arrived, a photographer in tow. A smile stretched her lips tight as her eyes flicked from Hunter to Bert. "I guess it's hard for you two to be apart, even when you're supposed to be working."

For the umpteenth time, Bert wished she could think on her feet and come back with a put-down. Hunter did his usual, ignoring a remark he didn't care to comment on. "Good morning to you, too, Vilma. How's the book coming along?"

Bert left Hunter to deal with the reporter and continued toward Julie. Clayton Davis, the Humane Society representative, was holding forth at the pen, intoning in his melodic voice, "So it boils down to one sample testing positive, number eighty-seven, but there's no record of a horse with that number." He shrugged. "Obviously, there's been a serious foul-up. Who numbered the tubes?"

"You know I did, Clayton." Julie's mouth was set in a heavy line, her face an ugly red.

He gave her a big smile, his rich head of white hair falling over his face, softening his scars. "Well, hey, we know you wouldn't make a stupid mistake like that. Why, you're the little woman who keeps the rest of us straight, right, boys?" Bert winced at the condescension.

"What's your point, Clayton?" DeWitt growled.

"Don't get your drawers in a knot." Clayton flashed a triumphant eye at DeWitt. "Correct me if I'm wrong, but there's a main log, isn't there, one with the history of each horse?" Julie nodded. "Did you count the horses in there and compare the count to the test-tube log?"

Julie and the state vet exchanged glances. "No, but that's a good idea," Greg said. The veterinarian for the state was one of the youngest men present—about thirty, Bert figured, with a broad, Scandinavian face and tinted glasses.

DeWitt picked up one of the logs, but Clayton waved him aside. "No need. I already did it. The main log has a hundred and ten horses. The cross-reference also has exactly a hundred and ten entries. Now, Greg, how many test tubes did you have total?"

Greg might be young, but he appeared very much at ease, the sun glinting off his glasses as he answered the Humane Society rep. "We had a hundred and eleven test tubes. Number eighty-seven was the only one to test positive. Clayton, I'm impressed you discovered this inconsistency, but where does it take us?"

The relief on Julie's face was palpable. She beamed at Clayton. "How would they end up with an extra test tube?"

Clayton smiled like a Cheshire cat. "Can't say I'm exactly certain, but I'd guess someone deliberately planted a sample of contaminated blood."

A murmur went through the crowd. Vilma Willit shrilled, "Why would anyone do that?"

Ernie Steingart leaned over and whispered something in Hunter's ear. With an impatient gesture, Hunter motioned Ernie up front, but Ernie shook his head, coloring to match his short, reddish blond curls. The chief resource ranger was painfully shy. Except for last Sunday with the ATV riders, Bert had never seen him speak before a crowd.

Hunter stepped forward, his dark hair glinting red in the sun. The vets towered over his five-foot-eleven. "Vilma, you know the boys are just theorizing. As soon as we have something definite, I'll be sure and inform you. Meanwhile, I'll be much obliged if you keep this confidential, as per our understanding. Wouldn't want to start any rumors." He turned to the others, raising his voice. "I'm fixing to have a meeting in the tent in five minutes. Appreciate it if all you rangers are there. I'd also like to see the veterinarians and all the reps for the state agencies and the foundation. That includes you, Ms. Piner."

For a moment, Bert didn't recognize the name, then realized he meant Julie. It wasn't until they'd all disappeared into the tent that Bert thought of a possible explanation for the extra test tube. She waited impatiently for them to emerge, glancing around at the other unchosen, who, like her, had been left feeling they didn't belong.

Uh-oh. That reporter was heading her way.

Vilma opened with a wheezy, "I must say, I'm amazed you're not in that tent with your boyfriend."

Imitating Hunter, Bert didn't try to counter. Instead, she asked, "Is this wind making your allergies worse? Or is it emphysema?"

Apparently, Vilma didn't like people to notice her problem. She took a deep breath and made a visible effort to speak without wheezing. "It's a condition I've learned to live with, even though it causes me a great deal of aggravation."

It was hard to feel sympathy for her. Bert headed toward the sergeant, hoping the woman would drop back, but Vilma skipped a step to catch up. "I'm asking for advice." She sucked air. "That is, if you can spare me a minute."

Bert noticed the heaving nostrils and, despite her dislike, had to acknowledge the woman's determination. "I'm only a volunteer. I have no official standing here, you know that."

"I'm talking about the count. You're aware, of course, they took duplicate blood samples—one set for the state vet and one for DeWitt Brigman." Vilma gave a small, dry cough. "Now, we all know DeWitt's set didn't show any horses infected with equine fever. How many tubes do you suppose the man worked on?"

"You're right," Bert said against her will. "If DeWitt only had a hundred and ten, that would pretty much prove someone did add a sample, wouldn't it? Yeah, but then . . ." Bert caught herself just in time. She'd almost told the woman about Shony. That would knock Vilma's theory to pieces.

They stood close to the horse pens, where the army team was counting ponies. Many of the remaining horses were clustered behind the wind fences put there for their protection. The sun glinted on their thick, furry winter coats, dappling them with red highlights. Two colts, one slightly behind the other, stood motionless like mirror images, their graceful manes blowing against the background of gold sand and blue—

Vilma interrupted her thoughts. "But what? What else is there?"

Bert groaned silently. The woman was quick, and good at her job. "I wonder if Triton got out." Anything to change the subject. "Sergeant," she called, "do you know if Triton is still here?"

"No, he ain't." The sergeant ambled over to the fence. "Good morning, Miss Bert. Morning, Miss Willit. Didn't nobody show you gals how to close a gate?" He threw back his head and guffawed.

Bert fell in with the spirit of the joke. "The question is, who taught the horses how to open it?"

The sergeant chuckled. "Looks like we'll be testing all over again."

That got Vilma's attention. "Really? What makes you say that?" She covered her mouth with a handkerchief.

Was she allergic to horses? Bert wondered. And doing a book on them?

"Equine fever ain't nothing to fool around with. They can't put them ponies out for adoption unless they's state certified. That means no horse in the herd can test positive for EIA."

"Hmm. DeWitt Brigman might be in a peck of trouble." Bert shot her a questioning glance. Vilma continued, "When DeWitt got himself fired from the foundation, it didn't do his business any good. Those foundation members are big landowners around here. I heard he was relying on the adoptions to get a big farm account."

"How would that help him?"

The sergeant answered. "When they adopt a pony, they got to agree to supervision for a year. Ain't just that." He eyed the reporter. "You heard about them starting some kind of gene pool?"

Vilma's lips stretched in her closed-mouth smile. "I surely did. Croatan Farm's fixing to bid on all the foals and give the job to DeWitt. I wrote that up last week. They're planning to build up a genetic base of the wild ponies. You know, in the event the Park Service takes it into their heads to kill off the mustangs again." She turned her blue eyes on Bert, smiling sweetly.

Damn the woman. Bert couldn't let that go by. "The way I heard it, the superintendent saved the herd by acting promptly, and sacrificed his job doing it. If he'd waited any longer, all the horses would have been infected."

"That's what the Park Service would have you believe. Why, the folks around here were so upset when the rangers put down all those ponies, they organized the Foundation for Shackleford Horses. The foundation got a law passed saying the Park Service has to keep a hundred horses on the island." Vilma cast a triumphant glance at Bert. "The park and the foundation have equal say in the management of the horses, you know. Lida Fulchard, our state representative, is going to see they do just that. You can count on it."

Just as Vilma walked away, satisfied she'd had the last word, Hunter and the rest of the rangers emerged from the tent. Young Purcell was hopping about like a bandy-legged stork, waving his hands and shouting commands. The sergeant's prediction was right. They were to begin retesting immediately.

Back in the pen with the army crew, Bert herded horses into the chute. DeWitt and Tanisha were already taking blood, Julie and Clayton marking and cross-referencing. A tall, slim man crossed the sandy area between the tent and the pens. Bert stared for a moment before she understood why he struck her as familiar. She waited for a break, then asked Julie, pointing, "Who's that man?"

DeWitt answered before Julie could. "That's the great James Blount, one of them important people that don't do anything."

"The head of the Foundation for Shackleford Horses," Julie added. "Why?"

"That's the man that told me Shony's name. He knows Shony existed."

Bert started to slide through the chute bars, but DeWitt stopped her. "You can talk to him later. We got a job to do and not much time. Got some weather coming."

Bert glanced at the sky. It was clear, with only a few high, wispy clouds. Except for the wind, there was no sign of trouble she could see. She wondered what NOAA, the government's weather division, was saying. But she didn't have much time to think. She helped the army drive a black stallion, Orion, and some of his band into the smaller pen. Bert and the sergeant were shooing one of his mares into the chute when another horse came charging toward them. Orion reacted immediately, rearing, front hooves flailing. The other stallion snorted, kicking and bucking, then pranced backward, shoving at Orion. Somehow, Bert found herself between the fighting stallions and the fence. She ducked just as a hoof came at her. The horse's rump, huge close up, struck the post by her shoulder; Orion was shoving the stallion into the fence—and her.

The sergeant roared, "Climb, climb!"

Bert grabbed onto the wire fence, which sagged toward her. Fortunately, the opening in the square weave fit her feet. A horse slammed by. She reached the top and felt it give, swaying under her weight. Somehow, she managed to swing her foot over and drop to the other side. Then, just as quickly as the fight had started, the horses were gone. The sergeant let the other stallion back into the main pen.

He lumbered over, his dark face gray through the wire. "He get you? You all right?"

"I'm fine," she responded automatically, hearing the quaver in her voice. "What happened?"

"Some fool let in a second stallion." The sergeant turned to his men and yelled, "Which one of you effing idiots let in that stallion? You could have got this gal killed."

A young soldier with a stubble of red hair answered, pointing at the men outside. "One of them vets told me to let him in the pen right away."

"Which one?"

"He's wearing one of them orange jumpsuits." The man looked around and shrugged. "I ain't sure which one."

"Find him and bring him over here."

"What's going on?" Tanisha yelled. "We're ready for another horse."

"Be right with you." The sergeant waved at Bert. "Why don't you go with him? Take a break."

Bert drew a deep breath. "I've always been told to get right back on the horse."

Eyeing her from under his brows, the sergeant nodded. "Let's get to work then." But Bert noticed that he stayed close by.

Soon, the redheaded soldier was back, shaking his head. "I can't tell who it was, sarge. He was behind the fence wearing that hood on his head. I never seen his face."

"How big was he?" Bert asked, glancing at the orange-clad vets and rangers. Most of them had their hoods up against the cold wind.

"He was taller than me, all right. Big as the sarge."

Bert sighed. That description fit most of the vets. "Beard?"

"I told you, I didn't get a look at his face. I was helping y'all, and he was talking at me from behind."

Bert walked to the chute, where DeWitt was down on one knee, pressing Orion to the bars as he drew blood from his neck. Orion twisted around, baring his teeth. "Aren't you afraid he'll bite you?" Bert waited to see if he showed surprise at her presence.

DeWitt glanced up, his green eyes laughing. There was straw in his black hair and stuck to the sweat on his cheeks. "Not as long as I'm below him. With these fellows, it's all hormones." He reached up and stroked Orion's muzzle. "Right, boy?"

It couldn't have been DeWitt. "Did one of you order the army to put the roan stallion in the pen with Orion?"

His eyes ceased being amused. "Is that what the commotion was about? I thought you had yourselves an ornery one. No one hurt, was there?"

Bert shook her head. "Sure scared me, though. If the sergeant hadn't yelled at me to climb out, I don't know what would have happened."

"No one in his right mind would put two stallions together in close quarters, not unless they was looking to make trouble." DeWitt removed the needle and motioned the man at the front gate to let the stallion through. "These horses been wild for two, three hundred years, some even longer. First ones come over with Columbus on his second voyage, you know."

74

DeWitt rose, patting Orion on the rump. "You don't got someone here that hates you, do you?" His Castilian green eyes glinted, as if relishing his words.

Chapter 8

Hispaniola, 1493

Jazmín

"*The Twenty-Third of May, 1493. Archive of the Indies. The King and Queen: Fernando Zarpa, our Secretary. We command that certain vessels be prepared to send to the Islands and to the Mainland which has been newly discovered in the ocean sea in that part of the Indies, and to prepare these vessels for the Admiral Don Christopher Columbus . . . and among the other people we are commanding to go in these vessels there will be sent twenty lancers with horses . . . and five of them shall take two horses each, and these two horses which they take shall be mares.*"

The master-at-arms hawked and spat. "*Basta.* I have heard enough."
Lowering the scroll so he could see the speaker, the Franciscan priest eyed the soldier from under bushy brows.

The master raised his head defiantly. "Our king will have our lancers riding mares?"

"Without mares to breed stallions, your lancers will soon be walking across *La Isla Española*." The ship's captain pushed back his chair. "The problem is not mares or stallions, but how to transport them."

"That is precisely my meaning," the master countered. "Equine mortality is already high on long voyages. But sailing west to the far Indies? We may be months en route. We need spare mounts, not brood mares."

The Franciscan interjected, "I have been told it will be a grand fleet, many ships, and they take colonists on this voyage."

"*Sí.* Also stockmen from Seville." The mate spoke for the first time. "The mares will be Jennettas of the finest quality. One is from the Noriega stables in Toledo."

"Then perchance they can tell us how to make the crossing with a hold full of such delicate cargo." The captain turned to the master. "Surely, it is easier to transport horses than slaves."

"*No es verdad,* not so. Horses require more food and water and take more space."

"At least the horses will smell sweeter," the priest said mildly, bringing a laugh from the group.

"*Cuidado!*" someone shouted in the mare's ear as the sling around her tightened, jerking her off her feet. She kicked, trying to regain the ground and escape the ropes. One of her hooves struck a sailor. He cursed, hopping back, but continued fastening the sling around her belly to the overhead bolt. Additional harnesses held the Jennetta mare suspended in the center of the tiny stall. Then the men hooked the open crate to a halyard swinging from the ship's boom.

"*Tire!*" shouted a sailor as he hauled on the pulleys.

Four more men worked the block and tackle from the ship's deck and the wharf below. The mare, blindfolded and hanging in the crate, spun slowly overhead as the lines were steadied to poise the creature over the hold.

"*Abajo*, down."

Lines jerked. The Jennetta was lowered, bumping to a stop that left her swaying in midair just above the hatch. Hands turned the crate to make it fit the square opening. Then she dropped into the void, the stall striking hard on the deck below. In a sweat, her stomach rolling, she squealed and fought the bindings. All about her were voices and men prodding.

The mare's nostrils flared. She snorted, ears back, ready for an opportunity to lash out or escape her tormentors. If only she could see. She tried to rub her blindfold off on her foreleg, but her halter was yanked up as a voice spoke in her ear, "Not yet, *chica*."

The runners bumped and scraped over the plank deck as the stall was dragged into position. More men surrounded the mare, shouting commands.

"Keep them midships—less roll."

"Put the feed in the bow."

Suddenly, the ropes were removed and the sling lowered so her hooves touched the deck. The tightness around her lungs eased. She squealed again. Somewhere, a stallion answered with a whinny.

"*Estás bien, estás bien*," crooned the same voice in her ear as he patted her heaving flanks. But the band around her belly still held her prisoner, her hooves scrabbling as she tried to move forward. The youth continued to stroke her until others called him away. "*Maldito*," he cursed. "Do not despair, *chica*. All will be well. I, Marco of Seville, am here to care for you."

Although blindfolded, the chestnut mare knew by the slow roll of the deck, the splash of water, and the salt in the air that she was on a ship again. All about her was activity as other horses were loaded, snorting and squealing. The hours passed. Her throat grew dry and her stomach cramped. She had not been fed or watered since being taken from her stable in the middle of the night. Finally, she heard the soft voice of the boy and felt his hand on her neck. "*Hola, chica*. Drink first, and I will take off your blind."

The Jennetta sucked deeply of the cool water held to her muzzle. Then she blew. The boy laughed as his hands removed the cloth about her eyes. She shook her head, blinking to clear her vision. At first, she could see nothing except dark. Slowly, shapes began to emerge. A solitary beam of light full of dust motes radiated from an opening overhead, far to her side. She was in a large room with curved walls. All about her were other horses. Some of them she recognized from the stable. Like her, they were all trapped by bands around their bodies attached to the crates. Fear rose again to her throat as she scrabbled uselessly to escape the sling.

"Easy, easy. You must accept that which you cannot change." The stable hand continued spreading a thick layer of hay over the wood floor of her crate.

She turned her head to stare at the boy, pleading.

"Ay yi yi, but you are a beauty." Marco's callused brown hand stroked the trumpet-shaped white blaze that ran from her forehead to her nose. "You are well named—Jazmín, flower of the stable that produced Triton, son of Nejmah. Come, I bring you feed, too, but you are not my only charge."

Jazmín did not eat. One did not feed in time of peril. But as the light gradually diminished, she realized no one was coming to set her free. Finally, she munched some of the bran in her manger and lowered her head slowly. Her legs ached from being in one position.

Before the light faded completely, new sounds came from above. Feet clattered on deck. The overhead hatch was battened down, and total darkness reigned. More shouts and thumps came from above, and the ship began to pitch.

The mare took a shuddering breath. The last time she had been transported by ship, she had stood on the open deck, rolling with each wave. It had been cold and wet, but they had reached their destination before nightfall. This, too, would come to an end.

But Jazmín soon learned she was mistaken. The seventeen ships set course for the Canary Islands, and it was a fortnight before they reached their first destination. The fall weather was unpredictable. Sometimes, the wind was strong, and the ships forged ahead pitching and rolling. Other times, they sailed smoothly over calm seas. On the seventh day, the wind picked up, rapidly escalating into a savage storm, accompanied by fearful sounds below deck. Masts groaned in their steps. The bilge pumps, manned by the exhausted sailors overhead, banged constantly.

"Quick, loosen the slings!" Marco shouted.

"Why? They will hold the horses up."

"Horses can keep on their feet in rough weather, if they are left free to balance. The slings are to keep the weight off their feet in calms and to prevent them from lying down. There is not enough space for them to kick back to their feet in these stalls."

After adjusting the slings, the stable boys rushed about, frantically adding hay to the crates to help secure the horses' footing.

For three days, the small carvel pitched and rolled, tossing the horses about despite their four legs and low center of gravity. Necks and backs were wrenched, hocks cut. Only the hay Marco had spread saved the Jennetta from more serious injury. She was also plagued by thirst, for no man dared enter the hold during a storm.

The open stalls, built of heavy, rough-cut timbers, had been tightly tied together and secured to the decks with netting and lines. On the third day, somewhere near the stern, a stall broke loose. It careened about the hold, sometimes upright, sometimes on its side, while the doomed stallion struggled to free himself, squealing so loudly he could be heard in the sterncastle. Soon, the stall was reduced to deadly posts that flew throughout the hold, piercing horseflesh. The stallion, still attached to the wooden brace with both his forelegs broken, was tossed back and forth until he was reduced to a grizzly mass of red meat, but not before two more stalls were crushed by his crate, their inmates also suffering the same fate. Jazmín, at the opposite end of the hold in the bow, escaped injury from the splintered wood, but she was tossed about in her sling until her flanks were bruised and bleeding. All the horses were in stages of dehydration.

The moment the sea began to calm, the boy, Marco, red-eyed and crusted with salt, was at her side with a pouch of water, letting her drink her fill. After he had watered the other horses and helped the bo's'n slit the jugulars of the moribund stallions, he returned to rub the dirt and salt from Jazmín with old rags and fresh water.

"You are mad, Marco. If they find you wasting water, it will be the lash," Marco's friend Costa, a dark-skinned Spaniard of Moorish blood, hissed.

"They do not care—yet." Marco's voice was confident. However, he scanned the dark hold. "The storm has helped. We are only two days from the Canaries. There is still water aplenty." The fourteen-year-old nudged his small friend, whispering. "You, too, would do well to pay extra attention to the mares."

"Why? What do you mean?"

Marco crouched at Jazmín's feet, motioning Costa to do the same. "You know Don Nicholas?"

"Sí." Costa shrugged. "He is the rich settler."

Marco's Castilian green eyes were bright in his smudged face. "He plans to start a hacienda at Navidad."

"So what is that to me?"

"I'll tell you what it means, *stupido*. It means if I bring these mares through this voyage not only alive but healthy, he promises me a position in his stable. So what do you think of that?" Grinning, Marco placed a palm on his friend's chest and pushed.

Toppling over on his rump, the smaller boy stared at Marco, open-mouthed. "You would leave the ship? Never return to Seville?"

Marco's smile vanished. "Return to what? There is nothing there for me. My father sold me for four months' wages." He stood and began getting the feed ready. With his back to the Moor, he said softly, "You, too, could buy your freedom and have a position as a groom."

Still sprawled on the manure-soaked planks, Costa stared. "Me? How?"

Marco bent as if to pull Costa off the deck. "You help me groom the mares after we water and feed the stallions. I will put in a word for you."

Costa shook his head as Marco offered his hand. "Don Nicholas would not want one such as I."

"It will be different there. They have *Indios*. You will be thought of as a Spaniard, not a *Morisco*."

His brows and mouth twisted in concentration, Costa pondered.

Then he took hold of Marco's hand and pulled himself to his feet. "What must I do?"

"Tell them you sleep down here. We groom them, pick their feet, brush and rub their legs, sponge their nostrils and eyes. But most important, we keep the scuppers clear so the decks stay dry. I plan to let the slings down, too, so they can exercise when it is calm, but I need help for that."

Both Marco and the mares were soon thankful for the extra hand. To escape the storms and rough seas, the ships detoured south when they left the Canaries. But they went too far south. Suddenly, the wind stopped. The tossing, white-capped seas flattened to an oily, slick calm, and the sky grayed with a haze of heat and humidity. For days, the little flotilla was becalmed, helpless.

Neither Marco nor Jazmín had ever experienced heat like this. In the battened-down hold, the temperature rose to unbelievable levels. The horses had been left to stand in their own manure and used hay. Trampled down, it was matted into a thick rug, giving them good footing. Now, these piles began to decompose in the heat, and the ammonia from the urine that slopped in the scuppers burnt their eyes and made breathing impossible. When Jazmín had sweated all the moisture from her body, dehydration began to take hold. To each side, horses dangled limply in their slings. Seeing what was happening, the captain ordered the overhead hatch opened. But since there was no wind, it had little effect on the conditions below.

"Drink," Marco said. He held the water sack to Jazmín's face, but she was too hot to care. He poured some of the precious water over her forehead and again tried to get her to drink, but she would not. The boy groaned, "Jesus, Maria, help me." He glanced about the dank hold. It was not the lack of water but heat that was killing his mares. His sweat-blinded eyes fixed on the oblong crack on the side of the ship. It was a large porthole or side hatch cut into the wall of the hold, used to load and unload from lighters when the ship was anchored. It had been tamped shut for the voyage.

Soon, Marco was back, a distinguished, gray-haired man sweating in his wake. "*Mira*, Don Nicholas, *mira*. If we open, the horses will have air. They are being cooked alive." He pointed to a stallion hanging dead in his harness.

Jazmín was only vaguely aware of the arrival of sailors with their hammers. The porthole was opened, immediately forming an updraft with the top hatch. As the fresh sea breeze rolled in, the mare slowly revived. Marco stood at her side, murmuring words of encouragement, wetting her down with buckets of seawater hauled up from the new port and offering her fresh water to drink. Throughout the hold, other stable boys did the same.

Later that evening, when the night air had cooled the horses even more and Jazmín was fully recovered, she nipped the sleeping Marco's shoulder gently. He laughed for the first time in days, cradling her head against his too thin chest.

When the wind returned, the porthole was battened down. The ships raised their square sails and resumed their westerly course. Three weeks later, they put into the port of Navidad on the isle of Hispaniola.

"*Qué pasa?* Don Nicholas goes back on his word?" Costa demanded, punching the downcast Marco.

"We go back to sea," the boy grimaced, leaning against Jazmín's crate.

"They do not put the horses ashore?"

Marco shook his head, matted locks flying over green eyes. "The fort is burned, the soldiers all dead."

"The *Indios*." Costa blinked dark, thick lashes. "This I feared. I think I do not wish to stay in the Far East."

"That is why we sail on, to find a better place."

Costa's eyes opened wide. "How do you know this? Even if we sail to another port, what is to say the *Indios* of that place will not kill us while we sleep?"

Marco hesitated, then put his lips to his friend's ear. "While I was sleeping, under the captain's port . . ."

Costa grunted. "*Sí*, sleeping, to be sure."

Marco flashed a smile, exposing crooked teeth. "I heard say it was the soldiers who provoked the *Indios*. They stole their women."

"And what is to stop that happening again?"

"The settlers are not like the soldiers," Marco answered. "They will keep the peace. Don Nicholas himself promised the *capitan general*."

Three more weeks passed before the flagship, *Maria Galante*, carrying the *capitan general*, discovered an area that was to his satisfaction. Three weeks of heat and flies and misery. Weakened by lack of exercise, disease, and malnutrition, several more horses died. Their bodies, trapped in the rear stalls, were left to rot. The air became putrid and heavy, the corpses so infested with maggots that they appeared to breathe and move once more.

Finally, one day, the men again opened the side wall. The ship moved slowly toward shore, towed by two shallops. It dropped anchor near a long, sandy beach lined by green palms. At the head of the harbor, a river discharged a small amount of water. Behind the palms extended a rolling, green plain.

Men pried Jazmín's stall open, removing her sling to let her stand on the deck unaided. All about her, other horses were also being loosed, many stumbling as their swollen feet and rotting hooves refused to hold their bloated bodies. Under the light of day, they were a pitiful sight. The slings and ropes had rubbed much of the hair from their bodies; open sores and swollen legs were evident on many; and all were emaciated and had bloated stomachs from the minimal diet.

Marco stroked Jazmín, his green eyes glinting with pride. "You can stand, *mi amor*, because I have taken good care of you. Now, you must trust me once again." He led Jazmín to the opening, letting her sniff the air and eye the clear, calm, turquoise water just below the porthole. "Now, my brave one, you must swim ashore." Marco let loose the lead, at the same time slapping her rump, the age-old signal to move forward.

Jazmín froze, forelegs locked, ears back.

Marco's hand was on her hindquarters, his voice high, urgent,

"Jump, jump. Otherwise, it will be worse for you."

Out of the corner of her eye, Jazmín saw men approaching. They carried sticks, raised and menacing.

"Go now." Marco once again slapped her rump.

Taking a deep breath, the mare kicked forward, plunging through the opening into the warm sea. For the first time in her life, she was completely underwater. Instinct told her not to breathe, and instinct also told her how to kick to the surface. Then she was on top, blowing salt from her nostrils, paddling easily to stay afloat. The cool, clear sea washed the months of sweat and dirt from her hide, revitalizing her spirit as well as her body.

From behind came splashes, shouts, and frantic squeals. Something large crashed down nearby. Jazmín kicked away from the ship and the leaping horses. She paused to take in the surroundings. The sweet scent of fresh water, grass, and green leaves floated over the surface of the sea. She turned and swam to shore.

Once on the sandy beach, the mare bucked, tossing her head with a triumphant nicker. Then, neck and tail high, Jazmín trotted across the gleaming sand to vanish among the tall palms and lush vegetation.

Chapter 9

A doe-eyed, delicate filly with a beautiful face nuzzled Bert's hand. Patting her withers, Bert led her into the chute. She was still thinking about what DeWitt had said. Could that stallion fight have been deliberately engineered? Why?

The vet still mystified her. DeWitt had been gentle and kind with Orion, but if someone had set up the fight, DeWitt was the most likely culprit. She or anyone on the army team could have been hurt. Bert glanced at the redhead. It was also possible the young soldier had made a mistake and was blaming it on an unidentifiable person.

Once Bert got over her adrenaline overdose, time flew. She enjoyed the horses. No two reacted the same. Some fought their return to the chute. Others wanted to go inside. Many just fixed their big eyes on their tormentors, seeming to say they'd do it, if only they understood what was being asked of them.

The spotter plane had been out, broadcasting the locations of the escaped horses. Meanwhile, the wind picked up. Bert caught glimpses of men unloading bales of hay from pitching boats onto a rubber raft to feed the penned-up herd.

It wasn't until they broke for lunch that Bert remembered James Blount. The scare with the stallion had driven him out of her mind. Before she could locate the director of the Foundation for Shackleford Horses, Lida Fulchard, state legislator, arrived, accompanied by the local television station. The boats had to stay offshore, so wading would have meant getting as soaked as the unfortunate maintenance men. The Honorable Lida Fulchard flatly refused to be loaded into the pitching, wet raft with the hay. Finally, Rudy brought her in piggyback, the TV crew slogging alongside, cameras high and rolling.

"That should make the news tonight," someone muttered. "Lida rides a ranger."

Bert chuckled, looking for Hunter. She spotted him ducking into the tent with the reporters. Apparently, James Blount was there, too. Bert couldn't find him anywhere.

"Looking for someone?"

That bass voice could belong only to Clayton, the Humane Society rep. He should be on radio, Bert thought again. "Do you know if James Blount's in there?" she asked, pointing to the tent.

Clayton gave her a warm smile, but the effect was spoiled by the way his bad eye wandered. Bert tried not to notice. "Why don't you go in and see?" Clayton said.

"Can I? I didn't want to interfere."

"Well, hey, why shouldn't you? You're working as hard as anyone."

Bert stuck her head inside. She spotted Ernie Steingart standing alone in the rear of the tent. He slouched gracefully on one leg, his tight, perfectly fitted trousers hugging his rounded butt. However, there was no sign of the foundation director. Puzzled, Bert edged over to

Ernie. "I'm looking for James Blount. Do you know where he went?"

The chief resource ranger shifted his weight to the foot farther from Bert, then gave her a small smile and shook his head. Like many truly fair people, his lashes and brows were close to invisible. She caught a glimpse of blue eyes under his reddish blond hair before he looked away. She could sympathize with his shyness. Bert had been shy as a child and still had stage fright speaking before a crowd. It helped when she concentrated on making the audience feel good, rather than worrying about the impression she was making.

"I can't find him anywhere," Bert whispered. "Do you know if he went out with the roundup crew?"

Again, Ernie shook his head.

She grimaced, annoyed. He must have noticed, because, eyes fixed somewhere around her waist, he said softly, "Only rangers and vets ride the ATVs."

Now, it was her turn to flush. "Wish I knew where he went." But Ernie's attention was back to Hunter and the reporters.

Wondering how a man that shy handled his job, Bert ambled back to the testing table. It was time for lunch, but her cooler was at the front of the tent, and she didn't want to walk past all the reporters to get it.

DeWitt was by the chute with Julie. "Hey, Bert," Julie called. "Did Hunter talk to you yet?"

"Uh-uh. What did he want?"

Julie ducked her head. "I don't know how you're going to feel about this." She gave a small laugh. "I volunteered to stay another night."

"Oh?" Bert's lips closed tightly. No way. If Julie was feeling bad because of the mixed-up test tubes, that was her problem. Bert wasn't staying another night so Julie could soothe her conscience. She had been counting the hours to five o'clock. After working with the horses and sleeping in her clothes, she was sandy, sweaty, sticky, and ready for a long shower. Besides, she needed to talk to Hunter about whatever was going on, and about what Vilma Willit had said. Time with Hunter was growing short. Monday was back to work for her.

It must have shown on Bert's face, because Julie pleaded, "Only for tonight, until they can line up some volunteers to take over. Hunter knows."

"Can't one of the rangers stay?"

"I suppose Purcell could." Julie rolled her eyes.

Bert grinned. She pictured Julie in her clinging long johns, buttocks rolling, heavy breasts swaying as the rather naïve Purcell blushed to his eyelids. "You could always ask Vilma or Lida."

"C'mon, Bert."

"It's just I'm so dirty."

"Take a swim." DeWitt pointed at the sound.

Bert hadn't realized he was listening. "I'm not that desperate."

"Do you good." He cocked his head, eyeing them. "There's a way to get a hot bath, you know."

Both women swung around. "How?"

"You got a propane burner in there, right?"

"Right," they chorused.

"Take one of the water tubs and put it on the burner. Best if you have the stove on the ground. Fill it up with water. Do it now, 'cause it's going to take a couple of hours to heat. Warm the tent up for you, too. Then find yourselves a bucket or something to stand in. Get all nekkid," he leered. "Now, all you need is a pitcher to pour the hot water."

"That would work." Already, Bert was looking around for a likely tub.

Julie smiled up at DeWitt. "I swear, that's the best idea I ever heard."

"Ain't my idea. The Eskimos in Alaska came up with that four thousand years ago."

"You've been to Alaska?"

Bert stopped herself from grinning at Julie's dulcet tones, but DeWitt seemed to be enjoying the attention. He straightened. "Been lots of places. Anchorage, Kodiak, Munivak, Barrow."

"Really? What were you doing?"

"What I should be doing now, that's what." DeWitt scowled, turning to Bert. "You staying or not? We got to make arrangements."

Hunter did have a meeting tonight. Bert sighed. "I'll stay—if you help me get that tub." She glanced around the work area. "What I really need to do is find James Blount, right now."

"Not around here, you won't," DeWitt said. "He went back to the mainland."

"Oh, no! Why? Did you ask him about Shony?"

The big man rubbed up against a fence post, scratching his back like a bear. "Don't know if you heard, me and Blount ain't exactly on speaking terms."

Julie leaned forward. "He said he had a plane to catch."

"Why didn't you ask him, Julie?" Bert snapped. "You know how important it is."

"I'm sorry, Bert. Blount was here for just a minute, and we were real busy." She spread her hands over the empty test tubes. "Went clean out of my mind. After the mix-up, I wasn't thinking of anything except the numbering."

And now Blount had gone again, probably out of state. Dammit anyhow. Bert walked away to stare at the water and to calm down. The wind was beginning to sound like a gale, and she was stuck for the night.

That was no way to think. Maybe she and Julie could go back out for another ride. Meanwhile, she'd better find that tub and start it heating before the sarge called her back to work.

The rangers and reporters emerged from the tent just as Bert reached it with her freshly scrubbed tub. Hunter caught her eye and signaled her with a finger to stay put. While she waited, she moved the camp stove down to a tarp on the sand floor. Then she filled the tub with one of the watering hoses. She was just lighting the stove when Hunter returned. He dropped the flap and took her into his arms, his palms firm and hot on her back, spreading warmth up and down her body. She leaned up to his chest and flat belly, putting her lips to his neck. He had the best hands of any man she'd ever known.

"Hear you're leaving me again," he breathed into her ear.

Damn, why did she agree? Bert pressed her cheek to his. "It was blackmail. They even told me how to fix a bath."

With a sigh, he let her go, eyeing the tub of water. "Is that what you're doing?"

She ran a light hand down his chest. "Hunter, what's your schedule?"

"I got to go off right soon." He looked at his watch. "Fixing to check out the dredge with some state officials."

"About the turtles?"

He nodded. "Ernie Steingart's coming, too. Rudy and the others got a law-enforcement meeting at Hatteras. Good thing you two can stay. Purcell's the only ranger free, and he's got duty tonight."

"You still have tomorrow off?"

"Far as I know." He gave her his lopsided smile. "How about I pick you up in the morning? James Blount was going to see about sending over some more volunteers from the foundation."

"Oh, no! Did you talk to him, too?"

"Not really, just long enough so he authorized the retesting." Hunter shook his head. "Going to cost some."

"Damn. I wanted to ask him about Shony." Bert made a face. "Blount was the one who knew him."

Hunter's brows rose. "So?"

Bert wasn't sure how to start. "You know how the state has an extra blood sample, a hundred and eleven total, but the logs only show a hundred and ten? No horses are missing, so they think it was planted."

"What you getting at?" He cocked his head, listening to some approaching ATVs.

"Hunter, this is important. There is a horse missing—Shony. With him, the count would be a hundred and eleven."

Now, Hunter was all attention. "You sure? No chance you could have mixed him up with another foal? Think on that a minute."

Bert shook her head slowly, going over the events. "That's why I wanted to get hold of James Blount. He saw the foal. And that's not all. He knew his name."

"There's no record of a foal by the name of Shony in any of the logs."

"I know." Bert grimaced. "If only I'd cornered Blount when I saw him this . . ." She stopped, palm to Hunter's chest. "You don't suppose . . . ? You don't think someone put that stallion in the pen deliberately to stop me from talking to Blount?"

"Slow down, hon. I'm not following you."

"This morning, while you were having your first meeting." She told him about the two stallions. "But how could they figure that would stop me from getting to the foundation director?"

"If it was deliberate, and I'm not saying it was, they might have done it to distract you until Blount left. It worked, didn't it?"

"That would mean someone knows Shony exists and wants to keep me from proving it."

Hunter frowned, his heavy brows jutting over his nose. "Maybe me and Ernie better stay over tonight. I don't like the sound of all this."

"Why the concern now? You knew someone let the horses out, or did you think we were careless?"

He eyed her, still frowning. "There's some that don't approve of the roundups, say it stresses the horses. Figured it was one of those do-gooders. They're usually harmless."

"You mean someone boated over in the dark?"

"Not necessarily. Those bolts look closed even when they're not. Gate could have been left open by one of the volunteers or workers. Tell you what, let me check with Ernie about tonight."

Bert was in the tent eating when Hunter returned. "Seems we got state reps driving in from Raleigh. If we cancel the dredge inspection, it could take a month to reschedule."

"That's too bad. It would have been fun with you here. We could take another ride out to the beach."

Hunter guffawed and sat down next to her. "If we stayed, you gals would have been gone." Then he added, "Rudy wants to let Purcell stay over."

"Then who's going to be at Harkers in case there's a problem on one of the other islands?" Bert patted Hunter's thigh. "You know, we could run some chains with padlocks around the gates. That would stop anyone from letting the horses loose again."

That was the way they left it. Julie and Bert would spend the night. Hunter made sure they had a radio and a cell phone. "You call me and Purcell, both of us, if a horse even snorts real loud. You understand?"

"I promise, Hunter. Really, I do." Bert was standing by the dock as the boats prepared to depart. It was only three o'clock, but the worsening winds had the captains concerned—not over the boats' seaworthiness, but the danger of an accident while boarding. Just down from where Bert and Hunter stood, Julie was arguing with DeWitt, her hands flying. It was about time. Julie usually agreed with everything the vet said, to the point of being sickening.

Hunter glanced at the sky. "Calling for small-craft warnings the next couple of days. You're going to get wet coming off tomorrow, for sure."

"But I'll be headed home for a long, hot shower."

His raised a brow, eyes laughing. "I reckon maybe I'll save my bath for when we both get home."

Bert smiled back, nudging him discretely. "You have the whole day off, right? Don't tell anyone, okay?"

Full of energy born of anticipation, Bert filled the horses' watering tubs after Hunter departed. The rangers had returned most of the escaped horses. Not surprisingly, Triton and a few others were still at large. After she and Julie secured the gates with the padlocks and chains, they went to check on their bath. The tub was steaming.

"You want to go first?" Julie asked.

"I thought we could ride down the beach. I'll bet Triton's back where we found him the first day."

The heavy blonde shook her head. "I can't, Bert. I want to review what we did today, and I have to get the test tubes ready for tomorrow."

Bert objected only long enough to be polite. After two days of being constantly with people, she was going to enjoy riding alone. They agreed Julie was to have the first bath.

Soon, Bert was speeding down the island. The beach was protected from the worst of the wind. She drove past the 51 to the 53, scanning the berm for signs of the missing Ridley carapace. There was always a chance it had been covered by sand, not stolen. But the wind had exposed no new treasures.

The dredge was still offshore, its bulky, gray outline looking strangely out of place on the tossing ocean. The pitching of the top structure was obvious even from where Bert sat on the ATV. Poor Hunter. There was nothing like explaining beach nourishment to a shipload of seasick VIPs. She'd read that the nourishment project was on a strict deadline. All the pumping and the grading of the beaches had to be completed in the next two months. Although the turtles' nesting season didn't begin until May, the loggerheads returned to the cape in early spring to mate, causing the incidence of dredge-related drownings to rise drastically.

Returning to the 51, she parked her Honda on top of the ridge of beach dunes. That way, if she wandered off course in the swales, she would still be able to see it.

It was quiet among the sandy hills sheltered from the wind. Bent, headless sea oats lined the primary dunes. Farther in, the dormant dune grass glistened gold under the cloudy light. Here and there, small cedars struggled to grow, leaning trunks and twisted branches sweeping toward the sound in mute testament to the constant offshore winds.

A long, dark head appeared silhouetted on a dune. The horse stood patiently, his shoulders higher on the slope than his rear, head and ears up, face and eyes turned toward Bert. She recognized the spiral white blaze with a start. Triton! She had not expected to find him this easily. Dropping her eyes, she waited, but the stallion did not resume grazing. Instead, he tossed his head and snorted, much as he'd done the first time she'd seen him, when he'd ordered his band to move. But this time, there was no band. With a swish of his tail, he turned and slowly walked away.

Bert clutched her camera and scurried behind the horse. To her surprise, instead of trotting off, Triton maintained a leisurely pace. Every once in a while, he turned his head to see if she followed.

Bert stopped. She didn't want to chase him away. She knew she'd better go back now, so Purcell could come get Triton in the morning. But even though she was no longer close behind, the horse did not stop to graze. Instead, Triton continued his slow pace to the wood line, pausing every hundred feet to snort and paw the ground while twisting around to look at her, almost inviting her to come along.

Chapter 10

Bert couldn't resist. She didn't believe Triton really was trying to get her to follow, but the idea was intriguing.

The horse waited until she was within a hundred feet, then turned into the woods. As Bert trotted down the narrow path behind him, fear began to build. Just what did he have in mind? She'd been nipped on the shoulder once by a stallion being too friendly.

Suppose Triton felt threatened and decided to turn and charge? The scrub trees were thick but too short to climb. Myrtle, cedars, and dormant, thorny blackberries enclosed the path, blocking passage. Well, better to get scratched than stomped by a horse.

Bert slowed, rounding each bend carefully, listening for hooves.

As she came around one turn, there he stood in a clearing not fifty feet away. Behind the stallion and a twisted cedar, she could see the blue water of the sound. Triton's brown eyes were fixed on her. Bert forced herself to look away, stomach contracting. She froze in place, not even breathing, sure he could smell her fear.

But once the stallion was satisfied she wasn't moving, he began to paw the ground. The sand was full of hoof marks and piles of dung, as if he'd been here before. Avoiding eye contact, Bert watched, fascinated. Using his front hooves, Triton was digging a hole in the loose mix of sandy earth. She'd heard how horses dug holes to find water. She smiled. Was this part of the courtship, offering his date refreshment?

Her amusement vanished as the horse raised his head and gave a high-pitched squeal, like the cry of a child. He danced backward, away from the hole.

It was an invitation one did not refuse. Bert moved forward slowly, her eyes on Triton. He stood still, head and tail up, ears forward, watching. With another anxious glance at the chestnut stallion, Bert looked down at the hole, expecting to see water. But it wasn't water Triton had uncovered. It was some kind of cloth. No, not cloth, it was hair— a pelt. Oh, no, an animal?

Triton nickered, then whirled and trotted to the beach, where another horse waited. Apparently, he'd managed to bring one of his mares along on his escape.

Bert dropped to her knees. The pelt was reddish. This close, she caught a faint odor of decay. Not wanting to touch whatever lay dead in the hole, she searched for something to scrape away the sand. That hunk of wood would work. As she scraped, deliberately not thinking about what she might dig up, she wondered how it got buried. It was too sheltered here for coverage by wind-swept sand, and too far from the sound for the tide to reach, except in a storm surge. She glanced up dubiously. It was possible this animal had been washed up during a storm. From its size, she was sure now it was a horse. Maybe the high surf that tossed it up had also buried it.

Suddenly, Bert sat back on her heels, her stomach heaving. She had uncovered part of a mane. It was a foal—with a blond mane. No longer worried about touching something long dead, she used her hands to brush the sand away from its face. Then she tugged at its head until she pried it from the grave.

Bert moaned. Stretching all the way from his forehead to the tip of his nose was the conch-shaped, white blaze, just as she remembered it. Now, the smell of dead animal rose in waves, forcing Bert to lean away to inhale. Shony's large, brown eyes were full of sand. More sand was clumped at his neck. Blood. She knocked it off. A thick, raw stench enveloped her. The neck gaped, showing an open cut caked with sand and black, congealed blood. Greenish black muck oozed from his nose.

Bert dropped the head, whimpering and gagging. Nearby, the two horses snorted and raced down the beach, their hooves resounding on the wet sand. She'd frightened them.

Trembling, Bert backed away. Shony had been killed, and not by another horse. That was no bite or hoof mark, nor was it the result of an accident with an ATV. Someone had sliced his jugular. Bert moaned again, hand to her stomach. How could anyone do this? How could anyone hurt a poor, little animal?

Maybe they didn't. She stumbled back down the path, barely conscious of where she was going. It didn't have to be a knife wound. Maybe he got hung up on the fence. Of course, that was it. Somehow, he climbed the fence, or wriggled through, but got caught and sliced himself badly. Bert shuddered to think of the foal struggling silently.

But if he hurt himself on the fence, how did he get all the way down here? She stopped. It wasn't possible. He didn't bury himself. Someone killed him and tried to hide his body. Oh, poor Shony.

Back at the primary dunes, Bert straddled her ATV and started up the beach. She forced herself to concentrate on driving. After a bit, she calmed, soothed by the open spaces and the big expanse of sky with its tumbled layers of clouds backlit by the sun. Her breathing slowed. She shivered, pulling her hood tight. She was damp with sweat, born not of exercise but of fear and nausea.

The ride back to camp had never seemed longer. Gearing down and driving right up to the door of the tent, she leapt off the four-wheeler, yelling for Julie.

The tent was empty.

Bert ran to the dock. Julie was just coming off the pier. The tide was near high. Water reached all the way to the grass, only a few rims of sand showing. If anything, conditions were even rougher than when Bert had left. Small breakers washed the shore, splashing high off roots and driftwood. Deep in the sound, a boat tossed.

Bert ran toward Julie, shouting her news.

For the first time since Bert had met her, Julie's face lost its flush, turning yellow-gray. "Are you sure, Bert? Ponies die every season. It's not unusual to find their bodies."

"Come with me. I'll show you." Bert ran into the tent and grabbed the radio. "But first, I've got to call in."

"Wait." Julie followed her inside, breasts bouncing under her tight sweatshirt.

Bert frowned. No way was Julie stopping her again. But the blonde pointed at the cell phone. "Use that. More private."

Bert called the park number and got a recording. It was after five. Purcell's message directed her to his cell, his home number, or, in case of emergency, the sheriff.

There was no answer at either of Purcell's numbers. Bert tried Hunter's cell phone, knowing he was still on the dredge offshore. She left messages for both Hunter and Purcell on the park's voice mail and at their houses. "I'm going to have to use the radio. Purcell's got to be somewhere around the cape," she told Julie. "He's on duty."

After several tries, Purcell's voice finally came back, barely audible, giving his call number first, then his location. "Three-one-two, back of Drum Inlet."

"Three-one-two, this is five-four-three. We have a problem. Can you give us a call?"

"Did not copy. You are broken."

"Purcell! This is Bert. Call me," she yelled.

There was silence. Perhaps she could transmit better from outside. Bert ran out to the end of the dock. Drum Inlet was almost thirty miles north. Purcell must have had some kind of emergency. This time, she got an answer.

"Three-one-two, I'm in the boat. Had to turn off the motor to copy. What's the problem?"

"This is Bert. Can you call me?"

"Negative. Cell phone's out. I'll call when I get in."

"Can you come here? I need you."

"You're breaking up."

"Come to Shackleford."

There was silence. Then the radio coughed static. "Take me near an hour. Sun's setting now. I'm in the skiff."

So that's why the contact was so bad. The skiffs didn't have built-in radios. Purcell was on his hand-held. Each branch of the park set its own priorities and budgets. Apparently, communications was not high on the list with Resource. It had the worst radio equipment in the park.

"What's your problem? Horses get out?" he asked.

How could she tell him without letting the world know? "It's Shony. I found him."

"So we'll pick him up tomorrow."

She had to make him understand. "No, Purcell. He's dead."

There was a long silence. "Hold up. Drifting. Got to move the boat. Can't hear you with the motor on."

She paced the dock, waiting. Finally, he came back. "Tried the phone. Not working. Battery's low. Guess I better come over."

He didn't sound enthusiastic. She didn't blame him. He had to be wet and tired and looking forward to a hot meal. "There's not really anything you can do. But I promised I'd call. Purcell, can you get Hunter?"

"You're breaking up again. ETA is six-thirty. Get an ATV on the dock, and turn on the headlights. I'll call in when I'm near. You copy?"

"Copy. Can you call Hunter?"

"Negative. Cell phone not working."

Of course. Stupid of her. "Ten-four. Will be waiting with the ATV. Five-four-three out."

Bert walked back to the tent. Already, the sky was darkening. There were too many clouds tonight for a sunset. Inside, Julie was on her cot, papers all about. Bert edged by her and picked up the phone to try Hunter again. Too bad the park wouldn't let them get cellular voice mail. It was a matter of money, as usual. The phone was warm to her touch. "Did Hunter call in?" she asked.

Julie looked up, surprised. "No, I would have called you."

"The phone's hot. Were you on it?"

"No. You were, just a minute ago."

More like fifteen minutes. She'd left the phone on so Hunter could reach them. Usually, they turned it off to conserve power, using it only to initiate calls. Maybe it heated up when it was left on. In any case, it was uncomfortably hot in the tent with the bath water steaming. Bert turned the burner off. "Did you get your bath all right?"

"It was truly a treat. I put some more water on. If you're ready, I can leave."

"No. I'm not in the mood right now."

"Shony?"

Bert nodded. "I never should have started petting him."

"Now, Bert. How could it be your fault? Could you tell what happened?"

"He was all the way down by Bald Hill, and I know what happened, all right. Someone cut his throat."

Again, Julie paled. "Cut his throat? Are you sure?"

"No mistake. They buried him, too, so we wouldn't find him."

Julie seemed to sag, her shoulders collapsing. "It can't be. No, that's wrong. There must be a mistake."

"Go look for yourself."

Julie said nothing for a minute, then rose slowly. "We'd better get something to eat. Didn't you say Purcell was on his way?"

Bert had never felt less like eating, yet her spirits did improve after a cup of hot tea. She was halfway though a cold steak-and-lettuce sandwich when the radio blared. "Five-four-three, ETA five minutes. Do you have lights on?"

Jumping up, Bert grabbed the radio off the table. "Be right there. You're early." She looked at her watch. It was barely six. "How did you get here so fast?" But there was no answer. Jamming the radio into her pocket, she started out the door. They weren't supposed to be on the air any more than absolutely necessary.

"Need help?" Julie asked.

"All I have to do is take the ATV out on the dock. Maybe you'd better stay here in case Hunter or someone returns our calls." She put her cap on under her hood and made sure her jacket was closed all the way up her neck and chin. The wind hadn't died down as it usually did at night. Leaving the wet warmth of the tent would make it feel even colder.

It was tricky taking the ATV out in the dark. On Portsmouth, the dock was larger and lined with pilings. But the Shackleford dock was just wide enough for the four tires. They'd have to back up to get the bike off. Better someone else than her. The trouble with ATVs was that the thumb-fed gas didn't flow smoothly. Between that and the gears, they had a tendency to jerk at low speeds.

She reached the end of the dock with a sigh of relief. Honda headlights worked only when the motor was on, so she had to gear down. With the engine running in neutral, the beams shone nicely over the water, bouncing off the chop and higher waves.

Behind her, the surf was breaking on the shore, unusual for the sound side of the island. The moon was hidden above the low ceiling, gleaming like a spotlight behind the rolling, churning clouds. Bert listened for Purcell's boat, but all she heard was the Honda, the whistling wind, and the splash of waves. The air was cold but clean and fresh. Across the sound, the lights of the mainland coastline danced for miles—red, green, and shades of white. What made all the different shades of white? she wondered. Some of the streetlights seemed to be yellow, while others had blue tints and some even a soft pink. A green glow moved on the water. Purcell's boat? Sure enough, it turned and headed toward the dock, its green and red lights coming directly at her. Then it stopped. Bert frowned. Why was he stopping? The tide was high enough for him to reach the dock, especially in the skiff.

Bert clicked her tongue—stupid. The tide was on its way out. He'd get in, all right, but not out again.

She heard, or thought she heard, the rattle of an anchor chain. Then the boat's lights went off. Bert reached for her radio. "Purcell, is that you?"

There was no answer. The ATV's headlights didn't reach as far as the boat. So when a huge, shaggy shape suddenly materialized in the yellow beams, Bert jumped. The form lumbered toward her, water to its waist, flashing a light ahead.

Damn, it was deep out there. Purcell would be soaked. Really, she shouldn't have made him come. There was nothing he could do for Shony tonight. Heat flushed Bert's face as she hailed him. "Hi. What can I do?"

Purcell grunted, emerging from the water. He had on a bulky, waterproof jacket over what looked like chest-high waders, the kind crabbers used, the boots built-in. His face loomed dark and very full. Was he wearing a face mask?

Wait a minute. That wasn't Purcell.

Chapter 11

That wasn't a face mask. It was a beard—a wet beard. Besides, even in waterproof gear, Purcell wasn't that massive. Bert ran down the dock. "DeWitt, is that you?"

"Who'd you think it was, Santa Claus?"

"What are you doing here? I thought you were Purcell." She walked back to the ATV and cut the motor, which turned off the headlights. Fumbling for her flashlight, she shone it at DeWitt.

He'd reached the dock and was shedding water like a seal, puddles spreading out from where he stood. "You got me instead. Now, what's the problem?"

"Aren't you freezing?" Bert stared at the big man. "Julie's inside. She's got a towel."

He grunted impatiently. "I don't need mothering. What's so important you got to bring a man out here in these seas in the dark?"

Damn. She knew she shouldn't have called, but she'd promised Hunter. "You know that little foal that was missing?"

"That you said was missing," he corrected, striding toward the tent.

"He was missing, all right," Bert said as she trotted behind. "I found him, dead." Trying to shock DeWitt, she added, "Someone slit his throat."

Apparently, the man was unshakable. "You don't say." He lifted the tent flap and stooped to get in. "You a forensic expert now?"

"DeWitt!" Julie was on her feet. "What are you doing here?"

"You called for help, didn't you? Now, let's have a look at this pony. Where is it?" He shrugged off his slicker. Underneath, he wore a heavy knit sweater, the colors all matted together.

"Down by Bald Hill somewhere. She found it." Hand to her mouth, Julie glanced at Bert. "I don't like this."

Bert blinked, sensing an undercurrent. What was going on? Had Julie been on the phone with DeWitt earlier?

"Can't say I care for night boating in January myself." DeWitt patted Julie's arm, then pulled the straps of his bib waders off his shoulders. One was missing its buckle. Shoving them off his hips, DeWitt sat on a cot, still shedding water. Wincing, Bert grabbed her sleeping bag before it got wet. The vet bent over, yanking off his muddy waders and slipping on a pair of shoes he'd produced from somewhere. Damn. He was making a mess of the tent with all that water and mud. Bert pulled her backpack away from the cot. He rose, dumping his gear in a corner. "Ready?" He eyed her from under his dark brows.

"Who, me?"

"Who else? You found him, didn't you?"

Just then, the cell phone rang. It was DeWitt who reacted first and picked it up. "Shackleford ranger station." He held the phone to his ear. "That's me, all right. Heard the women on the radio." He listened for a moment, then shrugged. "We all got issued radios today. I hung onto mine." DeWitt's mouth twisted under his beard. "How long you figure?"

Another pause. "Best if I go on ahead." He handed the phone to Bert. "It's him."

It had to be Hunter. It was. "You all right, hon?"

"I'm fine. Hunter, I found Shony, but he's dead. That's what I was calling about."

"So I heard, from three different people. Sorry about the cell phone. Can't use it on the dredge on account of their equipment. Purcell there yet?"

"No. I thought it was him coming in, but it was DeWitt. Purcell should be here pretty soon."

"You got lights on the dock so he can find his way in?"

"I'll go turn the ATV back on. Where are you?"

"Just leaving Morehead."

"Then how did you know I called?"

"Checked for messages soon as I came off the dredge. I've got Ernie and Clayton with me." He sounded tired. "It's going to be awhile till we get back to Harkers. Rudy took one of the Parkers to Hatteras, so I'm not sure what boats are left." Cape Lookout had two Parkers—those were the big cabin cruisers—and one small cruiser. The rest of the park boats were open-hull craft, mostly skiffs.

"Hunter, there's no reason for you to come out. There's nothing anyone can do until tomorrow anyhow. I just wanted you to know."

Bert could hear voices in the background. He had to be talking to the other men. Then he came back on. "I'll talk at you when we get to Harkers. Tell DeWitt to stick around until he hears from me. And Bert, you did good calling in. You take care now."

DeWitt waited until she hung up. "You coming?"

Bert stared. "Hunter said for you to stick around until he gets to Harkers."

"I'm fixing to stay the night. No sense taking chances on the water. Let's go."

"But—"

"O'Hagan told me to have a look. I'm a vet, remember?"

"Sorry. I didn't understand. Julie, you coming?"

Julie jumped up, smiling, but DeWitt shook his head. "One of you's got to wait for Purcell, and Bert knows where the pony's at, right? You best go turn them lights on. And stay there, hear me? Don't want that ATV stalling out."

Bert watched Julie's face fall. Too bad. Julie would have loved to go with him, whereas Bert wanted only to find out who or what killed Shony. But she had to admire Julie's technique. The blonde stood, slipped on her jacket, pocketed the radio, and turned to DeWitt. "I've never driven an ATV at night. Is there any trick to turning on the lights?"

Bert turned away so DeWitt couldn't see her grin.

The bearded vet stood and put his palm to Julie's back as he ushered her out the tent door. "Nothing to it. Got to have the motor running or the lights won't go on." Then he shouted back at Bert, "You want to get the other four-wheeler up and going? Take it over to the wagon. I'll meet you there."

The wagon, an ATV trailer for hauling hay, was kept by the well on the ocean side of the pens. A small shed housed the well's generator. While she waited, Bert sorted through the posts, posthole diggers, mallets, and PVC pipe heaped inside the shed until she found a shovel. She tied that and some rope onto the ATV, gathering up the spiked flags she'd knocked to the floor. Then she investigated a stack of cardboard boxes against the wall. They contained shells, a horse skull, assorted bones, a turtle carapace, some old egg casings, and the skeleton of a nutria with its orange teeth. The rangers used the shed for equipment and educational materials.

This close to the pens, Bert could smell the ponies. On the whole, they were quiet. Occasionally, one would neigh or snort. She checked her watch. It was almost six-thirty. Purcell should be arriving any minute. She didn't begrudge Julie her time with DeWitt, but she did wish the vet would get here. She'd like to get back before Hunter called in from Harkers.

What did DeWitt plan to do when they found Shony? Bring the carcass back with them? Bert shuddered. She hoped not, but she wouldn't put it past him. That's why she packed the rope. She'd shared ATVs with strange cargoes before. The worst had been the ripe head of a small whale that washed ashore after the hurricane last summer. She'd taken the National Fisheries biologist out to it. The woman had insisted on hacking the head off on the spot and bringing it back. The smell was the nastiest Bert had ever experienced, and she didn't want to test it against the pony.

Finally, she heard footsteps. Bert turned on her flashlight so DeWitt could find her.

"No sign of Purcell," he grunted, taking the driver's seat on the ATV. "Must have got himself lost."

Soon, they were speeding down the beach. At least he didn't smell bad, damp wool sweater notwithstanding. He drove like a maniac in the dark. Bert ducked, taking as much shelter as she could behind his broad back. His hair, beard, and sleeves were wet, some of the moisture blowing back on her. She figured his pants had to be damp, too. Well, he was big enough to have a nice layer of insulating fat. At least he wasn't whining about being cold.

When they reached the 51 mile marker, he turned inland, cutting across the dunes and sand flats on the four-wheeler, against all Park Service rules. Bert didn't protest. Walking in would have taken them forever. He skidded to a halt at the edge of the woods.

Bert stared at the deep, shaggy shadows of the brush, dark against the lighter sand. Only the immediate scrub illuminated by the headlights was visible. "Damn, I should have marked it. I'll never find the path."

DeWitt turned off the motor—and the lights. "You brought your flashlight, didn't you?" Bert nodded. He snapped on his light. "Take your time. We'll just walk around. Look for hoofprints."

They searched the edge of the woods, turning into paths that cut through toward the sound. But none seemed familiar.

"Was it a wide trail? Narrow? Where was the pony exactly?"

"Narrow, but it had been used a lot," Bert said.

"Dung piles? They mark their territory that way."

Bert nodded. "Then it opened up by the sound. I could see water behind Triton, and the beach where the mare was."

"Let's try over here." They walked northeast to a path DeWitt apparently knew. He was reputed to know every trail on the island. This path was the right width and had plenty of bends but no splits. They reached a clearing close to the water. The sand was more disturbed than she remembered, the dung piles overturned. "Look familiar?"

"I think so, but when I left, Shony's head was showing. Stunk, too." She sniffed, scraping at the sand with the side of her shoe. "All this loose stuff . . . The horses wouldn't cover him back up, would they?"

DeWitt plunged the shovel into the sand. Soon, he was down a foot, but no carcass appeared. He raised his head, eyeing her sardonically.

"I think he was more over here." Bert pointed with her foot.

Muttering, DeWitt moved. Again, sand flew. He dug down past his knees and stopped, leaning on his shovel, exasperated.

She was almost sure this was the right place. Bert knelt, scratching in the sand. Under the hoof marks, the ground was soft, like it had been recently excavated. This had to be Triton's clearing.

Meanwhile, DeWitt broke off a green branch to use as a probe. He poked around the clearing. "How deep did you say he was?"

"I didn't, but not more than six to eight inches."

"He ain't here."

"Maybe this is the wrong path."

"Maybe. Want to go back and try again?"

They'd just come from the woods when DeWitt's radio sounded. "Five-four-three, two-four-one."

"That's Hunter for me," Bert said, reaching for DeWitt's radio, clipped to his belt.

He grabbed it first. "Come in, two-four-one."

"What's your twenty?"

"Bald Hill with five-four-three. Where you at?"

"Just coming into the east-end dock area. Thought that was five-four-three on the dock with the ATV. You find what you were looking for?"

"Nope," DeWitt said.

"Meet you at the 51."

"Might as well stay put," DeWitt said. "Ain't nothing more to be done here tonight." Bert let out a protesting grunt, reaching for the radio. DeWitt shook his head. "Got the world listening in."

"Oh, right." That was why Hunter had used her call number. On the islands, with poor television reception and no cable, people entertained themselves listening to radio broadcasts. She'd done it herself.

Now, DeWitt called Hunter. "On our way back. Don't make no wake coming in. I got a cinder block anchoring the boat." He signed off.

"Why's that?" Bert asked.

"Somebody ripped me off. Lost my anchor."

"Around here?" They were walking back to the ATV.

"Gloucester." Gloucester was a small fishing village near his clinic. "First time for everything."

When they reached the four-wheeler, DeWitt jumped on and started the motor as Bert scrambled to climb on the back. Chivalrous he was not. All conversation ceased as he geared up and roared back at full speed.

DeWitt shut off the Honda as they reached the tent. Another motor droned by the dock. Bert ran toward the lights. Hunter was backing an ATV off the pier. When he had it on land, he dismounted and pulled Bert to his side. "Just fixing to come after you. You okay, hon?"

"I'm tired, but it feels good to have you here." His hand was firm and comforting on her waist. She leaned into him. "You've got to be dead. How was your meeting?"

It was too dark to see his face, but she heard the tension in his voice as he hugged her. "Different. Tell you later. Take it you and DeWitt couldn't find the foal."

"It's hard at night. I thought we had the right path, but then . . ." Bert sighed. "The ground was all messed up, like the horses had dug it up, but nothing was there."

"We'll find him in the morning. A dead horse isn't going anywhere."

"You're staying overnight?"

Hunter shrugged. "We'd all have to come back in a couple of hours anyhow."

"We?"

"Clayton and Ernie came over, too. They're concerned that someone might be killing ponies."

That figured. Ernie was the chief resource ranger. Resource took care of the park's fauna and flora but had little to do with the public—which was just as well, considering Ernie's reclusive nature. Clayton's job was to oversee the treatment and care of the mustangs.

"Where did they go?" Bert asked as they walked toward the tent.

"Ernie's in with the horses. Don't know where Clayton took himself."

"There's not enough cots or sleeping bags."

"We got some stuff in the boat. Don't you worry, we'll manage. Good thing that's a big tent."

They found Clayton inside. He'd turned on the propane heater and was eyeing Bert's bathtub on the camp stove. "You mind if we move that? I'd like to make some coffee."

"No, go right ahead." So much for her Alaskan bath.

Just then, both radios went off. "Three-one-two, east end. What's with the lights?" It was Purcell.

Hunter activated his mike. "Gave you up for lost. Have the lights on in five."

Bert looked at her watch. It was nine-thirty. "What on earth happened to him? He was supposed to be here hours ago."

Hunter motioned her to come with him. "Good thing you didn't have a real emergency." He kicked the ATV into gear and rode it back out on the dock, Bert walking behind. Purcell's running lights were in view. "There he is."

Soon, he was wading ashore. Bert had never seen a more miserable-looking human. He was shivering, his hair plastered to his head. He took off his waders and poured water from them, his trousers dark and clinging to his skinny legs. "You're soaked," she said. "What on earth happened?"

"Ran aground, don't you know," he muttered. "Thought I was all right. Kept to the right of the marker but guess I turned too soon. Got sand up the intake. She started stalling on me. Had to keep stopping to clean her out."

"Where, Shingle Point?" Hunter asked, slipping off his jacket and offering it to Purcell. "You didn't try to get it off the shoal by powering the motor, did you?"

The young man waved away Hunter's coat. "I'll just get it soaked."

When they reached the tent, Bert dug in her backpack for an extra sweatshirt. "Here. It's a large." The ranger peeled off his wet jacket and shirt and took Bert's offering, then Hunter's jacket. Bert eyed his trousers. "Maybe Julie has something that'll fit. Where is she anyhow?"

Clayton, the Humane Society rep, was sprawled on Julie's cot, sipping from a mug of the coffee he'd brewed. He shrugged, silver hair gleaming in the lantern light. "Haven't seen her since I got in. I thought she was with you."

"Not with us," Bert told him. "She stayed here with the ATV, to show Purcell the way in."

Hunter's bushy brows jutted in a frown. "There was no one about when we got in. Just the ATV running on the dock with the lights on."

Chapter 12

"That's weird." Bert spun around, half expecting Julie to materialize. "Maybe she got cold waiting for Purcell and went inside to warm
up. I bet she's with DeWitt now." Zipping up her jacket once more,
she unlatched the tent flap and stepped into the darkness. The wind
had dropped slightly, but it was colder than ever. Lights flashed near
the pens. At the fence, she found DeWitt holding forth while Ernie
listened, nodding. "Have you seen Julie?" Bert aimed her Maglite at
them.

"Uh-uh," Ernie grunted, ducking his head.

"Come to think of it, haven't seen her since we got back." DeWitt
peered at Bert. "Tried the john?"

"If she's been in there all this time, she's suffocated by now." To be sure, Bert trotted over. As before, the porta-potty was empty. The door banged when she released it, sounding loud in the dark, blustery night. Behind her, a horse whinnied.

Bert hadn't been concerned until now. Julie had disappeared off and on since they'd arrived, but this was once too often.

She went back to the tent. Within five minutes, Hunter had the men organized into search teams. Leaving the others to comb the pens, Bert and Hunter took the ATV to check the path to the beach. As they reached the dark, swaying walls of myrtle, Hunter turned off the motor and shouted Julie's name. Three times, he stopped and called. By now, Bert envisioned Julie sprawled somewhere, hurt, unable to walk or shout for help.

Finally, they came out of the dark corridor onto the beach. The surf gleamed a ghostly white. Even though the stars were partially obscured by the cloud cover, the ocean and sand reflected enough light to pick out shapes and shadows. There was no sign of Julie.

"You don't suppose she went after y'all, do you?" Hunter asked.

"Why would she? All she had to do was call if anything came up. She has our radio. I can't see her walking this far without a good reason. She's not big on exercise."

Hunter picked up his hand-held radio, then thought a moment and passed it to Bert. "Don't want to get people on Harkers upset. Could be she just wants some time to herself. You want to see if you can raise her? Make it sound natural."

"Julie. Come in, Julie. This is Bert. I'm on my way back. Where are you?"

The radio remained silent. They drove to the top of the dunes and tried again, then rode up and down the beach several miles—as far as Hunter figured Julie could get on foot in two hours.

"Maybe she's back at camp."

Hunter shook his head. "I told them to let me know if they found anything." He stopped the ATV. "Don't rightly know what to do next except call in for help."

"Search and rescue?"

He nodded. "I'm thinking she might have passed out on the dock and gone in the water."

"Oh, I never thought of that." Bert winced. "Maybe she slipped while she was waiting for you and hit her head."

"Doesn't have to be life threatening, but we need to find her quick, before exposure gets to be a problem." He revved up again. "Thing is, we could be driving right past her and not know it."

"Does she have any medical conditions?" Bert yelled over the engine.

"Not that she admitted to. She say anything to you?"

They were back in the corridor. Bert leaned forward. "Hunter, stop."

He pulled up. "You hear something?"

"No, but if she's disabled or something, we'd still hear her radio, wouldn't we? She had it in her pocket."

He nodded, sliding off the bike. "Two-four-one, three-one-two."

Purcell answered immediately. "Three-one-two." He recited his call numbers singsong, dropping a note in the middle, as did most rangers.

"Running a series of radio checks. Stand by, three-one-two."

"Copy."

They walked back to the beach, then turned and headed toward the tent area, broadcasting every hundred yards. Bert stayed well behind Hunter, listening for his voice to come in over Julie's radio. She'd just about given up when she heard an echo. "Hunter, do it again."

"Three-one-two, how do you copy?"

"Three-one-two, east landing. Hear you loud and clear."

Bert caught up and grabbed his arm. "Over there."

They pushed through the sparse myrtle. Hunter called again. Purcell's voice came at them not only from Hunter's radio, but also from someplace dead ahead.

Bert ran forward, flashing her light. "Julie. Julie. Are you there?" She stumbled over a grassy rise.

"Watch it." Hunter reached out, steadying her. He aimed his light ahead. It picked out a mound, dark on the lighter sand.

"Oh, God," Bert gasped. Both her flashlight and Hunter's illuminated the still form. "Julie." Bert dropped to her knees. "Can you hear me?" The light showed the woman's heavy windbreaker streaked with sand.

Questions fired through Bert's mind one after another. What was wrong? Why was the sand in streaks? Blood! Sand stuck to streaks of blood. There was nothing sharp around. Hemorrhage?

She was still holding her breath as Hunter's light traveled slowly up Julie's chest to her face. Bert stared, numb, shaking her head. No. It couldn't be. That wasn't Julie's face. Just raw meat, crushed, meat with pieces of bone and teeth showing. She moaned, letting out a little air as Hunter's light found an eye. The lid was partly closed, a half-moon of white peeping out beneath. A strand of Julie's hair lay bloody and matted across her face.

Hunter was pushing her aside. "Call the others. We're gonna need the stretcher." He felt Julie's arm, then slid his hand to her neck, looking for a pulse. He jerked away, shaking his head.

Bert knelt, staring at his hand. It was covered with blood. Julie's blood. Then his hands were on Bert's shoulders, pulling her up. All she could think was that he was getting Julie's blood on her jacket. "She can't be dead," Bert whispered, knowing she was. That slightly opened eye had told her. "She was alive just a minute ago. DeWitt knows how to resuscitate."

Hunter kept his arm around her as he used the radio again. "Purcell and Ernie. Bring a blanket and the cot, beach road." He turned to Bert. "Can you walk?"

"I'm fine," she said automatically. He turned her away from Julie. She resisted, saying, "Where are you going?"

"To meet the men."

"We can't leave her. That's not right."

"Just for a minute, hon."

"No." Bert planted her feet. "I'll stay with her."

"You sure?"

"Yes." She gave him a push. "Go get them."

"Be right back."

She could hear his steps in the sand, bushes rustling in the wind, even a motor starting up in the distance. Bert swung her flashlight back to Julie. Suppose she wasn't dead? Bert crouched. One of Julie's hands lay on the sand. The skin was unbroken, not even bloody. There were no defensive wounds; her fingernails were white and rounded. Hesitating, Bert reached out and touched the hand. The skin wasn't cold, but it wasn't warm either. She turned the hand over, resting her fingers on the vein at the wrist. She really didn't have to do it. There was something about the texture of the skin that told her life was gone.

Bert stroked the still hand. "Julie. Oh, Julie. I'm so sorry." She reached over and plucked the strand of hair from the broken face. Tears choked her. Julie had been so alive, so happy, and now she was dead, gone. Suddenly, Bert was filled with dread. Whatever had killed Julie could kill her, too—or Hunter. Somehow, you thought you'd live forever, or at least until you were very old and wanted to die. But it wasn't true. Some stupid accident could kill you just like—

Voices. Hunter was back with help. She squeezed Julie's hand and let it drop.

The men were silent and efficient. Having brought the lantern, they knelt to examine Julie carefully. "She's dead, all right. Been dead for at least an hour," DeWitt said. He started to slide a hand under her.

Hunter stopped him. "We can't move her until the medical examiner gives an okay. Ernie, will you go back and give Dr. Patel a call?"

"He ain't going to come out in this weather." DeWitt climbed to his feet, grunting.

The men waited silently. By the time Ernie returned, Bert's teeth were chattering.

"I told the doctor it was an accident, with a vehicle probably," Ernie reported in his low, jerky speech. The resource ranger wore his dress trousers and jacket, the wind plastering them against his long, muscular body. He blinked pale lashes as DeWitt raised the lantern. "The doc said to bring her in. That he'll meet the ambulance in Morehead."

An ATV accident? How? She and DeWitt were riding one machine. The other was on the dock. Bert shook her head.

Apparently, DeWitt didn't agree with Ernie either. "I thought you was supposed to be smart. She'd have to drive face-first into a tree to do that to herself. How you figure she done it with no trees or bikes around?"

Ernie said nothing, but Bert, standing slightly behind him, saw him make a quick gesture. She blinked. Had the quiet resource ranger just given DeWitt the finger?

Soon, they had Julie on the canvas cot. Bert tugged at Julie's jacket, noticing she still had on her shoes. There was blood on her pants, too. Bert pulled the blanket over her, leaving Julie's face exposed. The wool would stick to those terrible wounds. Someone else could cover her face.

But the men carried Julie back to the tent as Bert had left her. Inside, they crowded around the body and opened her jacket. Bert saw DeWitt point at something as they bent over her. "Hoof mark."

"No. You think a horse killed her?" Bert choked.

No one answered. Hunter came over and took Bert's hand. "Looks like it. Did you hear any horses?"

"No. Nothing around here." Then Bert remembered. "Oh."

DeWitt swung around. "You did see a horse?"

"Not today, but yesterday, after the horses got out."

"Go on."

"I went to check the other gates, and when I came back, Julie was gone. I found her coming back down the corridor. She said she'd seen something. She thought it was a horse, but it got away." Bert stared into DeWitt's angry eyes. "You don't suppose it came back, and she went after it again?" Bert clutched her stomach. "Oh, poor Julie." A horrible vision came to her mind—a horse rearing and coming down, again and again. "She must have been so scared."

Hunter took Bert by the shoulders and pushed her down on her cot. "When something like that happens, hon, you're too busy reacting to be scared. Think back to how you felt in the chute."

She hadn't been scared, Bert remembered, not until it was over.

Then she heard DeWitt's angry growl. "Told you that stallion was going to kill somebody. I should have taken care of him myself."

"You're crazy." Bert swung around, her voice high. "That's not true. Triton would never do that."

DeWitt shrugged. "What else? He's the only stallion loose."

"That's so, Bert," Hunter said, his voice low.

"Shit happens," Clayton intoned.

Bert's heart hammered in her chest. She stood up, her gaze going from one man to another. "No. You don't even know what killed her yet. Maybe it wasn't a horse. Maybe it was one of you." She had to do something. They seemed ready to shoot Triton on sight.

The stares she received made her quake deep inside, but she met their eyes defiantly. Hunter's face held an anxious expression. He obviously thought she was hysterical. DeWitt's eyes formed two angry slits, and his lips were clenched in a tight line. Clayton's bad eye was darting back and forth, his scar red and pulsing. Ernie's face was turned away, but a muscle in his jaw twitched. Purcell's mouth hung open. He stared at Bert, blinking. Why, he almost looked frightened.

Chapter 13

"It doesn't have to be Triton that kicked Julie," Bert insisted. "Maybe someone let another horse out, or a bunch of them. We don't know if they're all in the pen. Maybe that's why Julie wasn't waiting at the dock. She rounded up the horses and got hurt by accident." Bert voiced another thought, although the idea made her stomach crawl. "Do you suppose she got hurt in the pen and was trying to get help?"

Hunter glanced at DeWitt, who shook his head, saying, "Her head's stove in good. She wasn't walking nowhere."

The men's faces no longer showed anger. At least she'd put doubt into their minds. They'd have to prove it was Triton before they did anything.

Just then, the cell phone rang. Purcell exhaled, bending at the waist to pluck it from Bert's camp cot. He handed it to Hunter. "Sheriff's on the line." Events on park property came under federal jurisdiction, but Hunter had put through calls to the civil authorities as a matter of courtesy and because Julie was from the mainland.

Unable to sit still, Bert wandered over to Julie's cot. The men had apparently just tipped her things off the canvas bed onto the floor when Hunter called for a stretcher. Concentrating on the immediate task, and keeping her eyes away from the still form under the blanket, Bert rolled up the sleeping bag, shook out Julie's bath towel, and tucked it into her backpack.

Behind Bert, Hunter talked first to the sheriff, then to the Coast Guard. They agreed they would wait until daybreak to transport the body. Once it reached Harkers Island, the sheriff would send an ambulance to transport it to the medical examiner. It would be up to the foundation to notify her family.

"You'll let me know what the arrangements are, won't you?" Bert managed to keep her voice steady as she spoke to Ernie Steingart. He sat by Hunter, writing in a pocket notebook. As chief resource ranger, he'd be coordinating the park with the foundation. Suddenly, it seemed very important she attend the services. "I'll finish putting her things together. Her family will want them," she told Ernie. He looked up and nodded, giving her a quick smile. It was strange to think of Julie with family. She knew Julie wasn't married, and that she lived in New Bern, but that was all.

Bert gathered Julie's soap and toothbrush, shaking off the sand. She opened Julie's pack. Inside were several Ziplocs with toilet articles. When Bert pulled one out and added the toothbrush, she noted that her hands were shaking. She remembered her mother cleaning out her father's closet less than six hours after he died. Must be some kind of outlet for nervous energy.

Under the plastic bags, Bert uncovered a pair of sweatpants. Purcell was still in his soaked trousers. Bert pulled the sweats out of the bag. Walking over quietly, she held them up. "Here, I think these will fit you."

The young resource ranger's face contorted. He backed away, hand up. "No way. Forget it. I'm not wearing those."

Bert put them back in the sack. She could understand his reluctance, but Julie would have been the first to offer. "They're here if you change your mind. It's going to be awhile before you get off."

All too soon, Bert had the rest of Julie's things, including her cooking utensils, packed and ready. "I'm not sending back her food. Might go bad before someone unpacks it," she told Hunter.

He nodded. "Just do what you think best. I'm sure they'll appreciate it."

"What's going to happen now?"

"It's only two. I'm thinking we might as well get some rest."

Bert's lips tightened. "With her here?"

"Ernie brought in a body bag and a stretcher from the Parker. We'll put her behind the table."

She'd forgotten the park kept those bags on hand. One of a ranger's least pleasant duties was picking up bodies washed ashore. Bert nodded grimly. "There's no way I'm going to be able to sleep. Are you?"

He gave her his lopsided smile. "I said rest, not sleep. Might even doze off a little."

Bert took the cowardly way out and left the tent while the men bagged and moved Julie's body. When she returned, Clayton had appropriated Julie's cot, and Ernie and Purcell were unrolling their sleeping bags on the same tarp Bert had used under the stove. Swallowing, she wondered if they'd wiped up the water from Julie's last bath—or the blood on the cot. Suddenly, it was as if Julie had never been.

Hunter was going through his backpack, and Ernie was huddled on a cooler. "Where's DeWitt?" Bert asked.

Purcell nodded toward the tent door. "Went out to check the horses. See if any more got out."

So they were buying her theory that some of the penned horses could have escaped. Bert joined Hunter on the cot, watching as he rolled out his mat by her feet. It wasn't until he dimmed the lantern that she slipped into her sleeping bag on the cot.

Gradually, as Bert warmed up and relaxed, she decided Hunter was right. It did feel good to lie down and rest. But what was keeping DeWitt? It was probably hard to count horses in the dark. Bert stirred, suddenly uneasy. Whatever had killed Julie was still out there. But what could it be? A crazed horse?

As she drifted in that dark state that comes just before sleep, Bert's mind formed a nightmarish picture of a horse stalking people, leaping on them, feet turned into claws, teeth elongated and coming to points. As the monster crouched to attack her, a gold stallion appeared from the breakers. Trumpeting, the horse charged the beast. The clawed horse cowed before the magnificent stallion, dissolving into the sand until only a funnel of dust remained.

When she woke, the tent was quiet. The temperature had dropped considerably. The wind was roaring, but someone was snoring over it. Bert tried to see who it was without sticking her head out of the sleeping bag's hood. Hunter was stretched on the floor by her cot, so it had to be one of the other men. Would Clayton's snores be as melodic as his voice? she wondered sleepily. Maybe it was DeWitt.

That thought jerked her up from the warm sleeping bag. Had DeWitt come back? She scanned the tent, exhaling in relief. Opposite Clayton and the two resource rangers was a dark mass snoring rhythmically. DeWitt wasn't having any trouble sleeping, that's for sure. Bert again felt sorrow for Julie. Her friend might have been interested in DeWitt, but from his reaction to her death, her feelings had not been reciprocated.

Unable to go back to sleep, Bert lay waiting for the others to wake. When Hunter began to stir, she unzipped her bag, silently picked up her shoes and jacket, and crept outside. Hunter followed. After brushing her teeth, combing her greasy, limp hair, and splashing water on her face, Bert joined him by the dock. There was no pretty orange and gold sunrise this morning, just a lightening of the gray sky over the sand and shrubs. The water was dark and choppy. The wind gusted in their faces.

Hunter reached out a hand. She took it, sighing. "Please don't look at me. I feel an absolute wreck. I don't think I've ever been so dirty." Bert shuddered, thinking of Julie's blood on her jacket. "What happens now?"

Hunter stared at the three boats bouncing in the water. "First thing is to get her back to the mainland. Sheriff's office will be waiting. Then we got to take care of the horses. Need to map out a plan with DeWitt and Ernie."

She squeezed his hand. "Better you than me."

By the time they returned to the tent, the rest were up, and Clayton had the coffeepot going. Bert noticed DeWitt had appropriated her mug. He waved it in her direction. "Hope you don't mind." He tipped the rest of the contents into his mouth, poured some water into the mug, swirled it around, and dumped it on the floor. He wiped the mug with the edge of his T-shirt, exposing a hairy belly. Handing it back, he said, "Good as new."

I don't think so, Bert thought. Sneaking some water, she scrubbed it out discreetly, then offered the mug to Hunter. He shook his head. Bert helped herself. The hot coffee cleared her mind and revitalized her energy. Rinsing out the mug again, she handed it to Hunter. "Here, drink it. Make you feel better, and think better."

He grinned wryly. "Could use some clear thinking, all right." He pointed at a pack of Twinkies on the table. "Help yourself. There's some rolls somewhere, too."

Bert rummaged for the rolls, which turned out to be hot dog buns. She spread one with some leftover jelly. Ernie was munching a Twinkie. Purcell huddled on the end of her cot, white-faced and silent. It wasn't like Purcell to be so quiet. He'd barely known Julie. Was he sick, or did he feel intimidated by the presence of his boss?

Bert sat down next to him. "What's the matter? Don't you feel good?"

He shook his head. "Must have got a chill or something last night." Bert touched his brow. "No fever."

He pushed her hand away. "I'll be all right. I need to get warm."

Hunter walked over. "Tell you what, Purcell. Why don't you and

Clayton, no, better make it Ernie, take . . ." He glanced at Julie's body. "Just take her back in your skiff. We can beach it and load it from here. Easier than carrying her out to the Parker."

Bert didn't think Purcell could get any whiter, but he did. "No, please. I can't. Let someone else do it, okay?"

Hunter's brows lifted. He nodded and turned to Ernie and Clayton. But before he could say anything, DeWitt spoke up. "I'll run her over. It's the least I can do for her."

Again, DeWitt had surprised Bert. Just when she thought the man was totally uncaring, he did something nice.

"Take the skiff," Hunter said. "You want Ernie or Clayton to go with you?"

"I can use my boat," DeWitt told him. "Then I don't have to come back."

"We're going to need you back here. We haven't decided what to do about the horses yet." Hunter turned to Clayton. "Did you get hold of Tanisha and Greg?"

"Greg got the results from the blood samples we took yesterday— all negative. He drove them up to the Raleigh lab. But we're still missing samples from some of the horses," Clayton said. "We need to round them up. Can you take care of that, Ernie?"

Ernie nodded.

"I got hold of the park and asked for any rangers they could spare," Hunter said.

Eyes on his tented fingers, Ernie added in his slow speech, "I told them to call in the off-duty resource rangers."

"Tell them to come armed," DeWitt growled, "and to check Triton's hooves for blood."

Bert took a deep breath, but a warning glance from Hunter stopped her. He turned to DeWitt. "How far along are you with your test samples?"

"That's what I was doing when she"—DeWitt jutted his bearded chin toward Bert—"called last night. Expect I'll have the results in a couple of hours. Want me back then?"

Hunter nodded. "Should have the rest of the horses rounded up by noon." He looked at Bert. "Why don't you go in with him?"

Bert was caught off guard. She wanted nothing more than a real bathroom and clean clothes. On the other hand, she hated to leave Hunter alone. Besides . . . "What about Shony? Aren't we going to dig him up?"

There was a general groan. Bert caught a glance of annoyance in Ernie's blue eyes.

"Bert. That's just going to have to wait. If he's dead, he's not going anywhere, right?" Hunter tried to smile.

Bert didn't think that was funny. Suddenly, the import of what he'd said struck her. Shony *had* gone somewhere. He'd unburied himself and vanished, hadn't he? And if he hadn't, then why weren't she and DeWitt able to find him? It wouldn't kill her to be dirty a little longer. She marched to the tent door. "I still think what happened to that pony's important. Suppose I take an ATV and see if I can find him in daylight? You-all can do whatever you have to do."

Hunter shook his head. "Appreciate the offer, but Maintenance took the extra ATVs. Only have two left, and we're going to need them to round up the missing horses."

Bert grimaced but didn't argue. Dark lines were etched into Hunter's cheeks. He had enough to worry about.

An hour later, Bert was wading out to DeWitt's boat. Julie's body, strapped onto a stretcher, was laid out on a bunk in the tiny cabin. Apparently, DeWitt had cleared the bunk by shoving everything off the bare, stained mattress, leaving the small triangle of deck between the bunks heaped with life jackets, crumpled tarps, tangles of rope, and buoys. Bert stepped over a cast net, a soggy box of crackers, candy wrappers, and Coke cans. Tucked into the bow were several empty water jugs, a saddle, and two scarred and worn leather satchels. Bert assumed his veterinary tools were inside and hoped they were cleaner than the boat. Keeping her eyes away from the body, Bert slung her backpack and sleeping bag on top of the dirty blankets in the second bunk, next to Julie's backpack and a rusty toolbox.

As she returned above deck, DeWitt shoved the throttle forward so hard the boat dug in on its stern, bow completely out of the water. Bert lurched to the side, grabbing a rail. Julie's body started to slide off the bunk. The backpacks and toolbox crashed to the deck. "DeWitt!" Bert howled.

Somehow, he managed to stick a foot into the cabin and stop Julie. When the boat was on an even keel, Bert headed below, but DeWitt stopped her. "Take the wheel. I'll get her," he ordered.

After spending the past summer on the water, Bert had bought a small boat. Now, she blessed her limited experience as she guided DeWitt's cruiser along the few posts that marked the channel to Harkers Island.

DeWitt tied the stretcher down with some of the tangled lines in the cabin, shoving the black body bag around roughly. As soon as he took back the wheel, Bert went down to retrieve the backpacks from the damp, cluttered deck. As she made sure nothing had fallen out of her pack, she wondered why DeWitt had volunteered for this job. His careless handling of the boat and Julie's body negated his earlier remark about wanting to do something for her. Maybe he was just plain crass. Or did he have some other motive? He hadn't been happy about Bert's coming along. Was that because he didn't like her, or because he wanted to be alone?

She shrugged. She hadn't decided if she liked or disliked DeWitt, but one thing she knew: volunteering to transport Julie's body didn't seem to be in character. He had the tests to finish, so he didn't need an excuse to get back to the mainland. She stared at Julie's backpack. No. Could it be?

Suddenly, she was sure. Perching carefully on the side of the empty bunk so her body shielded what she was doing, she opened Julie's pack and began taking everything out, spreading it over the heaped-up junk on the soggy mattress. Most of it was clothes and toiletries in Ziplocs, but as she reached the bottom, she pulled out a small hand towel. Paper crinkled. She unrolled the towel.

Part of a photo was visible. Bert stared. It was a sheet of lined paper in a three-ring plastic page cover. At the top was a photo of a newborn foal with a long, blond tail. Bert gagged. Now, she did feel sick.

DeWitt was standing over her. "You ain't got no business messing with her belongings." He snatched the photo from her grip.

"It's Shony," Bert whispered. "That's the page from the log. Julie took it out."

DeWitt glanced at it. Suddenly, the paper was fluttering across the boat.

"No!" Bert shrieked, scrambling up to the slippery deck. But the paper sailed over the stern, tumbling into the waves. She whirled, hitting DeWitt with her fist. "You had no right doing that. Stop the boat."

"What's the matter with you?" He closed the throttle with a jerk. The boat's stern sank, the bow rising as it came off the fast plane. The wake caught up and threw Bert forward against the bulkhead. She slid to the deck, helpless. "You told me to stop," DeWitt said defensively, reaching out and yanking her back to her feet.

Bert pushed him away, searching the water. "That picture. We need to get it. It was Shony."

"You got horses on the brain." He circled the boat around the area where the picture was lost. "That was just an old file, a sample I gave Julie so she'd know how we worked."

Bert stared at the choppy water. There was no sign of the paper. She was so angry she was trembling. "You're lying. That's why you threw it away. You knew it was Shony."

DeWitt stopped the boat again. He turned so he was looking directly at Bert, his eyes slits, his mouth a tight line beneath his black beard. "You watch who you're calling a liar. Nobody calls me names. I don't care if you're sleeping with the superintendent of Cape Lookout or the head of the National Park Service in Atlanta, you don't talk to me like that. You hear me?" Spit shot out with his words.

Bert backed up, suddenly afraid.

His green eyes glittered. "I'm telling you, that was a picture of a horse I had years ago. The wind blew it out of my hand. I'm sorry about that, but that's all. You understand?" Hands on his hips, he advanced.

Bert dropped farther back. "Okay, okay, if you say so. It sure looked like Shony to me." She was certain it was Shony, but now was not the time to insist.

DeWitt snorted. "You think you're a park detective or something? You got no right going through a dead gal's things. Seems to me the sheriff's office is going to have something to say about that." He put the boat back in gear, throwing her another fierce green glance.

Bert hung onto the rail as DeWitt turned the boat back on course. They roared along in silence. As they reached the main channel to Harkers Island, they came out of the lee into a two-foot chop. Icy spray blew across the stern rails.

DeWitt cleared his throat. "No sense you standing way over there and getting wet." He spoke in a softer tone, not looking at Bert but staring through the cabin's windshield, chin up, beard stiff with salt. "I guess I owe you an apology. I got a mean temper, and sometimes it gets away from me." He darted a glance at her. "But you shouldn't have called me a liar. I ain't going to stand for no one saying bad things about Julie, and that includes a volunteer who thinks she's running this park."

Bert said nothing but edged toward the cabin.

He sighed. "Look. We got to come to an understanding on this." DeWitt's voice dropped and warmed. "I apologize for the things I said. Didn't mean nothing. It's just, when I get mad, I got trouble stopping myself." His mouth twisted under his beard. "My temper's cost me plenty in the past. Cost me a wife and son, and I'm sure you heard about me and the foundation director, Blount."

He waited. Bert hesitated, then moved forward a few more steps until she was out of the blowing wind and water. No wonder Blount fired him from his position as foundation veterinarian. But what about Julie? Had they fought? Could DeWitt get angry enough to kill? No. She didn't really believe that. He'd been kind to Julie, and she'd seen the way he handled the horses. Despite his braggadocio, his hands were gentle.

"I don't blame you for being put out with me. You're probably the best volunteer this park ever had. Guess I'm more upset about Julie than I realized." Now, he wanted to make up by flattering her."I come by it honestly, you know. My temper, I mean."

Temper or not, he had deliberately thrown away that photo of Shony. Or had he? Maybe it was an accident.

Now, he was saying something about his grandfather. " . . . reckon that makes me part Coree. My grandfather said his uncle rode a chestnut with a white blaze shaped like a whelk. He said it was a powerful sign."

She might as well accept his apology, or at least let him think she had. "Triton comes from the Coree?" she mumbled, trying to keep the residue of anger from her voice. "I thought they were extinct—the Coree, I mean."

DeWitt's big frame seemed to relax. "That's what some say, but it ain't exactly so. My grandmother was from Haiti—used to be Hispaniola, you know."

Bert nodded, still not trusting her voice.

After a moment, he sighed and continued. "My grandfather used to breed horses. Had a real way with animals." DeWitt gestured toward the mainland. "The Coree had horses on these islands long before the colonists got here. Stole them from the Spanish, you know."

Chapter 14

Cape Fear, 1527

Medeu

"A ship, a ship comes!" the Spaniard shouted, spurring his mount.

Twisting his neck, the stallion rolled an eye at his inexperienced rider. The horse had started to gallop long before the spur touched his side.

They flew over the uneven, marshy ground, soon arriving at the settlement. Still shouting, the rider charged through the opening in the crude palisade, pulling up at a row of mud-and-wattle huts. But his news aroused only mild interest. A few of the colonists went to their mounts, but most remained seated by their huts, shifting only to brush away a particularly vicious pest. The stench of feces and sweat rose about the stallion, along with the sweet-sour smell of pestilence.

Shortly, smoke from a beacon on the beach drifted over the rough huts. The people began to rouse, some even venturing from the gates of the new colony, clutching their muskets. Now, the stallion glimpsed the top of a sail off the nearby shore. As the ship approached, the excitement grew. The Spaniards began to stir, calling out and gathering their belongings.

Although the stallion longed for water, he remained by the gate, where his rider had dropped the bridle. Finally, the man returned, yanking the reins so viciously the bit cut into the horse's mouth. The stallion's foreleg pawed the air as he jerked his head, but he dutifully followed the colonist into the village. There, men attached a litter to the stirrups of his saddle, so it dragged behind him. They carried a sick man from inside one of the huts and tied him into the litter.

As the stallion passed from the gates of the settlement close to the marsh, the distinctive scent of tobacco leaves—the scent of the enemy—stung his nostrils. Trained to fight, he spun around to face the danger, tail and neck high. Again, the colonist jerked his bridle.

"*Qué pasa?*" asked the colonist's companion.

"Nothing. He imagines a lion in the swamp."

"He is not stupid, that Jennetta. More likely, he scents a murderous *Indio*." The two men paused, scanning the marsh. Seeing only the spiked tops of black marsh rush, they continued toward the ship.

There, a fierce argument brewed between the settlers and the ship's captain.

"I tell you, we have no room for horses. We do not even have space for your people."

"We number less than one hundred and fifty, and de Ayllon is dead," shouted one of the settlers.

The captain stared, open-mouthed. "One hundred and fifty? Out of five hundred? The *Indios?*"

"Partly, but mostly we die of the fever."

The captain crossed himself. "Pestilence?"

"No, no, the congestive fever. We grow too weak from lack of provisions to withstand its ravages," said a colonist.

"And only thirty of the eighty-nine horses remain," added a lancer.

The captain eased, shaking his head. "I regret, but I still do not have the space. Perhaps it would be best if you send a few chosen men to *La Isla Española*. They can hire ships to return to your assistance."

At those words, an outcry arose. The settlers began wading into the water, swimming toward the ship.

The captain shouted from his shallop. "*Atención!* I see I have misjudged the severity of your situation. I will not stop you from boarding, but for the love of Jesus, bring no possessions. The holds are full. You shall have to make the voyage above deck." He swung around to stare at the cloudless sky. "We must pray to the Virgin Mother that no storm arises before we reach Santo Domingo."

Leaving their bundles and clothing on the shore, the settlers swarmed up the sides of the ship, climbing lines and crawling aboard by any means they could manage. Soon, the decks were lined with passengers, some even hanging from the shrouds. With one last glance at the blue sky, the captain gave the order to sail.

From the shore, the stallion watched the ship move briskly down the river. As the bark drew away, he pawed the air and trumpeted to remind the men he was still attached to the litter.

There was a commotion on deck, and he saw fingers pointing at him. A woman's voice cried, "You cannot leave him like that! That was my husband's mount. He saved our lives from the *Indios. Por favor*, we must go back."

"The tide changes. We cannot delay if we are to pass below Cape Fear."

"Then have mercy on him. Do not leave him to die a slow death fettered by the litter. He's of the finest blood in *La Española*, from the mare Jazmín of the Marco de Seville hacienda."

"*Sí, sí*. She is right." The speaker broke open his musket, loading it. "I shall put the noble beast out of his misery." Several other men followed his lead, raising their weapons to the horse on the shore.

There were puffs of smoke from the ship and a spray of sand by the stallion's hooves. Then he heard the roar of the muskets. The stallion had been trained to carry men bearing muskets, and he knew when he was being fired upon. Coming about, he dashed away, the litter bouncing at his heels.

A safe distance from the ship, he paced about the settlement, waiting for the men to return. But no one came. From inside the pen, he heard the increased snorting and squeals of the horses. They needed food and water. Already, the younger stallions pushed at the makeshift fence. Many showed bloody wounds.

At the arrival of dusk, the marsh stirred. Then it appeared to grow as a man rose from the black rush grass. As he neared, the stallion scented the tangy herbs, grease, and tobacco that denoted the presence of an *Indio*. He also scented fear. The horse faced the threat, flattening his ears and setting his neck, ready to charge.

At his movement, the man dropped to the ground, becoming invisible. But when nothing else stirred, he slowly rose back to his feet. Again, he approached.

The stallion raised a foreleg, tail lashing. He jerked his nose up, mouth open, showing his teeth.

The man stopped, but he did not lower his gaze. Instead, he stretched out his hands, palms up, beginning a low murmur. "I am honored to meet you, great *mannitto*. I thank the Great Spirit that he has preserved your life and allowed me . . ."

Realizing his show of force was not stopping the man, the horse turned, assuming a defensive position. He raised his rear leg, ready to kick. But as he did so, he struck the side of the litter. Startled because he had momentarily forgotten his entanglement, the stallion shied.

The man took advantage, closing in, his hands still forward. "I am Pauk-sit, a Coree of the Lenni Lenape. I mean you no harm. You are a great and powerful warrior. You have killed many of my brothers, but my eyes have seen it was not of your doing. Since the hunting moon, I have watched from the salt pond. As they did with my father, Chicora, the firesticks have enslaved you. I, Pauk-sit of the tidewater people, ask you to look our way. Join with us, for we have done you no injury." The man took another step forward.

The stallion's nostrils flared. His eyes rolled.

Pauk-sit backed away. "I meant no disrespect, Great One, but merely to free you from your fetters."

The stallion stood still, ears flat, turning to better see the advancing danger.

Pauk-sit bowed his head. "I would lift you up from this place and set you down again in my dwelling." His eyes still lowered, he edged closer.

The man had acknowledged the stallion's superiority by looking away first. The horse's ears flicked, and his tail relaxed.

Pauk-sit sidled forward but came to a halt when the stallion's nostrils tightened. Neither moved. Then the horse lifted his head to the man's hair and, to familiarize himself, ran his muzzle down the man's face.

The Indian froze. After a moment, throat muscles working, he raised a shaking hand and touched the horse's nose. "Ei! You are as warm and silky as a spotted fawn." He scratched behind the stallion's ears and down his neck, growing bolder as the horse stretched and blew in pleasure.

When the stallion leaned into him, Pauk-sit reached around and took hold of the reins. "I will place you under my wing. I shall draw the thorns from your mouth." He put a finger on the horse's lips where the bit had cut. "And grease your stiffened joints with oil and wipe the sweat from your body. I will make you comfortable after your fatiguing journey, for you are a great *mannitto*." His finger traced the white, whelk-shaped blaze that decorated the stallion's forehead. "You bear the mark of the Medeu, and now you shall bear his name, too—Medeu, the wizard." Gently, he fumbled with the bit.

Medeu smelled the man's fear but tolerated his fingering, opening his mouth as he did for the stable boy. Finally, the bit was out, although the reins remained over Medeu's neck. The stallion turned to inspect the stranger, lipping the mud that covered his body, the tobacco pouch at his side, but no longer tasting fear. Behind them, the penned horses clamored.

The man, wearing only a breechclout, his black hair plucked at the sides and temples, glanced at the barrier surrounding the settlement. "I hear sobbing and sighing. This is a village of *machit*, evil spirits. The firesticks came and set themselves down in a dirty, wet place, never looking to see which way the wind blew." Taking his knife from his belt, Pauk-sit sawed through the lashings that held the litter to the saddle. "Come, Medeu, the path to our nation is open."

One of the mares squealed long and loud. Medeu stopped and lifted his head, neighing back. This elicited a series of snorts and nickers from the captive herd.

Again, the man squinted at the settlement, his fear tainting the air. He sighed. "You are indeed a *mannitto*. You know it is better to die as a man than to live as a coward."

With trembling hand, the Coree led the horse through the open palisade. He padded silently, crouching, his knife in one hand, the halter and his hatchet in the other. Circling so he did not pass near any of the huts, he finally reached the pen. There, he removed the two horizontal poles that secured the gate, freeing the horses.

The herd trotted to the riverbank to quench its thirst in the briny water. Medeu scented the relief emanating from Pauk-sit as they followed. At the river, Medeu drank while Pauk-sit cleaned the fear and mud from his body. Then the *Indio* turned to the west, the stallion close behind.

The other horses began to pasture, but once their hunger and thirst were assuaged, they huddled together, pawing and snorting. Darkness had fallen, and the scent of wild animals prowling about made the herd uneasy. As the moon waxed overhead, a flaxen-maned mare, mouth tight, nostrils flaring with fear and excitement, broke from the herd and began to trot along the dung-marked trail left by the stallion. The rest of the horses followed.

Pauk-sit was sleeping soundly, Medeu's halter tied to his foot, when the sound of beating hooves brought him leaping to the stallion's side. But as the horses arrived in the clearing with much nickering and blowing, Pauk-sit howled and danced with glee. "The Great Spirit smiles

136

our way. With such as these, my people will be able to travel to the north, far from the Savannahs who nip at our heels and the firesticks who swarm from the floating houses to the south."

Forty days later, during the month of the shad moon, Medeu and Pauk-sit swam across another great river while the Coree waited on the riverbank. It was a difficult crossing, the open water and rolling swells stretching as far as Medeu could see. But Pauk-sit was a good swimmer, kicking along Medeu's side, grasping his tail only when the current was particularly strong.

Finally, they reached a point of land guarded by water on three sides. They passed though a forest of live oaks, pines, and junipers laced with the tracks of deer, elk, and bear. There were ponds of fresh water and, as they neared the eastern shore, open ground with thickets of cedar, yaupon, and myrtle.

Perched bareback, for Pauk-sit had discarded the saddle when he saw it chafed Medeu's flanks, the man gazed toward the great salt sea. In front of them gleamed white sand such as they'd never seen. A small river of salt water flowed between the beach and a nearby island that sheltered this bay. The clear, calm waters teemed with fish, and the air was loud with the calls of waterfowl. To their side were flats of sweet-smelling salt meadow grass. There were marshes and fertile, sandy ground where the women could grow tobacco, maize, potatoes, and beans. Behind the guard island, other islands showed their undulating, green backs. In the distance, they heard the pounding of the great salt sea, with its fish and *tulapewi*, turtles.

Pauk-sit slid forward, hugging Medeu's neck. "The Great Spirit looks upon us with favor, for he has brought us to this bountiful land guarded from the winds of the *hurracon* by these islands. Here, we shall dwell in peace, and this land shall be known throughout the people as the banks of the Coree."

Chapter 15

"Core Banks is named after the Coree," DeWitt told Bert as he turned the boat into the park marina. "Once, there was horses and Indians from here all the way up to Corolla. Guess you knew that."

"Right," Bert agreed.

DeWitt gunned into a slip, threw the motor in reverse, and made the boat slither sideways until it lay against the dock. "Croatan got its name from the Coree. Same with Currituck," he said, stepping from the bouncing boat to the pier, a line in each hand. "That used to be called Core Tuck." He whipped the lines around two poles. "Wait here," he ordered. "I'll go see where they all got to."

Bert stared after his retreating back, shaking her head. The man was truly impossible.

Two hours later, Bert was standing in Hunter's shower, letting the hot water scour the dirt and cold from her body. But even the beating, sensuous spray could not stop her mind from churning like the steam that rose about her.

She had not been mistaken about the sheet of paper in DeWitt's boat. It was a page from the horse log with the photo up top and identification beneath. All she'd glimpsed was a poor-quality Polaroid of a newly delivered foal, but even so, she was sure it was Shony. He'd been facing the camera, and the spiral on his forehead had been clearly defined. Were there other horses with the same distinctive marking? She would have to check with the vets.

A frightening thought struck her. DeWitt said it was an old photo. Could it have been a shot of Triton when he was born? No, she didn't think so. But if it was Shony, then she had to face the fact that Julie had removed the page from the log and put it in her backpack. Not just put it there, but carefully secreted it inside a towel at the bottom.

Bert's hand shot to her mouth. Had her friend, who'd helped her look for Shony, hidden the proof the foal really existed? Had Julie also known he'd had his throat slit? Bert leaned against the wall of the shower. No, Julie couldn't have been part of that.

A series of pictures flashed through Bert's mind. Automatically, she turned off the shower and stepped out of the stall, her thoughts spreading like the water at her feet. Julie had pulled the photo from the log. She probably also pulled all the records for number eighty-seven. She'd fixed it so the test-tube counts matched. She certainly was in a position to do that, but why? And Bert's digital pictures . . . Of course! Julie had erased them to keep Bert from proving Shony existed. But it couldn't have been Julie who gave the command to put a second stallion in the chute. She didn't fit the description. The redheaded private said the person was as big as the sarge and wore a jumpsuit. Who, then, DeWitt? That was it! Julie had a thing for the vet, and he'd used her. He'd volunteered to take her body to the mainland so he could go through her things, knowing the file was there. He deliberately threw away the photo. But how could Bert prove it?

While she toweled the water from her body, Bert's mind climbed the next logical step. When she'd returned from finding Shony's carcass, Julie had been walking off the dock. There'd been a boat in the sound. DeWitt's? Julie and DeWitt had argued earlier. Had Julie experienced second thoughts about something and called DeWitt? Since the tide was up, he could have boated right to the end of the dock. He was returning to the mainland when Julie found out Shony had been killed. She panicked and called DeWitt again while Bert was on the radio with Purcell. That would explain the warm cell phone and how the vet got back so fast—he'd been just offshore.

Oh, Lord, then it had to be Julie who let the horses loose the night before. But she hadn't known Shony had his throat slit. Bert could still see Julie's shocked expression. That's probably what panicked her into the second phone call.

Bending over, Bert began to blow-dry her hair. What kind of story had DeWitt spun to get the vet tech on his side? And more importantly, why? It had something to do with that contaminated blood sample. Number eighty-seven must have been Shony, the horse that tested positive for EIA. Had DeWitt killed him to hide the fact, so the pony adoptions could go on as scheduled, then told Julie that Shony died of the fever? Was it worth that much to him, to risk his license and reputation?

Shit. Bert's stomach contracted into a cold ball as another thought erupted. Had Julie's death been an accident? If DeWitt could kill a horse to advance his business, could he also kill a person? If they got to arguing, that temper of his . . . Yes, he could strike out in anger.

She had to call Hunter. Barefoot, in bra and panties, she ran to the phone on the kitchen counter. She had just picked up the receiver when something thumped the picture window. Bert shrieked, ducking behind the counter. Someone stood on Hunter's deck, face pressed against the glass. A palm pounded the window.

Bert raised her head to peek over the counter. It wasn't DeWitt, thank God—too small. A woman. Long hair. Oh, no, Vilma Willit. Bert could hear the reporter's high voice shouting, "Hunter? It's me, Vilma. I have news. Let me in!"

"Just a minute!" Bert yelled. Still crouched, she ran back to the bathroom. All she could think of as she grabbed her jeans and fuzzy sweatshirt was that Vilma had found out something about Julie. The reporter had arrived with the ambulance shortly after DeWitt docked his boat that morning, but Bert had managed to sneak away, leaving DeWitt to deal with Vilma and the medical examiner. Even so, Bert had spent an hour filling out reports for the park and talking to the deputy at park headquarters.

Now, Vilma was banging at the front door. Bert rushed to open it. "What's the matter?"

Coughing, the woman slid past Bert into the kitchen. "Where's Hunter?" she demanded.

"He's not here. He's still on Shackleford."

"Then who was on the boat, the Parker?"

"The Parker's back?" Bert was beginning to feel like Vilma's echo. "I have no idea."

"What's going on around here? You're trying to keep something from me. Hunter and I had an agreement, but if he's not going to keep his side . . ." Snorting as she sucked air through her nose, Vilma planted herself on a barstool.

No way, Bert thought. "I don't know where Hunter is, and I think you'd better leave now."

"Not till I get some answers. Call the park and see if he's there."

Bert reached for the phone, then stopped. "Why don't you drive down and leave a message for him? I'm sure he'll get in touch with you when he can."

"Don't you start giving me orders."

Bert glared. "Who's giving orders? And don't you ever come around here peeking in the windows again."

"If you'd answer a polite knock on the door, I wouldn't have to resort to climbing." She rubbed her knee. "I learned long ago people don't hear doorbells, not when they don't want to."

"I was in the bathroom." Bert couldn't have heard the door, not with the hair dryer going. Some of her annoyance abated. "Look, Vilma. I don't think Hunter will be off the island until late. They had a lot going."

The reporter nodded. "I spoke to the deputy. He said they were sending Piner's body to the morgue at Carteret General. He thought it was some sort of accident with a horse. Do you know what happened?"

Bert shook her head, remaining silent. That way, she couldn't be misquoted.

Vilma stretched her lips into a semblance of a smile. "I didn't really expect you to tell me anything. I came here to see Hunter about something else."

"I'll tell him you were here."

"There's talk that they're going to order the dredging to stand down. They're saying National Marine Fisheries is accusing Southeast Dredging of a cover-up on turtle drownings. They're meeting now."

So that's what Hunter meant last night when he said the situation was different. As if he didn't have enough on his plate.

Bert's thoughts must have reflected in her eyes. Vilma leaned forward, exhaling noisily. "So you do know about it."

Bert stepped back, shaking her head. The woman's breath stunk like sour milk.

"They were all on the dredge last night. Heard they had some techs from Duke there, too. What did they find?"

"Vilma. I don't know anything. I'll ask Hunter to call you when he gets back."

"I heard they had two Ridleys wash up on Shackleford. Do they think the dredge killed them?"

Bert shrugged, opening the door. "Goodbye, Vilma."

The reporter spun around on the barstool. "You know I'm partial to the park. Hunter and I have a longstanding relationship." Vilma lowered her lids, which sent a shaft of anger through Bert. How dare

Vilma insinuate she and Hunter had been more than friends, as if she'd believe that for a minute. With a satisfied smirk, Vilma continued. "This beach nourishment is big. There are millions involved, and a lot of permits to be had. That takes political pull and big money. Hunter's bucking real power here. He needs me on his side." She slid off the stool. "You tell him that, you hear me?"

Vilma had been gone over an hour when Hunter walked in, trousers soaked, a day's growth of stubble on his face. He'd sported a curly, grizzled beard when Bert met him on Portsmouth Island the previous year, but he'd shaved it when he resumed his administrative duties.

"Oh, God, Hunter. You look beat."

He sank down by the bar. "I am. Ernie was late getting back, and I have to be in Morehead by seven."

"I've got dinner ready." Bert pointed to the stove, where she had Salisbury steaks simmering in a Cabernet with caramelized onions and Portabella mushrooms. She popped open a Coors, handing it to him.

He grinned, some of the weariness leaving his face. "Smells great. Let me get a shower and a shave, and I'll be right back."

Grabbing his beer, he vanished into the bathroom. He emerged a few minutes later to pile his wet clothes outside. "Come on in. We can talk while I clean up."

Bert perched on the toilet lid. Hunter, bare as the day he was born and just as unselfconscious, splashed hot water on his face. Lathering up, he began to shave. "Sorry I couldn't get back to you on the phone. Had too much to do. I figured you'd have left word if something was urgent."

Bert nodded. "Vilma was here. Did she get hold of you?"

Hunter waved his safety razor in the mirror. "Her and everyone in the state, and some from out of state, too."

"Julie or the turtles?"

"Both. I can stand lots, but this day beats all. Even had the governor on the line."

"Corps of Engineers put out an order to stand down?"

He blinked an affirmative, stretching his neck to shave.

"Is that what you're going into Morehead for?" Seeing Hunter couldn't talk, Bert figured it was time to tell him about Shony's file. "The reason I was trying to get you was Julie." She related what had happened in the boat with DeWitt.

When she got to the part about the photo, Hunter put down his razor and swung around. "Bert. You realize what you're accusing the man of? That's serious talk. You want to be sure."

Bert sighed. "I know. I've been thinking about it the last couple of hours. I could be mistaken. It could have been a photo of a foal just like Shony, but isn't that an awful big coincidence? The thing is . . . Hunter, are they going to do an autopsy on her?"

"Julie?"

"Uh-huh."

He shook his head. "Not that I heard. Far as I know, they're calling it an accident."

"Suppose it wasn't an accident? Suppose she didn't want to keep quiet any longer? Maybe she was upset about DeWitt killing Shony." Hunter waved his razor. "Yes, I know. We don't know he killed Shony. But if he did, he could have killed her."

Hunter leaned against the sink, his body a curved, white line, slim and muscular. She quelled an urge to run her hand down his smooth belly. "I don't know, Bert," he said. "He doesn't strike me as the kind of man who would kill a woman. Kill another man, yes, if he was provoked enough."

Bert grimaced. It was a new kind of discrimination against women. "I think you should ask for an autopsy, just to be sure." That reminded her. "How did they make out with the horses? Did they get them all?"

"Yes, and to answer your next question, no. There was no blood on Triton's feet. Understand, that don't mean a thing. He and Scylla were hiding deep in the forest when they picked them up. Never would have found them without DeWitt."

"DeWitt was there?"

"He didn't go ashore," Hunter reassured her. "When the pilot couldn't spot them, DeWitt took his boat down and pointed Greg to Triton's favorite hideaway, a wet area in the woods. Up to their knees in water, they were."

"But you could still tell, couldn't you? There would be some evidence imbedded in his hooves, wouldn't there?" She shuddered. Blood or bone fragments was what she was thinking.

Hunter rinsed his razor and wiped out the sink. "Possibly, but Clayton and Greg took a really good look. Heard they pared a couple of inches off his hooves to check. Don't you worry," he added at Bert's expression. "Doesn't hurt them one bit."

Lifting her chin, he gave her a quick kiss on the lips, then reached for her breasts, eyes twinkling. She slapped away his hand, laughing. So he had noticed her enjoyment of his naked state.

"No blood on any of the horses they rounded up," Hunter said over his shoulder as he disappeared into the shower.

Still smiling, Bert had Hunter's steak, mashed potatoes, and tiny green peas on his plate by the time he reappeared.

"What would it take to order an autopsy?" she asked after he started eating. "I mean, if she's buried and then you decide to do it, it's going to be a big mess. Wouldn't it be better to do it now?"

Hunter frowned. "You're back to Julie. I'm not sure I know. Tell you what. I'll check with Rudy tomorrow, have him call Hatteras and talk to Huff, the park's special investigator. Remind me."

"What's on tonight? What's the park got to do with Marine Fisheries?"

"Fisheries is responsible for the turtles in the water. On the park beach, they become our job. Also, we got rangers involved with the dredge."

"Rangers. You mean the turtle patrols?"

"I mean Purcell's been moonlighting as an observer for the dredge. Clayton, too. Clayton isn't anything to do with the park anymore, but he's been connected."

"They think the inspections aren't being done right?"

"Don't you say anything about that," Hunter warned.

"I won't. That's what Vilma wanted to talk to you about."

Hunter nodded. "She caught up to me. Wouldn't doubt she'll be there tonight." He pushed away from the table. "Don't wait up. It's going to be late."

After he left, Bert picked up the dishes, her mind still on the horses. Who was with them tonight? She'd forgotten to ask Hunter. Surely not DeWitt. The kitchen clean, Bert paced restlessly. Triton wasn't safe on Shackleford with DeWitt. She knew that as surely as she knew anything, but what could she do?

Chapter 16

Before she could sleep, Bert had to be sure DeWitt wasn't alone with Triton. Purcell was the horse ranger. Maybe he could help her. She picked up the phone, then hesitated. DeWitt's angry words from that morning came back to haunt her. She wasn't a part of this park and had no business meddling in its affairs.

As she walked away from the phone, Bert tried to think of what she could do outside of going to Shackleford at night, which was a definite no-no.

What if she went to see Purcell? She hadn't been to visit for a long time, and she could check on how he was feeling. He'd seemed down today. Yes, that would work. She'd take him the leftover steak and potatoes and the last piece of a three-day-old pie. Purcell was always in the market for food.

She frowned. Suppose he was staying overnight on the island with the horses? In that case, Triton would surely be all right.

Heading east down Island Road on Harkers, Bert turned her car onto a dirt road past the new Core Sound Waterfowl Museum. She took a right on another dirt road, where a sign warned unauthorized people to stay out. The park's residential gates were open and would remain so until late.

Driving past the maintenance shed—a misnomer for a huge, new building—Bert turned in by an elevated, hexagonal ranch home. It was unusual for a young ranger to rent a whole house, especially a seasonal ranger. She'd heard Purcell came from money and wondered if his parents were helping him out. The young ranger had absolutely no accent at all, like an anchor on TV. Private schools, she figured.

Bert parked, relieved to find Purcell's Jeep in the yard. He stood on the deck, his long body doubled over the rail. He'd obviously seen her headlights coming up the road. He waved. "Lost? Hunter's house is thataway."

"Sounds like you're feeling better. Brought you some dinner." Bert waved the plastic grocery sack as she went up the stairs. "Eaten yet?"

Purcell grinned, hefting the glass in his hand. "Drinking my dinner. Fix you one?"

It looked like Coke, but Bert guessed it was well laced with rum, Purcell's favorite drink. She shook her head. "No thanks. Gives me a headache. But I'll take a beer, if you have one."

Inside, the TV blasted. The living room was not really dirty—the female interns' houses were far worse—but it was cluttered, a stack of magazines scattered over the green carpet, dirty plates on the table, clothes on a chair, Purcell's park jacket and boots in a heap by the door.

"Want to leave it out?" she asked, setting the bag on the counter that divided the living room from the kitchen.

"What you got there?" Purcell reached inside, lifting out the Cool Whip container with the steaks. He pried open the lid and sniffed. "Stew?"

"Salisbury steak with mashed potatoes. Just nuke it for a minute or so."

Smacking his lips, Purcell slid it into the fridge. "I'll have some later. Not ready to eat now. Thanks, Bert." Stooping, he fished around inside the refrigerator, his pants sagging off his thin hips. Finally, he came up with a Bud from deep in the rear. "Okay?" His eyes were very bright.

Bert nodded, looking up. He seemed taller and skinnier than ever. "Hunter never got home until after five. What time did you get back?"

He slammed the refrigerator door. "Bastard made me stay on even after we got all the horses rounded up."

He must be drunk to be talking like that. "Who? Ernie Steingart?"

"Who else? All I did was ask to be put back on beach patrol. He's got me working the office day in and day out while he's running around outside."

"He's so shy. I feel sorry for him."

"Shy like a snake, don't you know." Purcell took a long swig. "I think he has a thing for Hunter. Ever notice how he imitates him?"

Bert frowned. "Come off it. You're just mad because he made you stay on. I saw Ernie ogling Tanisha the other day." Too late, Bert remembered the way Purcell, too, had been looking at the pretty vet.

The young ranger slammed across the room. "He'd better not get near her. I'll kill him."

Purcell must be farther gone than she thought. His eyes were like black marbles, his flat cheeks flushed. "Are you feeling all right?" Bert asked. "You look feverish."

"You saw how wet I was. Wouldn't be surprised if I have pneumonia."

Bert sighed. "I think it's time for me to leave."

Immediately, the young ranger became contrite. "You just got here. Finish your beer." He patted the sofa. "I'll behave, promise. Besides, I need cheering up."

Bert hesitated. Purcell put his hands together in a prayer plea. She grinned and sat down. "Who's with the horses now?"

"I'm not sure." He waved his glass. "Rudy was there when we got back with the strays. He and that new law-enforcement ranger had their sleeping bags in the tent. I think they were planning on staying."

"Isn't that your job, to make sure the horses are taken care of?"

"I do what I'm paid to do—or not paid enough to do. When I'm off, it's someone else's headache. I took this job to get on permanent. Now, the park is saying it's not going to be a full-time position. Screw them anyhow."

"Sounds like you have a problem." Purcell had been working as a seasonal employee for two years. It was one of the few ways for a white male to get a permanent job with the National Park Service, unless he'd seen active duty in the military.

He shrugged. "Ernie said maybe next year, but I'm not hanging around. Got another job promised, just as good or better."

Too bad. Purcell would make a good ranger. "I heard you were moonlighting on the dredge. You thinking of going with them?"

He swung around so fast some of his drink slopped over. "Where'd you hear that?"

"Hunter told me. You like the work?"

His small mouth tightened. "Not on a dredge boat. I want to get in with Marine Fisheries, don't you know. Pay's good." He waved at the room. "Hell of a thing when you can't even afford a dump like this without a second job."

Had his parents cut off his subsidy? Bert changed the subject. "What about DeWitt? Did he stay over?" She tried to be casual, but from the glance Purcell shot in her direction, she wasn't sure she had succeeded.

"What do you care?"

"I'm worried about Triton," Bert confessed.

"Oh." He seemed to relax. "Last I saw of DeWitt, he was picking up the samples we collected today." He slid down the sofa, extending his long legs halfway across the room. "Hunter wants the tests finished and the horses released by Monday at the latest."

Relieved that Triton was not in danger, at least for the moment, Bert changed the subject. "So where did you find Triton? Down by Bald Hill?"

"Clayton and Greg rounded him up. I'm not exactly sure where. That Clayton's a crazy man on an ATV."

"What do you mean?"

"He was airborne twice that I saw. You'd think he'd have more sense."

"You all ride like cowboys."

"Tell me, but he's got a plate in his head."

"Is that what happened to his face? An accident with an ATV?" Somehow, Bert had assumed he'd been kicked by a horse or steer.

Purcell gave a high-pitched snort. "It was no accident. He got beat up when he was in Yellowstone. Heard he was doffing the wrong man's wife. They went after his face on purpose, to mess up his looks." He leaned over, dropping his voice. "He used to work for the park."

"They fired him?"

"Not exactly. He was in law enforcement, GS-9. They moved him to maintenance."

"Why? Because of his eye?"

Purcell shook his head, giving her a secretive grin as he hunched over his glass. "He's got more problems than that."

"He does? What?"

Purcell hesitated. "Don't say I told you."

Bert waited, nodding.

"He blacks out. Can't remember things. He was in therapy for a long time, don't you know."

"No, I didn't know." Regretting the uncharitable thoughts she'd had about Clayton, Bert asked, "Couldn't he get compensation from the park?"

Purcell rose, going to refill his drink. "Not really. It didn't have anything to do with the park. He was off-duty, off the park grounds. They called it a barroom fight. Never got the men, but everyone knew who it was."

"So how come he's not working for Maintenance now?"

Purcell shrugged. "After being in law enforcement, I guess he took it as a demotion."

"Isn't he eligible for disability?"

"According to Clayton, yes, but it works like retirement. Disability pay's based on the years you had in. Clayton's only been in about ten."

"So he has to keep working." Bert paused, thinking that Clayton might well hold a grudge against the Park Service. "How did he get the job with the Humane Society?"

Purcell shook his head. "Beats me. Probably pulled a couple of strings. Lots of people felt bad for him, especially after he had to get married."

"Had to? He got someone pregnant?"

Purcell chuckled. "Didn't mean it like that. DeWitt came back from Alaska. Someone gave him a heads-up. He caught Clayton humping his wife. Marched both of them into his car, starkers, and drove them down to the sheriff. Wanted them jailed for adultery." He grinned at Bert's expression. "You didn't hear about that?"

She shook her head. That explained DeWitt's remark about Clayton not trusting his wife. No wonder the two men hated each other. "What happened?"

"Nothing much, except it was all over the county. Clayton married her after the divorce. DeWitt's kid ended up with his grandma in New Bern." He turned to Bert. "Ready for another?"

His black eyes weren't quite focusing. It wouldn't be long before he passed out. "No thanks. Time for me to go. Want me to heat up that steak before I leave?"

Purcell stared blankly for a moment, then remembered. "I'll get it later, promise. Sure you don't want a refill?"

Well, she'd tried to get some food into him, Bert thought as she backed the car out and started home. The park roads were dark. Purcell must be the only ranger living there in the winter. Bert stopped at the sign as she reached the main road. She could see the lighthouse blinking across the water. Actually, all that was visible was the beam, making a turn every fifteen seconds. Across the street, reflecting in the headlights, water crashed against the sea wall as the wind continued to blast. Bushes rattled, and something thumped rhythmically, sounding for all the world like the pounding of hooves on sand.

Bert peered toward Shackleford but saw only darkness. Along with the history of his grandfather, hadn't DeWitt said something about a black stallion that came from the sea each year and stole the best mares of the Coree?

Mist was beginning to grow and coalesce into shapes. Grinning, Bert made the turn onto Island Road. No wonder people believed in ghosts.

Chapter 17

Ocracoke Inlet, 1585

Diablo

The black stallion Diablo lifted salt-encrusted nostrils to the horizon. Invisible swells rolled under the ship as the breeze freshened. Despite the wind, the air remained heavy, full of moisture.

Back in Diablo's native Hispaniola, he would have been herding his mares inland. But there was no shelter here. Ten days ago, Diablo and his herd had been taken aboard this vessel. The stallion had been secured to a breast board amidships, facing forward. Although he could feed from his trough and had limited movement, a nose halter and blinkers prevented him from seeing or biting the horses to either side. Since his main defense was his ability to detect danger in time to avoid it, these restrictions made him uneasy. The crates of swine, fowl, and sheep separating the rows of horses added to his anxiety. Overhead, an old, gray sail flapped and cracked, shading the livestock from the sun, although as the day lengthened, the lowering rays would again reach under the rough cover.

Deep blue water lightened to turquoise off the port bow, and milky waves crashed on white-sand beaches. Ahead, wispy cirrus clouds streamed across the pale sky, while flock after flock of birds shadowed the coastline heading northwest, not south, as was usual in autumn.

The breeze remained light, but Diablo's hide rippled with static electricity, and his ears ached from the dropping pressure. He raised his head and squealed. The other horses joined in, snorting their warning: a storm was in the offing.

The commotion brought a young lancer to his feet. Hand shading his eyes, he stared at the large, black stallion. "I tell you, we carry a Jonah," he said to a group of mariners standing nearby. "This expedition has seen naught but calamities. Now, the captain fears a wind's a-brewing."

A wizened sailor muttered through black, broken teeth, "One blow offen Portugal, and the youngun's crying Jonah."

The lancer bridled. "Blow? It sank our pinnaces and scattered the fleet." His English complexion, burnt to peeling, raw splotches, flushed a deeper red.

"You've yet to see a real gale, m'boy." The old mariner, skin dark from years at sea and caked with a lifetime of dirt, gave a high cackle. "They calls them *hurracon* in this latitude." He leaned over the rail, studying the swells. "She'll be a solid screamer afore dark, but the worst'll pass to the south."

"Sir Richard searches for an inlet now, a passage the Indians call Wococon, discovered last year by Philip Amadas."

The old sailor spat expertly over the rail, eying the little fleet that trailed the flagship. "Not my place to speak ill o' another, but that Amadas weren't naught but a fledgling pushed out o' the nest. I'd not be relying on his say-so."

Even as the mariner spoke, the bo's'n appeared on the quarterdeck shouting orders. Sails were reefed. The watch climbed down the amidships hatch, hurriedly brushing past Diablo. He carried a lead line.

"Avast there. You want to be leaving that horse a wide berth." The mariner's warning came just as Diablo, haltered and blind, was startled by the man rushing past. He snapped at the offender. The seaman shied away, whipping his line across Diablo's face. The lead weight cut deep into the stallion's lip. Diablo squealed, rearing, but the nose halter jerked him down to his knees. He stumbled back upright with a groan, pain blinding him. Blood flowed from his mouth. His lips were the most sensitive part of his body.

From the quarterdeck above and behind Diablo, the captain was shouting commands. "Hard alee! Look sharp, lads, we come to Wococon Inlet." As the ship changed course, the captain leaned over the rail. "Each man to his station. We'll tack around yonder point. Mr. Wilkins, begin sounding."

From the bow came the voice of the watch. "Nine, eight, seven fathom."

Diablo held his muzzle up to ease the pain.

The HMS *Tiger* was the largest of the fleet of five carrying horses, livestock, and supplies for the colonists. One of the smaller vessels had already entered the inlet. Sails partly reefed, the three-masted flagship wound around the shoals guarding the ocean entrance into Wallace Channel, passing close to Portsmouth Island. Just when all thought they were safe, the lookout shouted, "Shoal, sir, dead ahead!"

"Port, port!" the captain ordered. Seamen scurried aloft, dropping canvas, pulling sheets.

"Lord God, shoal to starboard, too! That's land I could walk on, sir," the lookout bellowed.

"Haul the boom. Fast, you maggots, fast! Drop the sails."

The entire crew galvanized into action. Diablo snorted, alarmed at the activity. Behind him, geese honked and pigs squealed.

"Shoal dead ahead!" the lookout wailed.

A groan went up as the ship suddenly stopped its forward movement with just the slightest of shudders.

From the forecastle, Captain Grenville barked commands. "Mr. Green, lay out the stern anchor. You, helmsman, jettison the deck cargo. Send the livestock over the side. Mr. Jackson, take some men and go below. Check for leaks. Pitch the ballast and all we can do without."

Diablo felt the deck begin to tilt as each powerful swell shifted the ship broadside to the sea.

"Lower the shallop. All lancers off. Go to it, men. She's dead in the water with a falling tide. We've got to get her off fast or she'll break her back."

There were more shouts. Crates were thrown overboard. Then, suddenly, the old mariner was removing Diablo's nose halter and blinders. He yanked the stallion forward. "Move. Damn you for a black devil, move."

Diablo stood firm.

The old mariner did not hesitate. He clouted the stallion across his swollen muzzle, breaking open the sliced lip. "I'll learn ya to cross old Jack."

Diablo screamed, rearing, front hooves flailing. Two more sailors leapt to the mariner's aid. They dragged the stallion, still dazed and bleeding from the blow, across the deck. The ship's gangplank had been laid through an opening in the rail. They pushed Diablo onto the ramp.

The gangplank ended in midair, the sea far below. Diablo snorted, spraying blood. He moved up the ramp, but already another horse nipped his rump, squealing as it was prodded with sharp sticks from behind.

Diablo found himself being shoved off the gangplank. He resisted until the last, then leapt into the water. All about him, crates, bales, and barrels crashed into the inlet.

The two smaller carvels had come to the aid of the flagship. Men in boats were already gathering up the casks and the crates of fowl. Others attached lines to the vessel. Sheep floundered helplessly, but the swine lost no time paddling toward shore.

Diablo turned and followed the pigs, keeping a careful distance from the small boats, his muzzle smarting, his lip burning with the salt.

On shore, the black stallion discovered a marsh of tall reeds lining the beach. He had been ten days on a diet of old hay. The salt cordgrass was fresh and crisp and to his taste, although he chewed carefully, favoring his cut lip. Other horses followed. Soon, the entire herd pastured on the Spartina grass.

In the inlet behind the horses, the mariners worked frantically to free the carvel before the swells cracked her keel. Her cargo floating in Wococon Bay, the *Tiger* had reduced her draft enough to loose herself. The boatmen pulled at the oars. A cheer rose as she came free.

Fearing damage to the keel, Sir Richard Grenville ordered the *Tiger* careened on the nearby shore for inspection. The ebbing tide now in their favor, the mariners used halyards to keep her on her side as the water retreated.

Men were dispatched to round up the livestock and hold them safe until the ship was floated. Diablo watched the mariners as they approached. They fanned out, wading hip-deep in the marsh, cursing. The cursing translated into more blows. Diablo danced away, looking for an avenue of escape. He cantered down the beach, but men lined the sand to the water's edge. He eyed the waves. The surf by the ocean was much fiercer than in the inlet. Blue-green breakers higher than his line of sight crashed down in fearful roars.

"Head him off, Jack!" a man shouted.

The scrawny mariner ran toward him, waving a stick. "Ye be wanting another rap, devil?"

Crashing waves or not, the water meant escape. Diablo plunged into the surf, leaping and rearing to keep his head above the breakers. He heard angry shouts.

"Stop him!"

"You stop him. Them waves is dangerous."

"Take care. That be a devil horse. That's what his name means in popish."

Leaving the men well behind, Diablo bounded through the waves back onto the hard sand. Then, black mane and tail streaming water, sand flying, he tore south down the beach, away from the ships.

When he was sure he had escaped pursuit, he slowed to a steady trot, still wanting more distance between himself and the men. However, thirst began to plague him. He turned from the beach into the dunes, raising his head and fanning his throbbing lip to sniff for fresh water. It did not take him long to locate some small, brackish pools. After drinking his fill, he rolled about the sand, rubbing the sweat from his body. Then he fed on the sweet grass of the small meadow surrounding the pools, pausing to sniff for danger and to sight from the high dunes.

The sky grew dark as heavy clouds chased each other overhead. The wind accelerated, changing to the northeast and blasting sand into his face and eyes. Leaving the swales for the low shrubs and woods by the sound, Diablo continued to trot south on the island, ever distancing himself from the ships.

With the coming of dark, the wind blew a full gale. The stallion halted his journey to find shelter. He stood first behind a thick stand of woods, then in the lee of a small dune. He despised rain, but at least it wet down the sand and kept it from blowing. The wind whipped water into his eyes and nostrils, making it hard to breathe. Head low, sheltered behind the thickest stand of woods he could find, Diablo hunched his back and put his tail between his legs. Sand and water blasted his hide, lashing his mane across his face and into his eyes. At times, the wind buffeted him so hard he fought to remain on his feet. Chunks of deadwood and even small trees flew through the air, many crashing into his body. He forced himself deeper into the woods, holding his head low to protect his eyes and nose and letting the shrubs absorb the brunt of the flying objects. His eardrums popped. His forelegs, already sore from falling on the ship, ached fiercely. Then the water in the sound began rising, eating the sand from under his hooves. Twice, he was forced to move to higher ground.

By the time daylight arrived, the wind had changed to the southwest, bringing rain once more, but the gusts were abating. By midmorning, the wind had slowed enough that Diablo dared venture out. He was barely able to walk, his body bruised and cut, his muscles screaming from bracing himself in the soft footing. The wind had sucked the moisture from his body. He needed sweet water, but that proved a scarce commodity. The windblown sea spray had blanketed the narrow island. The ocean had overwashed the dunes in many places, the sound rising to invade ground already soaked with rain. Most surface water was too salty for him to tolerate. However, he was able to suck a few brackish mouthfuls off the top. Exhausted by the events of the last two days, Diablo found a hollow and lay down to rest. But soon, thirst drove him back to his feet. Another horse might have died, but his hardy Jennetta ancestry came to his rescue. Deep in the woods, he found a pool of potable water. He stayed nearby for several days until his flesh healed. By the end of the week, he had regained his strength.

Once again, he resumed his trek south, stopping to feed as he went. The barrier island was very narrow. He found that by standing on a dune, he could often sight from the ocean to the sound and spy the swales where the sweet grass grew. But the lack of shelter made him uneasy. After four days, he reached an inlet that was presently shoaled up. Indeed, Diablo crossed the inlet with water only to his knees, passing from Portsmouth and North Core Banks to South Core.

The storm had left in its wake downed wood and wrack on the beaches. The days were fresh, the skies full of fowl flying south, the breezes gentle and laden with sweet scents, the dunes full of butterflies. Diablo had never been as free. Besides the Spartina, he enjoyed the pungent marsh grass and the more delicate dune grass, thistles, and shrubs. He ran on the beach mornings and evenings and swam in the ocean to cool himself and to escape the pests when they grew too fierce. He learned to dig in the swales for water when the pools were empty, and to suck up the fresh water that lay atop the salt in the marshes. He was not alone, for he found deer, rabbits, and possums. Once, he scented bear. But he missed other horses. There was no one to nip his withers or rub his flanks. He rolled in the warm sand and rubbed against the trees, but it was not the same.

He continued south until he came to a great point extending deep into the ocean. On both sides, the surf crashed, powerful waves driving the water far up the sand as the wind howled unimpeded. Past a narrow channel of blue water, a maelstrom of white stretched into the ocean. Diablo had reached Cape Lookout and its shoals, which extended out to sea fifteen miles. Shrieking birds flocked overhead, feeding off the carnage left by schools of predatory fish rounding the point.

This barren, sandy spit was not a place that interested him. Quickly, he turned the point, following the beach as it curved inland. He crossed over a sandy tidal flat to Shackleford Banks. Now, to his delight, he reached higher ground. Soon, he entered a forest such as he had known in his native land. Only instead of banyans, this was a forest of live oaks with gnarled trunks that met overhead to form an impenetrable ceiling. Below, the ground had a soft mat of leaves. Here indeed was a place where he could shelter from both the sun and the wind.

For days, he explored the island. There were deep ponds of sweet water, sand to roll in, marshes full of grass, several thick oak forests, and an open beach to run. He lacked only one thing: companionship.

One day while he pastured at the west end, he heard the distant, musical neigh of a mare and the nicker of a stallion. It did not come from his island, but from across the water to the west. In a state of high excitement, Diablo waded into the sound, searching for a way to reach the horses. Day after day, he went from his island to smaller islands, thence to sand bars that lay offshore, until only one body of water separated him from the horses. Several times, he began the swim, only to turn back when he lost sight of land in the chop. But one fine day, both the wind and the current were favorable, and Diablo swam until he reached the other side.

The first thing he noted was the scent of man. It was not the same pungent scent as on the ship, but men meant pain, so Diablo took to the woods to observe from there. He spied a small band of men and women come to trap the fish at the shores of the sound. These people were dark of hair and face. However, it was not they who interested

Diablo, but the horses. The people had with them a dozen horses, both stallions and mares. All were well fed and in good condition. They were not penned, but free to roam and pasture to their liking while the tribe fished and smoked their catch. The horses were similar in size and shape to Diablo and his herd in Hispaniola.

One mare in particular took his eye. She was little more than a filly, with a rich, chestnut coat and flaxen mane and tail. On her face, she bore a huge white blaze in the shape of the whelk shells that lay in heaps on Diablo's island.

Diablo waited until the filly wandered away from the herd and her stallion. He approached from downwind, slowly, so as not to frighten her. Gently, he bumped against her shoulder, putting his nose to hers and letting her sniff his breath. To his relief, she appeared amenable, even laying her muzzle on his withers and snorting softly.

Edging her away from the herd and into the woods, Diablo continued his courtship, nipping her neck, working his way across her back, grooming her as thoroughly as he'd ever groomed a mare. She preened, stretching and nickering in pleasure and nipping him gently in turn. Finally, he trotted off, inviting her to follow. As soon as they were out of hearing of the herd, he stopped to let her feed and drink. Then he nudged her shoulder again, leading her to the edge of the sound. Stepping in, he pawed the water and snorted.

The mare, being Medeu's granddaughter, had no fear of the sea. Soon, the pair crossed the deep channel and stood on the sand bars that led to Diablo's island. The filly lifted her tail, let loose her aromatic water, and passed under his nose, showing the stallion her colors. Diablo could restrain himself no longer. He nickered, a low, forceful call, and began to prance around her. She tossed her head and gave an excited squeal. That was all the encouragement the stallion needed. Standing as tall as he could, neck arched, ears pointed up, head tucked in, muscles swelling, mane and tail elevated, Diablo began his courtship dance. Stepping high, he executed intricate movements in a powerful cadence as he pirouetted around the filly. She stood still, watching. When she raised her tail and flipped it to the side, Diablo knew she was ready. He came up behind, rubbing her rump with his shoulder, nipping and signaling her. She braced, and the stallion mounted.

Less than a minute later, they were again side by side, stamping and blowing. Diablo waited until the filly tossed her head, dancing off. Then, rearing and bugling, the black stallion led Jazmín's descendant, issue of the first Triton, across the last stretch of water to Shackleford Island.

Chapter 18

Bert woke with a start of regret when Hunter crawled into bed. It had been such a peaceful scene—horses playing on the beach, the ocean blue and calm, the sky full of fluffy clouds. Then she heard Hunter's sigh.

Hunter had no problem with Bert's not waiting up for him. In fact, he seemed to enjoy sneaking into bed and holding her until she woke. But tonight, he sounded tired.

She rolled over, lifting a hand to his chest. "You okay? How late is it?"

"Too late." He leaned over and kissed her forehead. "It's been one hell of a day." He exhaled, falling back on the pillow.

He was just as tense as she'd been earlier, when she went to Purcell's. The gossip about Clayton and DeWitt would have to wait. "Would you like something to drink? Milk or a shot?"

"Bert, food and drink are not the answer to everything, you know."

She stifled a laugh. "I know." She leaned on an elbow. "Roll over. I'll do your back."

"I'm too tired for anything tonight."

Bert tried to turn him over. "Just going to make you feel better, not start something. Promise."

She could hear the smile in his voice. "That'll be the day." But he rolled over.

She began rubbing her knuckles across his shoulders, then dug her fingers into his neck. Beneath her hand, she felt him relaxing. He snuggled down, giving a small moan of pleasure. "Always knew you had to be good at something."

She rapped his shoulder. "Thanks. I'll remember that. Want to talk about it?"

"Uh-uh. Do you mind?"

"That's fine, honey. Just go to sleep."

After a short silence, he said, "Get me up at seven, all right?"

"Alarm's set." After a few more minutes, she bent and kissed the back of his neck. She lay on her side, her hand still rubbing him, but lightly, rhythmically. Soon, she could tell from his breathing he was asleep. She cuddled in.

He grunted, then suddenly he was on top of her.

"Hunter," she laughed. "Are you jumping me?"

"You mind?"

"Never." She encircled him with her legs. "I thought you were bushed."

"Guess I was wrong."

"You definitely were wrong," Bert murmured quite a bit later.

"You say something?"

"Never mind. Go to sleep."

The next thing Bert knew, the alarm was ringing from across the room.

In less than half an hour, both were dressed. Bert leaned on the counter, sipping coffee and watching Hunter wolf a bowl of cereal. "So what happened last night? With the meeting, I mean."

"I'm glad you qualified that," Hunter said. "Hate to think you were asleep the whole time." His gaze caressed her for a moment, then darkened. "The Corps of Engineers told the beach-nourishment project to stand down until they investigate. Now, National Marine Fisheries has to show some kind of proof the turtle kills are connected to the dredging."

"That's Fisheries' problem, right?"

"It's everyone's problem," Hunter said. "We don't have the right to kill a species just because developers built houses where they shouldn't have."

Bert hesitated. "That's true, but five hurricanes in a row aren't normal either. People like me depend on the tourist trade. We need those beaches." She didn't want to sound heartless, but Hunter could be very "park" sometimes. "I like the loggerheads. They're fun to watch. But besides being part of the food chain, what good are they really?"

He shrugged. "Each time something goes extinct, we're the losers. No one thought horseshoe crabs were good for much, except to feed migrating birds during the spawn."

Bert tipped her head in question.

"Seems the crabs got copper in their blood—original blue bloods." He grinned. "We use it for leukemia and anemia. Now, the horseshoe crabs are getting endangered."

"So the park's going along with Fisheries."

"Right," Hunter said absently. "Too bad we lost those pictures of the sand. That might have helped."

Bert's lips tightened. That hadn't been her fault, but she still felt guilty. It did seem as if she was always making trouble for him. "What you need is to find that Ridley or have another one wash up." She smiled apologetically. "Not very nice of me to wish one dead."

"I know where you're coming from."

"Did you have a chance to do anything about Julie?" The minute she said it, she was sorry.

His face darkened, the lines coming back. Pushing away the half-finished cereal, he stood. "That's only one of the things I have to do this morning." He picked up his hat. "What are your plans today?"

Bert jumped up. "Hunter, what about Triton? And Shony?"

"I'll do what I can when I can." He reached over, rubbing her neck. "I'm sorry to be like this."

"It's okay. What time do you think you'll be back?"

"Don't look for me before dinner. I'll call, all right?"

She nodded, her mind already racing with an idea. "Look, I'm going to town for a while. I have to check some things at the restaurant."

"Don't work too hard. Bye, hon."

Bert followed him, glancing at the water as she watched him back down the drive. The wind wasn't as strong as yesterday, at least not yet.

If the rangers didn't have time to check out Shony's grave, there was no reason she couldn't do it. It should be easy to find the clearing in daylight. Bert was sure DeWitt had killed Shony and was looking for an excuse to kill Triton. It had something to do with EIA or the testing. Finding the carcass might provide an answer. All she had to do was pick up her boat. She had to stop by her apartment anyhow.

Twenty minutes later, Bert turned her car into a gravel parking lot on Route 70. After selling her restaurant in Swansboro, she'd bought an old concrete fish house that sat on a tiny prong of land in the North River. The building looked out on a wide creek surrounded by marshes, yet it was less than five miles from Beaufort and Morehead City.

Her plan was to turn it into a restaurant. Already, the kitchen had shelves and walk-ins, but the appliances had not yet been installed. The dining room was almost done. It had two walls of plate glass over the water and an outside deck shaped like a boat. As soon as the painting was complete, the floors would be laid. Then would come the furniture, fish-house décor, and a lot of greenery to make the place look tropical.

Bert swept up some chunks of plaster missed by the workmen and wiped off the solitary table and the few chairs she had brought over in preparation for Monday's interviews. She was not looking forward to them. Bert considered herself a poor judge of character and hated hiring. Linda, who'd worked for Bert at the old Swansboro restaurant, had done most of the preliminary screening, thank goodness. Damn, there was still a lot to be done before her Easter opening.

She went up to the apartment. In her junk drawer, she found a roll of survey tape left over from the construction. She pocketed it to mark Shony's grave, wishing she'd done that in the first place.

Going down to her boat, Bert told herself this had to stop. She didn't have time to be running around the park and spending a week with Hunter, as nice as that was. As of Monday, she vowed, it was back to the restaurant full time.

Pulling the canvas cover off her runabout, Bert connected the battery. Then she replaced the three black screws she'd removed from the carburetor for winter. Preening a little that she was able to do this, considering she didn't even understand what a carburetor did, Bert pumped the black ball until gas dripped out of the motor. Hitching the boat to her Toyota 4Runner, she drove back to Harkers Island.

Calico Jack's Marina was near the park entrance. As Bert expected, the ramp was empty but the gates open. Relieved that no one was watching, she backed the trailer and boat into the water. It took her only two tries this time.

Setting the 4Runner's parking brake, Bert climbed into the boat and started the motor. While she waited for it to warm up, she took a good look at the sound, feeling queasy deep in her stomach. It was still choppy, although there was no white water, thank goodness. She was always scared when she first set out in the boat. Once she got started, she'd feel better.

With a sigh, Bert trimmed the choke, backed the boat off the trailer, and tied it to the dock. As she stood in the stern, water gurgled at her feet. Water? Oh, my God, she'd forgotten to screw in the drain plug!

Hands shaking, she tried to untie the mooring lines. It seemed to take forever. Of all the stupid things to do. It was like driving across Death Valley with no water.

Bert didn't relax until she had the boat safely back on the trailer.

Then she had to pull it out, let the water drain, screw in the stupid plug, and put the boat back into the water again. Thank goodness there were no witnesses.

Finally, she had the boat ready and the car and trailer parked. Picking up her marine radio, she left the cell phone in the car. It wouldn't work on Shackleford anyway, and she was afraid she might get it wet. Back on the boat, she turned on the GPS, wondering if this trip was such a good idea. It was not getting off to a promising start. She sucked on her cheek. Of course, maybe this was her lucky day, since no one had seen her being stupid. That was the way she'd look at it.

Once Bert got over her nervousness, she found herself enjoying the water. Behind the shelter of Shackleford, the sound was smooth, the air fresh and clean, crisp on her cheeks. As always, the drop in temperature drove the algae from the water, leaving it clear. The deceptively beautiful pools of turquoise were actually white-sand shallows. And the lines of cobalt were not indicative of deep water, but rather of muddy weed beds. These could be easily confused with the royal blue channels of deep water and the blots of indigo where clouds shadowed the sound.

Right now, she was following the red and green posts marking the Harkers Island channel, which bisected the wide but shallow sound. Bert shoved the throttle forward. After ten minutes, she keyed to the chart on her GPS, squinting to see the tiny digital screen. Bald Hill was halfway down Shackleford near Bottle Run Point, a series of small bars that ran deep into the sound.

Bert slowed, watching the arrow that showed her location on the screen. She was pretty sure this was the place. She searched for any kind of marker—pound nets and crab pots usually indicated deep water—but saw nothing. She'd just have to wing it. It was too bad Hunter was so busy. He would have enjoyed this.

The water to her left, shaded all colors of blue and green like an artist's palette, darkened as she drew closer. This must be Bottle Run Point. She turned in. So far, so good. Between the sunlight and her polarized glasses, it wasn't hard to pick her way through the shoals.

They showed as greenish tan smears under the water. Up ahead, the water lightened to a pale aquamarine.

Stopping, she stood on the bow to sight. To her left, close to some marsh grass, a labyrinth of royal blue branched and wove back together again—a river within a river. Hopefully, this was a channel of deep water—unless it was weeds.

To her delight, it was deep water. Soon, Bert was threading her way through a maze of channels. A few times, she had to turn around when a passage petered out. She searched the approaching shore for clearings.

When she was as close to shore as she could get, Bert slipped on her hip boots and went over the side. She dropped a mushroom anchor and carried the bow anchor forward so she could pull the boat closer to shore as the tide rose. Before she left, she put the radio and a bottle of water in her coat pockets.

Making sure the line was tied on tight—she didn't want any more stupid mistakes—Bert slogged ashore. Her waders sank into the mud. Pulling up one foot only forced the other deeper. She had to go slowly so as not to lose her balance. Finally, she reached the beach and removed her hip boots. They were big for her, making it all the harder to walk through that soft mud.

Looking to both sides, she wondered which way to try first. West, toward Bald Hill.

A few minutes later, she spotted a double-trunk cedar between the sound and a clearing. She'd forgotten that weird tree. This was Triton's clearing. Not only that, but this was the same place she and DeWitt had found the other night. The dung piles were still here, all churned up, but the sand had been smoothed. She frowned, trying to remember if DeWitt had filled in the pits he'd dug.

As she passed under the twisted cedar, Bert slowed. It was so quiet in the hollow—and spooky. Suppose something was here? Or someone? She told herself not to be stupid. There were no boats around, no ATVs. She was alone.

What about the horses?

Hunter said they caught all the horses. That's why it felt so quiet.

Slowly, she walked around the clearing, taking shallow breaths, afraid she'd inhale something vile. She knew horses would stay around a sick or dead horse, trying to nudge it back to life. All animals did that, but she'd never heard of them moving a body. Could DeWitt have somehow dug around Shony's body the other night, or had he sneaked over before he arrived at the dock?

A picture of DeWitt yanking off his waders and spraying mud all over the tent flashed through Bert's mind. Had that mud been from here? But he wouldn't have had time unless . . . Of course. That had been DeWitt's boat in the sound when she got back from finding Shony. Maybe Julie called him, or he heard Bert on the radio telling Purcell about the dead foal and rushed to Bald Hill in his boat to move the carcass. He knew his way around. Since the tide was high, he could have run right up to shore. But he wouldn't have had much time. Had he dumped the foal in the woods somewhere?

Bert walked around, sniffing. There was no smell of dead animal in the air. Surely, he'd be pretty strong by now. Before she searched the woods, she'd better make sure the foal wasn't still buried. DeWitt could have moved Shony to a different spot in the same clearing. That would have been the quickest way to hide the carcass.

Bert dropped to her knees and began to dig. She'd find Shony. He had to be here. Then they'd know who killed him—or rather, why DeWitt had slit his throat. This was something she had to do for the little foal.

But nothing was here. First, Bert dug with her hands. Then, cursing herself for not bringing a camp shovel, she peeled a branch from the myrtle and began to probe the soft sand, as DeWitt had done, or pretended to do, the night Julie was killed.

DeWitt. Had a horse killed Julie, or had it been DeWitt? He couldn't have done it. He'd been with Bert that night. No, not all the time. He'd taken off with Julie to show her how to work the lights on the ATV, and he'd been gone at least a half-hour. At the time, Bert thought he was flirting with the vet tech, but now she wondered. No one saw Julie alive after that. Half an hour was long enough to have an argument, long enough for DeWitt to kill her and make it look like a horse did it. He could fake a wound to look like horse hooves, and he was strong enough to carry Julie's body from the water to the beach road. But what about all the blood? Dozens of blue tarps covered the bales of hay between the dock and the pen. He could have wrapped her in one of those.

Bert sat on her heels, frowning. She could see DeWitt striking out and killing Julie accidentally, but somehow she couldn't quite imagine his being able to calmly get on the ATV with Bert and drive all the way down to Bald Hill right after murdering Julie in a mad rage.

But he'd been wet. Bert remembered thinking it was from his trip over on the boat. Was he wet from washing off the blood? Ugh!

She'd hold that thought for later. Right now, she was here to find Shony. Maybe discovering the carcass would provide some answers. Bert stood and moved over a dozen feet, away from where Triton had been digging.

There was something here. Ah, thank God, she'd found the pony. Dropping, Bert scrabbled at the ground with her hands. The sand was damp, but at least it didn't smell. It must be cold enough to preserve things. There, now she was down to the pelt. It was darker than she remembered—wet, decomposing? She brushed more sand off, bending down. It didn't feel like hide—too smooth, more like rubber.

Scooping sand in big handfuls, Bert wondered if DeWitt had buried a tarp with Shony. No. This wasn't plastic, more like the kind of rubber they used on those big, black waders. Had someone hidden a pair of waders here with the horse? Why? Shit. A ball of cold grew deep in her stomach. She should have waited, or come with someone.

Sand flew as Bert opened up the hole, uncovering the bib of the wader. The buckle was missing, the wader strap knotted over the loop. It was DeWitt's. She remembered seeing it that other night. But what was it doing here, and what was underneath?

She shrieked, eyes bulging. Jerking away, she lost her balance and sprawled on her back, shrieking again. There was an arm under the wader, part of a shoulder, and a matted wool sweater.

No. It couldn't be DeWitt. How could he be dead? He killed Julie.

Chapter 19

There was someone here, under the sand.

Then Bert was on her feet, backing away. Sweat dripped down her forehead. It wasn't DeWitt. She'd been with him yesterday morning. He couldn't be in that hole. She had to be mistaken. Those were just his clothes in the sand.

But that was an arm inside DeWitt's sweater. No, maybe it was Shony's leg she felt. She hadn't really seen anything except clothes.

But how did the clothes get here? DeWitt had been wearing that multicolored sweater the last time she saw him. When was that? Yesterday morning? God, it seemed longer.

Reaching the sound, Bert hoped to see someone, anyone. Nothing moved. The beach and Bald Hill Bay were barren of life except for a wintering heron and a few gulls on the water.

She had to do something. Call Hunter. How? Bert charged down the beach until a water-filled cut stopped her. What was she doing? There was no help around. She'd left her cell phone in her car, and her marine radio wasn't on the same frequency as the park radios. She'd call the Coast Guard then. And tell them what? That she'd found some old clothes and thought there was a body inside? Suppose it was Shony? If she called the Coast Guard, the newspapers were bound to find out.

She walked back, glad no one had been around to witness her hysterical flight. Shaking her head, she stared at the twisted cedar that marked the clearing. She wasn't going to do that. She wasn't going back to make sure. That wasn't her job. People were supposed to leave the crime scene for the pros, right? What she should do was call the Coast Guard. Let them call the park and the sheriff.

But what if it wasn't a crime scene? She'd be a joke.

Even as she tried to talk herself out of it, her feet were already taking her back to the clearing. Lips clamped, walking on tiptoe over her own tracks, she approached the spot where she'd uncovered the waders. She glanced around for something to dig with, determined not to touch what was in that sweater again. To the side lay a flat slab of wood. Was it the same one she'd used to uncover Shony?

A sick feeling in her stomach, she began pushing the sand aside.

Oh, shit! It was a person. That was a hand, with fat, hairy fingers and spatulate nails cut short, black with grime. She touched the hand with the tip of one finger.

"What the hell are you doing?" a resonant voice boomed from behind.

"Clayton!" Bert yelped. She scrambled to her feet. "I didn't hear you."

He brushed past her, looking down. "What the hell?" His mouth opened, his bad eye jumping from side to side. "What have you done? Who's that?" He backed away, silver hair flying. "What's going on? Are you crazy?" He fumbled in his pocket. "I'm out of here." Whirling around, he loped off.

"Clayton, wait!" she shouted, running after him.

Clayton spun and dropped to a crouch. He lifted his hand, showing a large clasp knife. "Don't come any closer, you hear me?" The scar across his nose was red and pulsing.

Bert almost laughed. Clayton—trained in law enforcement and towering over her five-foot-five—was afraid of her? He must think she killed DeWitt. "I didn't do anything," she told him. "I was looking for Shony, but I found . . . that. I think it's DeWitt."

"DeWitt? He's dead?" He straightened up. The shadow of a smile flickered across his face. "DeWitt's dead?"

Most people felt guilty when something happened to someone they hated. Clayton's attitude made her stomach turn. She'd been thinking that DeWitt killed Julie in a fit of rage. And she was positive he killed Shony. Yet despite it all, there had been something likable about the vet. "I'm not sure, but it's his clothes. Clayton, do you have a park radio? We really should call someone."

Clayton jerked a thumb over his shoulder. "Back on the ATV." He stepped forward, frowning, his bad eye still jumping. "How'd you get here? Where's Hunter?"

"I don't know where Hunter is, but we need to get hold of him quick. Should we call in or what? I can call the Coast Guard on my marine radio." She lifted it from her pocket and waved it at him. Somehow, just having someone else to share her fears made her feel better. She was starting to think a little more clearly. "Maybe you should go back to camp and call the park on the cell, and I'll radio the Coast Guard. What do you think?"

"What happened to him? You didn't kill him, did you?"

"Of course not," Bert snapped. Suddenly, she was aware that it could look bad for her, being found at the grave site digging up the body— or burying it. She pointed. "He's been there awhile, at least overnight. Go feel him. He's cold."

Clayton shook his head, a shock of white hair falling across his forehead in a shiny wave. "No way. You don't contaminate a site." His good eye stabbed toward the clearing. "Can't say I'm surprised. He's a . . . He was a mean son of a bitch. Always figured he'd get it someday."

Bert remembered how Clayton had backed down when DeWitt

made the crack about not trusting his wife. Was Clayton jealous of DeWitt? Was he glad someone had killed him? "What are you doing here anyhow?" she asked.

"Well, hey, I just came down to, uh . . ." Bert caught a flash of panic in his eye. He shook his head. "I was doing a patrol on the beach, and, uh, I thought I heard a yell. Came to check."

She was sure he made that up. She remembered what Purcell said about him having blackouts since his accident. Could Clayton have . . . ? No. She shook her head. "Did you see DeWitt's ATV? How did he get here?" Bert exhaled. "We're wasting time. I think we'd better notify someone. Where's your ATV? Your radio's there, right?"

He waved vaguely. "By the edge of the woods."

How had Clayton known which path to take?

That question was partly answered when they got to the ATV. She saw more ruts leading across the dunes than his bike could have made. Were these tracks she and DeWitt made the other night?

Bert heaved a sigh of relief when Rudy, the chief law-enforcement ranger, answered her call on the radio. "Rudy, this is Bert. I'm at Bald Hill."

"You come over on your own?"

"Yeah. Rudy, listen, I found the clearing, and . . ." Bert hesitated, not wanting to inform the entire county. "There's something here you need to see, right away."

"You caught me just leaving Shackleford. I'm on the boat. Clayton's down there somewhere. How about I try to raise him for you?"

Clayton grabbed the radio. "I'm here. You come on down to Bald Hill. Now."

"Copy. On my way. Four-two-two out."

Bert grimaced. Rudy had signed off pretty quickly. She bet he was ticked off at the way the Humane Society rep ordered him around. She reached for the hand-held.

Clayton hesitated. Bert stared, holding her hand out until he finally handed over his radio. "Who you calling now?"

"I need someone to leave a message for Hunter." Bert was back on the air with Rudy. After she asked him to tell Hunter where she was, she said, "Where is he, do you know? He may want to come over."

Rudy was beginning to get the idea that they'd found more than a pony. "He's at a meeting. I'm not sure what his schedule is. Ernie's here with Tanisha. Want to talk to him?"

Ernie was second in command when Hunter wasn't available. "Thanks, Rudy. I'll wait until I hear from Hunter. How long will it take you to get down?"

"ETA fifteen minutes. Pulling out now. Four-two-two."

Taking a deep breath, Bert sat on the back of Clayton's bike to wait. Suddenly, she realized how tired she was. Her hands were shaking. Maybe she wasn't as much tired as shocked and scared. She still couldn't believe DeWitt was dead.

Maybe it wasn't DeWitt who killed Shony. Maybe he found him, dug him up, and got killed for his trouble. Was Shony still there, buried under DeWitt? Well, they'd know soon enough.

They went out to the beach to meet Rudy. When Clayton told him what was in the clearing, he just shook his head. "That's a new one for the Sea-born Woman." Bert had been born at sea, and the park never let her forget it. According to local lore, sea-born women had a special affinity with the islands and the sea creatures. "Didn't realize part of your talent was sniffing out bodies like a pig digging acorns."

"That's not funny, Rudy." At least he hadn't accused her of killing DeWitt.

"You found Julie, didn't you? And the woman last summer, and—"

"We were all looking for Julie. Besides, Hunter was with me," Bert protested.

They had reached the clearing. Rudy motioned Bert and Clayton to stay back.

After taking some pictures, Rudy crouched next to the body, slowly uncovering the face. "It's DeWitt, all right." The vet's beard and hair were gray with sand, his forehead smeared with dried blood. Bert turned away as Rudy scraped around his head. "Looks like he got his skull bashed in," she heard him say. "Clayton, can you do me a favor?"

"What?"

"Call Ernie on your radio and tell him he's needed here. Then run the ATV back to camp and pick him up. Is that all right with you?"

As soon as Clayton left, Rudy and Bert went to the sound-side beach, where Rudy had left his ATV. While he was on the high-frequency cell making a series of phone calls, Bert walked out on the berm to check her boat. The tide was coming in. It almost reached the clumps of wrack that lay on the sand in brown heaps. The sun was hidden behind thickening clouds, and the wind had picked up. Rudy joined her. "They're coming over. Be about an hour and a half. It'll be up to them from here on in."

"Who's coming?"

"Alton Huff will fly into Beaufort. He's the National Park Service special investigator. The county sheriff's office will pick him up at the airport and take him to the Beaufort dock. The park will boat them over from there—quicker that way. Joe Patel—you met him, didn't you?"

Bert shook her head.

"He's the medical examiner. He'll be coming, too."

"What about Hunter? Does he know?"

"Hunter's in a meeting with Representative Lida Fulchard, the town councilmen, Fisheries, and some others. I left a message telling him about DeWitt—and you."

"What's going on in town?"

"There's Cain being raised about that stand-down. It's not just Carteret County that's affected. They've shut down all dredging in the Southeast, from Oregon Inlet to Cape Canaveral. That's putting all kinds of pressure on Marine Fisheries and the park to back off and let dredging resume. Got Florida senators involved, as well as our two."

"Oh, shit." Bert remembered something else. "Did Hunter have a chance to talk to you this morning?"

"I spent the night here, on the island. Remember?"

"So he didn't say anything to you about Julie?"

Rudy cocked his head. "What was he supposed to tell me?"

Bert hesitated, then reminded herself that an opportunity missed was an opportunity lost. "I was wondering if a horse really killed Julie, and—"

A rumble from Rudy interrupted her. "First thing I thought of when you told me about DeWitt."

Bert propped her butt on the fender of the ATV. "Rudy, are they going to do an autopsy on her?"

He shrugged. "Don't know. But in view of this, I'll drop a word to Patel."

"I thought it was DeWitt that killed her."

Rudy raised a brow.

While Bert explained about Julie and DeWitt, Rudy began stringing yellow crime tape across the path. Did they carry rolls of that tape in their packs?

Tying off a strand, Rudy eyed Bert. "Can't say I buy DeWitt killing Julie, besides the fact he's ended up dead, too. I've known him since we were in fourth grade. DeWitt was in the marines, same as me. He nearly killed a man in a fight once, but . . ." Rudy shook his shaggy, flaxen head. "Going to take a lot of convincing before I believe DeWitt would do something like that."

They heard the grind of an ATV. Rudy swung around. "Wait here. I gotta tell Ernie what's going on and get some information from him and Clayton. Ernie's going to be put out you didn't call for him instead of me."

Bert's eyes widened. "I never thought of asking for him. He seems so out of it."

Heading out the path, Rudy called back over his shoulder, "Don't you be selling him short. He's smart and knows his field, and he's a good worker. He just doesn't know how to put himself forward. Wants everything just so, then gets upset when it isn't."

So Ernie was a perfectionist, whereas Purcell was casual about things. No wonder they didn't get along. Rudy had reached the curve when Bert remembered what she wanted to ask him. "Can you check the clearing, once you're done with Clayton and Ernie?" she called.

"You mean to see if that horse of yours is buried there?"

"Yes."

"Sure will."

Bert stayed on the beach. She heard their voices and caught glimpses of them through the trees. Ernie must have insisted on viewing the body. Finally, Bert heard the ATV start. Ernie and Clayton must be returning to the horse pens. When Rudy didn't appear, she went back to the tree by the clearing, where the crime tape began. Rudy was at the far end, away from the body, probing much as DeWitt had done the other night.

He heard her and looked up. "Your horse isn't here."

"How do you know?"

"He's not under DeWitt. Sand's too hard. I've checked this area in case the weapon was here. No hunk of wood made that hole in his head."

"Oh."

"Someone hit him. From behind, I'm guessing."

Bert winced. "But not like Julie, right?"

Rudy's head jerked up. "I never saw her. But I heard tell she had her face mashed in good. It could have been done with some kind of hammer, I reckon."

"Not a horse's hoof?"

Rudy shrugged. "That's a question for the medical examiner. I'll pass it on to Patel and the special investigator." He sighed. "Can't say I'm looking forward to telling DeWitt's kid the news."

"I forgot. Purcell said DeWitt had a child. He lives in New Bern, right?"

Rudy nodded. "With his grandmother. Big, just like DeWitt, only don't have his temper."

"His grandmother has custody?" Bert asked.

"Things got real dirty during the divorce. DeWitt said his wife was a tramp. She accused him of beating on her and the kid. Grandma was a compromise."

Did that mean Clayton and his wife could now get custody? Would the ex-wife be in line for DeWitt's estate or insurance? What had Clayton been doing down at this end of the island? And if Shony wasn't here, where was he?

Chapter 20

"What was Clayton doing down here? Did he tell you?" Bert asked Rudy.

The Parker had finally arrived and disgorged its load of officials. Bert and Rudy were waiting for the special investigator and the medical examiner to complete the body and site examination.

"Clayton said he was just taking a ride down the beach while Tanisha and Ernie were updating the logs," Rudy told her.

"You believe him?"

Rudy shrugged.

"What's going on with the ponies?" Bert asked after a short silence.

"Ernie's ready to set the horses free." Rudy leaned his massive rear against the side of the Honda. "He needs an okay from Hunter. I was heading for Beaufort when you called."

"Really? All the tests were clean? Did DeWitt get his blood samples sent in before . . . ?"

"You think that has something to do with him getting killed?"

Bert nodded.

"That's a stretch." Rudy eyed the clearing. "But to answer your question, DeWitt got his tests finished yesterday. Came in negative, same as Greg's. No EIA. Ernie and Tanisha were culling foals for adoption when I left."

"Oh." Bert had assumed the adoptions were off. "Who'll handle the adoptions now, with DeWitt gone?"

"Good question." The chief ranger scratched his beard. "Tanisha, probably. I'm not sure what kind of facilities she has. Greg's tied up with state business. They tried to get him to do it before they hired DeWitt."

"Does . . . Did DeWitt have a partner?"

Rudy snorted. "Not him. That was his trouble. Couldn't work—or live—with anyone. Too headstrong."

"Then his practice will go into his estate?"

"I'm not too sure how much he was worth. That man didn't give a dang about money, except when he needed some." Rudy stood. "Looks like they're ready to take our statements." He led Bert toward the path, where a man stood. "Agent Huff, Bert Lenehan."

Next to the National Park Service special investigator, even Rudy was puny. Bert estimated the investigator stood close to seven feet. He had to weigh at least two hundred and eighty pounds.

Pushing lank, dark hair off his forehead, Huff gazed directly at Bert with mud-brown, bloodshot eyes. Then he began to introduce her to the cluster of men emerging from the clearing. "This is the Carteret County sheriff, Ed White, and Detective Ramirez. Although this is officially a federal matter, not a county affair, I've asked them for an assist."

The sheriff, a fair, mustached man with a round face and clear, deeply tanned skin, bounced up and shook Bert's hand. "What he really means is, there's no residents on Shackleford, so chances are this is going to end up in our jurisdiction anyhow." He gave Bert the toothy smile of the perennial politician, then motioned toward a slim, young man with black hair. "Dr. Patel."

Bert glanced curiously at the doctor. Although they had never met, he'd been involved in the Portsmouth murder last summer. He apparently recognized her name, too, inclining his head gravely, his black eyes assessing her from under thick lashes. His dark, straight hair was beautifully cropped and styled. Both he and the detective had swarthy skin, but the doctor's was smooth, whereas Detective Ramirez's was pocked with the purple scars of old acne.

Alton Huff took Bert's arm. "I need to ask you some questions, if you don't mind."

"Sure." Bert tried to hide her sudden tension. It was like being called to the principal's office—you were uptight even when you hadn't done anything.

"Why don't we go out there, so they can get on with their jobs?" He guided Bert down the beach. "You live on the mainland, by Beaufort, right?"

She nodded.

"What were you doing on the island?"

"I, uh, I was looking for one of the horses."

"That your boat out yonder?" The agent inclined his head toward the sound. No neck was visible between his face and shoulders. When he tipped his head, his jowls spread like a hood of flesh.

"Yes."

His thin brows arched. "You came out here by yourself, alone?"

"Right."

"In January, in a boat, to look for a horse? Why?"

Bert squirmed. She'd hoped to keep Shony out of it. "One of the foals was missing. I worked on the roundup and was trying to find him."

He stared at her for a moment. "That doesn't explain how you came upon the body. Was he sticking out or what?"

The NPS investigator might be a ballplayer gone to fat, but he was no dummy. "Um, the foal, Shony, was dead. I was trying to find where he was buried."

Alton Huff said nothing, but his eyes never left her face.

Bert pushed her hair back, trying to come up with a logical explanation. "You see, someone had buried the pony."

"Here?"

"Yes." Bert avoided looking at the clearing, where the men were taking pictures. She was going to have to tell the whole story. "I'd found him, but when I came back with DeWitt, the foal wasn't there."

At the mention of DeWitt, the agent's brows rose.

Bert added hurriedly, "That was two nights ago. That's why I came over today. I thought we had the wrong clearing. I wanted to see if I could spot it in daylight." The agent's eyes grew smaller. Did that mean he didn't believe her? Bert felt the tension in her shoulders. "Look. DeWitt was dead when I uncovered him. He's been dead for quite a while, hasn't he?"

The special agent turned and motioned Bert back toward the clearing. He paused by the cedar, watching Detective Ramirez and the medical examiner bag DeWitt's body. "Any idea how long he's been dead?" he asked.

Dr. Patel stopped zipping the body bag and dug in his pocket for a cigarette. "What do you need?"

"Give me a rough estimate."

The medical examiner pinched a fold of skin, then picked up the corpse's hand and let it drop slowly through his fingers. "Time of death was about twenty-four hours ago, perhaps less. I'll narrow it down later."

"Thank you." Agent Huff turned back to Bert. "I don't recall it saying anything in the report that you were out with DeWitt the night Ms. Piner was killed." At Bert's astonishment, he added, "The sheriff faxed it to me. Read it on the flight over."

Ah, shit. "I didn't think this had anything to do with her." Bert glanced toward the sound, where her boat bounced. She wished she were on it. "I've got to get out of here before it gets dark."

"We'll get you back, don't worry." He turned his entire body to stare at her boat, then swung back to her. "If the foal was buried, how'd you know where to dig?"

Double shit. How much pull did Hunter have? Suppose they arrested her . . . "Look. I didn't want to say anything and embarrass the park when no one was sure. There's been so much publicity about the horses already. . . ." She trailed off, hoping for a nod, but his face remained expressionless. "One of the foals was missing, only we weren't sure he was missing, because there was no record of him." Damn, Huff was going to think she was crazy. "I'd kind of made him a pet. That's why I was looking for him."

"That doesn't tell me how you found him, if he was buried."

Bert swallowed a groan. "Triton took me there."

"Triton?"

"He's a stallion. Shony's father. He dug him up. Then he led me there." Bert waited, bracing herself for the explosion.

To her surprise, Huff nodded for the first time. "I've seen mustangs do that in Wyoming. When a youngun dies, they stay close for a week or so nudging it, like they're hoping it'll come back to life."

Bert exhaled in relief. "At first, I thought Triton was digging for water."

The special investigator nodded again. After a short silence, he asked, "You heading back to Harkers?"

"Calico Jack's Marina. I really should get going."

"We'll be glad to take you, if you'd like."

"Oh, thanks." Bert gave him a big smile. He did not respond. "But I don't want to leave my boat here. Just keep an eye out for me along the way, in case I have any trouble." Why did he make her feel she was babbling?

"You sure?"

"I have GPS," Bert said. Did this mean the interview was over? "Better get started." She walked over to her waders and began pulling them on, Huff following her movements with his eyes.

Please, don't let me screw up in front of him, Bert prayed as she hauled the line, bringing the boat closer to shore. She'd sounded like one of those dumb-blonde jokes while he was questioning her. The last thing she wanted to do was confirm that impression.

The sound was choppy now. A cover of clouds obscured the sun, changing the surface of the water to an opaque slate. It was a good thing she could follow her tracks on the GPS, although it wasn't all that accurate in narrow channels like these.

Bert soon found out how true that was. Twice, she hit bottom. Both times, she was able to free herself by tilting the prop and poling off. She was halfway to the Harkers channel, over by Bottle Run Point, before she hit ground again. But this time when she tilted the motor, the wind and current immediately swept her higher onto the shoal. Bert tried to pole off, knowing it wasn't going to work. Fortunately, she hadn't taken off her waders. Dipping her pole into the water to make sure it was shallow, she slid over the side and began walking the boat to the cut. It was going to be tricky getting off. At times like this, it was nice to have a second person in the boat, ready to gun the motor.

She glanced back at the men. She could barely see the park boat. Apparently, they weren't off yet. Good. Bert wanted to get going before they noticed her predicament. She suspected that Alton Huff didn't think much of women—women on the water, at any rate.

The water rose from her ankles to her knees and changed color ahead. The chill radiated through her boots, making her feet feel wet. Edging forward, Bert pitched her anchor out as far as she could. She let it sink, then drew it back slowly. The anchor slipped at first, then dug in. Feeling more confident by the moment, she climbed back on board and pulled the boat forward with the anchor line until there was enough water under the stern to lower the prop. Soon, she was back in deep water. She started the motor, then eased forward to bring in the anchor.

It was stuck fast. Bert geared up, advancing until the bow was directly over the line. She tugged hard at the Danforth, an anchor that could be loosened easily if pulled from directly above. But not this time. It was caught on something.

Her bare hands were freezing, but she didn't want to get her gloves wet on the line. Biting her lip, Bert gave another hard yank. Nothing.

Okay. Maybe if she circled around and tried from the other direction. Carefully keeping the line taut so it didn't get tangled in the prop, Bert steered the boat.

Still fouled. Well, there was nothing to do except try to force it loose. If that didn't work, she'd have to cut free. This was one of the reasons she and most weekend boaters carried a large clasp knife. Tying the anchor line to a cleat, Bert throttled up and started to pull. At first, the anchor didn't move, but as she advanced the power, she felt it give. Whatever it was caught on was coming, too. Bert continued forward, looking back curiously but at the same time keeping an eye on the GPS track. She didn't want to get back on the shoal.

She could see something dark to the side. What on earth? A tree? Bert slowed as she watched the shadow rise. Then she cut the power and hung over the side, pulling in the line.

The angle of the boat gave her some visibility through the water. Whatever it happened to be, it was as big as Bert—long and bulky, with extensions to the side. It was dark, too, shades of brown and purple, the water making it undulate, the legs moving as if trying to swim sideways, the body grossly swollen.

It was alive! She could see the lips fluttering, the teeth gleaming as it swam up to her. Its eyes stared, dark holes in a long skull, yellow-green hair floating like seaweed.

Bert was too scared to scream. Paralyzed, she hung over the side of the boat, unable to tear her eyes away. Deep down, she fought for logic and sanity. It was not alive. The refraction, plus the ripples from the boat's prop and the current, were making it undulate. She knew what it was: a dead horse, probably Shony. Someone had tried to hide his body in a deep hole. They would have succeeded, too, if she hadn't run aground.

It wasn't until her lungs screamed for her to exhale that Bert realized she'd been holding her breath. Where were the men? She looked back. The park boat was still at the shore. God, it seemed like she'd been here for hours.

Bert snatched up her radio with numb fingers. Right now, she didn't care who heard her. On sixteen, the hailing channel, she called for Alton Huff, knowing the park boat's radio would be keyed to the marine channel. Seconds later, his deep voice told her to switch to channel ten.

"Can you come over here?"

"You got trouble?" the investigator drawled.

Two could play that game. "Yeah."

In a few minutes, she watched the Parker take off, circle well past Wade's Shore into the sound, then come to her from the mainland side. That didn't surprise her. A boat that size could never have negotiated the channel she used. But as she pulled on her mittens, a little voice told her that DeWitt's boat could have.

The Parker came in slowly, one of the men hanging over the bow, signaling with his hand. "What's wrong? Suck up some sand?"

That was the biggest danger of getting on the shoals. Bert shook her head, pointing at the water behind her.

The cruiser pulled alongside. Agent Huff swung over the rail, dropping into Bert's boat. She reached for the console, yelling a warning. As his weight hit the deck, the little boat rolled steeply. If the cruiser hadn't been there, Huff would have been pitched into the water. As it was, he bounced heavily against the fiberglass, grabbing the rail to steady himself.

"Small boats," he complained. "What you got there?" He shuffled to the stern, the boat rocking with his every step. "How'd you latch onto that?" He actually smiled—not a big smile, but a smile nonetheless.

"Got my anchor caught on it getting off a shoal."

"Looks like a dead horse."

"I think it's Shony, the foal I was looking for. We need to take him back."

He tipped his massive head sideways, jowls rolling like jelly. "Why would you want to do that?"

"He didn't die naturally. Someone slit his throat. It may have some connection to what's happening." She waved a hand toward the park boat and DeWitt's body.

He nodded, apparently not surprised at her revelation. Then he

190

reached down and uncleated the anchor line, passing it up to one of the men on the cruiser. "Pull it up gently."

He and Bert watched the grossly bloated body of the colt surface. It was so swollen the tough hide was cracked, the hair forced into spiky tufts, the belly ballooned. Small scavengers scuttled into the eye sockets. A lizardfish slid out. Dark green slime oozed from every orifice. Bert turned her face away, choking. Poor little horse. Now, there was decay in the air. A lot.

"Swing it over this way, fellows."

"To my boat?" No way did Bert want that decaying, bloated horse on her deck, even if it was Shony. "What about the Parker?"

"Gonna take some to haul it up there. Might break apart." He must have seen the reluctance on her face. "You can ride with us. Ramirez can bring your boat along, if you don't mind." He looked at the detective, who nodded.

Bert hesitated only a moment. It wasn't Shony's fault. She could hose off the boat. And right now, the idea of having someone else take over sounded heavenly. "Try to keep him off the seats, would you?"

She watched from the big boat as they dragged Shony over the bow. A stream of greenish black liquid shot from his anus. Bert gagged and Huff backed away as an overwhelming stench blanketed them. Below, the men had donned disposable face shields, a park staple, as they struggled with the pony. They freed Bert's anchor.

"There's another line here. Want me to bring it in?" Detective Ramirez yelled up at Huff from under his paper mask.

"Let's see what it is," was the slow reply.

"Well, now, looks like someone weighed the carcass down with a big anchor." Detective Ramirez hauled at the mud-covered line.

"DeWitt was using a cinder block for an anchor. He told me his got stolen," Bert said, afraid the special investigator was going to give the order to cut it free.

"Bring it along, and watch for prints," Huff told the detective. He gave Bert a dark glance.

"I'm sorry." Bert flushed. "I didn't mean to tell you what to do." She tried to change the subject. "Do you think DeWitt came here in his boat?"

"Didn't see any boats around—except yours, that is."

Then they were off. Bert tucked in behind the windshield on the cruiser. Her boat and Detective Ramirez followed in their wake.

"Where would you say is the best place for us to leave the carcass, so the vets can go over it?" Huff asked Bert as they approached Harkers. "The captain's taking us back to Beaufort."

"Oh." She hadn't thought about that.

"The park dock?" the agent suggested. "Can you ask someone to pick him up? I'll tell O'Hagan, soon as I catch up with him."

Bert nodded. That would be as good as anything. She'd just leave the boat docked there until tomorrow, then hose it off before she took it out of the water. Hopefully, the rangers wouldn't yell too loudly about her using their dock space.

By the time they let her off at the park, it was well after five. The visitor center was closed, and there were no cars in sight. Hunter was probably either at his meeting or waiting for Huff in Beaufort. The park operated on minimum staff this time of year.

She needed a phone. Her cell was in her car. Bert hesitated, wondering if it would take longer to get to her car at Calico Jack's Marina or to Purcell's house. She began walking to Purcell's. He could drop her off at the marina.

When she reached the elevated ranch, she was relieved to see the ranger's Jeep in the drive. But this time, no one was waiting on the deck. Bert banged on the door until Purcell finally cracked it open. From his rumpled appearance, she knew she'd gotten him out of bed. At five-thirty? "Hey, Purcell, let me in."

"Um, Bert. I'm not feeling well. Is there something I can do for you?"

"This isn't a social call. We found Shony. I've got him on my boat, and Alton Huff wants him somewhere safe."

Purcell stared, his dark eyes round and blinking. "Where's Maintenance? They take care of dead animals. Why'd you bring him back?"

Bert rested a hand on the doorframe. "Look. I'm tired and cold. I'm sorry I got you up. Let me in for a minute, okay?"

Purcell hesitated, then stepped outside, closing the door behind him. "This has nothing to do with you, understand?" He took a deep breath. "I've been the nice guy for too long. Now, that Ernie Steingart's going to see just how much I do. No more, 'Purcell, can you give me a hand with this?' "

Bert frowned. "You mean you're not going to help me?"

He looked embarrassed. "It's nothing personal, truly. Hunter knows where I'm coming from. Starting now, when I'm off, I'm off. Call the ranger on duty, why don't you?"

Bert hated being rejected. She couldn't brush it off. Determined not to let Purcell know how much he'd hurt her, she backed away. "You're absolutely right. That's what I should have done. Sorry I disturbed you." She swung around on her heels and ran down the stairs.

Purcell hung over the rail. "Where's your car? You need a ride?"

"No thanks," Bert called back, feeling some satisfaction. "Not from you."

Instead of walking back the way she came, Bert went through the Maintenance parking lot, located next to Purcell's house. From there, she took a shortcut to Calico Jack's. Passing between a truck and a blue car, she ducked through the wooden fence and trotted up the dirt road to her SUV. Once in the 4Runner, she turned the heater on full blast and took several deep breaths. What had gotten into Purcell? Was he really sick, or just hung over? She shrugged, too tired to worry about him now. She'd promised Huff she'd take care of Shony. Besides, she could imagine the comments if Maintenance discovered a dead horse draped over her boat in the morning.

Driving to the boat, Bert dialed the park on her cell. The recording gave her the number of the ranger on call. She got him on his cell phone and arranged to meet him at the dock.

"I've called for Maintenance," the duty ranger informed her when she arrived. "Got any ideas about where to put it?"

"The vets need to see it." At least he didn't seem put out by her call. It probably broke up a dull evening.

Soon, a white park truck bounced over the manicured lawn onto the dock where they stood. Carlos, Bert's favorite maintenance ranger, stuck his grinning, mustached face out the window. "What you want with a dead horse, Miss Bert?"

"Opening my restaurant soon."

"Kinda ripe, ain't he?" Carlos chuckled. Groping behind his seat, he produced some face shields, but the stench still filtered through. Coughing and taking shallow breaths, they rolled the carcass into a tarp and tied it tightly. Then, using ropes, they pulled and shoved the dripping bag into the truck.

"I'm going home to get a bath," the duty ranger grunted.

"Ay yi yi. You can smell him a mile away." Carlos slid into the pickup. "What if I leave the horse in the truck and put it in the garage for tonight? He stinks more than that whale that washed up."

Bert laughed. A partially decayed whale had washed up on the Shackleford beach last fall, drawing both tourists and sharks until Carlos bulldozed it away for burial. Right whales had once washed up in numbers on the Outer Banks, attracting rough men who processed them for their oil. There were a lot of stories about those whalers, including a strange one about an encounter with a returning patriot and his magnificent horse.

Chapter 21

Yorktown, 1781

Kerrygold

The horse's nostrils flared as the darting shadow closed in. Thrusting his head forward, he snorted.

With a stifled shout, the runner twisted away, stumbling over the dark mound at the stallion's feet. Already off balance, the man crashed to the ground.

The mound heaved, moaning.

The stallion charged, a pale blur in the Chesapeake night. He reared and slashed at the intruder with his iron-shod hooves.

Screaming, the runner rolled away. "What kine o' devil . . . ?" He bounced to a crouched position, shielding his head, blinking into the dark. Then the thin sound of his chuckle pierced the stallion's ears.

"You be no devil, you just a white horse." The soldier dropped his voice to a croon. "Easy there, I got no quarrel with you, horse. I be on my way now, iffen you don't mind."

Often mistaken for a white horse because of his flaxen mane and tail, the palomino remained alert, waiting for the intruder to make another aggressive move. The black man retreated, keeping low. Satisfied, the gold horse dropped his head to nudge the body at his feet.

At his touch, the tumbled heap groaned. "Help me."

The black soldier swung around.

The palomino snorted a warning.

The black froze. "Mistah, iffen I come any closer, yo horse gonna kill me."

There was silence. The man struggled to roll over, inching a hand to grasp the trailing bridle. "Steady, Kerrygold." A single epaulette gleamed.

Very slowly, the black man approached on his hands and knees. "I come to help yo master, horse. I don't mean no harm."

Kerrygold stood still. No tension rose from his master, nor did he scent fear in the intruder. The black crouched over the wounded man. "I can't see nothing, suh. Where you be hurt?"

The officer let Kerrygold's reins drop, moving his hand to his stomach. "Ball in me belly. Have you water?"

"Aye, suh, but water's bad for gut shot."

The officer laughed, breaking into a moaning cough. "Even laughter hurts," he panted. "I'm dying, soldier. Ease my way. Water, please."

Kerrygold's ears flattened at the pain in his master's voice.

Lifting the officer's head, the black man put his canteen to the injured man's lips. The lieutenant drank slowly, pausing to gasp for breath. Finally, he turned his face away. "You have my gratitude." After a minute, the officer asked, "You are a Negro, a slave, fighting with us?"

"I be a free man," the black growled.

"The British promise freedom to any slaves who join up with the loyalists. The patriots do not."

The black man was silent.

The officer sighed, moving restlessly.

"Do you wish for me to raise yo head, suh?"

" 'Twould be a relief, to be sure."

Muzzle tight, the horse watched the big Negro pile up sand to form a small rise. As the black gently eased the officer onto it, Kerrygold snorted, but his master made no objection. The soldier retrieved the lieutenant's tricornered hat and folded it under his head. "Water?"

The officer grunted a negative. After another silence, the horse heard his master speak again. "What was your regiment?"

"I never fight for the lobsters. Dat de truth. I were with Captain Tewes, Rhode Island Regiment," the black answered in a low tone. "Can't give you no good reason. When the New Bedford shipyard go belly up, I move to Boston. I be proud what the Minutemen do in Lexington. I join up then."

"Your brogue . . . You don't speak like a Northern Negro, or a Southern one."

The other man was silent. Kerrygold's ears pricked at the rising tension.

Sighing, the officer persisted. "I have a reason. What are you doing here?"

The black turned his head toward the bay, where fires still smoldered, although the guns were silent now. "They leave us to watch for the lobster longboats, iffen they come ashore."

"Go on."

"Well, suh, that British admiral, he send out two boats, thirty men. We work our way through the thicket to the edge o' the water. Soon as the boats get to shore, the captain gives the order to charge. Away we goes, water flying over our heads. They yell and start to fire. Dey is balls going every place. We only got ten men, but we fight hard. We push de lobsters back to de water. Something hit me. When I wake up, everybody gone. Den I fall over you."

"Are you hurt, private?"

"Got me a bash on the head and a cut on the ribs. That's all, suh."

"Thank the Lord." The injured man coughed, alarming the horse. "I must ask you again. Where were you born?"

This time, the Negro did not tighten. No waft of fear tainted his scent. The guarding stallion eased his stance, lowering his head.

"I from the Windward Isles, Martinique, suh."

"That explains the brogue. How long have you been a free man?"

"Long time, suh. My master give me my papers after I fight at his side, on the *Delight*."

"The *Delight*? A pirate ship?" The officer's voice weakened. Kerrygold turned his head, eyeing him.

"Yes, suh."

"You're an older man?"

"Aye, suh."

"Many joined after Lexington, then left. What made you stay in?"

The black man hesitated, then said, "Our boy, he be living with his relation in Boston. I promise my woman I bring him home safe."

Only the choked breath of the dying man broke the silence. "And?" he gasped.

The horse lowered his head, his lips inches from his master's side, the scent of mangled flesh thick in his nostrils.

"The sooner the war be done, suh, the sooner we go home."

The lieutenant's eyelids closed, then fluttered back open. "You have experience with horses?"

"Aye, suh. I take care of the stables and horses for the captain."

"Yes, I thought as much. Can you ride?"

"I ride horses since I be a wee lad, suh. Ain't nothing I can't ride."

"So this was meant to be." The lieutenant turned toward Kerrygold, who blew gently. "My horse must thirst. Can you . . . ?"

The black rose slowly and approached the flaxen-maned stallion with his hand outstretched, palm open. The horse lifted his head, ears flattening.

"His name is Kerrygold," the officer whispered. "He has been with me since this campaign started—indeed, before. My father brought him over from Ireland."

"Don't fret, horse," the black man murmured. "I gonna make you happy."

The stallion let him approach. The black was much larger than his master, but he made no sudden moves. Slowly, the man detached the water bag, filled it, and let the palomino drink his full.

From below came the officer's breathless voice. "In the saddlebag, there is a pouch. Fetch it out, please."

"Aye, suh." The Negro placed the leather purse in the officer's hands.

"This horse, he is well descended."

The soldier eyed Kerrygold, who stared back. "Yes, suh, I can see that. I ain't never seen a palomino horse wid black eyes before."

"He's an Irish draft, came from the Spanish hobby horse," the lieutenant whispered. "You know the breed, private?"

"No, suh. Do you wish for me to fetch help, suh?"

"No, soldier. I shall be dead soon, but before then . . ." The officer remained quiet a long time. "My horse, Kerrygold, I wish you to take him."

The stallion nickered, acknowledging his name.

"Take him, suh?"

"Yes. Ride him. I have seen Negroes mounted in the army."

The private did not reply.

"He's descended from the hobby horse of Ireland. Did I tell you that?" The lieutenant's voice was slow.

"Yes, suh."

"He's of the legendary stallion Finn-gall. His forefathers came from Spain. They were called Jennettas. They are known for their smooth gait. He can walk as rapidly as most horses trot, and march for hours." His breath was thick with phlegm. "My ancestor was said to be the first to breed them."

From the way both men eyed him, Kerrygold knew himself the subject. He raised his head, curling his neck.

"Dat a handsome horse, all right, wid dat long mane and tail."

"Yes, well . . . He is yours, in return for one thing."

"They not going to let me keep him, suh."

"I'll give you a letter." The officer gasped for air. Kerrygold snorted. "I was on a mission, private, when the shot felled me. This letter . . ." The stallion shied as his master pulled a rustling, sealed packet from the leather pouch. "It tells General Rochambeau, our French ally, we are badly outnumbered by Cornwallis and begs him to send reinforcements."

"But suh, Lafayette's troops been here for a while. We got lots of men."

"Yes, yes. I come from Lafayette's camp. This is to keep Cornwallis unaware of our true strength." The lieutenant motioned east, where the sky had lightened just enough to distinguish the horizon. The horse followed the gaze of the two men. The blackened, smoldering remnants of Admiral Grave's British ships could barely be seen. But nearer the horizon, gold glimmered like fireflies over a vast expanse of water as the invisible sun reflected off the sails of de Grasse's victorious French fleet. Letting the letter flutter to the sand, the lieutenant sighed. "I was trying to reach a special detachment of the Rhode Island Regiment. My orders were to engage the enemy and allow myself to be captured by the British."

The black man growled, reaching for the parchment. "We was sent to die, for this?"

"This coming battle could end the war. If it is not ended soon . . ."

The stallion could hear the call of seabirds, as if there were no encampments of men and horses only a few miles distant.

The black was still. Then he muttered, "There be no crops in the ground this year. Soon, all the men leave to go home." He pocketed the thick letter. "This war got to end. What you want me to do, suh?"

But the officer did not respond. The sand about him was dark and reeked of blood and bile. The private knelt by his side. Kerrygold jerked to attention, curling a foreleg. At that, the man stirred, opening his eyes. "I am not dead yet. But soon . . ." He paused, his breathing slow. "You must make it seem you try to reach General Rochambeau."

The black spoke slowly. "The sailors we fight, they back with

Cornwallis already. I got to make the English think dey catch me. That be the problem."

The stranger was too close to his master. Nostrils flaring, Kerrygold snorted.

The lieutenant opened his eyes. "Farewell, old friend," he said in a faint voice. "Soldier, give me your hand."

The two joined hands, stroking the stallion's muzzle, their scents mingling. The black broke the silence. "Suh, if I go to the English camp and say I wish to join, they believe me. They think I come to be freed."

The wounded man's eyes showed white as he rolled them in question.

The black smiled. "I ride yo stallion. They gonna ask where I get such a fine horse. I don't tell at first. They search and find yo papers. Then I say I find you dead and take yo horse. They gonna think I kill you." He shrugged. "It don't matter, iffen they think the letter be real."

With his eyes closed, the lieutenant nodded. "Yes, that may work." He was silent again. Then he opened his eyes. "You must leave now."

The big black man shook his head. "Yo horse not going to let me take him until you be dead, suh."

"Then we shall oblige him. My pistol, private." He glanced toward the saddle.

Kerrygold shied when the shot rang out, then cautiously nosed forward. He fanned his lips, sniffing the air and his master's broken remains. Blood from the living he could tolerate, but blood from the dead terrified him. He backed away, squealing and bucking.

The black man held onto his bridle, stroking him, soothing him with a stream of words, telling him his master had died a noble death. Grasping the reins, the soldier led him away from the lieutenant's body. He did not attempt to mount Kerrygold until they had crested the hill and the smoke of morning campfires choked the air.

In Cornwallis's camp, men wearing red coats with yellow linings, white shirts, and powder in their hair came to examine Kerrygold and his new rider. As they pulled the patriot from Kerrygold's back, the stallion reared. A soldier grabbed his reins and held him so tightly the horse could barely draw breath. They yanked off his saddle and shook everything out on the sandy ground. There was laughter as the lieutenant's possessions were divided. Then one of the officers opened the leather pouch.

Cursing, the officers converged on the black man, who waited silently nearby. One of the men in red brought his whip down upon the huge Negro, who cried out, explaining, "Please, suh. I don't read. There was a battle, suh, by the York River. The lieutenant were laying there dead, in the middle o' a heap of mariners. They was all dead, too. This horse here, he were standing by the traitor's side. That be all I knows. That is the God's truth, suh." He ducked another blow. "I take the horse. I hear the gov'nor, he promise we free if we joins up. Dey call me Goree. I come to fight, suh."

They sent Goree to the loyalist Negro camp, while Kerrygold was placed in a pen with other mounts. That night, the guns began sounding. Two days later, at dawn, the black man came to the pen. Kerrygold trotted up, whinnying a greeting. Goree smiled, showing white teeth and whispering, "Come with me, horse. De lobsters be sending us free Negroes on a mission. I got orders to take a mule to help wid the carryin'. Yo is a mule now, you hear me, horse?"

A group of blacks with bundles trudged down a path. Some were sick. Goree lifted two of them onto Kerrygold's back. One of them protested, "Stay away. It's the smallpox."

"They send us to spread the plague among the traitors," said the other.

Goree grunted. After that, he kept his distance from the plague-stricken men on the stallion's back. When they reached a stand of trees close to the campfires of the patriots, the two black loyalists dismounted. At nightfall, the sick men set off on foot to infect the patriot forces.

When they were gone, Goree mounted Kerrygold. "We done our duty, horse. I ain't fighting wid de lobsters. Captain Tewes be dead, and I ain't sure where to find the regiment. It be time for us to go home."

As they traveled south, the sound of cannons slowly faded. For days on end, they passed through thick marshes and pine forests, avoiding roads and hiding in the woods when they heard other deserters. Kerrygold found ample pasture, but his rider did not fare as well, stealing gourds from the fields and trapping a few fish in the rivers. Once, when they ventured over a lonely country road, they came upon a gruesome sight. The head of a black man had been stuck upon a sapling on one side of the dirt road, his hand tied to another tree across the road. As Kerrygold backed away, snorting and squealing, the soldier muttered, "Dat what they do when a Negro kill a white man."

That night, Goree did not hunt for food but rolled up in his blanket. While the black slept and Kerrygold dozed, two whites crept into their camp. They approached the blanket-wrapped form cautiously. One lifted his hand. Metal flashed.

Kerrygold charged, a blur of white and flying hooves. The thief attempted to defend himself with his knife, slashing at the horse. Screaming with rage and fear, Kerrygold kicked, striking the man's wrist and driving the knife into his thigh. Another hoof struck his face. The stallion rose, coming down again and again, until Goree's roars made themselves heard. "Enough, horse. He be stone dead."

From the side came a keening. It was the white deserter's companion. "Jed Salter weren't going to hurt nothing. Just wanted your horse, for his boy."

The black man whirled. "And that there knife, that were to scratch my arse?"

The deserter's mouth dropped at the sight of Goree's face. He clung to a tree. "Smallpox. You've the smallpox." Pushing himself away, he ran into the woods, crashing through the brush in his panic.

They left that night, but something was wrong with Kerrygold's rider. He slumped in the saddle, shivering. Other times, sweat ran down, soaking his body and dripping onto the stallion's flanks. The patriot cursed. "Live through six years of war, eight battles, to die o' the pox.

Dear Lord, let me live long 'nough to see my woman and tell her where de boy be. This be my dying wish."

They forded yet another river and came to a huge marsh. The man faced east, patting the stallion. "We be even with Portsmouth, but it be too far for a horse or a sick man to swim. We got to cross to the south."

They did not stop but marched through the night, passing the outskirts of a town Kerrygold's rider called Beaufort. As they reached the edge of a large salt lake, the black man appeared to revive. He guided the stallion to the water's edge and then, dismounting, led him into the chilly sound.

Seeing another shore nearby, Kerrygold swam easily across the water. His rider, fast weakening, clung to his mane. Soon, they were on the far shore. They crossed more water, but none so deep they had to swim again. Then they reached the lee of another large island.

"Shackleford," the black exhaled, sliding off the horse's back. "We've only two days' ride to Portsmouth." He swayed, clutching at Kerrygold. "The fever addles my senses. I can't go to her wid de pox." He sank to the ground, shivering. He beat at the sandy soil with his fist.

For a moment, Kerrygold stood over him, nudging. Then the stallion backed away, raised his head, and gave a long neigh that culminated in a grunt of despair.

Shortly, the woods began to rustle. Head up, ears forward, lips fanned, Kerrygold whirled to face the approaching danger. A child stepped from the trees. When he saw Kerrygold, his mouth and eyes grew round. He made a sound of pleasure and ran toward the stallion.

The black lifted his head. "Where you come from, boy? Best you leave, quick."

The boy stopped, staring at the man. "Are you sick?"

"Aye, dat de truth. It be catching. Be gone now, I tell you."

"That's a fine horse."

"Aye." Goree rose up on his elbows. "Why you on the island? It be too early for whaling. Yo family here to fish?"

The boy nodded, edging closer to Kerrygold, who stood firm.

"A little young, ain't you?"

The boy stuck out his chin. "I'm eight years old." His hand touched the stallion.

"And yo name?"

"Jeremy Salter. Are you a runaway slave?"

"I be a free man, and don't you forget it." The black man frowned. "I got a son. He be called Jeremy, too."

The boy laughed, his mouth close to Kerrygold's nose. "There ain't no slaves called Jeremy."

"Go 'way, boy."

"Can't make me."

Without moving, the Negro growled, "What you want wid me?"

"My daddy's bringing me a horse, when he comes back."

Goree said nothing.

"My daddy went to war."

The soldier groaned. He eyed Kerrygold, who was watching him. Then he shook his head, muttering, "No, Lord. Don't make me tell it."

The boy sidled closer to Kerrygold, lifting a hand to his mane, letting the long, flaxen strands flow through his fingers. "I never seen a palomino with black eyes before," he whispered, his hands gentle, his breath sweet on the horse's muzzle. The stallion turned his head, nuzzling the child's neck. Laughter came from the boy.

"Take him," the soldier growled.

"What?" The boy's head snapped up, gold curls flying.

"Take him. He's yours."

"But . . ."

The black man pushed himself up on one arm. Open sores leaked pus down his cheeks. The skin on his swollen face was tight and shiny with fever. "Leave me now," Goree said through cracked lips, "before I think on it."

The boy grasped Kerrygold's reins, backing off.

At the edge of the woods, Kerrygold balked, nickering. The black called out in a firm voice, "Better you go wid him, horse."

Understanding that this was something his master wanted him to do, the stallion let the boy lead him into the oaks. Then he heard the patriot's voice one last time. "His name's Kerrygold. He be bred from the stallion Finn-gall. Yo father, Jed Salter, sent him. Don't you forget dat, Jeremy."

Chapter 22

Had the whalers kept the stallion on the island? It was said that the ghost of a horse with a silver mane still roamed the Shackleford beaches. Bert chuckled as she drove to Hunter's house, envisioning a four-legged apparition charging from the surf.

She was hoping Hunter would be back, but the cabin was dark and lonely. Bert flipped on the lights, turned on the stereo, and headed for the shower. Hunter arrived while she was toweling off.

"You just get here?" he asked, sticking his head through the door. She nodded. "I'll be done in a minute."

"Got to make a couple of calls anyhow." Hunter continued to talk from the kitchen. "Heard you been busy again, pulling bodies off Shackleford like they were in season."

"You saw Rudy?" Bert shouted back, reaching for her hair dryer.

"And Alton Huff. Had to get him accommodations." His tone became serious. "Can't hardly believe someone would have done that to

DeWitt. I was thinking it was him that was making the trouble." He stuck his head back through the door. "Hon, I don't want to be telling you what to do. . . ."

"But . . ."

"I just don't want to be worrying about you being out on Shackleford by yourself, not till we catch the killer. All right?"

"You and me both." She bent over, brushing her hair. "I only went to look for Shony. I had no idea DeWitt was missing."

"What did y'all do with the foal? I told Alton I'd get Greg and Tanisha to check him out tonight."

"Oh, good. I was afraid you'd think I was being stupid, bringing him back," Bert said. "Carlos put him in the garage, by the shed." She should have more confidence in Hunter, she told herself as she pulled on a shirt. When would she learn he wasn't like her ex-husband?

Hunter was on the phone when she came out of the bathroom. Bert opened the fridge and peered at the shelves in the forlorn hope that a meal would materialize. If only she hadn't given that steak to Purcell. She could defrost some chicken and make piccata, or they could—

Hunter leaned over her shoulder. "I just called for takeout. That all right?"

Bert slumped in relief. "Oh, that's great. I'm whipped." She eyed him. "Looks like you are, too. Another bad day?"

Instead of answering, he gave her his lopsided grin, then lowered his mouth to hers. As always, Bert felt that instantaneous response, her body leaning and melting into his, flowing into every hollow as his hands pressed her to him, wide palms gently—

The phone rang.

Hunter moaned and picked it up, still holding her tight. "O'Hagan." He held his hand over the receiver. "Greg Statler," he mouthed to Bert. Statler was the state vet. He was saying something about Tanisha. "You can't raise her either?" Hunter asked. "They left the foal in the garage, across from the maintenance shed. Yeah. Meet you there in five." He hung up. "Sorry, hon." He looked at his watch. "Captain's Choice will have our order ready at seven-thirty."

208

"I'll pick it up."

Hunter dug into his pocket for money. Bert waved it away, but he pressed it into her hand. "My turn tonight."

He'd no sooner walked out the door than the phone rang again. Tanisha was on the line. Bert gave her Hunter's cell number and told her where he was, in case she couldn't raise him. There were a lot of dead-air spots around Harkers.

"I'm here on the island," the vet told Bert. "Maybe I'll just run down there."

What was Tanisha doing on Harkers? Bert wondered as she hung up. The vet worked out of Morehead City, and she'd been on Shackleford all day with Clayton and Ernie. Bert would have expected her to be home by now. It was lucky she wasn't. Maybe they could have some answers on Shony tonight.

The next phone call was from Vilma Willit, who sounded annoyed that Hunter was not immediately available. "You have him call me this evening," the reporter said. "I don't care what time, you hear me?"

Bert picked up the takeout and was keeping it warm in the oven when Hunter returned—with Greg and Tanisha in tow.

"Sorry, hon," Hunter said softly while the vets dropped their coats in the bedroom. "It was just too cold to stand around talking in that garage."

Hunter had ordered chicken fingers, hush puppies, and slaw. Bert passed the containers around. Hunter and Greg both grabbed, but Tanisha waved the food away. "Ate already," she smiled, patting her flat middle. "Steak with wine gravy and mashed potatoes."

Bert swung around, mouth open, then quickly glanced away, hoping no one had noticed her reaction. She slid off the barstool and walked to the window. There was a small, dark blue car parked in the drive, like the one she'd seen at Maintenance. Bert choked back a laugh. So Tanisha had been at Purcell's. Not only that, but Bert had dragged the ranger out of bed, probably at a crucial moment. No wonder he'd acted so strangely. The idiot. Why didn't Purcell just say he had company, instead of making her feel bad?

Suddenly, her amusement cooled. Was there a more sinister

reason for hiding the fact Tanisha was there? Had Purcell and DeWitt fought over the woman? She could still see Purcell's glare when DeWitt had put his arm around the young vet's shoulders the last day of the roundup. Or was he afraid his parents would disapprove?

Greg was saying something about Shony. ". . . throat cut. Some minor rope marks and scrapes, probably inflicted after he was dead. No other trauma, except for the scavengers and decomposition."

"Do you know when?" Hunter asked.

Greg shook his head. "At least three days ago." He glanced at Bert. "Probably sometime right before Bert missed him. That would have been either Tuesday night or Wednesday early, right?"

Bert nodded. "Can you tell how long he was in the water?"

"I'd say not more than twenty-four hours. Except for his eyes, there was very little scavenger damage. The bloating would have started shortly after death."

Soon, both vets were gone. Bert collapsed on the stool next to Hunter while he finished eating. "Some week." She nibbled another piece of chicken. "I can't believe tomorrow is Sunday already. Have you heard anything on Julie?"

"Guess they haven't released the body yet. Weekend delayed things."

Bert waited until he'd finished eating, then said, "Don't forget to call Vilma."

"Better do that now." Hunter picked up the phone and dialed her number. Apparently, he knew it by heart. Vilma must have been sitting next to the phone, as he began talking immediately. "That's right, Vilma. There's been no decision yet. The town has offered to hire two turtle trawlers, to use baskets, and to have an observer approved by Marine Fisheries on board at all times."

Bert picked up the dishes and got the coffeepot ready for morning.

"Yes, that's it exactly. If they'd spent the extra money from the start, chances are they wouldn't have this problem. I'll do that. Take care."

He leaned over and grabbed Bert, pulling her onto his lap. "Now, it's time for some serious business."

Bert woke up naked, her head on Hunter's shoulder, his arm around her. God, it was nice having sex with a man you loved and waking up all relaxed like this in the morning. But what was that noise? The waves under their window tended to muffle sounds. She lifted her head to eye the red dial on the alarm. Only five-twenty. It rang again. Oh, the phone.

She reached over Hunter for the receiver. He groaned, coming awake and stretching out his hand.

"No!" she heard Hunter exclaim. He bolted up, swinging his legs over the side of the bed. Bert sat up, too, leaning against his back, her head on his shoulder so she could hear. "Greg," Hunter mouthed.

". . . began the Coggins test last night," Greg was saying. "Drove up to Raleigh, had a friend meet me at the lab. We finished it up just now. No doubt about it. The foal tested positive for EIA. Already faxed the USDA."

"Shony?" Bert whispered.

Hunter nodded.

"I'm checking the blood against that first sample we had, remember?" Greg said.

"The extra one." Hunter scowled. Things were starting to make sense. "I'm betting you find it's all from the same horse—Shony." He stood. "And DeWitt had to know. That's why he killed the foal, dammit to hell." The phone to his ear, Hunter paced, stark naked. "The culled foals. We got to let them go, quick." Bert could no longer hear Greg's side of the conversation. Hunter nodded, then said, "Can you get Tanisha to confirm the blood test? She's the foundation vet. I got to find Ernie. We have to turn those babies loose, before it's too late."

Well, so much for their last day together. "What did you mean, 'before it's too late'?" Bert asked Hunter while he dressed, careful not to show her disappointment.

"The dams won't take the foals back, not if they've been separated too long. They're too little to winter alone. They need their dams."

"You mean they can't be adopted? Even though it was just one horse that tested positive?"

"Any one of those horses could be incubating EIA. We'd have to wait two weeks and retest all the horses. If even one showed up positive, we couldn't get a state certificate." Hunter shook his head, frowning. "Couldn't keep them penned that long, so we'd have to round them up again, and we're already way over budget."

"So the adoptions are off."

"Looks that way, unless they can raise the money for another roundup and testing later this year."

Bert reached for her slippers. "DeWitt would have known the adoptions would be canceled. But what was so important about twelve adoptions that he'd kill Shony and falsify records to cover it up?"

Hunter sat to lace up his high-sided leather shoes. "Shony would have been put down or removed the minute we found out he had swamp fever, even if it was in remission. DeWitt knew that."

"So he could have justified the pony killing to himself that way. But why take such a risk? I would think the veterinary association—or whatever they have—would take his license."

"What's worrying me is that those mustangs could have infected mainland horses. I can't believe DeWitt would be that irresponsible. He was one of the best vets around."

"Maybe he was planning to keep them quarantined until the two weeks were up."

Hunter started down the circular stairs from the loft. "I hope you're right. It still don't explain why he got killed, or Julie." He heaved a sigh Bert could hear all the way up the stairs. "Senator from Florida told me last night I better pay more attention to park business and less to outside interests. Looks like he was right."

"I assume he was referring to the nourishment negotiations, not me." Bert grabbed her robe and followed him down. She could see a couple of lights twinkling across the water. Otherwise, it was still dark outside. "What's with the dredging? When do you meet again?"

But Hunter was on the phone to Ernie, talking about the horses and foals. "Might as well just let them all go. We'll have to keep an eye on them, particularly Triton's band. If any go missing or sick, then we bring them back in for testing."

Bert felt sick to her stomach. She hadn't thought of that. Triton, that beautiful horse, could be in danger. When Hunter got off the phone, she asked, "Isn't there anything you can do? Vaccination or something?"

"No. Good thing it's winter. There aren't as many flies around, and EIA isn't all that contagious. We might get lucky. Besides, DeWitt always said Triton was immune."

"Then where did Shony get it?"

"Ernie said another horse went missing out of that band earlier this year, Charybdis's foal. Could be he died of it. Greg's taking Tanisha out this morning to get samples from all of Triton's family again before—"

The phone rang. Hunter reached. "O'Hagan. Yes, Ms. Fulchard. I'm sorry to say it's true, but how did you—?" Hunter listened, brows rising. "If we do that, we can't bring them over. We'd have to keep the twelve foals penned up on the island for at least two weeks. Cost some extra to keep staff there. The problem is, if another horse tests positive after the quarantine, it'd be too late to let them go."

Bert could hear Representative Lida Fulchard's voice from across the bar.

Hunter shook his head. "Lots of cold weather still to come. When they're with their bands, they run around, shelter in the woods. We don't have a barn, and they won't get exercise. That's going to put them at risk for pneumonia." Hunter listened, his mouth a straight line. He held the receiver away from his ear, took a deep breath, and exhaled. "Yes, ma'am. I certainly appreciate your support. I'm sure you understand I'm not in a position to make decisions for the National Park Service."

Lida went on about something at length.

Hunter shook his head, looking furious. "I, uh, I don't see how I could do that, Ms. Fulchard. Not when I have reason to believe—"

Even from where she stood, Bert heard the representative's raised voice. Finally, Lida paused.

"Yes, I understand they're bringing in a turtle trawler. Should have done that sooner."

Again, Lida Fulchard spoke at length.

Hunter's scowl deepened. "That's true. The tests did come in negative, both sets, but—" He listened in silence. "That's right. There's no record of another foal, but we believe the records were tampered with." Finally, he said slowly, "I understand your position. I'm certain we'll both continue to do what we believe is best for the public. Yes, ma'am. I appreciate what you're doing. Good day to you." He hung up the phone slowly and remained deep in thought. Finally, he raised his head. "How much of that did you hear?"

Bert shrugged. "Only that she was mad and doesn't want the adoptions canceled." Damn, that did it. No day off.

"Nothing else?"

"Uh-uh."

"Too bad. Would have been nice to have a witness."

"She tried to bribe you?" Bert wasn't surprised. Lida Fulchard's election campaigns were particularly vicious.

"More like threaten. If I recommend the dredging be resumed, she'll support me on canceling the adoptions and turning the twelve foals loose. Seems the project in Canaveral took some Ridleys, too. Take's up to six for the season, and seven's the limit." He reached for the phone again. "Now, she's saying Shony wasn't from Shackleford. She's saying someone dumped his body and that the park's causing problems where there are none. I gotta get hold of Blount before she does."

Bert ducked into the guest bedroom to pull out the clothes she planned to wear. Emerging, she asked, "You find Blount?"

"Left a message. He's in Detroit right now. Since he's director of the Foundation for Shackleford Horses, I'm sure he'll go along. Blount knows we can't risk infecting any mainland horses, and we can't leave the foals penned up all winter." Hunter had changed from his dress shoes to his work boots.

"You going out to the island?"

"I'm going to wait to hear from Blount. Then I'll open the gate myself. That way, if there's any trouble, they can't lay it on anyone else."

"You're expecting trouble?"

Hunter nodded. "Wild horses make headlines. The politicians know it, and so does the media. Lida Fulchard is going to turn this into a political football. Good thing the new superintendent hasn't been appointed yet. She'd have him fired before he began."

Bert watched Hunter climb into his car. It might be a good thing for the new superintendent, but it could go against Hunter.

How had Lida Fulchard found out about the foals so soon anyway?

Chapter 23

From the window, Bert watched Hunter's truck back down the driveway. Today was his day off, the last day of their week together. Sighing, she turned. The waters of the sound were dark, reflecting her mood.

Suddenly, Hunter's Mazda revved back up the drive. Bert glanced around, wondering what he'd forgotten. But when he came through the door, he looked at her.

She tipped her head in question.

He gave her that lopsided grin, holding out his hands. "I just realized it's Sunday."

"That's okay." Her voice was soft. "With all this going on, you have to go in. It's not a problem."

Pulling her into his arms, Hunter breathed into her ear, "I'll try to

216

get back early. Maybe we can drive into Beaufort for dinner, to that place you've been wanting to check out."

Bert snuggled up, pressing her hips against his. "Let's see what time you get home."

"You're right. First, the governor's calling. Next thing, I'll have the president himself on my back." Hunter's slate eyes bored deep into hers. "It's been good having you around, you know." His gaze shifted sideways for an instant, then returned to caress her. "To tell the truth, I don't want it to end." His chin nuzzled her hair. "You don't suppose we could make it permanent, do you?"

Bert jerked in surprise.

He winced. "I know this isn't the way to do things, but the problem is, um, I don't want you to move out tomorrow, and I might not have another chance to tell you."

Bert pressed her cheek to his shoulder. "I love you, too," she whispered into his jacket. She needed to hear him say it.

He chuckled. "Got it all wrong again." His arms tightened around her. "Hon, if you don't know by now I love you, you'll never know." He kissed her, his lips warm and coffee-flavored. "What do you say? Think you could stand to live here?"

Was he asking her to marry him or to live with him? Bert didn't want to press, afraid she'd be forcing a proposal. She wasn't ready for that, not with her history of falling for men with problems. Then she realized he was tense, waiting for her answer.

She brought her head up to gaze into his eyes, now a warm gray. "Oh, Hunter, there's nothing I'd rather do. I don't want to leave either. But what about when the restaurant opens? I work nights. You work days."

He held her tightly. "Don't you worry, hon. We'll find a way to be together. I promise."

"We have to figure out finances, too."

He grinned. "Come to think of it, you might be buying trouble. I could be out of a job by next week."

"I'm hiring tomorrow."

The phone rang.

Hunter held her tight for another moment, then broke away. "I just left, all right?"

Bert held the phone so he could hear, their bodies still meeting. It was Ernie.

Rolling his eyes, Hunter took the receiver from her. "I'm on my way." He started to put the phone down, then raised it again as the voice said something. Hunter tapped his forefinger against his thumb to show Ernie was running at the mouth, which was unusual for the reserved ranger. "Right. I figured we'd go over soon as I get the okay from Blount."

Ernie's voice rumbled.

"If you say so." Hunter frowned. "You don't have to go to the island. Probably better if I go it alone." Bert felt Hunter inhale deeply. Then he blew out before he spoke again. "I guess it won't hurt to wait until tomorrow. I was thinking the sooner the better, before Lida Fulchard makes more trouble." He nodded at something Ernie said. "You're the resource man. If that's how you want it, that's the way we'll do it. The vets are fixing to do more tests on Triton's band anyhow."

Hunter hung up and stared at the phone. "Strange. A minute ago, he was all for releasing the horses. Now, he wants to wait till tomorrow."

Bert barely heard him. Already, she was thinking of what she'd have to do to move in. "Maybe he had plans for today," she said. She could rent out the apartment, but not right away. There might be times she'd want to spend the night there, especially when she first opened up.

"Right. That's what he said." He put his arm around Bert. "You think he has a girl?"

"Who, Ernie? Purcell says he's got a thing for you. Ernie shaved off his beard when you did. Should I be jealous?"

Hunter sighed. "Back awhile ago, I tried to help him out some, but it didn't work. The man reads too much into everything."

"Oh?"

"He was raised in foster homes, you know. Ernie done good,

though. Worked two jobs and put himself through college and graduate school. Reckon he never had time for friends." Hunter's hands, moving over her back, were hot through the satin of her robe. "I feel for the man, but he's too intense, you know what I mean?"

He pulled her close and kissed her. As the kiss deepened, his hands tugged at the opening of her robe so Bert's bare breasts were pressed against the rough wool blend of his park shirt. When they finally broke for air, Hunter stepped back, running his hand slowly along the curve of her jaw as his eyes dropped to her breasts. "If I don't get going, I won't be able to leave," he said hoarsely.

"If you leave now, I'll kill you. Besides, I don't think it'll take very long."

Hunter chuckled, fumbling with his belt buckle. "I do believe you're right at that."

A little later, Bert again watched Hunter back down the drive. This time, he did not return.

Still wearing a smile of contentment, Bert showered, dressed, and sorted through her clothes, enveloped in that warm, confident glow that comes after making love.

How had Hunter known she was feeling bad? She'd been very careful not to let on. And then he'd come back to ask her to move in. She'd been thinking about it but had been afraid it was too soon. She'd learned with her husband and in two other relationships that seemingly minor problems—like Hunter's guilt over his wife's death, and Bert's insecurity because she was older than Hunter—could become major issues later.

Since they met last summer, Bert had been busy setting up the restaurant, and Hunter had been away to endless park meetings and training programs. Until this week, the most time they'd spent together was four vacation days in Charleston. Both their lives had been hectic and were probably going to stay that way. That could be trouble. But at least they'd have moments when they were home at the same time. And they'd be able to share a bed for part of most nights.

The phone rang. It was Rudy for Hunter. "You got the TV on?" he asked. "Lida Fulchard's on twelve."

Bert hit the remote. When she saw Lida's overly red mouth and too-white teeth, she pressed the record button on the VCR, in case Hunter wasn't watching.

The camera zoomed in on the state legislator. "I've been in touch with the acting superintendent at Cape Lookout," Lida Fulchard announced. "Although EIA is a dangerous disease, this isn't a serious outbreak. Only one horse has tested positive, a small foal. It died, but not from the fever, and I've requested an investigation. Until more studies can be made, the adoptions will go ahead as scheduled." She leaned forward and lowered her voice, as if imparting a secret. "Since the news was released, I've received many calls from constituents who are concerned about the wild horses. James Blount, director of the Foundation for Shackleford Horses, has assured me there will be no exterminations as were done in ninety-six."

Damn, Lida had gotten to Blount before Hunter did. Her staff probably found out where he was staying and got him out of bed. Hunter was going to be upset.

How had Lida Fulchard found out so soon? Only Greg, Hunter, and Ernie knew about the foal's testing positive. So it had to be one of them or someone they called. Greg was going to phone Tanisha, and Ernie probably told Purcell. But which one of the four called Lida? Purcell, maybe? He seemed to be carrying some kind of grudge against the park. Tanisha? Bert could think of no motive, unless it was connected to Purcell. That left Greg and Ernie. Would Greg, as veterinarian for the state, be looking to curry favor with Lida Fulchard? Why had Ernie changed his mind about letting the horses loose? Did he call Lida and let her reaction influence him? But what was in it for him? Would a state representative have enough influence over a park ranger to have him playing informant?

Bert walked to the phone, then stood undecided. She couldn't very well dial Greg, a state veterinarian she barely knew, and ask him whom he'd told about the tests. He'd tell her to mind her own business. Even

Ernie scared her a little. As a GS-13, the same pay level as Hunter, he ranked second in command. After what Rudy and Hunter had said, she didn't want to hurt his feelings or offend him. Purcell and some of the younger rangers sometimes amused themselves betting on who could get Ernie to say a complete sentence. From the glances he'd shot at them, Bert suspected he knew what they were doing.

Ernie was in the park meeting with Hunter. Maybe she could catch him after they were done.

Bert drove to the visitor center, circling around to the rear. There were several white government vehicles in the lot, along with Hunter's Mazda, Purcell's Jeep, and two other cars she didn't recognize. She parked between them, hoping one of them was Ernie's.

She was about to give up and go back to the house when Ernie emerged from the building. He walked with a natural grace, his jacket blousing just the right amount. Bert wondered if he had his uniforms specially tailored. She waited until he neared, then slid out of her car and started down the walk, as if she were on her way inside. She stopped, giving the ranger a big smile. "Hey, Ernie. Is Hunter still here?"

The ranger flushed, nodding his head.

He wore a wide-brimmed park hat, his short-cropped reddish curls cupping his ears and curling down his forehead, the edges of his front teeth visible between his lips, the tip of his nose bright pink. He reminded her of a well-dressed white rabbit. Bert blinked away the thought. She was here to get information. "What did you and Hunter decide to do about the foals?" Let him try to answer that with a yes or no.

Ernie frowned, pained. "We're waiting for Mr. Blount."

"Oh, you mean you haven't got hold of him yet?"

Ernie shook his head and tried to sidestep around her.

Bert put a hand on his arm, effectively bringing him to a stop. "Did Hunter tell you Lida Fulchard called?" she asked, looking up into his face. His eyes were a soft, clear blue, like a child's. Was it the pink rims and invisible lashes that made him appear so innocent, so vulnerable? Bert found her courage. "I've been wondering how she found out so soon.

Did you talk to Purcell or Vilma Willit or anyone after Hunter called you?"

The resource ranger ducked his head, cutting her a quick glance. "I called Purcell, to be certain he could cover."

"No one else?"

He shook his head.

Damn, she had to remember to stop asking yes-or-no questions. "So what's going to happen now?"

Ernie's pale brows rose slightly, his eyes darting toward the park building. "You want me to tell Hunter you're here?"

Nice comeback on his part. "Thanks, but I'm on my way in." Then Bert remembered something else. "Do you know when Julie's funeral's going to be?"

He shook his head again, as if that was all he was going to do, but then said in his soft, hesitant voice, "Why don't you, you know, call the foundation?"

"I still can't believe she's dead. It seems like just yesterday we were riding the beach." Bert cast around for something else to say, anything to prolong the conversation and get something from him. She'd ask about the turtles. That was his specialty. "Any more turtles wash up?"

He shrugged.

"You found the other one, didn't you? Julie said she saw you with the Ridley." For a moment, Bert thought she'd gotten under his skin.

He blinked, lips parting.

"Strange, that turtle just vanishing, isn't it?"

Damn. Her strategy to get him talking wasn't working. Ernie stepped off the concrete walk, glancing at his watch. "I don't mean to be rude. I have to be someplace."

"Yes, well, nice talking to you. Have a good day."

Again, his face softened as he looked down at her. He touched his hat in an old-fashioned gesture. "You, too."

That went better than expected, even if it didn't net her much information. Hopefully, she could do as well with Greg Statler.

An engine roared and tires squealed as Ernie hot-dogged out of the parking lot. Bert grinned. Apparently, he changed from a rabbit to a tiger behind the wheel. Or did Ernie have a hot date, after all?

Bert drove back to Hunter's and spent the next fifteen minutes trying to find a phone number for the state veterinarian. She hated looking up government listings. Finally, after three calls and endless choices of confusing options, a recording told her Greg was on the dredge in Morehead City and gave a number for the port authority. At least he was back from Raleigh. Bert started to call, then stopped. She'd been wanting to see how a dredge operated anyway. This was her chance. Not only would it give her an excuse to ask Greg about Lida Fulchard, but she could find out exactly what Clayton and Purcell did as observers.

Chapter 24

Bert drove to Morehead City as fast as she dared, hoping Greg wasn't in the eastbound lane headed home. As she crossed the Beaufort high-rise bridge, she could see the port's pastel blue water tower. A couple of freighters were docked near a mountain of wood chips. Behind the administration building, Bert glimpsed the dredge's bulky outline. She made a hairpin left at the railroad tracks onto a gravel road. As she drew up to the gate, a policeman, nattily dressed in navy blue and gold braid, stepped out.

"I'm looking for Dr. Greg Statler. His office said he's on the dredge." She tapped a manila envelope on the seat—the job applications for tomorrow—hoping the guard would think she was a secretary.

With a friendly smile, the guard stepped closer. "We're on orange alert, you know. Only authorized cars and trucks allowed, unless you have an okay from the chief of police. You speak with him?"

Bert shook her head. Damn Homeland Security and their cover-their-ass panics. What color would they use when something serious happened? "You mean I can't go inside? I have to deliver this."

"I can't leave my post or I'd take it." He frowned, then glanced up. "You know the chief?"

"No." Bert had an idea. "But I know the sheriff. Would that help?"

Her ID in hand, the guard called the sheriff, who got on a three-way with the chief of police. "Blonde, long hair." The guard peered at her. "Yup, hazel eyes. Don't look fifty-five." He winked at Bert. "Sure thing, chief." Pocketing his cell phone, the guard leaned on the open window and pointed to the right. "You can go in. Over there, berth six. But you can't go on board unless the captain gives us a written permit. Can't do that over the phone."

"I just have to give this to Dr. Statler."

"Follow the tracks under that derrick and around to warehouse three. You can park there." He gave her another smile. "How long do you think you'll be?"

Bert hesitated. She wasn't good at this. "I'm not sure. I guess it depends on what he wants me to do with these."

That seemed to satisfy the guard. "Go ahead. I'll be looking for you."

The port was a big square; except for the entrance road, it had four sides to water. Overhead, truck tires hissed as traffic crossed the bridge connecting Morehead City to Beaufort.

Minutes later, Bert was on the dock. Close up, the dredge was massive—a three-hundred-foot black barge with a four-story, dirty superstructure in the bow. From below, she could see several men inside the glass wheelhouse. Bert waved, yelling.

Two of the men came out. The larger one with glasses was Greg.

"Hey, Greg. It's Bert."

The state vet waved back and clattered down the metal ladder to the main deck. He leaned over, his collar-length brown hair blowing across his face. "Something wrong?"

"I was wondering if I could come aboard and look around. Hunter told me the next time I saw the dredge tied up, just to ask." She wasn't really lying.

Greg yelled up at the man on the flying bridge. "Okay if she comes aboard?"

The captain peered over. "I'm supposed to sign you in first."

"She's just wants a quick look, right, Bert?"

Bert nodded, waving the manila envelope. "The guard said it was all right for me to give this to Greg."

The captain said, "Okay, make it quick, and watch your footing. Don't want any liability suits." He pointed to a gangway leading to the bow.

Bert scrambled on, walking past the huge, flat center to the rear structures.

Greg followed her line of sight. "That's the hopper, or belly. Big pit down to the hull. Holds the sand they bring up. There's other kinds of dredges, too. Sidecasters—that's what you usually see in the inlets—have a cannon that shoots the sand over the side. And cutters. They're platform drills, like oil rigs."

Greg was bigger than she'd realized. "Are those what they use to suck up the sand?" Bert looked at the fat, black pipes along the side of the barge.

"Those pipes are called drag arms. Have a drag head attached to the end. See it?" Greg leaned over the rail, pointing. "Works just like a vacuum cleaner."

At the end of the drag arm, under the water, Bert could see something about the size of a Volkswagen. "No wonder the turtles have a problem. That looks big enough to swallow a killer whale."

Greg laughed, a high, soft laugh for such a large man. "The drag head lies flat against the sand. It's hard for anything big to get under it, just like a regular vacuum. There's a cowcatcher on the head, like the plow on a train, to push things out of the way."

"How do they get the sand to the beach?"

"When the belly's full, they go to a pipeline connected to the shore and pump everything out."

An officer came down the stairs. Greg introduced her to the captain, a tall, slender man with a military bearing. Bert thanked him for letting her come aboard. "I can't stay long, but I'd love to get an idea how this works."

The captain led the way down a fixed metal ladder. He motioned Bert ahead along a narrow corridor and through an oblong metal door. Inside, they crammed into a small space occupied by a chunky young man. "This is one of the mud suckers, our chief engineer. He can tell you about the machinery." The captain pointed behind the engineer.

To Bert's surprise, considering the worn exterior of the dredge, the machinery appeared new, the pipes all painted cream, the area brightly lit—no oil spills, rust, or dirt. After some small talk, the engineer explained how the impeller pumps and suction worked.

Bert listened patiently until he got to the part that interested her. "Doesn't the noise scare the turtles away?" She glanced at the diesel that drove the pump.

"We think they come in to feed on the stirred-up sand." Greg said. "That's how they get sucked up."

"What happens when one gets caught?"

"It usually gets chopped into bits by the impeller, although sometimes a small one comes through without injury." The engineer drew a rectangle, then ran a line across it. "Everything gets pumped through a big pipe with holes in it that runs over the belly. The water and sand drop out, but the big stuff, like shells or turtle parts, is forced to the end of the pipe and into metal cages."

"We get a lot of flounder and skates still flopping and alive," the captain added. "We throw them back. Sometimes, I imagine the flounder thinking, what in the hell was that?"

Standing practically under him, Bert glanced up, surprised by his flash of fantasy.

Encouraged, the captain continued. "You'd be amazed at what we bring up—lead fishing weights, musket balls. We picked up some human bones just last week."

That caught Greg's attention. "What makes you think they were human?"

"It was part of a backbone with a steel rod holding it together, about so big." The captain spread his hands.

"Where did it come from?" Bert asked.

He shrugged. "We have graves washed out all the time around here."

"They use steel rods to treat scoliosis." Greg had a distant look in his brown eyes.

The captain nodded. "Scoliosis, that's what the sheriff said."

"Do you think there was more, and it got chopped up?" Bert visualized a skeleton going through the impeller.

The engineer smiled at the look on her face. "We checked the baskets. There wasn't anything else."

Bert caught Greg looking at his watch. She'd better get them back to talking about the Ridley. "If nothing big can get under the drag heads, then what kills the turtles?"

Some kind of silent signal passed between the officers. Then the captain spoke. "The main problem is that when turtles get scared, they bury themselves in the sand. That's how they get sucked up." He turned to Greg. "We just welded bars across some of the drag heads. We're hoping that'll help."

Bert tipped her head. "The main problem? Are there other ways they get caught?"

The captain turned to the engineer, who took over. "The drag heads have to be winched off the bottom with big cables. If the vacuum mechanism is shut down before they're lifted, there's no danger to turtles."

The captain leaned forward. "That's where the trouble comes in. When the drag arms are full of sand, they're very heavy. It takes longer to winch them up, and it's hard on the cables. It's much quicker to lift the drag heads off the bottom while they're running. Flushes out all the sand."

"Flushing them would speed up operations, wouldn't it?" Greg said dryly. "The contractors would get their bonuses, right?"

"We told you we want full-time observers aboard," the captain said to Greg.

"National Marine Fisheries is taking care of it."

The captain nodded. "About time. We spend two thousand a day for turtle trawlers, nets, cages, and all. The company's been studying to find some kind of noise, like a mating call, to lure them away from the dredges. Even hired a professor to come on board and help sight turtles. We stop dredging the minute we see one."

"You actually want the observers aboard?" Again, the captain surprised Bert.

"I'm tired of being blamed for everything."

"Like what?" Bert asked.

"Had a bunch of seaweed come on the beach when we were offshore," the captain said in his flat tone. "They blamed it on us. Got chased by peacekeepers last fall." He turned to Greg. "Shrimpers killed ninety turtles off the coast of Georgia in one month, but they didn't get told to stand down."

Greg's broad face reddened. "I'm just here to show the men how to spot turtles and how to treat an injured one. But we'll have a full-time observer on board before you resume operations. Marine Fisheries is interviewing now."

Was Purcell one of them? Bert wondered. "How long do you stay out at a time?" she asked.

"We come in only for fuel and repairs—and when we get told to stand down," the captain growled. "We have two crews."

The engineer added, "Men are the most expensive commodity on a dredge. We work in shifts."

"It's ten thousand dollars off our contract every day we go over," the captain told Bert. "That's bonus money the crew's losing."

"It's costing the town a hundred thousand a day to have you stand by," Greg snapped.

The captain's brows raised. "Not my doing. In Florida, state law says all dredged sand has to be put on a beach or a spoil island. Saves a lot of money."

Bert multiplied a hundred thousand by five days, then by five again—the number of dredging jobs that had been ordered to stand down between North Carolina and Florida. That was two and a half million so far, plus half a million for each additional day. It was a lot of money—more than enough to bribe someone to hide a turtle.

"Do the observers get a bonus, too?" Bert asked as they climbed back above deck.

Greg shook his head. "Observers are paid by Marine Fisheries. Their pay has nothing to do with the contractors."

Would Lida Fulchard be able to influence the hiring of someone like Purcell by Marine Fisheries? Probably not, but as a legislator, she had a hand in the distribution of state monies. Bert turned to Greg. "Did Hunter tell you Lida found out about Shony and the EIA? She was on the news this morning."

Greg's brows lifted higher than the captain's. "Who told her?"

"That's what I was wondering," Bert said. "Did you call anyone after Hunter?"

"I called Tanisha. Sent her back to the carcass to run another test. Then I crashed and slept until ten."

"When did you do that? Call Tanisha, I mean."

"Right after I hung up with Hunter at five in the morning." Greg gave his high-pitched laugh. "She was spitting mad. Guess I got her up. I also reported the positive Coggins by fax to the Greenville office and USDA Veterinary Health."

There went that lead. Any one of them, including the agencies, could have called Lida Fulchard. Bert looked at her watch. "I'd better get back before that nice guard sends Tom Ridge after me." She paused, waiting for the captain to catch up.

"Did you learn anything?" Greg asked after they thanked the captain and were walking off the gangplank.

"Not really. I was hoping to figure out what happened to that missing Ridley."

"The one the spotter plane reported last week?"

Bert nodded. She'd forgotten about the plane. "If only it hadn't disappeared."

They picked their way over the tracks and around rusty container cars. Greg stopped by Bert's car. "Tide get it?"

Bert shook her head. "They pulled it up past the tide line. Hunter figures someone came by in a boat. I thought it might have been the dredge's Zodiak, but I don't anymore." Somewhere, a quantity of spilled menhaden meal stunk like rotten fish.

"You're right. Not while the captain's around. He's a good man." Greg looked thoughtful. "The wind's been making for some real high tides, you know."

Bert's eyes widened. "If the tide took the turtle, where would it go, down the beach?"

"No. Someone would have reported it by now." He tipped his head to the side. "Current could have taken it through Barden Inlet into Back Sound. Be hard to spot in there."

"Think anyone's asked the Hatteras pilot to keep an eye out for it? He's been flying down almost every day with Alton Huff."

Greg shrugged. "Give him a call."

As Bert crossed back over the drawbridge to Harkers Island, she realized she'd forgotten all about her boat. Tomorrow was Monday. Between Maintenance and the rangers, they'd be needing all the boat slips. The spotter plane would have to wait. The pilot wouldn't be working on Sunday anyhow.

She'd just changed into jeans and was putting on her shoes when Hunter walked in. Bert jumped up. "All right! Are you done for the day, or do you have to go back?"

"I got a couple of calls to make, but I'm fixing to do them from here. No messages?"

"Nope. I figured you picked them up."

"I did." He scowled. "Called Blount three times. Can't believe that man never checks his voice mail."

"What are you going to do? About the horses, I mean."

Tipping his stool back against the counter, Hunter leaned an elbow on the bar. "That's the problem. We got the twelve foals to be adopted separated and ready to come off the island. But we need a certificate of clean health from the state before we can transport them."

Bert nodded. "Which you can't get, since Shony had EIA."

"You got it." Hunter sat up. "I need to get the foals together with their dams before we release the herd. Otherwise, they'll never find each other, not to mention they'll be apart too long."

"And Blount has to agree to this, right?" She was beginning to understand the predicament.

He sighed. "The park and the Foundation for Shackleford Horses share management of the ponies. I can't call off the adoptions or let the foals go until I get their approval."

"But you can let the other horses out of the pens without their permission, right?"

"We already agreed to that. Fact is, I was supposed to let them go soon as the testing was done, but I held off, trying to find Blount."

"Doesn't the foundation have a second in command?" Bert asked.

"They got a new gal. The board appointed her just last month. I went to see her today, all the way to Newport. Didn't do any good. She wants to wait until she sees Blount. Says it won't hurt to leave the ponies in the pen another day." Hunter took a long breath. "I don't believe she understands all the problems. I'm also thinking someone's talking at her."

"Do you have a meeting tonight?"

"No. They wanted to have one, but I told them there was no way I could make it." He grinned. "Can't leave you alone the first night of our living together, now can I?" He jumped up and kissed the back of her neck. "How did your day go? What did you do?"

Bert leaned into him. "I tried to find out who told Lida about Shony."

"Any luck?"

"Not really." Bert told him about her trip to the dredge, then remembered her boat. "You know what? My boat's still at the park dock. I was just leaving to get it when you came in."

"Guess we'd better pull it quick, before I have to give you a ticket."

Bert glanced out the window. The sky was beginning to change color. She grabbed her jacket. "Let's go, then."

Between the two of them—one in the boat, one in the car—they had the little runabout out of the water in minutes. Back on land, motor flushed, boat hosed off, straps secured, Hunter leaned against the car, facing the sound. "Looks like we're getting a sunset tonight."

Birds circled a sand bar, outlined by the setting sun. The sky above was piled high with ragged, fluffy clouds colored flaming red and orange, extending far over their heads and bathing them with a fiery glow.

They ambled to the narrow sound-side beach. To the left was Core Banks, almost invisible over the salmon-tinted waters, save for the lighthouse rising from a smudged line near the horizon.

"I don't like winter, but at least it gives us spectacular sunsets," Bert murmured, slipping her arm around Hunter's waist. "That lighthouse is a picture." Its black and white diamonds were pink under the reflected glow; its light sparkled like a diamond against the deep red clouds.

"People been saying that for a hundred and forty-four years now."

Bert did a little mental math. "You mean it was built before the War Between the States?"

"Right before. This was the first of the big lighthouses. The original one was only a hundred feet high. The standing joke in those days was that by the time you saw the light, you were aground."

"They take the old one down?"

Hunter shook his head.

"What happened to it?" The sun was sinking over Beaufort Inlet, the reds turning into purples.

"The Confederates held Fort Macon until 1862. They had pickets at the lighthouse. When the Union soldiers came nosing around, our boys would pose as locals and give them all kinds of misinformation." Hunter grinned. "Then, after Fort Macon was taken in sixty-two, the Confederates had to get out in a hurry. But before they left, they vandalized both the lighthouses. Problem was, both were still standing, and the Federals had the light back up and running in no time."

"The Confederates must have returned." Bert stared at the single tower.

"Took them until sixty-four, but our boys came back, all right. Why don't we head to the house? I'll tell you about our Confederate spy over dinner. We got reservations in Beaufort for seven."

Chapter 25

Cape Lookout, 1864

Finola

"What devilment do the scum plan now? We're almost to Beaufort."

Finola pricked her ears and turned her head to see what concerned her mistress. A corpulent man blocked the center of the road, legs spread, a long rifle cradled in his arms.

The mare's rider leaned forward, muscles tightening. Finola's mistress had been anxious ever since they'd left Colonel Whitford, constantly fingering the packet that rustled under her riding skirt. But the girl did not tug on the reins or tell the mare to slow. So Finola continued her rapid canter, not coming to a stop until her chest was within feet of the armed guard. Gravel and sand sprayed in a most satisfying manner.

Jumping away, the paunchy bluejacket and his companion spat curses and shouted at them. "What you think you is doing?"

Finola's rider gave a little gasp, her heel digging into the stirrup.

The palomino danced back, ready for flight. "I do apologize, captain," the girl said in her prettiest tone. "I cannot fathom what gets into my mare when she sees those uniforms. I trust none of you brave gentlemen were harmed by that little bit of grit."

"Sergeant Johnson," the guard growled, not mollified by the increase in rank. "Get down off that horse. Now." He glared from dark eyes buried in fleshy folds.

Now, fear emanated in waves from the girl. She took a deep breath. "Whatever for, sergeant? Why, I passed through here just yesterday."

"Orders," the Northerner snarled. "Ain't no one going through 'cept they gets searched." He jerked his head toward a rough plank building. "They got a woman inside to do the likes of you proper." He signaled the private to approach.

Trembling slightly, Finola's mistress rested her hand on the mare's neck. "If you'd be so kind as to hold her steady . . . She's a mite skittish today."

As the soldier reached for the bridle, the girl tapped once on Finola's neck.

Finola knew what that meant. Snorting in the soldier's face, the mare reared, her forefeet raking the man's chest as he jerked back. She continued to buck around the soldiers, alert for the order to bolt.

The bluejackets leapt out of her way with angry cries while her mistress pulled on the reins and shouted for Finola to stop. But the mare paid no heed. This was all part of the game.

The sergeant lifted his rifle, the long bayonet flashing in the sun. "You get that horse quieted, or so help me, I'll run her through."

"No, no. Don't." The girl jerked on the reins, at the same time tapping Finola's neck three times. "Whoa, girl, whoa," she said.

The mare came to a snorting halt. With a pleased shake of her head, she waited for the praise that always followed this maneuver. Instead, the sergeant was yelling at her mistress. "Get down 'fore I pull you off!"

Finola's rider lifted her knee off the horn and slid off the sidesaddle, landing in a heap on the ground. The sergeant stepped forward. Finola made a head thrust, snorting a warning. "No, Finola, friend," her mistress breathed, scrambling to her feet as the sergeant lifted his bayonet.

Leaving Finola by the guard post, reins dangling to the ground, the girl walked across the road, the Yankee close behind, his weapon still at the ready. The mare watched her go, torn between the desire to protect and the need to follow commands.

A soldier came slamming out of the plank headquarters building. He was a sturdy, young bluejacket with shiny black hair under his cap, trousers neatly tucked into his boots. Finola nickered a welcome. He always had sugar for her and a smile for her mistress.

He jerked to a stop, shading his eyes to stare at the horse and the party crossing the road. Then, waving his cap, he loped toward the sergeant and his prisoner. "Where have you been, Miss Mary Frances? I had given you up for lost."

Finola's mistress started at his use of her name, but she straightened her shoulders and called back, "My dear friend, I am very happy to see you. There appears to be some kind of misunderstanding. This brave officer"—she indicated the sergeant—"says I must be searched. I do believe he takes me for a spy. Can you imagine?"

"They haven't frightened you, my dear, have they?"

"You know this woman?" the sergeant demanded.

"With all due respect, sergeant, this *lady*"—the young soldier emphasized the word—"does not come to cross the line. She comes to see me, Edward McMurray. Right, my sweet?"

The sergeant scowled, lower lip protruding. "Why didn't she say so?"

Mary Frances ran to the young man's side. "I feared to say too much, sir." Taking the soldier's arm, she raised her face to the sergeant with an apologetic smile. "Folks about here don't take kindly to their women visiting with y'all." She glanced pointedly toward the headquarters building. "I thought it wise to be discreet."

Finola ambled toward them. She wanted her treat.

The bluejacket leaned over and bussed Mary Frances's cheek. "She risks being ostracized to see me. Am I not a lucky man, Sergeant Johnson?"

Mary Frances twirled away, laughing. "You must not take such liberties, my dear Edward. Whatever will this good man think?" She smiled up at the sergeant, then bowed her head modestly, letting her golden curls tumble forward.

"He will think I'm a very fortunate man." Tucking Mary Frances's hand under his arm and picking up Finola's bridle, the soldier turned to Sergeant Johnson. "Is that not so, sergeant?"

Rifle butt resting on the ground between his legs, the sergeant watched with narrowed eyes. Then he turned away, grunting, "Women got no place on the line. Be gone."

Two hours later, Finola preened and blew as Mary Frances wiped her down in hurried, nervous strokes. "I was so scared, Uncle Charles. Why, if that nice young man had not come to my rescue, I would be in prison this moment."

"Damn Yankees." The balding man helping Mary Frances curry the flaxen and gold horse looked up. "Is he a sympathizer?"

Mary Frances shook her ringlets. "Not to my knowledge. He's just the politest man, and he always carries a treat for Finola." Blushing, the girl picked some pebbles from under Finola's shoe. "I believe he's sweet on me."

"I don't blame him," the man said. "Tell me, what would this Yankee do if he discovered you carry letters for Josiah Bell?"

Mary Frances jumped, her eyes darting. "Hush, uncle. Pray, do not even say the name. I came to Beaufort rather than travel directly to him."

"The sergeant had you followed?"

"I'm not certain, uncle." Mary Frances scratched the mare's withers. "I thought I heard a horse behind me. Once, Finola looked around and neighed, and there was an answering whinny." At her uncle's exclamation, she added, "But it could have come from any stable in the vicinity."

"It's time you give up this activity."

Mary Frances dropped her voice. "First, I must deliver this packet.

There are urgent arrangements to be made." Her serious demeanor turned to laughter as Finola tried to steal a toffee from her pocket. She threw a blanket over the mare. "I have a favor to ask of you, dear uncle. Could you send a messenger? But not from this house, for I fear it is being watched."

"Of course, my dear. I know just the man." He rapped his cane against the floor, startling Finola. "It aggravates me I cannot do more."

Two weeks later, Finola and her mistress waited in the dark woods. They had been standing in the drizzle of the April night for several hours. Finally, they heard the clink of metal and then the tramp of many feet. Mary Frances leaned forward, sighing her relief. "Speak, Finola," she whispered.

Tossing her head, Finola gave a loud neigh, followed by two snorts. Shortly, an owl hooted twice. Mary Frances waited until the men appeared in the path. Then she and Finola led the way up the road to Crow Nest Plantation.

Stopping at a small barn, Finola and her rider entered, followed by a line of tattered men carrying rifles. Once all were inside, they shut the door. Only then did Mary Frances light the many lanterns that had been left in readiness. "There are Federal sympathizers among us. We must take precautions," she explained to the captain. "I dare not house you at the plantation."

"Do not fret, my lady." He motioned to the pallets, blankets, and clean hay that had been set out for the men. "We have been on the move for three days now. Just to sleep dry will be a great comfort."

The miasma of stale sweat and fusty swamp mud that rose from the soldiers was soon made worse by the smoke of their tobacco. Finola snorted repeatedly, but no one took notice. The men dropped to the pallets, some curling up under blankets, shivering. The soldiers revived, however, when Mary Frances's father arrived bearing two flasks. Tin cups suddenly appeared in many hands.

Mary Frances bent over a youth in a ragged gray uniform to examine the wrappings on his feet. Many of the soldiers had been limping. One lay tossing under a spread coat while his comrade offered his canteen.

Sipping from his cup, the captain joined Mary Frances and her father. "It has been a terrible hard trek from South River."

"Mother, preserve me," added the Confederate soldier with the bandages. "We got in swamps with two foot of water and mud that sucked the shoes right off our feet."

"We suffered from the pests, too. 'Tis a wonder we got blood left to stain a bandage."

Standing in the center of the barn by the lanterns was a ruddy-faced, older man in civilian dress who had arrived after the soldiers. He examined the Confederate detachment, eyes bright under bushy, gold brows. "Have you no boots for the men?" Josiah Bell asked the captain.

The captain spat. "We've not seen the clothing wagon for three months. We have no boots, no shoes, no tents, not even munitions for this raid. And now, less then half my men are fit for duty."

"No dynamite? Then how do you propose to destroy the light-houses?"

"Gunpowder, friend Josiah." He jerked his head toward the door. "My men had to wrest a hundred-pound keg and one of fifty pounds over ten miles of the worst terrain I've seen—damned near impassable. We forded a river where the water was saddle-seat deep. Past there, the marsh bottom was very bad."

He gestured at the man tossing under a blanket. "The mule gave out, and my men had to carry the powder kegs the rest of the way. Half the detachment was taken with chills and fever. We were compelled to throw off the third keg of powder and some of our munitions."

Finola whinnied as Mary Frances approached, but the girl paid her no heed. Instead, she addressed the ruddy-faced man. "Mother attends to a hot meal for the men right now."

The captain touched his hat. "Our eternal gratitude, Miss Mary Frances. It is fine Southern ladies like you and your mother that make our hardships bearable."

"How long will you stay?" At the captain's hesitation, she added, "On occasion, a runner gets through the blockade with shoes."

"You can speak freely before Miss Mary Frances. She has risked death carrying our letters across Yankee lines," Josiah Bell told the captain. Then he turned to Mary Frances. "They're fixing to leave for the cape tomorrow night, providing all is quiet in Beaufort."

Finola blew. Mary Frances circled her arm about the mare's neck. "Oh, my, I can scarcely believe it slipped my mind. Why, I promised to attend church with my Beaufort cousins. After the services, we shall take a little stroll along the waterfront." She winked at Josiah, who sighed but nodded his approval.

Finola and Mary Frances were back at Crow Nest Plantation before noon the next day. Josiah Bell and the captain awaited their return at the end of the long entrance road.

"I am told the two Federal gunboats remain anchored in Lookout Bight. I saw no steam, not even from the widow's walk atop my cousins' house," she informed the men. "The bluejackets were strutting about the waterfront as usual." A gleeful smile appeared on Mary Frances's lips. "I trust they'll not be bragging this time tomorrow." She eyed Josiah, who held Finola's reins. "I have been thinking."

"That is a dangerous thing to do, Miss Mary."

"Do be serious, Josiah. How, may I ask, do you plan to get the powder kegs to the lighthouses? Those men are plumb wore out."

"I have fishing boats waiting downriver. They're fixing to carry the men to the cape."

"Yes, to be sure," Mary Frances said, caressing Finola's forehead. "But where will you put in?"

Josiah eyed her from under his bushy brows. "There's a slew north of the light, about two miles, I reckon. Why do you ask?"

Mary Frances slid off Finola's back. "Seems to me they could use a horse to carry that powder." She busied herself loosening the saddle girth.

"Lord, Henny, God!" Josiah exploded, startling Finola. "You will do no such thing. If need be, we shall take a mule over."

Mary Frances smiled, removing the saddle and giving Finola a pat on the rump. Finola nickered and trotted to the water trough as the trio watched. Her thirst satisfied, she wheeled, nosed open the stable door, and entered.

"Does she close the door, too?" the captain laughed as they followed her into the stable.

"Finola is the cleverest horse Down East—in the entire state, I dare say." Mary Frances reached in her pocket for a toffee. "She comes from the Salters' Kerrygold, you know. My granddaddy said he was out of an Irish stallion named Finn-gall."

"Clever play on the name Finn-gall, Finola." Josiah approached and stroked the mare's nose. The palomino stood still, not responding until Mary Frances nodded. Then she lipped his hand, making him laugh.

"She will not utter a sound, not a whinny or a snort, when she is so instructed. Can you find a mule who will do that?"

"You have my answer, dear girl. Do not waste your time arguing."

Mary Frances laid a small hand on Josiah Bell's sleeve. "With all due respect, sir. My horse and I have ridden dusty roads. I have swallowed my mortification at the hands of the Yankees and among my own acquaintances. Indeed, I have taken pleasure in doing so. But now that they search all who pass through the Union line, my usefulness is ended." She clutched Finola's neck and looked up at Josiah. "I want a chance to see one mission to the end. I will stand back and leave with the first boat. There are no Federals at the lighthouse, and you expect no resistance, true?"

"There are two gunboats with over one hundred soldiers within shouting distance."

"We shall be gone before they can get up enough steam to leave their anchorage, and they cannot follow our boats into the sound. The Drain is much too shallow." There was triumph in Mary Frances's voice.

Josiah sighed, shaking his head. "The explosions and fires will be seen along the mainland for miles. We must get the men ashore before the Yankees have time to muster a detachment. You can rest assured they will search every road, every house, and every barn. This is no time for poling a raft that carries a horse."

Mary Frances drooped, her weight on the mare's neck. Then she straightened. "There are many horses on the islands. Some are wild, some belong to the Ca'e Bankers, but all run free." She hugged Finola. "You shall run wild for a fortnight. It will do you good, my sweet."

Josiah threw up his hands. "Lord, have mercy. You're harder to reason with than a stump."

"You agree?"

"No. Your father would come after me with his pistol. He barely speaks to me now."

Mary Francis pouted, combing Finola's long, white tail. She said hesitantly, "Pray, take my horse then."

Josiah raised his brows. "Take your mare?"

"Name me an animal more suited. You know the islands are rife with Federal sympathizers. She will not jeopardize the mission with a whinny or neigh."

"That is a mighty generous offer." He rocked back and forth on his heels, then shook his head. "Your mare will not obey me or a stranger."

"But she will listen to Sonny."

"Your stable boy?"

"He rides and trains her." Kissing his cheek, Mary Frances smiled at the older man. "It is the solution, my dear Josiah."

That evening, having been delivered to the cape by raft the moment it grew dark, Finola stood in a small clearing whisking mosquitoes and munching thistles. Around them, dogwood bloomed in ghostly drops, night herons called, and mockingbirds sang from the thickets. But her mistress was ill at ease. She paced the sand, peering through the pine branches and slapping at the pests. Sighing, she tucked several strands of gold hair back under the checkered stable cap she wore.

Finola gently nipped her neck, then hung her nose over Mary Frances's shoulder, rolling back her upper lip to savor the strange smell that rose from her mistress's clothes.

With a chuckle, Mary Frances reached up and hugged the horse. "You don't understand why I'm in Sonny's clothes, do you?" She sighed. "Josiah will be furious. Moreover, if we fail, they will blame me. I'm scared that if by any mischance someone reports our boats, the Federals will be waiting at the lighthouse."

She cupped Finola's face in her hands, laying her cheek to the horse's nose. "I fear for you, too, my love. I cannot take you back. But I will return for you, I promise."

Finola nuzzled her mistress, blowing but not making any sound, as she'd been told.

The moon shone over nearby Shackleford. Through the fragrant pines, Finola spied a herd of horses across the tidal flat known as "The Drain." She wanted to neigh to them, but after a quick glance at Mary Frances, she tossed her head instead. Then she heard the sound of water slapping wood and scented the men from the barn. She nudged Mary Frances, who leapt to her feet.

The girl drew some canvas lashings from the brush and began to strap them onto Finola. The mare curled around curiously. She had never seen anything like this. Her ears pricked, and her tail went up. This was far more fun than standing around.

A few minutes later, Finola no longer thought it was fun. The soldiers tied two great kegs to the canvas bags. One weighed far more than the other, making it difficult for her to keep an even gait. Not only that, the barrels bounced against her ribs with each step. The mare eyed her mistress.

"It's all right, girl," Mary Frances whispered into her ear, keeping her blackened face low. "I'll be right at your side."

Finola followed her mistress through the woods, then onto the berm of the sound beach. The kegs hung heavy on her back and bruised her ribs, and the canvas straps chafed her belly. Twice, she stopped to bite them loose, but Mary Frances was quick to soothe her and rub her nose. "I know, I know, but just a little farther."

They reached a beach bisected by water. "It's The Drain," her mistress breathed into her ear. "Quiet, Finola. Quiet."

The wet sand was soft under her hooves. Soon, the water lapped her knees, the mare's hooves sinking into the mix of mud and sand. Between the ooze that sucked at her feet and the unbalanced kegs dangling from her sides, Finola staggered like a man in his cups. Mouth tight, afraid she would fall, she rolled a pleading eye at her mistress.

Suddenly, the worst happened. As she pulled up one hoof, the big keg on the opposite side dragged her down. She stumbled forward, only to sink deeper. Then she was down on her side, the barrel digging into her ribs.

Mary Frances was in the water with her, holding her head up. "Get up, girl. You can do it."

Sucking air, Finola rolled off the keg. She gathered herself and kicked up on her front feet. With her hindquarters still down, the hated barrels slipped farther back.

Mary Frances tugged at the reins. "Up, girl, up."

Water lapping her rump, Finola crouched and sprang. She stumbled, fought for balance, and managed to remain on her feet. Through ringing ears, she heard her mistress's soft voice. The mare's flanks heaved, and her legs trembled. Mary Frances was at her neck, patting and whispering, but Finola had had enough. She hung her head, her body stiff.

"Please, girl, you can do it."

Finola shuddered.

"Mary Frances?" A voice hissed like a snake. Josiah splashed up and yanked off her cap. "Arrgh! Your father will have my hide."

He threatened her mistress? Nose tight, muscles swelling, neck rippling with effort, Finola took a step forward, then another. Then she curled around to glare at the man next to Mary Frances. But they stood close together smiling and applauding her effort.

After a moment, Finola lowered her head and plodded forward again. The water began to recede, the bottom grew firm, and soon they were on dry sand again. She almost whinnied her relief, but a quick, whispered "Quiet," stopped her.

The kegs were removed, the cinch belt taken off and buried in the sand. Finola could no longer see the soldiers, but she heard them as they made their way to a tall, dark shadow that ended in a glow of light brighter than any lantern or even the moon. Off to the side, an old tower, shorter, stood silhouetted against the starlit sky.

After an interval, the brush rustled and snapped, the sand squeaking as several men approached. Finola alerted Mary Frances, who stiffened, squinting into the night. But as the people reached the clearing, Mary Frances relaxed, whispering greetings to the keepers of the light.

The keepers and Mary Frances stood motionless, facing the towers, their breathing rapid and shallow. Sweat born of fear filled the air. Their anxiety made Finola uneasy.

Then came a flash of light, followed by another flash and two tremendous explosions that shook the ground under Finola's feet. She reared and whinnied before she could stop. Ashamed, she hung her head, but Mary Frances did not seem upset. Her attention was on the crackling sounds.

Feet thumped the sand as the raiding party retreated to the beach, where the others waited.

A gigantic tongue of fire shot into the sky. The entire wooden frame of the smaller lighthouse was burning, sending flames high into the air and lighting up the beach. Smoke and the sharp smell of gunpowder filled Finola's nostrils. The fire glowed so brightly Finola could see beads of sweat glistening on the soldiers' faces.

"The Fresnel is out!" the captain hooted as he arrived. "We destroyed the light." Rebel yells resounded.

The beam of the new lighthouse was gone. Not only that, but oil-fired flames enveloped the brick tower and spread from the fuel sheds. A jagged crack, pulsing red from the inferno inside, ran up the side of the monolith. Nearby trees smoldered; one burst into flames. Fire roared, and heat-generated wind tugged at Finola's mane.

They could not stay to admire their success. Finola, with Mary Frances astride, trotted back toward the boats, the soldiers jogging behind them. But when they reached The Drain, Mary Frances slid off her back. Holding Finola's face in her hands, she kissed her on the nose, then pointed across the flats to the island where Finola had seen the herd. "Go," she said in a choked voice.

Finola turned her head so she could see her mistress clearly. Mary Frances nodded, tears flowing. "Go, Finola. I'll come back for you. I promise."

Behind them, footsteps crashed through the brush. On the water, the steamboats' lights, once so far away, were now very close. Angry voices shouted, and guns cracked.

Mary Frances's hand slapped Finola's rump. "Now, go. Go."

This must be a new game. Always eager to learn, Finola curved her neck, holding her head in tight, her ears forward. Then, with a swish of her tail, she leapt over the now-dry tidal ditch and galloped into the night.

Spring passed into summer. One clear June day, Josiah Bell found Mary Frances riding a large, brown horse along the bank of the North River. He reined up, and Mary Frances slowed to a walk. "I have just come from your stables. Finola's paddock is empty, and you ride a strange mount. Something has happened to her?"

Mary Frances turned her large, blue eyes on him. She shook her head mutely.

"Then your father is punishing you?"

"No, he does not know. No one knows."

Josiah raised bushy brows. "You did return to Shackleford after the fury was over?"

"Yes, I returned."

"You could not find the mare?"

"I found her, Josiah," Mary Frances whispered, "but I could not bring her home."

"Why ever not?"

"I found her in a meadow with the most beautiful stallion I have ever seen, a chestnut with a flaxen mane just like hers and a whelk-shaped blaze on his forehead. He had one foreleg resting on her back, like a lover would put his arm around his beloved, and they stood with noses touching." Mary Frances wept as she spoke, but there was wonder in her voice. "Do you think I shall ever find a love like that?"

"I do not doubt it for a minute," Josiah assured her. "As a matter of fact, I am here to ask you to dine with us this Sunday. A friend of my wife, Elijah Hancock, will be visiting. I do believe you two shall get along splendidly."

Chapter 26

Had Elijah Hancock and Mary Frances fallen in love? Bert awoke spooned into Hunter, her arm over his waist. The name Elijah brought to mind black frock coats and stovepipe hats.

"What time is it?" he mumbled.

"About five of, Monday. The alarm's going off any second." She cuddled in. "Whatever happened to Mary Frances? Did she ever find someone as nice as you?"

Hunter chuckled. "I wouldn't know about that, but she did marry Elijah Hancock."

"In that day and age, I'm surprised they let her ride around alone."

"Well, now," Hunter drawled, "I took a few liberties about the cape part."

"Don't tell me." She thought for a minute then asked, "But they did destroy the two lighthouses?"

"All that was left of the old lighthouse was some of the brick that was under the wood frame. Next time you're over there, walk around back. You can see the mound where it was. After the war was done, they fixed up the new one, put in another Fresnel lens, metal stairs, and all that. But it didn't get painted with black and white diamonds until seventy-three." He rolled over and planted a kiss on her mouth. "You want to get your shower first?"

By eight-thirty that morning, Bert had the restaurant open, the heat on high, the files spread out. She paced around waiting for Linda, her dining-room manager, to show. Even though the sky was overcast, the two floor-to-ceiling glass walls let in a lot of light. They let in cold, too. Bert pulled her jacket tighter. She didn't plan to have the restaurant open in the winter anyhow.

Outside, the landscape had taken on the characteristics of a black-and-white picture. The water shimmered silver as the sun leaked through leaden clouds, glinting on oily waves. The lowlands lining the pewter bay formed a dark, rolling border, clumps of bare trees fanning out like skinny, dead mushrooms. High overhead, a wedge of pelicans glided in formation.

Bert spun around. The spotter pilot. This was the perfect time to catch him before he took off for the day. She'd been meaning to express her regrets about Julie anyhow. After all, he was Julie's cousin and a park employee.

Bert had to go through a number of people to get connected to the hangar. "Jerome Piner," the pilot finally answered.

Stumbling, Bert told him how sorry she was about Julie and asked if the funeral had been scheduled. Then, feeling like a turd for using her friend's death as an excuse, she led into the turtle. "The other thing I called about was to ask if you'd seen any turtle carapaces around Back Sound, by Barden Inlet."

"How many do you want? Big one on Hunk of Hair Island, been there for years."

Bert chuckled politely, still uncomfortable. "There's really an island called that?" Then she added, "I didn't mean an old carapace. I meant a dead turtle, a Ridley."

"You mean like the one on Shackleford, across from Bald Hill Bay? What happened? I heard they lost it."

"We were thinking maybe the tide washed it up somewhere around the inlet, where the boats couldn't spot it."

"I'd report anything like that—horse carcasses, dead dolphins. That's my job. Had a small whale stranded by Ocracoke two days ago."

"Did they get it off?"

"Sure did. They had it on TV and all. You know, I'll be bringing Agent Huff down later today. We'll take a quick . . ."

Gravel crunched. Linda was pulling in, another car right behind her. Their first interview.

The pilot was still talking. ". . . or would you like me to call you?"

"No, that's all right. Just let Cape Lookout know if you see anything." Bert thanked him, vowing to herself to make an effort to look him up at the funeral. She hung up as Linda walked in.

Linda had worked for Bert in Swansboro and, to Bert's relief, was helping with the interviews. Bert was swayed by first impressions and hated to say no if someone really wanted a job, even when she knew it wouldn't work.

"Sorry I'm late." Linda handed Bert a penciled form. "I took this one on the fly. He came knocking at the door just as I was leaving. He looked good, so I had him fill out an application and follow me here."

It was a high-school senior by the name of Goodwin. Of average height and sporting hair cut above his ears, he seemed quite self-possessed for his age. To Bert's surprise, she saw on the application he'd been working as a stable hand for DeWitt.

"I'm free nights and weekends. I graduate in May. Then I'm available anytime." Goodwin gave her a brilliant smile full of white teeth surrounded by smooth, golden skin.

"You're not planning to get another job after gradua . . . ?" Could that question be considered discrimination? There was so much you couldn't ask, even about their health.

"I'm going to college in the fall. Got into the N.C. State vet program. That's like premed." He gave the women another large smile. "I can work summers for the next four years, maybe longer. And I'll be available to help out holidays. That's when you're the busiest anyhow, right?"

Linda was nodding. They hired college kids as extra hands during the summer rush.

Bert said, "I see you were working for DeWitt Brigman. What if whoever takes over his practice wants to keep you on?"

The boy shook his head. "His lease was up. There's a feed store coming in. But even if he hadn't died, my job was done next month."

"Really, why?" Linda jumped in.

"He wasn't firing me or anything," the boy was quick to explain. "He was moving to Croatan Farms. They hired him full-time, built him a lab and all. But they didn't need me. Croatan Farms has their own hands."

"Lab?" asked Bert.

Goodwin nodded, leaning forward. "That's why I was working for him. My major is veterinary science. DeWitt was into genetics and bioengineering."

"Cloning?"

"No. More on dominant traits and inherited immunities. That's what he was doing in Alaska."

"I didn't know that." Bert started to say something else, but Linda coughed. "One more question, then back to business. If he was closing his practice, where was he going to keep the Shackleford ponies?"

"He'd planned to keep them in the stables next to his new lab."

Bert almost missed it. Then his use of the past-perfect tense sank in. "You mean he changed his mind?"

The boy hesitated. "Look. The man's dead, and he was my boss. I don't want to say anything I shouldn't."

"I'm glad you feel loyalty toward your employer. That's the way it should be." Bert dropped her voice. "I'm the one who found DeWitt's body. This is not about a lawsuit or getting him in trouble, but it's important to me."

Goodwin frowned, thinking, then said, "It was just a phone call I overheard. He asked the foreman if he could keep the ponies in the west-end pens instead of by the lab. I thought it was kind of strange. That's miles from anywhere."

Relief flooded Bert. DeWitt hadn't been totally irresponsible. He was planning to keep the foals isolated until he was sure they were free of EIA. "That's great news."

The boy's dark eyes narrowed.

"I'm just relieved to hear he was making provisions for the ponies."

"Whatever."

"Linda, if he could get along with DeWitt, I'm sure he'll do a great job for us. And we get the services of a scientist in the making."

Linda smiled. "Are you over eighteen?"

"Will be by Easter." The boy bounced up. "Does that mean I'm hired?"

Linda was good at this, Bert thought. You couldn't ask how old they were, just if they were over eighteen, so they could carry drinks to the tables. Employees had to be twenty-one to bartend.

"You'll start out bussing and work your way up." Linda pulled out a sheet and began going over the restaurant's policies and procedures.

They were finished before two. They'd pushed the last applicant out the door with the woman still running at the mouth. Going up-stairs to her apartment, Bert flipped on the TV to catch the weather channel while she folded her wash and packed some clothes to take back to Hunter's. She watched the announcer pointing out a gray mass of clouds off the Florida coast. They were overdue for a northeaster. Sure enough, that's what the weatherman was predicting. A northeaster was expected to reach the Outer Banks sometime tomorrow.

Back at Hunter's, Bert had to find room to put her things. The small guest-room closet accommodated most of her clothes, and the dresser would do as a makeshift desk for her laptop. By the time Hunter walked in the door, she had a Thai curry with coconut milk, pink shrimp, and sugar peas simmering on the range, the stereo playing mood music in the background. He came over to the stove and nuzzled the back of her neck. That reminded her of the first time they'd made love on Portsmouth.

He must have thought of it, too, as he made a point of glancing out the window. "Better close up tight," he laughed. "Looks like some tall weather coming." That's what he'd said to her that evening.

"You heard there might be a nor'easter on its way?"

"It's a given. NOAA says conditions are ripe for a good one. Big cold front dropping down, another coming in from the southwest with some strong, upper-level winds to suck the moisture up from the gulf." He walked to the phone, raising a brow at Bert.

She shook her head. "Vilma wants you, and you had a couple of other calls—dentist on Wednesday. Nothing from Blount."

Hunter played the messages, then got on the phone and dialed a series of phone numbers from a dog-eared scrap of paper. At each, he left a message for the foundation director, telling him a nor'easter was expected by noon the next day. Finally, he put the phone down, only to have it start ringing a minute later.

At Hunter's nod, Bert answered. It was the detective at the sheriff's office. She handed the phone to Hunter. "It's Ramirez. Says Agent Huff asked him to call."

Hunter listened, nodding. Then he exclaimed, "You don't say!" Bert jumped up. He held the receiver slightly open, so she could hear.

". . . left it out to drift. If Miss Bert hadn't dug up that body, we'd have taken it for an accidental drowning. They's going over the boat now for prints." Ramirez might be of Hispanic origin, but his speech was pure North Carolina.

"Now, that's right interesting," Hunter said.

"We got some findings on the autopsy, too. Want to hear them?"

"Go ahead."

"Like we thought, DeWitt Brigman was killed by a blow on the back of the head by some kind of blunt metal object. Found some rust chips. They think maybe a hammer or mallet. Agent Huff's got some rangers checking the tools in the shed. He asked them to check the mallets they use for pounding in the stakes."

"What about Ms. Piner?"

"Dr. Patel said he figures she was done in by the same weapon, only they used something else to mess up her face so bad. He found bone chips and pieces of hoof. Says they were from a dead animal. Dead a long time."

"There's a box of horse bones in the shed."

"You might want to pass that on to Agent Huff," the detective said.

"I will. Appreciate your call."

"One more thing. DeWitt Brigman had some kind of bruising on his thighs and one arm. The medical examiner said it occurred before death."

"Any idea what did it?"

"Nope. Scrapes, like he was hit. His waders got ripped."

"Like they fought?"

"More like he was running away."

"Is that so? I can't see DeWitt running from someone. You don't suppose it was a horse, do you?" Hunter asked.

"I didn't think of that. I'll be sure to ask the doc."

"Detective Ramirez, I'm much obliged to you for keeping me updated."

"Always glad to lend a hand. Sheriff says to call if there's anything else we can do."

"I'll do that. Have a good evening."

The minute he hung up, Bert started serving their meal. The rice was lukewarm, the pea pods limp.

Hunter didn't notice, eating automatically. He pointed his fork at Bert. "This still don't make sense. Why would the killer bury DeWitt in the colt's grave, then go to all that trouble to let the boat drift so we'd take it for a drowning or a suicide?"

"Suicide?"

"Get quite a few, mostly men. They drown themselves to make it look accidental—on account of the insurance, you understand."

"Maybe the killer didn't know it was Shony's grave."

"If that's true, then DeWitt had to move the foal before the killer got there."

Bert poured some coffee. "I think DeWitt brought his boat over to see Julie while I was out digging up Shony. When he heard I'd found the foal, he motored down fast to move the carcass. It was half an hour before DeWitt arrived at the dock, and he was all wet and muddy. He was showing a green light when he came in. That would mean he was coming from Bald Hill, wouldn't it?"

Hunter raised a brow. She'd always been envious of that ability. "He could have overshot the landing. Easy to do." He leaned back in his chair. "What I don't understand is why DeWitt would go to so much trouble just to hide one infected foal."

"I might have the answer to that." Bert told him about Goodwin and what she'd found out concerning DeWitt. "You know, if you could get the foals off the island, maybe Croatan Farms would let you keep them in those west-end pens."

"There's no way Croatan would let a contaminated horse anywhere near. Back in ninety-seven, we had some EIA horses in remission. The foundation wanted to take them off the island to a secluded location, so they didn't have to put them down. We were months in planning and had to get special permits from the state. Had a lot of objections from horse breeders. Croatan Farms was the loudest." Hunter gave her a small grin. "I reckon we know now why DeWitt went to so much trouble to keep that pony hid."

"They wouldn't have let him bring the foals to the farm."

"You're right about that. The farm's incorporated, stockholders and all. They're paranoid about contagious diseases. They'd have put the adoptions off and waited until the herd tested clean for at least five years. Don't blame them any either, not with all those thoroughbreds. I reckon that's why they were funding DeWitt's research."

"What research? You knew about this?"

"I didn't know Croatan had fixed up lab facilities for him," Hunter said. "But I did hear DeWitt go on about how he believed some of the Shackleford horses—Triton, for one—were immune to EIA. He didn't know if it was a gene or what, but he said he planned to find out someday."

"That's so sad." Bert visualized DeWitt's face when he'd talked about Alaska. "To lose all that talent . . . He had so much to contribute. Julie, too." Bert was silent for a moment. Then something else occurred to her. "If DeWitt didn't kill Julie, then who did? I can't imagine a stranger boating up in the dark to kill her with all of us around." An image flashed into her mind. "Purcell should have been at the landing long before you, and he was soaked when he finally did arrive. You don't suppose . . . ?"

"I can't see Purcell killing anyone, but he had the opportunity, all right. Come to think of it, we all did."

"What do you mean?" Bert asked.

"There wasn't anyone at the dock, not when we got there. I stayed back with the boat. Ernie went off to check the horses, and I don't know where Clayton took himself. He wasn't around when I got to the tent."

"How long were they gone?"

"You mean, were we apart long enough for someone to kill Julie?" Hunter thought, then spoke slowly, counting on his fingers. "The fellows got off first. I stayed back to button up the Parker and set a second anchor. Checked DeWitt's boat, too. Took me about fifteen minutes, I reckon. Then I dropped my gear off in the tent, shucked my waders, and got ready to come after you. I was backing the ATV off the dock when you and DeWitt got there." He tapped his palm. "I'd say it took me half an hour, all told."

"Long enough for someone to hit Julie over the head and drag her body into the bushes?"

"Before you go jumping to any conclusions, you might want to check with Ernie and Clayton. Could be they were together and can alibi each other."

Bert sighed in relief. "You're right. I'd hate to think it was either of them, or Purcell." She grinned. "It must have been you."

"Didn't know what you were getting into, did you?" Hunter glanced toward his picture window, where the increasing wind was rattling the panes. "Tell you what. Let me check NOAA for the latest, then we'll go to bed—that is, if you dare."

He turned on his radio. NOAA was already issuing small-craft warnings for the Georgia coast. The storm was expected to become a nor'easter by morning. "That means we won't be seeing anything around here until one o'clock or so." Hunter turned off the radio.

"This storm isn't going to be bad, is it?"

"Can't say. The question is, what am I going to do about the horses?" He walked to the window, staring out at the sound.

"You're going to let the main herd go, aren't you? Even if you have to keep the foals culled for adoption penned up?"

"Yup. But I'm fixing to wait till the last minute. I'm still hoping to hear from Blount. If he says it's all right, I can let the little ones loose at the same time. That way, they can get back together with their mothers."

"And if he doesn't call?"

Hunter was silent.

"You're going to let the twelve foals go, too? I don't understand. I thought you said you couldn't."

"I can't. Congress legislated back in ninety-six that the Park Service and the foundation share management of the horses." Hunter paced the living room. "If I leave them penned up three days in a nor'easter, I might as well take a gun to them. Be more merciful." He sighed. "I'm caught between the rock and the whirlpool. Either I go against a congressional mandate or I kill twelve horses."

There had to be a solution. Scylla and Charybdis were the rock and the whirlpool—Triton's mares had refreshed Bert's memory on that—but who was the hero of that myth? "What did Odysseus do?"

"He looked for another way out." Hunter grabbed the phone. "Of course."

Bert watched him wide-eyed as he ran his finger down a list until he found the number he wanted. "Clayton, this is Hunter O'Hagan. Sorry to disturb you so late. How you doing?" Hunter tapped his foot as he went through the niceties. Then he laid the problem before Clayton.

Suddenly, Bert felt better. Clayton was the rep for the Humane Society, a national agency. They knew the laws regarding animal suffering and death—and how to get a court order to have the foals turned loose.

Clayton said something.

Hunter snapped back, "I thought that's why they sent you here, to be sure the horses are treated in a humane manner. Leaving a dozen foals penned up in January during a major nor'easter don't fit my idea of humane." Hunter listened. "I'm telling you, get me a go-ahead and you'll be the hero of the hour." He scowled. "What time does the office open? I got until noon at the latest." Then his scowl relaxed. "You do that. I'll be waiting like a bride at the altar."

Bert hugged him as he hung up. "That was a great idea. Will he do it?"

Hunter shrugged. "You heard me. He has to call the home office. Then they have to get their legal department on it. He doesn't know how long that'll take."

"If a judge says it's okay to let the foals go, will that get you out from under?"

"It won't hurt any. You be sure to get word to me when he calls, all right, hon?"

Bert blinked, then realized what he was saying. "You're going to Shackleford. Are you going to stay overnight?"

"Not if I can let the foals go in time."

"I'm coming, too."

"No way."

"Hunter, if it's safe for you, it's safe for me."

"I'm not allowed to jeopardize civilians. That's park policy. If you got hurt, it would be the end for me, in more ways than one. Now, what say we try to get some sleep?"

Bert didn't argue. Six years ago, Hunter's wife had drowned when his boat broached, and he still blamed himself for staying out too long in deteriorating weather.

As Bert lay in bed watching him undress, she wondered where he'd be tomorrow night. Hopefully, the foundation director would show, or Clayton and the Humane Society would come through. Then Hunter could let all the horses go, foals included.

Hunter turned off the light, but Bert could still see his silhouette by the window.

"It's all going to work out," she said softly. "You'll see. Those horses have been in lots of storms, and they always seem to come through just fine, better than people sometimes."

"That's because they got more sense than to go out in a boat when there's trouble brewing," Hunter said bitterly. "But the horses don't always come through. Diamond City was leveled by the hurricane of eighteen ninety-nine. Killed three quarters of the animals on the banks, all the way from Shackleford to Ocracoke." He dropped onto the bed.

Bert reached over, touching his back. "They're not predicting anything like that this time, are they?"

Chapter 27

Diamond City, 1899

Demon

The greatest hurricane on record started near the Cape Verde Islands, where the blazing August sun beat on the already warm waters of the Atlantic Ocean. Overheated, moisture-laden air rose until it reached the cooling layers of the upper atmosphere. There, it condensed into billowing clouds. A growing low-pressure trough began to flow like a river, drifting slowly west. It sucked up the clouds and built them into towering, black thunderheads.

The storm raced west with the trades, the earth's spin bending the winds into a counterclockwise rotation. Like dogs herding sheep, this circling kept the clouds together, intensifying the pressure and helping it to greedily suck even more energy from the evaporating waters. Now a full-fledged hurricane covering hundreds of square *miles, the monster continued its erratic course toward the warm Caribbean south of Shackleford Island.*

White rims surrounded the stallion's maddened eyes. Foam flecked his lips. The man on his back clung like a tiger. Mired in the mud as he was, the horse had no leverage. He shook and tried to buck.

The man hung on, forcing the horse's head away from the edge of the mud pit. Instinct told the stallion he was in mortal danger. Soon, the tiger-man would dig in his claws and bite through his backbone. Then he would feed on the horse's helpless body.

The man roared, waving something that caught the corner of the stallion's eye and spurred him to one last, fierce buck. His heart pounded wildly as his system tried to fuel his struggle, but he was weakening. He had only a few moments left to rid himself of this thing on his back, or he would be defeated. Nose tight, mouth rigid, eyes showing red, the stallion dropped under the mud.

The tiger-man loosened his hold. Sensing victory, the stallion rolled and kicked back to his feet. He had knocked the thing off his back. But he still had to get out of this trap. He leapt up, scrabbling with his hindquarters to get purchase on the steep side. Men rushed toward him, swinging ropes. He kicked, scrambled, and rolled. He was out of the pit, but before he could get to his feet, they came at him from all sides.

Two men sat on his neck. He struggled, groaning, but could not shake them off. They wrapped him in a net of ropes. With a long grunt of despair, the stallion dropped his head to the sand, flanks heaving, nostrils flaring, mud dripping off the side of his tight muzzle.

"Lemme at him, goddamn devil horse. I'll learn that no-good bastard to roll." A small man, so covered in sticky, black mud that only the whites of his eyes showed, stomped toward the stallion, pole in hand.

Someone jumped in front of him, arms forward, palms up. It was a boy just a few years short of being a man. "No." Determination jutted his chin and clenched his lips.

"Get out of my way, Jason," the small man spat.

The boy flinched but held his position. "Let him be. He's beat."

"He's beat, all right. I'm fixing to teach that black devil a lesson he'll never forget."

"He's mine. I caught him in the roundup."

"I ain't arguing, I'm telling. Move, boy, you hear?" The man lunged. Jason ducked, dirty blond hair wild around his face.

The stallion followed the action with one eye.

Before the man could bring his pole down on the horse, the boy grabbed it. Letting out a howl of fury, the small man shoved the boy to the ground, then began to hit him. Knees to his chin, the boy covered his head with his hands as the pole lashed his back. He didn't make a sound.

The crowd began to shift. A murmur grew.

"Youngun's wild as the stallion," said one of the men.

"Looks like Amos got two to tame," grunted another.

"Stop it!" cried a woman.

"Mama, he's hurting Jason!"

The Core Bankers parted, and a grossly overweight woman waddled through. "You fixing to pull them nets alone, Amos?" she shouted, hands on hips, lank, black hair hanging over a yellowed face. "Tide's up three feet in the sound, and them is storm swells pounding the beach. Beat on him later, why don't ya?"

The man grunted but reached down and yanked the boy up by his collar. "Your ma's right. We got work to do. But you's going to be sorry, boy, better believe you is." He shoved Jason toward the stallion. "And get that horse in the roundup pen afore I get cleaned, or I'll shoot him. You got that?"

The boy stood dazed until one of the younger men clasped his shoulder. "Come on, Jason. I'll give you a hand."

The stallion flinched, rolling his eyes at the boy as they bent over him.

"I'm sorry, Demon," Jason said. "I tried to stop him." He began wiping the mud from the stallion's face and nose.

"Best let him wash off in the sound," the young man said.

"Ain't got time." The boy pulled off his shirt and used it to scrape, all the while speaking in a soft tone. "You was almost ready to ride, wasn't you? I had you carrying feed sacks. If he'd just waited a little longer, I'd of had you broke nice and easy."

"Your dad were just trying to help."

"No, he weren't, Tim." Jason gazed with narrowed eyes in the direction his father had gone. "He were showing off. That's what he were doing." He crouched, whispering in the stallion's ear. "I'm glad you beat him, Demon."

The stallion lay motionless, flanks rising and falling, breath rasping, mucus dripping from his nose and mouth.

"Jason, we better get this horse to water. He don't look good."

Boy and man untied the ropes that held the stallion until only his front legs remained hobbled, the bit still on.

"Up, Demon." Jason shook the reins. "It's all right, boy. We ain't gonna do no more horse breaking."

"Not for a spell, that's a fact." Tim pointed at the sky, where line after line of pelicans flew north. Below them, cormorants swooped in black drifts. To the east, clouds of terns, gulls, and other seabirds covered the sky.

But Jason had no interest in the birds. "Please stand up, Demon."

Demon didn't even raise his head.

"I'll fetch some water."

When Jason returned with a bucket of water, he dribbled some over the horse's mouth. The stallion lifted his head long enough to shake it off. Jason stared for a minute, then said, "You done asked for it, horse." He dumped the bucket over Demon's head.

The shock brought the stallion to his feet, but as he tried to bolt, the reins and hobbles stopped him. He eyed the two men, ears back, head low, a line of drool coming from his mouth.

Jason picked up his lead. Demon followed. They cut along a path to the town. From the marsh, they could see Yellow Hill, the huge dune that sheltered Diamond City from the ocean winds.

Soon, Jason had the stallion watered and back with the other horses captured in the recent roundup. Demon meekly let the boy remove his hobbles, but as Jason reached in his pocket for a scrap of hard sugar, Demon trotted into the center of the herd of horses. The boy stood in the pen, the sticky chunk still in his hand, until someone shrilled his name. With a sigh, he pocketed the sugar and left at a run.

The monstrous hurricane now covered the sea from the West Indies to Florida. Spinning like a dervish, it roared over Puerto Rico, killing thousands, then went on to ravage the Dominican Republic and Haiti. It was one of the most powerful storms of the century, this leviathan, the San Ciriaco.

Already, wind-generated swells reached the Outer Banks, and thin clouds streamed through the high atmosphere. Behind the horse pen, silhouetted by a mackerel sky, a towering black-and-white monolith dominated the landscape. A narrow stretch of water known as The Drain separated the lighthouse from Diamond City. Rushing tides ran through the cut, eating away at the sand.

The black stallion charged around the perimeter of the pen, scattering the herd. After several runs, he stopped, rolled his upper lip to the wind, squealed, and pawed the ground.

"What ails you, horse?" Jason called as he tramped down the path. "Here, I brung you something."

Demon ignored him, ears and tail flicking.

Jason lifted his sister onto the rail. "Reckon he's still iller at us."

"Ain't that." An old man stood nearby. "He smells the storm. They's all fretting, and they ain't the only ones."

"What you saying?"

"I just come on." The man nodded toward the mainland. "Been up North River. I'm telling you, that were a sight to behold."

The children drew closer to the oysterman. Demon, drawn by the scent of the rutabaga, also neared.

The old man talked on. "Them finny tribes was all running upriver, so thick you could dip them out by the bucket. Gave me the chills, it did." He shook his head. "Tell your daddy this gonna be a bad one. I done hauled my boat out of the slew."

Demon edged up to the fence, where Jason held a delectable treat.

One of the other horses, also attracted by the smell, trotted up but backed off when the stallion made a head thrust. Delicately, Demon took the vegetable from the boy's hand.

Jason, face caked with salt and sand, smiled as he leaned wearily on the rail. Caressing the stallion, he glanced at the oysterman. "You reckon it'll be as bad as the storm of eighty-four?"

The man reached over and cuffed the boy. "What you know about that? You wasn't even birthed yet."

"Mama told me the tide come into the house and my daddy scuttled the floor with an ax. Still got the water marks." He grinned. "You reckon it'll do that again?"

"Equinoxes ain't no fun, boy. Salt poisoned the wells. Couldn't grow nothing for years." He eyed the hunk of rutabaga in Jason's hand. "Washed out the oyster beds, too. Mess of Ca'e Bankers went off and never come back."

"The horses, they gonna be safe?"

"Sure 'nough." The man spat tobacco juice. "Little bit of water don't hurt them none. But you don't want to be leaving them penned up, even iffen they be newly caught. You see any critters round?"

Jason swung his head to look. "Where'd they go?" Free range was practiced on the Outer Banks. The residents fenced their homes and gardens not to keep their livestock in but to keep it out.

The old man shrugged. "Wade's Shore, I reckon. Plenty of high ground there."

Jason's little sister poked the last chunk of root through the fence. Demon lipped it carefully from her small fingers, huffing to show his pleasure. She laughed and placed her warm palm on his nose. The food gone, he waltzed away and trotted around the perimeter of the fence, stopping to paw and toss his head.

Spent by the havoc it had wrought in the Caribbean, the San Ciriaco followed the life-giving waters of the Gulf Stream north into the Atlantic. Gathering nourishment from the warm waters, it grew strong again, spreading over thousands of miles like a big, white belly with an umbilical hole in the center. Then, for some unknown reason, it slowed, turned, and headed directly at Shackleford Island.

As the hurricane neared the Outer Banks, the winds from the northeast forced the waters of the Pamlico, one of the largest inland seas in the world, into narrow Core Sound. Unable to handle the tremendous volume of water, the inlets turned into raging rivers. The Drain was a mad torrent. By dawn, the sound tides had risen over the sea walls and wooden docks. Boathouses floated off. Skiffs were sunk by the very lines that held them to their moorings.

The waters wound their way over the marshes and around the eroded dunes of east Shackleford, spreading deep inland. Soon, streams of salt water reached from the sound to the primary dune line. Imprisoned by the high dunes of the barrier island, the sound had no place to go but up. By dawn, the pen was under two feet of water. A river ran down the main street of Diamond City.

Few people in Diamond City slept that night. Before dawn, Jason went outside to help his father nail down the shutters, which strained at their fastenings. Then they moved the traps, nets, feed, and tools from the bins to the shed loft. He didn't rest after that.

Through a broken slat in one of the shutters, Jason watched the water rise over the path and reach the steps. The air was solid with sand and water beating against the cabin. He wasn't sure if it was rainwater or spray from the waves that pounded the beach. He could feel the crash of breakers through the floor under his feet.

The plank cabin shook with each blast of wind, but even worse was the roaring. They had to scream to be heard. First, it rained. The water found each crack and crevice, running down the window sills and seeping under the door. When the rain stopped, the wind increased. Now, fine, dustlike sand sifted through the walls. It swirled around the room and layered the wooden table.

Jason's mother slid a rag rug across the planks with her foot, pushing it up against the door. Two chickens, alarmed at her movement, squawked and fluttered across the room. "Look." Jason poked May, who was curled in the bed at his side, sucking her thumb. "They's so scared they's pooping."

She took her thumb out to giggle. "Are you going to bring Demon inside, too?"

Jason heaved a sigh. "He's too big." He again peered through the slat. The water was up past the steps. How deep would it be in the pen?

Demon stood in a huddle with the other horses, rump to the wind, the foals on the inside, under their dams. All had their heads down, ears back, tails tucked as far under as they would go.

It wasn't the wind that made Demon's heart pound, it was the water that flowed like a tidal stream up past his knees, eating the sand from under his hooves. The tide reached the bellies of the foals. If it got any higher, they would not be able to keep their footing.

Taking advantage of a temporary lull in the wind, Demon raised his head for a quick check. He blinked, trying to clear some of the sand crusted around his eyes.

A small figure, bent almost double against the wind, splashed through the water. He staggered to the pen and lifted one of the rails that barred the gate.

Backing away from the herd, Demon trotted over and stuck his nose over the fence. The boy reached up and patted him, saying something. Then he fumbled under the water to remove the last of the gate rails.

Hesitating, Demon passed through. He was outside. Tossing his head, he neighed low and loud, ending in a commanding grunt.

The horses did not move.

Jason started to enter the pen. The boy was his friend now, part of the band. Nosing Jason away from the gate, the stallion splashed back inside. He nudged the nearest mare. She twisted around to see what he wanted. Lowering his head and extending his neck, Demon shoved and nipped the rumps of the mares and colts until he had broken up the huddle and had them moving through the gate. A brown mare with a white, shell-shaped blaze took the lead. Ears back, tail still in a protective position, she instinctively headed for the big dune. Demon brought up the rear, herding both the foals and the boy to the center of the band.

As they wound through the village, heads down against the fierce wind and blinding water, Demon heard pigs squealing. Unlike most of the animals, they had been penned to fatten and now stood with water over their backs. Two goats, loosed from their stakes, joined the small herd as it passed through.

It took the horses a long time to traverse the village. Often, Demon stayed back to help a foal or the boy across deep water. There were times when the wind gusted so fiercely it made them skitter sideways, as if dancing. One of the foals was swept away. His dam chased after him. Neither returned. Another horse, injured by a wind-driven plank, fell and could not rise. Two more wandered off.

As the herd passed a small cabin that leaned to the south, Demon felt a tug on his mane. The boy yelled something. Then he left Demon's side, wading to the porch. Once there, he beat on the wall, his thin voice screaming over the wind. The door crashed open. Hanging onto the jamb, a man came out, cursing. He yanked the boy inside, slamming the door behind them.

When the herd reached Yellow Hill, the brown mare began to climb to the lee side of the dune, but the hundred-and-fifty-knot wind was too strong. She was forced to stay low and circle the hill until the herd reached the sheltered, ocean side of the huge mound. Below, breakers boomed, surging over the beach dunes to lick at the foot of Yellow Hill. A handful of summer cabins tilted precariously as the ocean undercut their foundations.

Several hours later, just as one of the foals collapsed from exhaustion, the wind suddenly ceased and the sun came out. Above the horses, the sky was blue and clear. The herd, which had been clustered together for protection, broke apart. Most wandered off to dung or graze. Others rolled in the sand to relieve the hundreds of scrapes and scratches they had sustained.

But Demon did not let them go far. Surf from the ocean was sweeping up to the foot of Yellow Hill. Massive breakers cracked like thunder and shook the ground under his feet. Static electricity coursed through his hide. He could not stand still. He paced, ears pricked, tail high. He was not the only one. Several of the mares, including the brown, were tense, shuffling about instead of grazing or resting after their ordeal.

With no warning, the wind changed to the southwest and blew harder than before. The clouds closed overhead, thunder roared, and wind blasted the sand so strongly it penetrated their hides. Heads low, unable to see through the wall of sand, they stumbled blindly back around the dune. What had been the sheltered side was now exposed.

Two more of the herd disappeared as they plowed their way to the Diamond City side of the dune. The sound tide had reached Yellow Hill and was eating at its banks. The horses huddled in a hollow overlooking the village.

Despite the storm, Demon kept careful watch. Diamond City was mostly underwater. There were not as many buildings as before. Of those left, some were tipped, parts of them gone. Roofs, timbers, animals, and even a boat rocked in the water.

He saw something move in the tossing waves. Then the stallion heard the boy. "Kick, May, kick! We're almost there." Clinging to a rafter, the boy who had let him out of the pen and the little girl were being swept back by the wind even as they fought to reach the hill.

Demon watched for a moment, then slid down the dune. Water midway up his flanks, he made his way to the children, careful where he stepped. The most dangerous thing about water was getting a foot trapped or cut by some hidden object. He splashed around behind the boy, using his chest to push Jason against the current, as he would one of his foals.

"Wait, Demon, wait!" Jason yelled, letting go the timber. Up to his neck in the water, he shoved the little girl onto the horse's back.

The stallion stiffened, but her scent was familiar, and the child's small hands did not threaten. Instead, she clung, making soft noises like a foal looking for its mother. The horse rolled an eye at the boy, who raised his chin and reached for the stallion's mane. "Go on. I'll hang on and walk."

Demon started back to the dune. Here, they were more exposed to the wind. It blew the sand and water into their eyes and stole the air from their lungs. The current had reversed, joining the wind to keep them from the dune. Demon was a strong stallion in his prime. He could stay on his feet even in a heavy current. Not so with the boy, who stumbled and fell, saved only by his grip on the horse's mane. Each time he fell, it took him longer to recover, until Demon was dragging him. Finally, the stallion came to a halt, bringing his head around.

The boy staggered back to his feet. "I'm all right," he gasped. "Go on."

Demon stood still, eyeing the boy. The wind whipped his black mane over his forehead. He neighed, nosing up.

The boy's lips trembled. "What's the matter? You want me to let go?"

May patted the horse's back. "He says get up with me."

Half sobbing, Jason scrambled onto the stallion's back behind May. With a shake of his nose, Demon bent his head and plowed through the flood tide back to Yellow Hill and his herd.

Once in the lee of the big dune, Jason searched his pockets. With a cry of triumph, he offered a small carrot. "It's not much for what you done, but it's what I got." He stroked the horse, a continuous stream of words pouring out. "The water were up past the doorknob. My daddy chopped a hole in the roof, and we stood on the table and crawled through. Had to put a chair on the table to get Mama out. When the wind stopped, Dad was taking us over to Uncle John's house. I had May on my shoulders, and he were helping Mama. We weren't halfway there, then the wind come up all of a sudden. Next thing I knows, there's a shed coming right at us. I yell and jump away. Me and May both went underwater. Don't know what happened to Mama and Daddy." Jason rubbed his eyes. "I hollered and hollered, but I couldn't see or hear nothing in that wind. Couldn't hardly draw breath neither. Anyhow, I just wanted to tell you, you is a hero now." After a quick hug, Jason dropped to the sand, where May was already asleep.

Demon and his herd were no longer the only occupants of Yellow Hill. Sows with young, a lame cow, chickens, goats, and a few cart horses kept in stables had made their way to the dune, as had many of the Bankers. But the storm was not finished.

As the hurricane traveled over the Atlantic, it sucked up a dome of water over twenty feet high and a hundred miles wide. Monstrous, foaming breakers swept over the beaches, cutting away the primary dunes and rushing inland until they met the waters of the sound. The only land visible on the east end of the island was Yellow Hill.

Now, the hissing, racing surf ate away at the giant dune, undercutting and sucking up the sand. Soon, there was a cliff forty feet high on the ocean side, as piece by piece Yellow Hill split off and slid into the ocean. The people and livestock retreated down the lee side of the dune, closer and closer to the sound. Then, for the first time since the eye passed over Diamond City, the wind began to abate.

Suddenly, Jason jumped to his feet. Cupping his eyes against the sand and spray, he stared into the sound. A checkered jacket lay bunched on some sort of raft. "Daddy." He bounced up and down, waving. "Look, May, it's Daddy!" The boy stilled, frowning. "Pa?"

The man floating on the roof lay face down. Demon drew near to see what alarmed the boy. As he did, the man stirred. One hand lifted, only to drop back.

The boy clung to the stallion. "We got to go get him, understand? Please, Demon, help me." Slowly, making friendly sounds, the boy climbed on his back. Demon turned his head to look at him. His rider lifted an arm, pointing. Then he leaned forward, making little clicking noises.

The boy wanted him to go into the water. Demon considered this a moment, then slowly stepped forward. Soon, he and the boy were working together, the boy guiding him around obstacles he might have missed. Following the boy's hand and the way he leaned his body, Demon reached the bobbing raft.

As he approached downwind of the roof, the stallion jerked back, his ears flattening. Never would he forget the scent of the tiger-man who forced him into the mud. He danced away.

"Demon, please," the boy begged, but Demon backed up farther.

Then the boy slid off his back and swam toward the roof. Climbing on, he bent over the man. "He's hurt bad. You got to help me, Demon."

Torn between his fear and his desire to keep the boy safe, Demon drew near. As he approached, the boy stroked Demon's muzzle, smiling and talking. Then, before Demon realized what he did, the boy slid the small man off the roof and draped him across the stallion's back. Demon snorted, ready to rear. But the boy was astride his neck, crooning and patting. "He ain't gonna hurt you, I promise. It's all right. Easy, boy."

The man did not move. Demon ceased trembling. He whirled about and plowed back to the dune, careless of where he stepped. All he wanted was to reach land and get the man off his back.

Having watched the rescue, the Ca'e Bankers hurried over to help the injured man. Soon, the children were in the center of the villagers.

The brown mare with the white trident on her forehead greeted Demon's return with a nicker. She stayed by his side, grooming his back and withers. Yellow Hill was no longer a hill, just a low hump protruding from the water. People, dogs, livestock, and even nutria all huddled on the shrunken dune.

As the winds continued to drop, the floodwaters retreated with amazing speed. By nightfall, the villagers were able to return to the shambles of their homes. Jason, his father, and his sister were offered shelter in one of the cabins.

Demon, satisfied the wind had really stopped, began herding the mares down the island to the woods. But the maritime woods were no more. Trees lay fallen by the hundreds. Their roots loosened by the high water, they had been unable to withstand the winds. Those that remained standing had been stripped of their leaves and soaked with salt spray that would kill them in the heat of the sun.

The herd, half the size it had been that morning, plodded head down in a single line over the sand. It gave wide berth to the bodies of horses, cows, swine, and people that lay scattered over the island. Caskets sprawled open. Bare bones dotted the beach, as did drowned mariners. Seven ships wrecked off the banks that day; six others vanished without a trace.

The hurricane had reduced the sea oats to stubs and torn away the cedars. There were no shrubs left on the island. All had been buried by sand or would wither and die. Only marsh grasses, roots, and tree bark remained. Had most of the grazing livestock not drowned, Demon and his herd would have starved to death.

Several weeks later, Demon and the brown mare stood knee deep in the sound feeding on salt-meadow grass and watching the residents of Shackleford migrate to Harkers Island. For days, a fleet of houses—some whole, some sawed in half—had been floated on rafts over the sound. As a rowboat pulling a small cabin passed near the stallion, he heard a shout.

A boy bounced on the boat, waving his cap. His dirty blond curls blew in his face. "Look, Dad, it's Demon!" Then he stilled. "We ain't gonna take him with us, are we?"

The father shaded his eyes. "That horse got my brand on him. I reckon that means nobody 'cept me's got the right to bring him off."

Jason stiffened.

His father cuffed him. "And we don't need no devil horse in the Promised Land, right, son?"

"You hear that, Demon?" Jason whispered. "Ain't nobody gonna bother you ever again."

Shackleford Island belonged to the horses once more.

Chapter 28

Wind rattled the panes and rain beat against the glass, but by the time Bert's alarm went off, the cold front had passed. She glanced at the outside thermometer as she poured coffee and stuck two bagels in the toaster—twenty-six degrees, cold enough to snow.

The computerized, strangely accented voice of NOAA was broadcasting warnings for the Atlantic coastline. A nor'easter was pounding Myrtle Beach, generating eight-meter waves. The storm had a central pressure of 998 millibars, whatever that was.

An orange jumpsuit flew into the hall as Hunter, buried in the closet, tossed out his equipment—heavy gloves, goggles, a small tent, long underwear, neoprene socks, and other cold-weather gear. Noticing Bert's frown, he said, "Not to worry. We train for this, in worse weather yet."

"You're looking forward to it, aren't you?" Bert asked, amused but also mildly annoyed.

He paused, grinning. "You might be right at that. I'll get a break from all the politicking and butt-kissing."

"Don't you think there should be two of you, in case something happens?"

"There will be. That's park policy. I'll take Ernie or Purcell."

"Take Ernie, will you?"

Hunter's brow raised.

The bagels popped up. Bert put them on a plate and tried to explain. "I meant to tell you before. Purcell and Tanisha have a thing going. At least I think they have." She told Hunter about Saturday night. "Do you suppose he and DeWitt had a fight over her?"

Hunter guffawed. "Purcell and Tanisha! Good on him." His tone turned serious. "Couldn't have been a fight with DeWitt, that's for sure. Purcell's still alive and in one piece. DeWitt would have mashed him flat as a fritter."

"Someone hit DeWitt from behind, and Purcell's been acting strange lately."

"You saying that because he's sleeping with Tanisha, or because he's applied for another job?" Hunter glanced out the window. "I'm hoping there's not going to be any reason to stay overnight." He strapped his sleeping bag onto the backpack. "There's one good thing. I don't have to sweat out the beach nourishment. They're not going to be dredging in this weather, no matter what I recommend."

Bert was shocked. "You were thinking of going along with Lida Fulchard? To get the culled foals turned loose?"

"That's my hold card if Clayton and the Humane Society don't come through. I'm thinking Lida's fed the foundation and Blount a pack of lies about Shony and the foals. That's why Blount hasn't called. If I have to, I'll tell her I'll go along with the dredging—if she asks Blount to release the foals. Once the foals are loose, it's a done deed."

"She'll never forgive you."

Hunter grinned, throwing out his hands. "So what else is new? I got lots of enemies."

"Hunter, I almost forgot. Guess what I found out when I was on the dredge." She told him about lifting the drag heads while they were still running, and how turtles could be sucked up.

Hunter whistled. "Now, that's right interesting. Too bad we weren't informed of this."

"Couldn't you recommend they be allowed to continue dredging, provided the observer makes sure the drag heads are properly shut down?"

He rolled his eyes. "I could use that to make Representative Fulchard think I changed my mind about the dredging."

"You wouldn't."

He became serious. "The Ridley that disappeared would have made the seventh of the season. That's an automatic shutdown for all the dredging, no discussion. I don't believe someone stole it 'cause they wanted a pretty shell."

"Greg said the tide took it, that we had real high tides that day."

Hunter shook his head. "Ernie wouldn't have left it where it could be swept away. He knows where the tide line is."

"It washed up overnight, right? Who would have seen it there? The dredge contractors couldn't have found out that quick."

Hunter finished loading his pack. "You're right. I'm thinking it had to be someone on the island who knew a seventh Ridley meant trouble."

Bert blinked, pursing her lips. There was something else, something someone said about the turtle that she meant to check out, but what was it?

Hunter was still talking. "That's the morning we rounded up the strays. Must have been forty people on Shackleford."

"How would they get rid of a turtle? They all came on park boats."

He considered her question before he answered. "The way I see it, they either buried it or pushed it back to sea."

"You said Ridleys weigh about a hundred and fifty pounds, didn't you?"

"Right. Unless they had an ATV, they couldn't have taken it far. Besides, there were too many people about." He drummed on the counter. "But we checked all around there."

"If someone shoved it back in the water, would it drift out to the ocean? Greg said it might end up in Barden Inlet."

"I reckon that's possible. The currents around here bring most everything back sooner or later." Hunter reached for a bagel. "Someone would have reported it if it washed up on another beach."

This might be a good time to confess. "I asked Jerome, the spotter pilot, to keep an eye out for it." Hunter cut Bert a glance. "I called him to see if Julie's funeral had been scheduled," she added quickly.

"Right, to be sure."

Bert cast about to change the subject. "If the currents bring everything back, then how do coffins get washed out to sea?"

"What in tarnation do coffins have to do with pilots or turtles?"

"They sucked up a human backbone on the dredge. Said it probably came from a coffin."

"That happens. We've picked up a couple of them, mostly after storms."

"They still wash out?"

He swallowed a mouthful before he answered. "Just the old graves, like the ones on Portsmouth. There's part of an old cemetery underwater by Evergreen Slew, you know."

Bert mulled that for a moment. "But these bones are newer. The captain said they have a metal rod holding them together."

Hunter's head jerked up. "He say anything else?"

"Greg said they use rods like that to treat some kind of disease. That's what made me think it was from a recent burial."

"Scoliosis."

The sibilant whisper made Bert look up. Hunter's mouth was set in a hard line, his eyes focused over her head. "What is it, Hunter?"

He exhaled, making a thin, high sound. "Was it scoliosis?"

"I think that's the word Greg used. Do you know something about it?" A horrible suspicion was dawning.

Hunter gripped the side of the counter. "They find anything else? How old were the bones?" He raised his voice. "Tell me."

"I don't know," Bert said, backing off.

He pushed himself to his feet and stood staring at his hands. "It can't be," he muttered.

"They took the bones to the sheriff," Bert whispered, cold spreading from deep inside.

He reached for the phone. His hand shook. Mutely, his eyes begged her to dial. She picked it up, then realized she didn't know the number. Hunter recited it in a hoarse voice.

The sheriff confirmed that the bones were human vertebrae from someone who died between five and ten years ago.

"Ed, Rhoda had scoliosis and a steel rod in her back." Hunter's voice was gruff.

"Oh, Hunter." Bert laid a hand on his arm.

He shook it off, turning away. "Her family used Dr. Stanley. I reckon he still has the records."

Bert stared at her hand and at Hunter's arm, the sick feeling in her stomach growing. She stepped back, tears high in her throat.

Hunter was muttering something into the receiver. Then he dropped it on the cradle and crumpled on a stool, shoulders shaking.

Bert didn't know what to do. She wanted to comfort him but didn't want to intrude, afraid he'd brush her off again. She watched in an agony of indecision.

Now, he was standing and saying something. ". . . to go down. Call the park. I'd be obliged if you'd tell them I have a personal emergency." He walked out the door.

Bert stood frozen as the truck backed down the drive. Tears blurred her vision. She wandered around the house, staring out the windows but seeing nothing. Finally, the sound of the phone brought her out of her trance.

It was the contractor. He was at the restaurant looking for someone to let him in. She stammered that she was on her way, her thought processes slow.

Once outside, she found the boat still hitched to the SUV. She uncoupled the trailer, relieved to have something physical to do. Hunter had pushed her away, then left. He didn't want sympathy from her. His wife was separate, sacrosanct. She was not allowed to intrude or to help him with his grief. Like a whore is kept apart from a man's family.

No, that wasn't fair. She was overreacting. Shivering, Bert started the car. Hunter had just received a terrible shock. It must have brought everything back like it happened yesterday. But even as Bert told herself this, she knew it wasn't true. Hunter loved her, but not the way he loved Rhoda. Could she live with that?

She drove off the island and over the drawbridge, wishing he'd taken her with him. He probably never thought to include her. It was a very masculine trait.

Her mouth twisted. That might be true, but it didn't help. She felt lonely and rejected. He didn't need her, except . . . Oh, Lord. Bert braked, pulled into a gas station, and turned around. The only thing he'd asked her to do was tell the park, and she was so busy feeling sorry for herself that she'd forgotten.

Feeling the need to deliver Hunter's message in person, Bert used her cell to call the contractor. She told him she couldn't make it and to bill her for his time. He said cheerfully that he had more work than he could handle anyhow, and to yell when she was ready. The sound of a friendly voice made her feel better.

Inside the park headquarters, the long corridor leading to the Law Enforcement and Resource offices was dark, as was the second-floor balcony that housed the administration offices. Because of budget constraints, many of the rangers worked an eleven-month year.

Purcell was hunched over a computer behind the reception desk. He glanced up when she came in, then turned back to the screen. The cold ball in Bert's stomach tightened. She didn't belong here. Like DeWitt said, they only tolerated her because of Hunter.

Bert waited. Finally, the young ranger raised his head and gave her an unsmiling glance. "Hunter sent me." Her too-loud, unsteady voice echoed in the large room. "He had a personal emergency. Said to let you know."

Before she could tell him what the problem was, Purcell shrugged. "I'll pass it on." He swiveled around to the computer.

Bert stared at his back, lips pressed together. After a moment, she walked out through the heavy glass doors into the leaden light. Now, Purcell was ignoring her, too. Why? What had she done to deserve this?

Why didn't she ask him? Why hadn't she asked Hunter? She knew why—because she was a coward and despised confrontations. Her parents had fought constantly. She'd hated it then and hated it now.

Bert hesitated, took a deep breath, and went back inside. In a rush of courage, she asked, "Purcell, have I done something I shouldn't have? You're acting as if you hate me."

Purcell made a half turn, glancing toward the dark corridor behind the reception area. "Didn't mean to be rude, but I got to get this to Ernie before ten."

Bert leaned on the counter.

He didn't look at her but instead stared at the computer screen, which now was flashing concentric circles. "I do what I'm told," he muttered. "I can't afford to buck the administration like some people I know."

So she wasn't the only one hurting. Bert dropped her voice. "What's the matter? Are you in some kind of trouble?" This was not the Purcell she'd known last summer.

He rose, put both hands on the wide counter, and bent until his face was close to Bert's. "I can't talk now," he whispered. "Catch you later." His breath was heavy with the acrid stench of digested alcohol.

Well, she'd tried, and it had helped to think of someone besides herself. Bert turned toward the entrance, only to spot Vilma Willit struggling with the big doors. Fear clutched at Bert's belly. Had the reporter come to ask questions about Hunter's wife? She couldn't handle that, not now.

Behind her, Purcell hissed, "Effing woman. Help me get rid of her. Please, Bert."

She winced. "I can't."

But it was already too late to escape. As Bert tried to duck around Vilma, the reporter sidestepped, blocking her path. "I was thinking you'd be here. I've been chasing after you all over the island."

Bert retreated to the counter.

Sucking air, Vilma peered at Purcell over Bert's shoulder. "Are you the ranger I talked at earlier? Did you give Hunter O'Hagan my message?"

Purcell straightened. Bert could see him putting on his park manners. "I tried to reach him several times, Ms. Willit." He darted a glance at Bert. "He's apparently out of contact for the moment."

Vilma slapped the counter. "Try again, boy. Does he know he's been relieved as supervisor?"

"What?" Bert said.

"Don't make like you didn't know."

"I haven't seen Hunter since eight this morning. What happened?" All Bert could think was that he'd resigned.

The reporter stared at Bert, eyes hooded. "You weren't around when he was talking with Representative Lida Fulchard?"

Bert shook her head.

"Seems they had words about the dredging and the horses. I don't know what he said to her. Surely wish I did." She coughed. "Lida Fulchard got the governor to make a formal complaint to the National Park Service in Atlanta. I heard they relieved O'Hagan and appointed Ernie Steingart as acting superintendent." Vilma stepped closer to Bert, dropping her voice. "Tell Hunter that woman's out for his head."

Bert groaned. When had Hunter found time to talk to Lida Fulchard? He must have called from his cell phone on the way to the sheriff's. Or had Lida called him? That was probably it. And he'd been too upset to be diplomatic. Damn. She should have insisted on going with him. She'd let her fear and pride take over, instead of following her instincts.

Vilma pulled out a notepad. "Can you kind folk tell me what's happening with the twelve foals? Did the foundation director get back yet? Blount's due in today, you know."

Bert felt as if she were being attacked from all sides. "The foals," she echoed. In her concern for herself, she'd forgotten the horses. What about Hunter? Surely, he'd do something about them even if he'd been relieved. But he was in Beaufort. She looked at her watch. It was only nine-thirty. There was plenty of time before the storm winds reached the island.

The reporter's voice pierced her thoughts. "Cat got your tongue?"

She tipped her head like an inquisitive bird.

Bert hesitated. Things could hardly get worse. What mattered now wasn't Hunter's wife or Bert's hang-ups, but rather the horses. "Hunter was waiting for the Humane Society. They're looking into the possibility of a federal court order for the horses' release."

Vilma chortled, choking halfway through. "Good thinking. Did they say when?"

The woman might be crass, but she wasn't stupid. "I don't know. Clayton was to call the Humane Society office after eight."

"Well, speak of the devil . . ."

Clayton was loping up the long walk. Both women watched the lanky, silver-haired man enter. He smiled a greeting, glancing about. "Where's the boss?"

So he hadn't heard about Hunter's demotion yet. Bert rushed to answer before Vilma could tell him. "He had to go to Beaufort. Did you get hold of the Humane Society office?"

Clayton nodded. "Been calling O'Hagan for the last twenty minutes. He's not answering his cell." His good eye flashed toward Purcell. "Can you get him on the radio?"

After Lida, Hunter had probably turned his cell off. "What did they say about the horses?" Bert asked.

Clayton smiled down at Bert, his shock of fine hair haloed by the window. "You ready? The judge said to turn them loose right away. Foals, too. How's that for action?"

Bert blinked. There was something appealing about his triumphant, scarred face.

Vilma scribbled in her notebook. "Have you informed Representative Fulchard of this? You're from the Humane Society, right? Clayton Davis?"

Clayton turned his attention to Vilma, his deep voice booming. "That's Clayton E. Davis. Been on the phone since eight this morning."

Bert leaned over the counter. "Can you raise Hunter, Purcell? We have to let him know."

Purcell hesitated. "I got to ask him first."

"Who?" Vilma asked.

Purcell jerked his thumb toward the dark corridor. "Ernie."

"Ernie Steingart's back there, in the dark?" Bert said.

"He's in his office with the door closed."

"Well, hey, get him," Clayton demanded. "This is important."

Purcell vanished. Clayton began telling Vilma how his prompt action had saved the herd. There was not a word about Hunter instigating the call.

It was a few minutes before Purcell returned, shaking his head. "No can do."

"What?" Clayton said.

"Why not?" Bert asked simultaneously. "Clayton's got a federal court order to release the foals and all the horses."

The young ranger lifted his hands. "Hey, I'm only a seasonal. I do what I'm told." Dropping his voice, Purcell mimicked Ernie's slow speech. "He said, 'There's no need to call O'Hagan to the park. I've taken care of the problem with the horses.' "

"Let me talk to him," Clayton growled.

Purcell rolled his eyes toward the dark corridor. "He said you'd want to see him but to tell you he had some 'important matters' to take care of first. He'll get to you later and explain."

"My orders are to see the horses are let loose, and I've got instructions from Superintendent O'Hagan to get hold of him as soon as I've talked to my boss. You get him on the radio now, boy."

"O'Hagan's not the acting superintendent anymore," Vilma chirped. "Ernie Steingart's the new superintendent."

Clayton swung around, open-mouthed, his bad eye jumping. "No shit. That's all I need."

"We have to get hold of Hunter anyhow," Bert said, fighting to keep her voice steady. She was close to tears—tears of fury and frustration at Hunter, at Ernie, at Purcell, and most of all at Hunter's dead wife, Rhoda.

Clayton ignored her. "You tell Ernie what's-his-name to get out here now. I have to deliver this mandate."

"Too late." Purcell pointed at a car speeding through the gate. "I can leave it here for him, or make a copy."

Clayton sprinted toward the door as if to wave Ernie down, then realized it was impossible. He banged his palm with a fist. "Well, hey, that does it! What in the hell am I supposed to do?"

Bert pointed at the radio. "We'd better make sure Hunter knows about Ernie and the Humane Society." How on earth was Ernie going to manage the park if he ran like a rabbit every time someone wanted to see him?

Purcell opened his mouth, but before he could say anything, Clayton boomed, "Head office said to turn those horses loose before noon today, even if I had to do it myself." He squinted at the sound. "I have to get out there."

Both he and Bert swung around to Purcell. "Not me. I'm not taking you over. Ernie told me to stay here and keep off the radio, in case he needs to get hold of me. Besides, he said he's taken care of the horses. I think he's gone to meet James Blount."

"Did he happen to mention which airport?" Vilma asked.

"New Bern."

Vilma picked up her notebook and dropped it into her large carry-all. "I'm thinking maybe I'll take me to the airport. I'd like to hear what the Foundation for Shackleford Horses is fixing to do."

Bert watched the reporter walk down the concrete path, storm clouds piled up behind her. Then a ray of light broke through. "Vilma." Bert ran after her. "Can you make sure Blount knows about the court order and the danger to the culled foals?"

To Bert's surprise, Vilma gave her a wink. "You better believe I will."

Bert stared after her. Maybe Vilma wasn't so bad after all.

Clayton headed for his car. She couldn't let him go. He was the horses' only hope. Bert stopped him with a hand on his arm. "Wait till she's gone, will you?"

Clayton smoothed his hair. "Why?"

"You still want to get over to the island?"

"I don't want to. I hate boats. But I can't afford to mess up this job." He gave her a smile. "My boss can be a mean son of a bitch." He bent, lowering his voice. "You got an idea?"

He was turning the charm on her. She dropped her hand, stepping away. "Let's check with Maintenance. They take boats over all the time."

But only Clyde, one of the senior workers, was at the shed. "I'm sorry, Miss Bert," he said. "They's all out at the cape buttoning up for the storm and checking for fishermen and campers. Got two crews to the lighthouse. The others went to Atlantic and Portsmouth, and I got to go to Morehead to pick up a part for the other Parker—been giving us trouble." He pointed at the big boat moored to the dock.

Bert sagged, then got an idea. She knew that someone stayed with the horses while they were penned. "Mr. Davis here needs to be sure the horses are set free. I wonder if there's anyone on Shackleford. Could you check?"

Clayton's head jerked up. Bert nudged him to shut up before he said something about Ernie's orders.

Clyde's creased, brown face broke into a smile. "Be glad to, Miss Bert." He went over to the mike hanging off the shed wall and began broadcasting for Shackleford Island. No one answered. Bert expected Ernie to cut in and tell him to get off the air, but it was as if all radio communications had been terminated.

Finally, Carlos answered from the cape. He sounded far away. "Clyde, we pulled the two volunteers off Shackleford already this morning. There ain't nobody there. Super was supposed to come on."

Hanging up the mike, Clyde pointed at the water. "If O'Hagan's out yonder, he don't have his radio turned on. Could be he's on the ATV. Can't hear over that motor, you know." He must have seen the disappointment in Bert's face, as he added, "Iffen you want, I'll try him when I get back from Morehead, but he'll be here by then. Ain't no boats supposed to be on the water after noon today."

Bert and Clayton strode back to their cars.

"Well, hey, that does it," Clayton said, an edge of relief in his voice. "They can't say I didn't do everything I could."

It was time to swallow her fear of another rebuff. "My cell's in the car. Let me call the sheriff and see where Hunter is."

Detective Ramirez answered. "He and the sheriff left to see Doc Stanley. That sure is something about those bones turning out to be Mrs. O'Hagan, isn't it?"

Bert's stomach sank. "Then they're sure?"

"It's Stanley's work, all right. They're out checking records to see how many of those operations he did. Doc thinks all his other patients are alive."

After getting the number from Ramirez, Bert called the doctor's office. They'd all left. She then called the recorder at Hunter's, but there were no messages. Clayton stood first on one foot, then the other. He sighed loudly as she punched off.

Exhaustion set in as Bert tried to think of some other way to contact Hunter. "He had to go into Beaufort to identify some remains," she told Clayton, hoping to appease him. "But I don't understand why he hasn't called in." Had Hunter's grief, augmented by his belief that he'd caused his wife's death, driven all else from his mind? Dammit anyhow. Rhoda had been dead for six years. He didn't have to act as if it just happened.

Clayton edged toward his car. "Well, hey. Like the kid said, maybe the horses have already been let go. That's probably where that Ernie fellow was headed."

Relief flooded Bert. Of course. That was why Ernie was in such a hurry. He wanted to let the horses loose before the storm. She started to exhale, then stiffened. "He can't be there. He left in his car. How would he get to the island?"

"Oh, right. You know, that ranger never did like those horses. Said they were exotics competing with the endemic—that's native plants and animals."

Bert's mind registered annoyance at his condescension, but now was not the time to protest. "Something's wrong. Hunter was expecting a message from you. He would have called in by now." The minute she said it, Bert knew she was right. No matter how upset Hunter was, or how single-minded, he would not have forgotten the horses. He would have found some way to contact Clayton.

"Well, it's up to the Park Service now." Clayton beeped his car locks open.

He was correct. This was park business. Ernie could have been going to meet Hunter somewhere. They were probably headed out to the island now. Dammit anyhow. She could understand Ernie, with his reticence, not stopping to explain, but the idea that Hunter had gone over without saying anything hurt.

But suppose they weren't on the island? In several hours, no one would be able to get over to Shackleford. Hunter would never forgive himself if something happened to those ponies, just as he hadn't forgiven himself for the death of his wife. But this time, his guilt would be compounded because he'd neglected his job to indulge his grief.

Clayton was here, and Clayton had a court order to release the horses. Bert would be within the law. She'd held back once today, and Hunter had suffered for it. She wouldn't do it again.

Bert took a deep breath. "There is something we can do. We can take my boat."

Chapter 29

Clayton recoiled, his scar pulsing red. "You're crazy. You're going over by yourself?"

Feeling better now that she'd come to a decision, Bert gave him a wicked smile. "Not alone. You're coming, too."

Clayton backed up, hands raised. "No way, José."

"You want to keep your job, don't you?" She remembered the carrot Hunter had used with Clayton. "I'll make sure Vilma Willit knows you went over in the teeth of a storm to save the horses. The home office'll love the publicity."

The red faded from his scar. She knew he was wavering. "Is it safe?"

"No problem. Winds are between fifteen and twenty. We'll be in the lee of Shackleford. And we'll be back long before the storm hits."

Mentally, Bert crossed her fingers. All they had to do was get to the island. They could follow Hunter and Ernie back—if they were there. If not, they would open the gates to the pens, get right back in her boat, and head home. It shouldn't take more than an hour, an hour and a half at most. She checked her watch. It wasn't quite ten. That would get them back by eleven-thirty. According to Clyde, Maintenance was keeping the boats on the water until noon. The park was ultraconservative, so that meant conditions weren't expected to get really bad until much later. If the weather grew too nasty, she and Clayton could just stay on Shackleford, though she'd better not tell him that.

It wasn't until they set out in the boat and passed the first buoy that Bert suspected she'd made a mistake. From the top of the sea wall and the shelter of the marina, the chop hadn't seemed as high as it did now. The wind wasn't churning up the water; these had to be front-running swells from the nor'easter. For a moment, Bert considered turning around. Then she reminded herself that she was always nervous at first. She was already halfway there, and the water would be calmer when she got out of the main channel. Besides, she had Clayton to help her.

But the chop was no better in the lee of the bars and small islands. Bert stood behind the low windshield. Clayton crouched in the seat beside her, knees together, clutching the rail so tightly his knuckles glistened white. Each time the small boat met an incoming wave, the bow slapped the crest, sending a curtain of cold spray over Bert and Clayton. A wave washed over the bow, swirling around their feet as it flowed down the bilge. Both Bert and Clayton had donned rain gear and waders before boarding, but even so, the icy water forced its way through openings Bert hadn't known existed. Already, her gloves were soaked and her hands numb with cold.

Clayton flinched as another wave washed over the prow. Bert had no time to waste reassuring him. She was braced at the wheel, scared that one of the swells would catch her unaware and knock them around. Thank goodness she'd had the foresight to make them both put on life jackets. If worst came to worst, they could swim or wade to one of the bars or islands before the cold got to them.

Again, she considered turning back, but from everything she'd been told, it was safer to continue forward, into the wind. Carefully, Bert worked her way closer to the island, squinting to spot the marker leading to the horse dock on Shackleford. "Clayton, help me. Can you see a pole ahead?"

"I don't believe this. Don't you know where you're going?" His voice broke. "Turn around. Go back now."

A fat lot of help he was going to be. "Relax! We're almost there," she shouted. "It's just hard to see with all this spray."

"Are we going to sink?"

"No way," Bert snapped. "But if I don't find the marker, we'll run aground and have to walk in through the surf."

Still clutching the rail, Clayton raised his other hand to his eyes and peered forward.

"You're not going to see anything from down there. Stand up. Hold onto the console." Bert slapped the bar that ran over the short windshield.

The boat lurched as he jerked to his feet. Just then, a wave came at them from the side. "Hang on!" she yelled, spinning the wheel and throttling up to meet the water. The boat flew into the air and crashed back. Clayton slammed onto the deck, howling in panic as a flood of freezing water washed over his head. "You all right?" Bert shouted, not daring to let go of the wheel.

Clayton groaned, then reached for the rail to pull himself up, only to collapse face down.

With one hand, Bert tried to grab his belt, but she couldn't reach it. "What's the matter? Are you hurt?" she yelled, wiping salt from her face and eyes. Something was sending spray high into the air. Thank God, the dock. She'd missed the marker but made it in anyhow. "Clayton, we're there. Can you get up?"

Her words must have gotten through, as the big man began moving. He drew his knees up beneath him and pushed himself to the bench. "Hit something," he moaned, clutching his side. "Think I broke a rib—again."

"Ah, shit!" Swells were washing over the dock. Without Clayton to help her tie up, she'd never get alongside. Besides, he might hurt himself even more getting from the boat to the dock. She searched the landing for signs of Hunter or Ernie. Incoming boats were visible from the pen area, but no one came running to toss her a line.

Cold knifed through her body. Not only was there no one on shore, there was no boat at the dock. Hunter wasn't here. She hadn't realized until now how much she'd counted on his presence.

Bert made her decision. "I'm going to beach her. Get back down, Clayton. It's going to be rough for a minute."

Paying no further attention to him, Bert sighted her course through the breakers that swelled and crashed on the shore. The trick was to get in the trough between them and motor in at the same speed as the waves. Holding her breath, hands frozen to the controls, she throttled up and closed her mind to what would happen if she made a mistake. Then all was white foam and noise. There wasn't enough space between the swells. She and Clayton shot ahead as if on a surfboard. The boat jerked to a halt, throwing Bert into the console. A wave broke over the stern, sweeping across the seats.

"Quick!" she shouted, tilting the outboard and switching it off. "Get out before she washes back."

Clayton yelped as she grabbed him by the waist and tried to lift. He struggled to his feet. Bert slid into the cold, shallow water, jumping away as the waves tossed the boat. She stretched out frozen hands. "Come on, Clayton, move."

He was standing, hanging onto the side of the boat, staring numbly at the foaming water. Another breaker lifted the stern into the air. He pitched forward. Bert grabbed him and pulled him headfirst into the surf. He howled, spitting water.

They staggered to shore. Bert stopped, shoving him forward. "I have to get the boat."

She turned back. The craft was sideways to the surf and rapidly filling. Grabbing the anchor line, she slogged ashore and tied it around the nearest tree. Hopefully, the waves would wash the runabout farther up the beach. She'd worry about how to get it off later. No way was she taking it back to Harkers Island.

Clayton hunched on the path, shivering. Bert started toward him. As she did, she glimpsed a white streak on the far side of the dock, close to shore. A skiff was being tossed by the chop. Relief coursed through Bert. Someone was here—Hunter, she prayed. He hadn't forgotten the horses. Somehow, that was terribly important to her. "Clayton, look." She pointed. "Hunter's here."

The presence of the boat had the same effect on Clayton as it did on her. Suddenly, the lines around his mouth loosened. He turned and limped up the path, Bert right behind.

"Hunter!" she yelled, but the surf and wind drowned her voice. Clayton added his bellow as they reached the volunteer tent. The tent was leaning and flapping. Hunter was right. It wouldn't hold up to a big wind. Teeth chattering, Clayton fumbled with the door snaps, but Bert knew it was empty. It had to be, since the outside fastenings were closed.

Behind her, horses squealed and snorted. She heard a metallic clang. Was that the horses ramming the enclosures, or . . . ? Hunter might be opening up right now. Bert dashed toward the pen.

No one was there. Then Bert remembered the foals. He'd let the babies into the main pen so they could find their dams before he set the herd free.

Behind her, Clayton yelled, "Where are you going?"

"To the foals. See if anyone's over there, will you?" She pointed toward the shed.

The twelve foals were still in the small enclosure, pressed against the fence separating them from the main pen. Several mares had their noses through the wire, nuzzling their offspring. Bert didn't hesitate. She climbed over the fence and opened the gate, jumping out of the way when the eager mares threatened to overrun her. "Whoa," she gasped, smiling for the first time since Hunter found out about Rhoda. "Don't kill the hand that frees you." She continued smiling as she watched the reunions. Several foals stretched their heads forward, teeth showing as they made mouthing movements, a submissive reaction similar to a dog rolling over on its back. The mares were blowing in their offspring's nostrils, nickering and nipping them gently. One by one, they left, until only four foals remained in the small corral. Bert shooed them into the main pen. "Go on, kids. Go find your mothers. Hurry up, so I can let you all loose."

Clayton was nowhere in sight when she returned to the tent. Nor was he inside. It shouldn't have taken him that long to check the shed. He'd been gone a half-hour at least. Bert had just started up the path when he appeared. Panting, he limped along, hugging his rib cage. "Couldn't find anyone," he wheezed. "But one of the ATVs is gone. Left fresh tracks."

He sounded as bad as Vilma Willit. Bert narrowed her eyes, giving him a searching look. His face was ashen, and his scar and lips had a blue tinge, but beads of sweat glistened on his forehead. "You don't look so good, and you're all sweaty. You weren't running, were you?"

Clayton forced a smile, leaning against the fence. "Well, hey, I don't feel so good either. Hurts like hell. May have punctured something."

"Here, let's go to the tent." She discarded the idea of offering him a shoulder. If he leaned on her, she'd probably crumple.

Thankful to find a full tank of propane in the tent, Bert lit the heater. "Wonder where he went to?" she mused.

"Did you let the horses go?" Clayton asked.

"We need to give them a little time first, so the babies can find their mothers. Then we'll open up." Bert frowned, going to the tent flap. "Did you check the john?"

"It's gone. Maintenance must have picked it up."

"Where's the other ATV?"

Clayton grimaced, shifting on the cot. "Hey, look, could you get my waders off? I hate to ask, but . . ."

"I'm sorry, I should have thought of that." Bert yanked his sand-covered waders. Water ran out. "You're soaked."

"You should know. You pulled me in."

Bert sighed as she removed his socks and shoes. "You'd rather have waited in the boat?"

He started to laugh but choked off, clutching his middle.

The volunteers had left blankets and sleeping bags in the tent. Bert pulled one over. "Let's get you into this. Would it help if we wrapped your ribs?"

Clayton shook his head. "They don't do that anymore. I just need to take it easy so I don't make it worse."

Bert helped him remove his wet jacket, vest, and shirt, spreading them out to dry close to the heater. If he wanted to take more clothes off, he could do it without her. She went back outside.

A walk around the entire perimeter of the pen revealed no one. If Hunter didn't get back soon, they weren't going to get off the island in time. She should call, but her marine radio was in the boat. Bert hurried to the sound-side beach to see if she could retrieve it. The boat was being tossed by the surf. Water filled the hull and sloshed over the radio. She tightened the line around the tree, hauling the little craft as far up the shoreline as she could. If she waited until the tide fell, the runabout would be high and dry. She could get the radio easily then, although she doubted it would work. In any case, she'd be able to reach only the Coast Guard, not Hunter.

She walked toward the dock until she saw the green logo stripe on the side of the boat. It belonged to the park, all right. The chop slammed the skiff against the dock and washed over the bow. But skiffs were unsinkable. Besides built-in buoyancy, they had scuppers just above water level, so any water coming in flowed right back out again. Bert shuffled onto the flooded dock, bracing herself against the wind and waves, hoping to see something in the skiff that would tell her who had come out. But everything had been carefully stowed in the lockers, and the ignition key was gone. Whoever was here would have his radio with him.

Let it be Hunter, she prayed. He must have gone to the beach, although she couldn't imagine why. He had to be alone. If he'd brought someone with him, both ATVs would be gone, unless they were riding double and expecting others.

There might be someone in trouble on the island. In Portsmouth last year, after the hurricane, Hunter had to direct the park plane to a landing spot near them. Perhaps there was a boat in trouble offshore, or a plane. That would explain Hunter's absence.

A plane! Bert's eyes widened. Oh, no, it couldn't be. She hurried over to the ATV. Jerome Piner had been bringing Agent Huff to Beaufort regularly. Had he been flying low searching for the turtle on his way home and been forced down? No, the wind was still under twenty-five miles per hour and steady, which would not be a problem for an experienced pilot. It was the front-running swells that made the water so choppy.

Bert stopped. That's what was bothering her, what she'd meant to check out. The spotter pilot had said something about the turtle before they got onto the subject of the stranded whale. He'd mentioned the Ridley's being across the island from Bald Hill Bay. Bert remembered the map Hunter drew in the sand on Sunday, when they'd taken the ATV down to look at the Ridley. Bald Hill Bay was even with the 51 marker, not the 53! That's why they couldn't find the turtle. It was two miles east of where they'd been searching.

Suddenly, everything fell into place. Bert knew who'd killed Julie, and why.

Chapter 30

It had to be Ernie. Ernie was the one who went out to investigate the turtle after it was reported by the park plane. When he saw it was another dead Ridley, he must have dragged it to the edge of the dunes by the 51 marker, planning to hide it inland. But Julie was on the ridge keeping watch while DeWitt went after Triton. Ernie had no choice but to bury the turtle on the beach. Then he'd lied and logged the location as being east of the 53, so a search of the area wouldn't uncover it. He'd even swept the sand at the 53 to make it look as if someone had taken the turtle and was hiding the tracks.

Bert bit her lip. She remembered the puzzled look on Julie's face when they were searching for the turtle. She'd said she thought it was farther up the beach, but Bert had paid no attention.

Julie must have said something to Ernie when he came ashore that night. Maybe they ran into each other at the horse pen or the shed, and Julie mentioned seeing him with the Ridley. It was even possible Julie tried to blackmail him. Whatever Julie said, Ernie panicked and struck, then tried to make it look like a horse had killed her.

After gassing up the ATV, Bert stopped by the tent. "I'm going after Hunter," she told Clayton, hoping it wasn't wishful thinking that made her so sure Hunter was on the island. "Give the foals half an hour to find their mothers, then let all the horses loose, okay?"

As Bert drove off, a frightening thought came to mind. Ernie had left the park office in a hurry. Was he going to meet Hunter? Was Hunter in danger? No, Ernie had no reason to hurt him. More likely, both men were on their way to the New Bern airport to pick up the foundation director. Had Ernie or Hunter dispatched another ranger to free the horses? If whoever it was didn't return with the ATV soon, they'd all be stuck on the island for the duration of the storm.

The sandy road was damp and showed fresh tire tracks. Bert followed them to the beach. At least it wasn't as rough as on the sound. The northeast wind blew at an angle, mostly to her back, which gave her some protection from its icy bite.

The tracks turned west, down the beach. Bert followed, noting how close the ruts were to the falling tide line. Whoever it was had come through less than a half-hour ago. She stopped to tighten the straps on her jacket. Unlike Clayton, her rain gear had kept her reasonably dry. Only her hands, hair, and neck were wet. Now, the damp areas leached the warmth from her body. She'd taken off the sodden gloves, but her fingers were still numb. Pulling her sleeves down over her hands, Bert gunned the ATV, expecting any moment to see a black dot down the beach. The wind burned her cheeks and made it difficult to breathe. She kept her face down, peering up from under her hood.

She couldn't quite believe the killer was Ernie Steingart. He seemed too introverted to inflict such violence, but aggressive driving was indicative of hidden anger. Because of her own shyness, Bert had read up on the subject. She knew shy people worried obsessively about things they or someone else said or did. The painfully shy, like Ernie, often overreacted, taking minor perceived rejections to illogically drastic conclusions.

And being raised in foster homes could leave a sensitive child with deep anger and guilt. Besides, his job as chief resource ranger had put Ernie in the perfect position to hide the Ridley. He'd lied about its location, and about its condition, too. It must have had fracture marks, and he was covering up for whoever was behind this. Ernie had probably hidden other mutilated turtles. But why? Money? A bribe?

Who'd brought that skiff over? Perhaps it had been left because of motor trouble. That meant she and Clayton were alone with a beached boat. Bert tightened her grip, feeding gas as she bounced along the damp sand.

Stupid! If she was alone, then who took the other ATV and made the tracks she was following? Someone was on the island. But why hadn't he let the horses loose while he was at the pen?

Of course! Hunter wouldn't know Clayton got approval. He might be trying to contact her right now. Sometimes, when radio signals were weak, the rangers used a high dune by Wade's Shore to communicate. Or maybe someone was in trouble and Hunter had gone out to direct the medevac copter.

Bert was so busy thinking up dire possibilities that when the tracks turned inland, she continued past. Realizing what she'd done, she wheeled too sharply and skidded. Finally, coming to a shaky stop, she started up through a pass in the dunes. The tracks were not as well defined here, the wind filling them in.

As she crested the primary dunes, she saw a flash of orange. Oh, thank God. Hunter was straight ahead on his ATV, pulling something up the hill. Was it a stretcher?

Bert fed gas and leapt forward, yelling. If she'd had a horn, she would have blown it.

He didn't hear her.

As she neared, Bert stood on the pedals to see what he was dragging.

Just then, Hunter heard the sound of her motor. He glanced over his shoulder, saw her, and speeded up.

Bert reeled as if she'd been hit. Hunter was running away from her. She shook her head, grinding to a halt. It couldn't be.

Hunter slowed and turned. He threw his hands out in an angry gesture she'd seen him use before, then started toward her. He was furious, and he was right. She shouldn't have come. He'd be even angrier when he discovered Clayton was hurt. Oh, God, another blot on his record due to her! Bert fought for control, turning away. She would not let him see her cry.

The ATV spun to a stop several feet in front of her. Hunter said nothing. Taking a deep breath, Bert raised her head. She blinked. Fear coursed through her body, yet somewhere she knew a spark of joy. It wasn't Hunter who had run from her.

Ernie crouched on the ATV.

So that was why Ernie'd left the park in such a hurry, to move the Ridley to a safer hiding place. He must have stashed a skiff at one of the marinas. It was perfect timing. There was no one around. And if he was seen, he could say he was releasing the horses.

He killed Julie, and now he'd kill her, too.

But he didn't know she knew. Perhaps she could fool him long enough to get away.

Bert forced a smile. "Ernie! Am I ever glad to see you." Her voice quavered deep in her throat.

Ernie's head cocked slightly under his orange hood. His pale eyes were fixed on Bert.

She couldn't just ignore the fact he was dragging a turtle. Bert swung around on the seat to stare at it. It was dark and streaked with sand, but it had its flippers and head. "What, did another one wash in?" She tried to sound casual. Her Honda was still running, but it was in neutral. If she slid her foot under the clutch, ready to go . . .

His shoulders relaxed. He nodded.

It was working. She edged her hand toward the throttle. "Not going to let the tide get it this time, are you?" Oh-oh, his eyes had narrowed, just a little. She better get off the subject. "Is that your skiff at the dock?"

This time, he spoke. "What are you doing here?"

The best way to lie was to stick to the truth as much as possible. "I brought Clayton over, to let the horses go. We told Purcell to tell you, remember?" She was babbling. Bert made herself slow down. "The Humane Society said to let them go." She risked a glance to the side. There was nothing in her way.

Ernie shook his head slowly, his eyes soft and sorrowful. "You know, don't you?"

"Know what?" Blood pounded. She tried to appear puzzled, rounding her mouth. "That you're superintendent now? Congratulations." She had to stay calm and not let her face give her away. "Did you tell Hunter?"

He stared at her silently. Bert steeled herself to meet his gaze, to let him see she had nothing to hide. Weren't killers' eyes supposed to be dead? His weren't. They darted around, anxious, unsure. The pupils were tiny, the irises large and icy blue. He blinked. There was sand on his pale lashes.

She forced a smile. "We should get moving before the storm arrives." Her voice was too high.

But Ernie had turned away. "You shouldn't have come, you know." Looking down, he picked at burrs on his orange pants. "I liked you."

Bert tried to say something, but all that came from her mouth was a croak.

"I'm sorry." His voice was soft, hypnotizing. "There's no other way."

She shook her head. Fear filled her throat, paralyzing her brain.

"I'll make it look like an accident with the ATV." He gave another sweet smile.

Bert fought not to flinch, her thumb on the throttle. She made herself speak. "Why?"

He hesitated, then shrugged. "I thought Hunter was my friend. I did everything he asked, and more." He spread his hands, palms up. "Just because I didn't want to take a transfer . . . He should have told me how important it was. I'd have done it if I'd known. He said I wasn't qualified for a promotion. Wasn't qualified, me! I have to see a shrink, he says." He wiped his nose with the back of his hand.

300

Her stomach churned. Ernie wouldn't be telling all this unless he was going to kill her.

"I'm not crazy," he said, as if he could read her mind. "I have my doctorate. Just because I'm not a social giant doesn't mean I can't be a leader." His mouth contorted. "It's like the military, you know. Getting passed over for promotion is death." He blinked rapidly, then continued in his normal tone. "Lida Fulchard doesn't think I'm crazy. She's making me secretary of the Department of Natural Resources for North Carolina, with perks." He smirked. "She knows I can handle a responsible job."

Keeping his eyes on Bert, he reached back and pulled on a rope. He'd released the turtle.

With a clang of gears, Ernie's ATV reared and charged at her. On an adrenaline overload, Bert hit the gas and changed gears at the same time, a big no-no. The bike bucked forward and up. Ernie struck her fender, throwing Bert sideways and almost knocking her off the seat. Somehow, she stayed on. Her only chance was the ATV. On foot, she was dead.

Bert fed gas. The bike jerked ahead. She squeezed the thumb throttle harder. Nothing. Ernie was turning.

Gear up, stupid. She was still in first. Finding the foot-activated clutch, Bert geared as fast as she could. She saw orange from the corner of her eye. Ernie was charging.

The ATV leapt forward, but not fast enough. He was gaining. She went into fourth gear but forgot to look where she was going. The bike bounced over a gully, went into a skid, and lost more ground. Struggling to straighten out, Bert looked down. Damn, she was on soft sand, the wheels miring. She wrenched the bike sideways, toward the ocean, holding the throttle all the way down. The turn gained her a little ground. Ernie had not expected it.

Unable to get down to the beach, Bert raced east along the back of the primary dunes, searching for a break. At this speed, the Honda jolted over every dip, threatening to buck her off. Bert found herself standing on the footrests, as if she were on a galloping horse.

Ernie was catching up. Now, she could hear the engine right on her. She didn't know ATVs were so loud. He was on top of her, shadowing her. Bert ducked, screaming.

Something passed overhead.

Dear God, it wasn't Ernie. It was a plane. She looked up. Hunter's face was pressed to the window. He was smiling and waving, pointing to the camp.

She shrieked, tossing a glance at Ernie. He was right behind, smiling and waving at the plane. Then she realized Hunter didn't understand what was happening. Bert let go of one of the handlebars and made a slashing motion across her throat, straining to feed gas and control the bike with the other hand. Now, the plane was ahead of them, rising. Had Hunter seen her signal?

The ATV jerked.

Ernie had rear-ended her. He'd gone mad. How could he kill her with Hunter on the island?

Easy, he had no choice. With her alive, he was dead.

Bert did the only thing she could think of. She turned the bike toward the beach. The ocean continually undercut the primary dunes, leaving sand cliffs up to fifteen feet high. Bert crouched like a jockey, praying the dunes here were low. If she could keep her seat on the Honda—and if it landed flat—she might be able to reach the plane before Ernie caught up. If not, well, she was a good swimmer.

As she reached the crest, she knew she was out of luck. It was one of the higher cliffs. Then she was in the air. But the Honda did not continue its forward motion as she'd expected, as she'd seen in countless car chases. The moment the wheels left the ground, the nose dove straight down.

As if in slow motion, Bert went headfirst over the handlebars. Her thigh caught under one of the handles, bringing her forward progress to a halt. The front of the ATV hit the soft sand, hesitated for an eternity, then slowly rolled over her leg.

For a minute, Bert couldn't breathe. Was she hurt? She couldn't feel anything. Her leg. Was it broken?

She heard Ernie.

Pushing on the seat, Bert tried to wriggle out. The sand gave a little. Ernie wouldn't dare kill her with Hunter so close, would he? Even as she freed one leg, she knew she'd made it easy for him by crashing.

Crouched on the ATV, head down like a crazed bull, Ernie raced up the beach.

Bert screamed for Hunter, for a miracle. Where had they gone? But she knew. They'd land on the beach by the horse pens and wait for her and Ernie to catch up.

The tires were close. Still screaming, Bert shrank back, trying to find shelter under the ATV.

So this was how she would die. She hadn't thought it would be so soon. Ernie would say she lost control waving at the plane, and Hunter would blame himself for her death, too.

She couldn't let that happen.

She shoved the bike up with all the strength she had. There, she was free, but it was too late. Ernie was coming right at her.

A blur of white shot from the beach, mane flying. A horse? Nose thrust forth, tail streaming, Triton charged at Ernie.

The huge, black tires were feet from Bert's face. She could see tiny shells caught in the treads.

Hooves pounded past, showering Bert with sand. Even as she blinked to clear her eyes, she watched Triton shoulder Ernie off the Honda, just as he'd done to DeWitt. Bike and rider tipped to the ground, skidding, coming to a stop next to Bert. Ernie rolled away.

The golden stallion pranced near the fallen vehicle. He advanced with high, exaggerated steps, baring his teeth and squealing. Bert froze, not even blinking. Even though she knew Triton could turn on her at any moment, she couldn't help wondering how he'd gotten here so fast. Clayton must have let the horses out early.

Something glistened. Ernie was up, a knife in his hand. He rushed, not toward Bert but toward the stallion. At the sight of the raised, glittering blade, Triton reared and shrieked, a prolonged, warning scream that made Bert's scalp crawl.

The knife came down, the point catching the horse's neck. Blood welled and dripped down the long, flaxen mane. Dark eyes gleaming, mouth open, the stallion thrust his head forward and lunged at his attacker. There was no doubt in Bert's mind the horse meant to kill.

Ernie leapt to the side, stabbing at the snapping teeth. He narrowly missed the muzzle. Screaming furiously, the stallion reared and, with flying feet, slashed at the man. One hoof caught Ernie just above his brow. It took his eye, his cheek, and part of his nose. Blood spurted. Arms bent over his face, Ernie staggered back. Again, the hooves slashed, this time crushing the side of his head. The man swayed, took a few blind steps like a headless chicken, and sank to the ground in a heap. The stallion roared and came down, flared nostrils smoking in the cold, eyes rolling, teeth snapping savagely. His white mane was stained with blood, but the flow had slowed.

Bert shouted, unable to turn away. "Stop, stop! He's dead. Oh, please, stop."

As if he understood, Triton danced back. For a moment, he remained poised, front leg raised, tail still lashing. He gave a little shake of his nose, as if to say, "See how great I am." Then, ears pricked, upper lip fanned, he stood motionless before the mangled man, his dark eyes searching for signs of life.

Bert wasn't breathing. He'd saved her, but would he come after her next?

Seeing no movement from the bloody carcass, the stallion turned away. High-stepping, he circled the fallen ATV, blew, and farted. Then he trotted off and disappeared over the crest of the dunes.

Bert stared at the red Honda, now on its side, black tires in the air. Triton had initially attacked the machine, not Ernie. Had DeWitt used that ATV to move Shony's body to the clearing?

For a long time, Bert did not stir. She was astonished to find her leg was no longer trapped. Then she remembered the final heave that had freed her. Her thigh ached fiercely, but there was no bleeding. She raised her heel off the ground. No new onslaught of pain. Still worried something was broken, she scooted over to Ernie.

The only part of him that wasn't bloody was his feet. Bert pushed up the leg of Ernie's jumpsuit. Where was the pulse on an ankle? Wherever it was, she could feel nothing, nor was his chest moving. He was dead, all right. He had no face left, just like Julie. Justice had been served.

Getting to her knees, Bert sighted up the beach, hoping to see Hunter. Stupid. She must be in shock or something. There were no ATVs left at camp. Using her downed bike, Bert pushed herself upright. She stood balancing for a minute before she dared take a step.

Her thigh hurt, but nothing grated. She was going to have a mother of a bruise. She made no attempt to right the Honda, knowing from experience it was too heavy for her.

Where did that horse go? She could use him right now. Bert grinned, her smile quickly changing to a grimace. She shouldn't be laughing in death's presence.

Who was she trying to impress? She wasn't sorry Ernie was dead. Actually, she felt triumphant, as if she, not Triton, had won the fight.

Gulls called, and wind tugged at Bert's hair. She spit sand from between her teeth. Her face burned with cold, and the ugly scent of blood and feces filled her nostrils. Her hands were numb. She discovered other places that hurt—a knee, her left arm, a shoulder. But she didn't care. She was alive, gloriously alive.

There was nothing for it but to walk back. She wondered how long it would be before Hunter started to worry and came after them.

Chapter 31

Bert had barely covered half a mile when she heard the plane. Smiling, she shook her head. She should have known Hunter would take the fastest way back when they didn't arrive.

The cliffs guarding the beach were high enough to flip an airplane, but the tide was almost all the way out, leaving an expanse of hard sand. Was it wide enough for them to land?

As soon as they spotted her, the pilot nosed down. Hunter hung out the window, his face a scowl of concern. He threw his hands open in question—the same gesture she'd seen Ernie make earlier. Bert made a circle with thumb and forefinger, the diver's okay sign. Then she pointed down the beach to the ATVs and drew her hand across her throat. The plane passed low over Ernie's body and landed on the beach facing windward.

Bert had already started back, limping faster, now that she didn't have four miles to hike. She saw three figures drop from the plane and run to Ernie's side. Minutes later, an ATV motor coughed, and Hunter was speeding up the beach.

He vaulted off before the ATV stopped rolling and gathered Bert in his arms, hugging, talking, and yelling all at the same time. But his hands were shaking. Holding her by the shoulders, he ran his eyes down her body, checking for blood or ripped clothing. Then he yanked her back to his chest and held her tight.

How could she have thought he'd run from her? Bert buried her cold face in his neck, ashamed she'd had so little faith. If loving Hunter meant learning to live with a ghost—a young, Southern ghost—then so be it.

"Are you all right? What in blue balls happened? An accident? It wasn't something we did, was it?" Hunter cupped her face with his hands. "Hon, hon."

His concern and sympathy undid what was left of her self-control. Bert began to cry. She never cried unless she was angry or feeling sorry for herself. Worse yet, she was scaring Hunter. "I'm fine. Really, I am. Oh, Hunter. It was Ernie. Ernie was trying to kill me." She felt him stiffen. "He went after Triton with a knife, and Triton . . ." Bert broke off as once again she saw blood spurting and heard Ernie's skull crack under Triton's hooves.

Hunter held her tight in his arms, rocking back and forth until she calmed. Then he led her to the ATV. Setting her on the seat, he held her hand between both of his. "You think you could tell me exactly what happened?" He glanced back at the plane. "I'd like to get a handle on this before we go back. That's James Blount over there."

Bert told him in spurts. She'd stop to explain something, then jump ahead. All the time she spoke, Hunter never took his eyes from her face, clutching her hand, stroking her arm. The warmth in his gaze thawed the frost from her fingers and the horror from her mind.

He didn't seem surprised the killer was Ernie. "You know he was Phi Beta Kappa? But no common sense. I told you about his family?"

"That he was brought up in foster homes?"

"Personnel records are private, but this changes things." Hunter threw a glance back toward the plane. "Seems Ernie's father was one of those family tyrants—real religious. Kept the kids home as much as he could. There was an older sister. She sneaked off to meet a boy, wearing jeans and makeup yet. The father had some strange ideas about discipline. Anyhow, he and his wife tied her up in a blanket and left her in a closet for two days. When they went to let her loose, she was dead. It was in all the papers up north."

Bert recoiled. "Oh, God. No wonder Ernie had problems."

"It gets worse. He's the one that turned them in."

"He told you that?"

"No. He never talked about it. Never said much about himself. But he had to know it was in his file." Hunter paused, staring over her head. "He was getting stranger all the time, that's for sure. He kept putting in for promotion, but he didn't want to take a transfer or any training. I told him just last month he had to go for counseling." Before Bert could say anything, Hunter clutched her arm. "Come to think of it, he and Lida Fulchard had their heads together at the Decoy Festival. I was wondering how she got Ernie to run at the mouth like that. Lida must have been testing the water."

"How would you go about asking someone to hide turtle carcasses? I mean, suppose he turned her in?"

Hunter grunted. "Miss Fulchard's too smart to come right out and tell Ernie to get rid of the turtles. I reckon she told him about the job, and that she thought he was the man for it. Then she probably mentioned how, if the dredging got done on schedule, she'd be in a strong position to appoint him. It wouldn't surprise me any if she let on that any more dredge kills could screw the deal." Hunter squeezed Bert's hand so hard it hurt, but that kind of pain she could live with. "Ernie and Purcell are the only two who check the turtles—"

Bert interrupted. "He took Purcell off the beach run after that first Ridley. Said it was because Purcell was careless locking up."

"That figures. All Ernie had to do was call it a natural death, and the investigation stopped there. I reckon Miss Lida has someone on the Atlantic Beach crew working for her, too." He reached over and wiped sand off Bert's face.

"You mean Ernie killed Julie for a state job?" Her teeth were still gritty.

Hunter shook his head. "I believe it happened like you said. Julie got after him, and Ernie panicked. Tried to lie his way out of it. She wouldn't buy his lies and threatened to tell. He lost it, and then he tried to make us think it was an accident."

"And Lida went along with murder?"

Hunter's brows drew together. "Lida Fulchard might have some suspicions, but I expect she just closed her mind to them. One thing I don't understand. Why was Lida so hellbent to get the dredging done?"

"That's easy," Bert said. "She almost got defeated last time she ran, didn't she? The only thing that saved her was all the TV advertising. Must have cost a fortune."

"You saying she was taking money on the side? Bribes?"

Bert made a face. "I don't know. But she was getting fat campaign contributions from people who wanted the beach nourishment to go through—contractors, realtors." Bert paused as she remembered something else. "You know what? Julie said Lida bought a beachfront motel, the one that got condemned after the ocean took the septic tank. She got it at a bankruptcy sale."

Hunter whistled. "That beach is on the west end of the nourishment project. Until it's filled in, she can't get insurance. The land alone would be worth ten million after nourishment."

"They'll be able to do something about Lida, won't they?" Bert asked.

His eyes darkened. "I don't believe there's enough evidence to charge her, not unless Ernie had something in writing. She's too smart for that."

"You mean Lida will get away with bribes and cover-ups?"

"Oh, I wouldn't say that. No, sir, I wouldn't." He glanced at the plane. "Blount over there isn't real happy with Miss Fulchard right now."

"Then she did lie to him."

"Told him Shony was a plant. She picked the wrong man to fool. Blount remembered the foal soon as I mentioned his name. That man's got a lot of pull in this state." Hunter sat down next to Bert, putting his arm around her shoulders. "That's not all. I'm fixing to let Vilma have an earful about our state representative. Some of the other reporters, too. Between the park, the sheriff, and Blount, we can get an investigation going on Lida Fulchard. I'll be surprised if they don't dig up a lot of dirt."

What had Hunter found out about his wife? Bert didn't want to ask and spoil the moment. She took a deep breath. It was time she learned not to run from her problems. "What happened with the sheriff? Was it her?"

Hunter's expression didn't change, but for a moment he closed his eyes. "The sheriff's office was still checking when I left. Seems Dr. Stanley wasn't the only one who used that medical supplier, but we're ninety percent sure. I asked them to do one of those DNA tests."

"What's next?"

Hunter's grip on her shoulders tightened. "I don't really know. We had a memorial service for Rhoda back then, after . . ." His voice broke. "We had to wait, in case the body showed up." He stared over her head. "They'll probably have some kind of service, just family. She has a headstone, you know, in Marshallberg. Her mother's taking it hard. I think she was hoping Rhoda was still alive. That's what kept me so long."

Had Hunter clung to a remnant of hope, too? Was that why he reacted so strongly? Bert touched his hand. "I'm so sorry, Hunter. Is there anything I can do?"

He shook his head. "Maybe later." He stood. "Think you're ready to go back? Need to get that plane out before the wind picks up any."

He still wasn't letting her in, but at least he wasn't pushing her away. They both had much to learn, Bert thought as they rode the ATV to the plane. Most of all, they had to learn how to open up to each other. But wasn't that part of living?

At the plane, they faced another problem. "This Cessna tail-dragger was built to land on beaches," the pilot told them. "But she can't take more than three besides me."

Hunter pondered for a moment, then came up with a solution. "We got to get Clayton back to the mainland. He's hurt. Think you can take an ATV back to camp?" he asked Bert. "Mr. Blount here doesn't ride." Hunter eyed the foundation leader. "Do you?"

James Blount shook his head. "But I've always wanted to learn."

"I'll go, Hunter. I'm fine, really." Bert edged toward one of the machines. It would be good for her to drive back—the old get-back-on-the-horse thing.

Hunter hesitated, then said, "That's the way we'll do it, if it's all right with you, Mr. Blount. Jerome here will fly you and . . ."—he indicated the body bag—"back to the mainland. You can pick up Clayton on the way."

Blount cleared his throat. "On one condition."

Hunter raised a brow.

"That you and this lovely lady let me buy you dinner Thursday and tell me the whole story."

"We'd be honored, I'm sure." Hunter turned to Jerome. "Better call ahead and tell them you'll be needing the coroner's wagon again. By now, I reckon they know the routine."

"I just called in for a weather update," the pilot told them. "The nor'easter's moving slower than they expected. How's if I meet you on the east beach in an hour?"

"Don't take any chances if the wind picks up, you hear?" Hunter checked his watch. "We can get along fine for a few days if the weather gets worse. Just leave my pack off when you pick up Clayton."

The wind remained steady, and Bert and Hunter were able to take off an hour later. The small plane lifted so easily Bert could hardly believe they were airborne. Pulling her jacket tight, she peered out the window, marveling at the shape of the island. "I never realized it was so wide. And the colors . . ." She pointed at an expanse of blue water. "Is that Mullet Pond over there?" They passed over Shackleford to the sound. "Wish I could see the shoals like this from my boat." That reminded Bert. She started to swing around, then decided to shift her entire body instead. She'd be moving slowly for a while. "I still don't understand why Ernie killed DeWitt. I assume it was Ernie." It was so cold in the plane her breath steamed.

"I don't expect we'll ever know." Bert was next to the pilot, and Hunter sat behind her. He rested his warm hand on her shoulder, cupping her neck. "I reckon Ernie thought DeWitt was a threat. Not sure why."

The pilot pushed his earphones away. "He was killed the day you were hunting the chestnut stallion with the white mane and blaze, right? By Bald Hill Bay?"

"You know something?" Hunter asked.

Jerome shrugged. "Could be. We were all trying to find that horse. DeWitt came down in his boat to point out the hideaway. I was directing the ATVs from above. I said something over the radio about DeWitt being directly across the island from the Ridley. I didn't know it was gone."

"So?"

"A couple of minutes later, I got a call on my cell from DeWitt. He wanted the coordinates for the turtle. I thought it was kind of strange."

"Oh-ho," Bert breathed, tucking her hands up under her jacket.

"It's coming clear now," Hunter said. "DeWitt figured out who killed Julie. Had to take care of it by himself. He never let anyone help him."

Trying to catch Hunter's eye without moving her head, Bert said, "I know someone else like that."

Hunter gave her his lopsided grin. "I guess you're right at that. Reckon I'd better mend my ways, before it gets me killed, too."

"You mean I got him killed?" the pilot exclaimed.

"Wasn't your fault, Jerome, no way. DeWitt's temper got him killed." Hunter sighed. "DeWitt used the coordinates to figure out Ernie lied. I reckon Julie told DeWitt she'd seen Ernie with the turtle. He put two and two together."

"Instead of telling the authorities, you think he went after Ernie himself?" Bert asked. A picture was forming.

"Ernie was working on the roundup with the others. I imagine

DeWitt called him on the radio or cell. Wouldn't surprise me if DeWitt was fixing to beat some on Ernie before he turned him over."

"That would fit. DeWitt liked Julie, in his way." Bert paused. "And Triton's hideaway was close to that clearing. It would have been the logical place to come ashore." She visualized an ugly sequence. "DeWitt must have accused Ernie. Ernie tricked him into turning away, then rammed him with the ATV. DeWitt wouldn't have expected Ernie to take the initiative."

"That would account for the marks on his back, all right," Hunter said. "I reckon he stunned DeWitt long enough to beat in his head. Resource always carries mallets, posts, and shovels on the ATVs."

"And then he buried him there, figuring nobody would find his body and people would think DeWitt drowned. Ernie didn't know it had been Shony's grave." Bert leaned back, silent for a moment. "Wasn't that the night you were so late? You said you had to wait for Ernie."

"Bastard said he had ATV trouble," Hunter growled. "All the time, he was taking DeWitt's boat around to the inlet. I'd guess he had to wait for the tide before he set it adrift. Then he hiked five miles back to his ATV. Small wonder he ran late."

The pilot spoke in a low voice. "I never knew Julie too well, but my mama always said she was a nice girl. I think they were hoping she'd get together with DeWitt."

"It's so sad they had to die." Bert fought to hide the sudden quaver in her voice. "Julie got cheated out of years of life, and DeWitt might have discovered a way to immunize for EIA." That made Bert think of the horses, a happier subject. "Did all the foals find their mothers?"

"Far as I know, they did. Clayton let them out of the pens before we got there." Hunter gave a short laugh. "Reckon Purcell isn't going to be sorry to hear about Ernie."

Bert started. She'd forgotten about Purcell. "Oh, poor guy. No wonder he was acting so strangely. Maybe he'll stay on now."

Hunter's grip tightened on her shoulder. "Tell the truth, that was one of the reasons I told Ernie to get counseling. He was harassing Purcell something terrible." After a brief silence, Hunter said, "One thing I got to know."

"What?" Ahead, Bert could see the mainland approaching. The heat in the car was going to feel good.

"You sure it was Triton that went after Ernie?" Hunter's tone was low, flat, and formal.

For a moment, Bert didn't understand. Then an alarm went off. The park couldn't take a chance on a horse attacking a visitor. If Triton had killed Ernie, even if Ernie drew first blood, they'd have to relocate the stallion off the island. He'd never be free again.

"Bert?" Hunter's voice nudged.

"I'm thinking, I'm thinking. It all happened so fast." She was such a bad liar. If she hadn't been able to fool Ernie, how could she lie to Hunter?

But was she really sure it was Triton?

"I never saw his face, you know," Bert said, mind spinning. "When he knocked Ernie off the Honda, I just assumed it was Triton. That's what Triton did to DeWitt." That much was true. "The horse went after the ATV. He didn't pay any attention to either of us until Ernie stabbed him. . . ." She shook her head. "Come to think of it, this stallion was a lot lighter. Triton's brown."

"Chestnut." Hunter's fingers tapped the back of her seat. "With you flat on the ground, the water and sand behind him, you'd have got mostly a silhouette. Light shining though his pelt."

Bert visualized the scene. "At first, I thought it was a white horse," she said slowly. "He had a white mane and tail, but when he got close, I saw he was gold."

"That can't be right." Hunter's brows jutted. "Gold and flaxen are palomino coloring. There's no palominos on Shackleford, not since I've been here. No duns either." Hunter ran his palm over her forehead. "You weren't knocked out, were you? Does your head hurt? How's your vision?"

Bert pushed his hand away. "I'm fine. The handlebars caught me in the middle, just winded me. I was kind of woozy, but I could see just fine." She'd even seen the tiny shells in Ernie's tires.

"You sure it wasn't the light reflecting on a flaxen-maned chestnut?"

Bert shook her head, picturing the stallion's rippling muscles and gleaming coat as he'd pranced.

After a moment, Hunter asked, "Which direction did the horse come from?"

"From the ocean side of the beach."

He leaned over so he could look into her eyes. "You're not trying to protect Triton, are you?"

"Uh-uh." The more she talked, the surer she became it wasn't Triton. "He was big, bigger than Triton even, and he had black eyes." Bert shivered. "Strange eyes." After a pause, she asked, "If there's no palominos here, where do you think he came from?"

The tension in Hunter's voice eased. "Could have swum over from the mainland, or someone let him loose on the island. That happens a lot. Maybe he's just got a good hiding place for the roundups." He squeezed her shoulder. "Had a white foal born on the island back a few years ago, but it died."

Bert heaved a sigh of relief. Triton was safe.

"Hey, Jerome," Hunter said. "How would you and Purcell like to hunt a horse after this storm is done?"

The pilot threw back a smiling glance. "Always glad for an excuse to get into the air, even when it's this cold. But I can tell you right now, you're wasting your time. There's no white horses on that island."

Hunter shook his head. Bert laughed. It felt good to smile again.

The plane dropped them off at the New Bern airport, where Hunter had left his pickup. With the heater on high, they started back to Harkers Island. Hunter filled Bert in on his morning. "Finally heard from James Blount. Would you believe he called while I was on the line with Lida Fulchard? Good thing, too. I'd kinda lost it with our state legislator." Hunter paused, shaking his head. "Blount said he was flying in to New Bern. No way I was taking a chance he'd disappear again, so I said I'd pick him up. Then I called and got the park plane to come down." His lips twisted. "Don't care if I ever have another morning like that. First was Rhoda. Then Lida Fulchard was threatening me with the Park Service regional office in Atlanta. Then I got Blount running at the mouth. I was still on the line with him when Atlanta called."

"What's going to happen with that? Did they really make Ernie acting superintendent?"

"He was the same pay level as me, so the job passed to him. Don't worry, hon. Atlanta told me to hang loose until things cooled off. They knew it was political."

"So it'll be all right?" Edging over on the seat until she could feel Hunter's body next to hers, she put her hand on his thigh.

He grinned, covering it with his. "It wouldn't surprise me any if Cape Lookout gets a new, permanent superintendent in the next ten days. Not going to hurt my feelings."

Bert sighed. "You mean you don't want to be superintendent?"

"Sometime, maybe. I'm not sure I'm ready to get stuck behind a desk just yet."

By the time they reached Morehead, the storm was rolling in, raindrops exploding on the windshield. Bert stared out the passenger window at the whitecaps on the sound, wondering about her boat.

As if he could tell what she was thinking, Hunter cleared his throat. "Meant to tell you, while we were in camp, Jerome and me pulled your boat way up on the sand and put some more lines on it. Should be all right till the storm's over."

Bert leaned happily against his warmth. "You know, I'd forgotten how nice it is to have two people taking care of things."

Hunter turned into the driveway. "This week wasn't exactly what I had in mind for us. The bright side is that things can only get better. Just give us a chance, okay?"

Bert didn't know what to say, but her smile and her body language seemed to satisfy him.

By the time they went to bed, the nor'easter was in full force. Rain rattled against the panes. The wind shook the house and whistled in the eaves. As Bert drifted off to sleep, warm in Hunter's arms, her thoughts turned to the horses. She'd always heard they hated rain. At least it would wash the blood out of Triton's mane before Hunter thought to check—if it had been Triton.

Bert smiled. She could still see that cloud of white hair flying like foam on the ocean, muscles rippling under his gold coat.

Bert bolted up, staring into the dark.

Immediately, Hunter came awake. "What's the matter?"

"Nothing. I'm sorry I woke you. Go back to sleep."

"Come on. Had to be something." He pulled her to his chest. "Tell me."

Bert kissed him, then raised just enough so she was gazing right in his eyes. "I was thinking about that horse, and how strong and beautiful he was, and then I remembered something." She grinned. "His coat was smooth. I could see his muscles rippling."

Hunter's brows drew in slightly. "I don't understand."

"The Shackleford horses all have shaggy winter coats. Remember? We had to shave them to see their brands."

After a moment, Hunter smiled.

"What?"

He pulled her down so his lips were on her ear. "It must have been a ghost horse. Maybe your guardian angel sent him—out of the sea."

It wasn't possible, was it?

The banks held many a secret.

Acknowledgments

My thanks go to the following people.

Patricia Deshinsky is my daughter, my reader, my critiquer, my idea person. Every time I write myself into a corner, Pat unfailingly comes up with the perfect solution. She's also responsible for the horses' names. My daughter Linnette designed my web pages and is my number-one fan. My sons, John and George, along with Jean and Debbie, contributed encouragement and enthusiasm.

Ruth Hallman took time from her own writing to go over my entire manuscript and make great suggestions. The last line is hers.

Carolyn Mason deserves thanks for her beautifully written internet articles, for the information she provided on the ponies, and most of all for her courage and generosity of spirit in her fight to preserve the Shackleford horses.

Katherine Muller of the Carteret County Public Library in Beaufort helped me with research, particularly in locating an obscure book on the transportation of horses overseas.

Dr. Walter Westbrook, Judy, and the rest of his staff at the Newport Animal Clinic provided the dope on vets, horses, and EIA. Here's hoping Barb doesn't read this and say, "No vet would ever do that!"

Paul Branch, park ranger and historian at Fort Macon, offered his expertise on the Civil War and provided me obscure leads, not the least of which was where to find the story of Mary Frances Chadwick.

The crew of the *Elizabeth II* in Manteo showed me around and answered all my questions about transporting and loading horses.

Detective Jason Wank at the Carteret County Sheriff's Department provided information on protocol and procedures, as well as some great details.

Supervisory park ranger Jim Zahradka, an old friend from my volunteer days, helped me with policy and procedure for rangers.

Dr. Larry Crowder of the Duke University Marine Science Laboratory on Pivers Island in Morehead City supplied expert information on endangered species and the responsibilities of the various governmental agencies.

Douglas Campen, the chief of police for the North Carolina State Ports Authority, and Lieutenant Wesley Collins of the authority's police department gave me information and showed me around the port in Morehead City.

A special thanks goes to the crew of the sidecaster dredge *Merritt*, pride of the fleet. David Cribbs, second engineer, showed me around the *Merritt* after a long day at work and gave me information on the various types of dredges. Any mistakes here are mine, not his.

Debbie Hackett dropped everything to get me the capabilities of a small airplane. I also thank the manager at Michael J. Smith Airport in Beaufort.

Most of all, I thank the patient members of the Carteret Writers genre groups, who critiqued and edited this manuscript word by word. They were very generous with their time, ideas, information, and even names, dialects, and phrasings.

And where would I be without the expert help, advice, and editing of the staff of John F. Blair, Publisher? I thank Carolyn Sakowski, Blair's great and efficient president; Steve Kirk, the best editor ever; Ed Southern, fun sales director; Kim Byerly, cool publicist; Sue Clark, the first to read and recommend; and the talented Debbie Hampton, Anne Waters, Margaret Couch, Heath Simpson, Jackie Whitman, and Betsy Bost.

Although I've been fortunate enough to receive excellent help from experts with various parts of this novel, my recollections and interpretations may not always reflect what they said or meant. Any mistakes in this novel should be attributed to my poor listening habits and not ascribed to them.